CARVED FROM STONE AND DREAM

A Los Nefilim Novel

T. FROHOCK

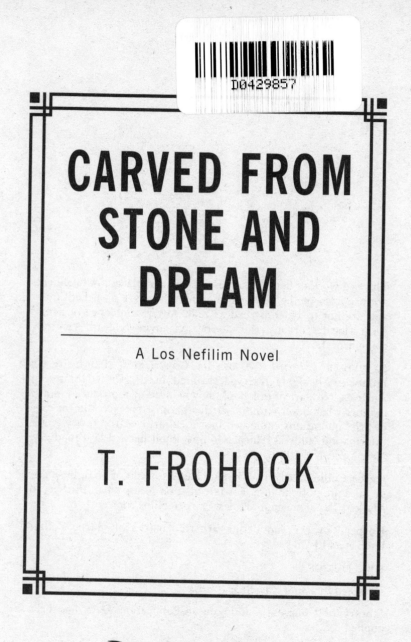

HARPER Voyager

An Imprint of HarperCollins Publishers

CARVED FROM STONE AND DREAM. Copyright © 2020 by Teresa Frohock. All rights reserved. Printed in the United States of America. No part of this book may be used or reproduced in any manner whatsoever without written permission except in the case of brief quotations embodied in critical articles and reviews. For information address HarperCollins Publishers, 195 Broadway, New York, NY 10007.

HarperCollins books may be purchased for educational, business, or sales promotional use. For information please email the Special Markets Department at SPsales@harpercollins.com.

Harper Voyager and design are trademarks of HarperCollins Publishers LLC.

FIRST EDITION

Designed by Paula Russell Szafranski

Library of Congress Cataloging-in-Publication Data has been applied for.

ISBN 978-0-06-282564-3

20 21 22 23 24 LSC 10 9 8 7 6 5 4 3 2 1

For Robert Dunbar, who graciously gave me the space on one of his forums to ask questions, and for Vince Liaguno, whose responses to those questions helped shape Diago's character.

And especially for:
Johnathan, Cushing, and Vinnie.
Thank you for letting me be a part of your lives.

AUTHOR'S NOTE

A quick note on the spellings used: the accepted spelling of the word is *Nephilim*. However, in Spanish the *ph* sound is replaced by the *f*, hence *Los Nefilim*.

This novel is primarily told from the points of view of my Spanish characters, so whenever I need to use the generic term *Nephilim* to indicate the species of Nephilim as a whole, I use the spelling *nefilim* (the lowercase *n* is intentional for plural *nefilim* as well as the singular *nefil*).

I also needed a way in which to distinguish the various nationalities of nefilim within the Inner Guard. Whenever you see capitalization—Los Nefilim, Die Nephilim, or Les Néphilim—I am referring to the Inner Guard's different divisions—the Spanish, German, and French, respectively.

While each of the Los Nefilim novellas and the novels can be read as stand-alone works, several characters and themes do recur. Likewise, those keeping up with the series might enjoy a mild refresher, as well.

The novellas (*In Midnight's Silence, Without Light or Guide,* and *The Second Death*) all served as an introduction into the world of Los Nefilim, as well as forming the basis for discovering the Key—the song that will enable the nefilim to open the realms as the angels do. The novels, which began with *Where Oblivion Lives*, concern Diago's actual composition of the Key. Somewhat like an opera in three parts, the story follows the crucial points that lead our heroes to the next act of the movement.

I understand that people might not remember the terminology from one story to another. With that in mind, I included a glossary in the back of this novel.

To remedy any memory gaps the reader might have, I'm also including a very brief, spoiler-free synopsis of the events from previous episodes. To be clear: each of the novellas and novels can be read as stand-alone works. However, I always imagined Los Nefilim as a serial, much like the old *Shadow* radio serial. In keeping with that tone, here is the story so far . . .

1931 (The *Los Nefilim* omnibus contains the novellas *In Midnight's Silence*, *Without Light or Guide*, and *The Second Death*.)

Diago Alvarez, a rarity among the nefilim in that his mother was an angel and his father was a daimon-born nefil, discovers that he has a six-year-old son named Rafael. Having never officially joined Los Nefilim, the Spanish Inner Guard, Diago has always lived as a rogue. He maintains a superficial connection to Los Nefilim through his husband, Miquel de Torrellas, who is Guillermo Ramírez's second-in-command.

Rafael's presence changes Diago's priorities. The only way he can protect his son from his daimonic kin is by joining

Los Nefilim. Diago swears an oath to Guillermo Ramírez, the king of Los Nefilim, who wants Diago to try to compose the Key—the song that will enable the nefilim to open the realms as the angels do.

1932 (*Where Oblivion Lives*)

Now a member of Los Nefilim, Diago leaves Spain in order to solve the mystery of his missing violin, which torments his dreams. It's his first official mission as a member of the Inner Guard, and he succeeds in both solving the mystery and in confronting his PTSD from the Great War. During the course of these events, Guillermo discovers traitors within his own ranks who serve his brother, Jordi Abelló, who has returned to undermine Guillermo's right to command Los Nefilim. At the end of 1932, Diago and Guillermo work together and finally compose the first notes to the Key.

Our story begins in 1939 . . .

PROLOGUE

TOP SECRET
Inner Guard Division: Los Nefilim
General Miquel de Torrellas
Servicio de Investigación Militar

15 March 1938
SIM Report No. 49477

Summary of Events 1936–Present

JULY 1936. Reports are confirmed that the rogue nefil, Jordi Abelló, brother to Don Guillermo Ramírez, Capitán General of Los Nefilim, did willfully and knowingly:

1. Instigate and coordinate a mortal civil war in the Spanish territories held by Los Nefilim;
2. Use his song to cause the death of the mortal General Juan Sanjurjo on 20 July 1936 for the sole purpose of installing General Francisco Franco as the leader of the rebel army that currently identifies itself as the Nationalists.

21 JULY 1936. Don Guillermo Ramírez commands Los Nefilim to guard the Republican government elected by the mortals. When German combat aircraft arrives to support the Nationalist advance (see SIM Report No. 37825), Los Nefilim evacuates valuable grimoires and artifacts from the town of Santuari to the Inner Guard's vaults at the University of Toulouse.

APRIL 1937. Jordi Abelló succeeds in uniting the Falangists and Carlists under the Nationalist banner to form a single army under Franco's leadership as caudillo.

26 APRIL 1937 (OPERATION RÜGEN). The Basque town of Guernica is bombed by the German Condor Legion. The town, which served as the communications center for Republican forces, is in ruins. Number of dead: unknown.

2 MARCH 1938. Los Nefilim receives intelligence that Santuari is the target for a Nationalist air strike similar to the attack on Guernica.

12 MARCH 1938 (OPERATION VERNICHTUNG). Los Nefilim's forces evacuate to Barcelona mere hours before a blitzkrieg attack by the German Condor Legion bombards Santuari. The rebel, Jordi Abelló, offers amnesty to any members of Los Nefilim who decide to join the Nationalist cause. Forty nefilim defect to the Nationalist ranks (names and profiles are listed in the attached addendum). To date, twelve have been captured and executed. We will watch for them.

COMMENT: All diplomatic efforts to acquire official intercession by the British and American nefilim have failed. The Republican mortals are losing the war. On behalf of Don Guillermo Ramírez, Capitán General, Los Nefilim, I have been instructed to request permission to establish a base camp for Los Nefilim in France in the event the Nationalist rebels temporarily take Spain.

INNER GUARD DIVISION: LES NÉPHILIM
Madame Sabine Rousseau, Capitaine Général
Direction Générale de la Sécurité Extérieure

20 March 1938
DGSE Report No. 12301

To the Honorable Don Guillermo Ramírez, Capitán General, Los Nefilim:

Members of Les Néphilim have finally persuaded the mortal government to reopen the French border on 17 March. The bearer of this report, Madame Lucile Perrault, possesses the seal to create the necessary passports and identity papers for your nefilim. Send your family and the closest members of your council with her to Paris.

DO NOT DELAY.

Madame Perrault bears the diplomatic credentials that will ensure your family is allowed to proceed across the border unhindered. The French mortals grow restless beneath the wave of Spanish refugees. After April, I cannot guarantee your nefilim will escape internment in the camps.

May the Thrones watch over you.

INNER GUARD DIVISION: LOS NEFILIM
Don Guillermo Ramírez, Capitán General
Servicio de Investigación Militar

26 April 1938
SIM Report No. 49495

To the Honorable Madame Sabine Rousseau, Capitaine Général, Les Néphilim:

At your urgent request, I am sending the closest members of my court into your safekeeping through Madame Lucile Perrault. It is in Los Nefilim's best interest that Juanita accompany our daughter, Ysabel Ramírez, with the retinue so that Ysabel can benefit from her mother's angelic guidance.

Until I can reach Paris, Ysabel is my voice in all matters regarding the Inner Guard and serves as my proxy. I've instructed her to establish a base of operations for Los Nefilim in Paris in order to facilitate the resettlement of nefilim displaced by the war. She will have my personal staff at her disposal. Although she is fifteen years old and in her firstborn life, she has trained for this role and exhibits sound acumen. Trust her as you would me.

The Republican mortals have planned one last offensive in the hopes of turning the war in their favor. We have advised them to pursue a different course, but the Popular Front suffers from continued infighting within its leadership. Achieving any form of accord between the groups grows more remote by the day. I will remain with Los Nefilim's milicianos to offer the mortals support for as long as we're able.

INNER GUARD DIVISION: LES NÉPHILIM
Madame Sabine Rousseau, Capitaine Général
Direction Générale de la Sécurité Extérieure

7 February 1939
DGSE Report No. 12595

To the Honorable Don Guillermo Ramírez, Capitán General, Los Nefilim:

The French mortals are overwhelmed with Spanish refugees. They are separating families at the border checkpoints and placing them in internment camps. Soldiers and able-bodied men are currently being sent to Argelès-sur-Mer. Conditions are horrific. Prepare your nefilim for this eventuality. Les Néphilim will watch for them and liberate them at the first opportunity.

INNER GUARD DIVISION: LOS NEFILIM
General Miquel de Torrellas
Servicio de Investigación Militar

10 February 1939
SIM Report No. 49785

To the Honorable Madame Sabine Rousseau, Capitaine Général, Les Néphilim:

Catalonia has fallen. Los Nefilim is in retreat.

Our intelligence has uncovered Jordi's plot to send assassins after Don Guillermo and his daughter, Ysabel. Diago Alvarez, Carme Gebara, and Feran Perez are assigned to escort Don Guillermo to the French border via an undisclosed route. We severed communications with Don Guillermo on 5 February 1939 for his own safety. His whereabouts are currently unknown.

Even in retreat, our unit remains under heavy artillery fire. The Germans and Italians bomb civilians as they flee the Nationalist advance.

My unit will continue to provide support to the mortal refugees in the eastern sector as they cross the Pyrenees. We will approach the border at Le Perthus.

Watch for us.

15
February
1939

Night

la retirada
(the retreat)

[1]

Winter hit the Pyrenees hard with ice as treacherous as postwar loyalties. Both could kill with a single slip.

Dark clouds smoldered over the jagged peaks, threatening a storm before the twilight ended. The wind blew in savage gusts, ready to rip all four nefilim from the old chamois trail and toss them into the valley far below.

As Guillermo navigated a difficult climb to the summit, Diago waited on a narrow ledge with Feran and Carme. Barely sixty centimeters separated the trio from a sheer drop. Three hundred meters below, coniferous trees hid the valley's floor. At their backs was a wall of stone that offered them no cover from either the wind or their enemies.

Feran, a Galician with light brown hair and fair skin, shifted his weight from one foot to the other as he stood between Diago and Carme. On the other side of him, Carme crouched and watched the opposite ridge with the studied gaze of a professional killer.

Above them, Guillermo caught hold of the ridge's crest. He pulled himself upward, digging the toe of his boot against the sheer wall.

Feran twitched and tightened his grip on his rifle's strap. Diago followed the lanky nefil's gaze, half expecting to see soldiers on the opposite ridge. To his relief, the trail remained empty. *Fucking Feran is infecting me with anxiety.*

Not that the younger nefil's skittishness was entirely unfounded. If the Nationalists caught up with them now, they made perfect targets.

A smattering of loose stones tumbled down the incline. Diago looked up in time to see Guillermo's heels disappear over the ledge. *Finally.*

Feran shifted his weight left again. In doing so, he managed to step on Carme's last nerve.

"If you've got to piss, Feran, just whip it out and go."

"Looking for a golden shower?" he shot back, terror sending his voice and his bravado soaring into the higher registers.

Not even the wind could tear the menace from Carme's words. "Just one nudge." She pointed down. "A quick push and over you go."

Feran's cheeks paled. "You wouldn't dare."

Carme's cold smile said otherwise.

"Don't test her," Diago warned. "From this height, your skull will burst like an overripe melon."

Feran squeaked, "Fuck you, Carme."

She lifted her finger in an obscene gesture and halfheartedly waved it in his direction while never taking her gaze from the opposite ridge. "Fuck Diago. He likes men."

"Are you crazy?" Feran's flush had nothing to do with the wind. "Seriously, Diago, no offense—"

"Jesus Christ, you two, pipe down," Diago muttered. He tuned out the bickering pair and wondered if his husband, Miquel, had reached France.

With communications cut, news had grown as thin as the mountain air. Rumors and carrion birds were all that followed battlefields. Their last missive from Queen Rousseau indicated Republican soldiers were being taken to an internment camp at Argelès-sur-Mer, although it was just as likely that Miquel might be in Paris when they reached the French border.

One step at a time. They would be together again soon . . . another week, maybe two.

Guillermo tossed down a rope. "Okay, lovebirds, Diago is next."

With a deep breath to steady his own jangled nerves, Diago stepped around a puddle of ice and pressed himself against the wall. Fissures zigzagged over the limestone beneath his feet. A small section near the toe of his boot crumbled and vanished into the thin air.

Diago froze. Fear sent a trickle of sweat down his back. He remembered dying in his last incarnation, a lingering death wrought by an insane angel. *At least this will be quick.*

Behind him, Carme's voice rose over the howling wind. "Keep moving, Diago."

The command snapped him out of his daze. He shuffled along the trail again and removed his gloves. The wind threatened to tear them from his hands before he could stuff them into his pockets. The incline grew steeper. Reaching up, he sought a handhold in the crevice between two stones. The icy rock leached the feeling from his fingertips.

He pictured his son, Rafael, waiting for them in Paris. *I promised him that I'd join him there.* Gritting his teeth, he dragged himself upward, bringing his body a few centimeters closer to the French border and his family.

As soon as he was within reach, he seized the rope and pulled himself upward. When he neared the crest of the hill, Guillermo reached down, grabbed his pack, and hauled him onto level ground.

"Do you think we've lost them?" Guillermo asked.

Rolling free of the precipitous drop, Diago scrambled to his knees and unshouldered his rifle. The scree bit through his worn trousers and into his knees. He scanned the opposite ridge, looking for any sign of movement, and breathed a sigh of relief when he saw none. Jordi's squad still hadn't caught up to them.

"No. We haven't lost them. They're just being more cautious after Carme shot one yesterday. Besides, it's almost dark. They may have decided to camp for the night."

Guillermo coiled the rope. His lips barely moved with his reply. "They've had multiple chances to take us down and they haven't. They're herding us, and that means they have a plan. The question is, where? And why?"

"Not for anything pleasant, I can assure you of that."

"No argument there." Guillermo returned to the ledge and tossed down the rope. "Move it, Feran!"

Diago surveyed the area with a glance. A few pines clung to the stony ground in defiance of the wind. The trees and rocks gave them a smattering of cover. Otherwise, there wasn't much to distinguish this hill from the one they'd just left.

Diago took shelter behind a wide outcropping. Dropping to his stomach, he balanced his Mauser's barrel on the rock's rim.

Through the scope, he observed a male figure creeping wraithlike along the thin trail on the opposite ridge. The man's red-tasseled infantry cap and the heavy wool poncho belted tight around his waist identified him as a Nationalist soldier.

Diago didn't need to see his eyes to know he was a nefil. The grace of his movements gave him away.

"We've got company."

"How many?" Even as he continued to pull Feran upward, Guillermo lowered himself to his belly to make a smaller target.

"One. Looks like a scout." Diago lined up his shot and squeezed the trigger. Just as he fired, the Nationalist skidded on a patch of ice and crouched to keep his balance. The bullet skimmed the top of his hat. The nefil dived behind a nearby boulder.

Goddamn it. "I missed. Get them to hurry." He chambered another round just as Feran reached the top of the ridge.

Feran wasted no time crawling behind a half-dead pine a meter away from Diago. He lifted his rifle and peered through the scope. "Position?"

"Ten o'clock," Diago answered.

"I see him."

Diago squeezed another shot. The Nationalist cowered behind the rock.

"You're wasting ammo," Feran snapped.

"I'm covering Carme." Diago noted a second Nationalist rounding the bend. Another nefil. Fur on the collar of his poncho indicated he was an officer. The man threw himself behind his comrade's outcropping just as Feran fired.

"Fuck," the Galician muttered. "I missed."

Two shots came from the other side. Carme shouted. Shock and pain collided in her cry.

A bullet struck the earth beside Guillermo. He twisted his head. "Hit them!"

Unperturbed by the thunder in Guillermo's voice, Diago watched the Nationalists through his scope. He almost had one in his sights. "Just a little more to the right . . ."

The nefil moved. Diago fired. His target's head jerked backward and sent a spray of blood across the gray stones. His comrade moved to catch him. Diago worked the bolt with supernatural speed, lined up the shot, and fired again. His next bullet caught the second Nationalist in the throat.

Diago focused on the nefil's face. Blood ceased to gush from the man's torn artery. The tempo gradually slowed until the nefil's heart no longer beat. As it did, his aura—slender threads of light the color of cream mixed with merlot—slipped through his lips. Soon, the second nefil's soul emerged in sepia vibrations to join that of the first.

Although Diago was too far away to hear them, the frequencies produced by the violent deaths manifested as dark sounds that clung to the mortal realm. As he watched, their auras faded into the coming dusk. Nefilim's souls rarely lingered on the mortal plane. To do so meant they might become trapped between lives—unable to be reborn into their next incarnation.

It was a fate he wouldn't wish on anyone, even his enemies.

Diago bowed his head. Half angel and half daimon, his dualistic nature enabled him to kill with precision and to see the souls of those who suffered from violence. In times of war, the talent became a curse.

For the benefit of his angel-born comrades, he announced, "They're dead."

"Good," Guillermo grunted as he dragged Carme over the ledge.

Her long face was the color of whey. She got to her knees. The left arm of her coat was wet with blood. "I'm okay," she gasped.

Guillermo didn't buy her stoicism. He helped her to Diago's side. "See to her."

Shit, shit, shit. Everything was going sideways at the worst possible time. First with Jordi's squad picking up their trail, and now this.

Diago eased Carme to the ground as he slid free of his own pack. He rummaged through his dwindling supplies and withdrew his medical kit.

Guillermo turned to Feran, who surveyed the ridge through a pair of scuffed binoculars. "Is that all of them?"

"For now."

But the others won't be far, Diago thought as he peeled back Carme's jacket.

"It's the healing that hurts," she whispered.

Diago knew the truth of that statement from his own experience. *And the older the nefil, the faster the healing.* But that speed worked against them, too, especially in cases of shattered bones. The body's natural ability to form blood clots and new cells around the fracture accelerated. Unlike mortals, who took months to heal, an old nefil's body shaped new threads of bone cells within days or weeks. If a thread of cells reached any bone splinters that were embedded in the muscle, the result was the creation of new bone structures. Untended, the new bones had the potential to leave a nefil deformed, or dead.

"Is it bad?" She twisted her neck, trying to see.

"Be still." Using his knife, he cut away a portion of her shirt. Fibers from her clothing were pushed into the entry wound, leaving her at risk for an ugly infection. *But that's the least of our worries,* he thought as he examined her. Bone shards embedded in muscle and skin dotted the gory mess. From the rapidly swelling tissues, he guessed the shot broke her humerus.

She'll be in constant agony until I can operate. "Damn it, damn it, goddamn it," Diago muttered. "We've got to get her under shelter."

She ground her teeth and glared at him. "I'll heal."

"Yes, but until you do, you can't depend on this arm." *Maybe not even afterward.* The roughest climbing lay ahead of them. He had no idea how they'd get Carme over the high mountains in Ariège.

We'll worry about it when the time comes. He just wanted to get her through the first twenty-four hours intact. Using her blood, he sketched sigils over both the entrance and exit wounds, and then charged the glyphs with a note made high by his anxiety. The viridian lines of his song pierced her flesh and sewed the loose skin shut. Between his spell and the icy air, her bleeding slowed.

"Thank you." Her dark eyes sparkled with an angel's fire. "The pain isn't as bad."

Diago didn't immediately call her on the lie. If there was a path into friendship with Carme, he hadn't found it and sincerely doubted he ever would. She carried the baggage of grudges from one incarnation into another and never forgave him for the transgressions of his firstborn life. He'd managed to prevent creating a deeper rift between them in this life by shutting his mouth and letting her believe in her own infallibility.

Times like these, he wasn't entirely sure that was a good idea. He exchanged an uneasy glance with Guillermo and parted his lips.

Guillermo merely shook his head and mouthed, *Let it go.*

Diago exhaled and released his warning on the wind. *I'm barely hanging on to my own sanity. I can't fix her—neither emotionally nor physically.*

Feran nodded at the trail. "There is a cave nearby. One I've used in the past. We can camp. Diago can stay with Carme until she stabilizes. Once Guillermo is safe beyond the Estany del Port, I'll come back, and then together we'll get Carme over the worst sections of the mountains."

Carme's grimace told Diago what she thought of that plan. Her voice made it even more apparent. "Who put you in charge?"

"It's not a bad idea," Diago said. Once Guillermo passed the lake, he would be in France. But not safe. *None of us will be safe until we're out of the mountains and well past Jordi's reach.*

Diago met his old friend's gaze. "Your safety is the priority."

"Exactly." Feran sniffed and wiped his runny nose with the back of his hand. "Although I don't understand why Jordi wants the ring. You still hold the blessings of the Thrones without it, don't you?" His voice cracked beneath the weight of his hope.

And that explains his agitation—he's terrified. If Guillermo lost the blessing of the Thrones, any members of Los Nefilim that supported him would be considered stateless. Without the protection of the Inner Guard, they would be hunted by their enemies.

Guillermo didn't hesitate to reassure him. "Of course I do. The Thrones have ordered me to join my forces with Rousseau's nefilim in France. This is merely a retreat so we can regroup."

Feran seemed somewhat mollified. "Then even if Jordi steals the signet, he obtains nothing but a symbol."

Guillermo drew his lighter from his pocket and thumbed the lid as he stared back the way they'd come. "Symbols are potent, Feran. They're emblems of rank and power. All Jordi needs to do is send me into my next incarnation. Then, with the ring on his hand and enough pressure, he can force my daughter to abdicate. He'll become king and take command of Los Nefilim again."

"And the Thrones will recognize him?" Feran asked.

Guillermo nodded. "In the case of abdication or death, yes."

And that was the crux of it. If something happened to Guillermo, then the danger to his teenage daughter, Ysabel, multiplied tenfold.

Carme glared at them. "Leave me behind. As soon as I'm well, I'll join you."

"No." Diago refused to consider her request. "If the

Nationalists find you, they'll make sure the Falangists have a go at you." He didn't need to elaborate. Carme had been with him when they'd found the women's bodies a week ago. Two had been raped and then murdered with grenades pushed between their legs. Others bore the Falangist symbol of yoke and arrows branded on their breasts.

The Falangists referred to all Republicans as "Reds," regardless of their actual political affiliation, and all Reds were seen as less than human—women doubly so. The luckier victims were given a bullet and a shallow grave. The less fortunate felt the dirt beneath their backs and suffered cruel indignities. At times, the mortal capacity for violence surpassed even that of the daimons.

A flicker of doubt touched Carme's eyes before her irises grew dark with rage. "Let them try. I'll give them something nasty for their trouble."

Diago had no doubt she would. Carme's sigils were nothing short of malevolent. He helped her to her feet.

"The cave is a good idea," Guillermo said mildly as he continued to examine the trail below their perch. "But we can't keep running. It's time to go on the offensive." He turned and faced Feran. "How far away is it?"

"About fifty meters." Feran pointed to a lip of rock shaped like a heavy brow. "See that shelf overhanging a bed of scree? There."

"Okay, get Carme under shelter, make her comfortable, and wait for us."

"Me?" Feran huffed and looked around. "Why me? Diago is the medic. Let him go. I'll stay here with you."

"I said go."

Feran lowered his voice, as if to keep Diago and Carme from hearing. "You want to keep the nefil who is most likely to betray you—"

Guillermo raised his finger. "You don't want to finish that sentence."

Feran lifted his hands in a gesture of peace. "I'm just saying he's daimon."

Carme's glare should have sliced Feran in two. "He's angel, too."

Diago couldn't believe what he was hearing. That was the closest she'd ever come to actually defending him. "Thank you, Carme."

"Shut up, Diago, I'm just stating a fact."

Christ, why do I even care what she thinks of me? But he did. Although he'd be damned if he intended to let her know it. His response mirrored her retort. "Good," Diago snapped. "I worried you'd become delirious."

Guillermo pointed at Feran. "We're not Communists. This isn't a committee decision. I gave you an order," he said in a way that made the air even colder. "Take Carme to the cave and wait for us. *Now.*"

Feran locked stares with Guillermo and fingered the trigger guard of his gun. For one scary moment, he looked as if he might keep arguing.

What the hell is wrong with him? Is he staging a mutiny? Diago's fingers drifted closer to his pistol's holster. If that was the case, Feran was about to find out exactly whose side Diago intended to take.

With one finger, Carme traced the first line of a deadly indigo sigil.

Feran glanced at the darkening sky. He shouldered his

rifle and surrendered to Guillermo's command. "Come on, I'll babysit you."

The wicked light drifted close to her palm. "I don't need your help."

"You need help," Diago muttered.

"Shut up." She started for the cave with slow, hitching steps. Feran hovered by her side, prepared to catch her when her pride could no longer hold her erect.

Guillermo waited until they were out of earshot. "Give me your pack."

"Technically, he's right," Diago said as he passed his rucksack to Guillermo. "I should be with Carme right now. What have you got planned?"

Guillermo retrieved his length of rope and then hid their gear behind an outcropping well away from the edge of the summit. "Assholes like Feran are why I can't let them see you using your daimonic song."

Diago grimaced. Using his daimonic nature wouldn't endear him to either of his comrades, even if it meant saving their lives. "Carme is no different."

"She clings to the memories of your betrayals from our firstborn lives. You and I, we're a long way from that incarnation. We've worked hard and moved on. Carme will, too." Guillermo spat. "In another couple hundred years or so."

"Swell." Diago's tone indicated it was anything but.

"Forget Carme. How much longer do you think we have before the rest of that squad gets here?"

"Those were scouts. The others are probably a half hour behind. They should be here any minute. I'm sure they heard the firefight."

"That will make them careful. They'll send another

scout." Guillermo pointed back to the chamois trail. "Did you see the fissures in the limestone as we came up?"

"I worried they'd break beneath us."

"Can you move the stone and shatter that portion of the trail?"

"Short answer: yes. But once a spell of this nature is set into motion, it's impossible to control. I might not be able to move away in time to avoid going down with them."

"I won't let you fall." Guillermo tied the rope around Diago's waist, cinching it tight.

Then he gripped Diago's shoulder. The fat signet bearing the fiery tear of the Thrones bulged beneath his glove. "I wouldn't ask you to do this if I thought there was another way, but I've used every trick I know to evade them."

"Okay, let's say I destroy the path. They'll simply find another way around the break."

"What if they're standing on it when you hit it?"

Diago didn't need to look over the edge. "They die." *And I'll have another nightmare to add to my queue.* Yet he couldn't think of another way. Guillermo was right: their backs were to the wall.

A light rain began to fall. An idea formed.

"If I work enough moisture into the cracks, I can widen them until the ledge breaks."

Guillermo's grip tightened on Diago's shoulder before he released him. "Where do you need me?"

Diago scanned the area. A nearby outcropping provided a clean view of the trail. *If I'm very careful, I can keep it outside the radius of my spell.* "There."

Guillermo played out the rope and settled behind the

boulder. He leaned his Mauser against the rock and withdrew his binoculars.

Diago followed the ridge until he stood over the fractured trail. Squatting, he touched the ground.

His silver ring caught the fading light. Similar to Guillermo's signet, but not nearly as powerful, the wide band was adorned with sigils carved into the metal. The setting held a crimson angel's tear, which was marred by jagged streaks of silver.

The hoary veins within the stone glittered as Diago moved his palm from one spot to another. Close to the ledge, he finally located the faint pulsation of soil shifting deep below the surface.

He eased himself onto the ground until he was prone. Vibrations from the falling rain colored the air in shades of gray. He gathered the deeper tones and shaped them into sigils.

As he worked, a slender line of silver emerged from the angel's tear in his ring. With no effort on his part, the magic entwined with his song, strengthening the timbre of the chant.

This spell called for darkness. *Terror and hate.* Not difficult emotions for Diago to draw forward. He thought of hollow-eyed children, wandering the ruins of their homes—their mothers taken to prisons, their fathers dead on battlefields. He knew their despair and fear. It wasn't hard to personalize those feelings, owning them so that they burned hot in his chest.

When he was barely five, he'd run after his father, begging him not to leave . . .

I'll be good, I'll be good, I'll be good . . .

Diago's gut clenched. His eyes burned. That was what he needed. Resurrect the horror, give it teeth, and let it bite. He allowed the emotions to crawl up his throat, where they emerged as a choked cry. The sound twisted and became a scorpion—the manifestation of his daimonic clan's song. The arachnid scuttled toward a crack between two rocks.

Diago nurtured the memories. Fear matured into hate, which easily splintered into the longing for revenge.

The darkness around his soul pulsed, glad to be awakened from its long dormant sleep. From the back of his mind, he heard Miquel's voice, chiding him with an urgency born of love: *These emotions are poison. Don't let them control you, or one day they will eat your heart . . . How can you live without a heart?*

Diago banished the memory. Restraint would come later. Guillermo's order took precedence, and this job called for poison. He traced another sigil.

As he retched the short, harsh notes of his pain and rage onto the ground, the scorpions grew in number. Strands of silver from the angel's tear outlined the shadowy forms and made them glow in the fading light. They dripped from his mouth and worked themselves into the earth, pushing the top layers of grit downward to compress the lower layers. Cracks spread through the sediment and extended through the limestone.

Diago joined a line with two ligatures and four large circles while digging deeper into his past, gouging every old wound until his song bled, first seven scorpions . . .

. . . *do as you're told and you will eat* . . .

. . . then twelve more passed his lips, one for each lash he endured that first day . . .

. . . they forced him to fight for his bread, and though he was small, he soon discovered viciousness trumped size . . .

. . . then twenty, one for each boy who beat him for being different . . .

. . . and in the brothel, he learned not to cry when strangers touched him, burying his hate deep where it smoldered, ready to burst aflame at the slightest provocation . . .

. . . and a hundred thousand scorpions poured from him into the ground, turning into a stream, a lament, a torrent, a dirge . . .

"They're here," Guillermo whispered, momentarily bringing Diago out of his trance.

He glanced up. Across the gorge, a soldier skulked around the bend at a crouch and wasted no time taking cover. They'd definitely heard the firefight.

Guillermo lifted his binoculars. "He's checking this side of the pass. Shit. Recon by fire." He hunched low behind the rock. "Keep your head down."

A bullet lifted the dust before the sound of the shot drifted across the gorge. The objective wasn't to hit a target but to instigate return fire so the Nationalist could clock their position. Four more shots followed. From the pattern, Diago guessed the sniper used the corpses' positions to estimate where their killers might have roosted.

Another bullet struck the rock Diago had initially used for cover. *He's good, too.*

Thirty seconds passed with no fire. Guillermo risked a look. He scowled through the glasses. "He is signaling his comrades . . . here they come."

A drop of sweat slid down Diago's brow. "How many?" He croaked the words, barely recognizing his own voice.

"There are only four left." Guillermo lowered the binoculars. "It's our friend Gunter Sitz."

Diago remembered him: a wiry little German with a face like a hatchet and a large mole on his cheek.

Guillermo stowed his binoculars and lifted his Mauser.

Returning to the spell, Diago checked the lines of his ward and then began to work again, conjuring the grisly events and broken pieces of his early life. He passed his childhood and moved into adolescence, when he'd murdered his first daimon-born keeper at the age of fourteen. *The same age as my son.* He shut Rafael's face from his mind. Like his husband, his son was a source of light and love. *And here I must have darkness.*

Guillermo whispered, "They're here."

Diago blinked and examined the sigils. *Close, but close only counts with hand grenades, and this isn't one.* "I'm not ready. Draw them nearer and stall them." He lifted himself on his elbows until he could peer over the edge.

When the squad was half a meter from the trail's fissure, Diago nodded. Guillermo stood. He angled himself so the rope around his forearm remained out of sight. Raising his Mauser, he aimed it at their point man. "Halt."

The soldier swung the barrel of his gun in Guillermo's direction. Sitz put his hand on the man's shoulder and motioned for him to lower the rifle. The soldier obeyed him.

The point at which they'd stopped was wide enough to allow Sitz to ease around his man. It was tight maneuvering, but the German managed to keep his heels on the ledge. "We just want to talk, Herr Ramírez. Please, join me."

"I'm fine up here."

Diago eased himself back to the ground and resumed his

work, shaping triangles within the circles, panting through dry lips as he vomited more scorpions onto the ground. The sounds he made were so low, the howling winds covered the throaty growl of his song.

Gunter's voice floated up to them. "Your brother needs you."

Guillermo laughed.

The image of Jordi's smug face filled Diago's mind. He hacked a fresh round of rage into the spell. The ward's lines shimmered to life, plunging deep into the earth. More silver threads from the angel's tear snaked behind the scorpions.

The rock beneath his body answered with a growl. A few pebbles clattered beside him.

Sitz made no sign he heard or saw the minor disturbance. "I've offered to negotiate on Generalissimo Abelló's behalf."

Generalissimo Abelló, my ass. Enraged by Jordi's pomposity, Diago coughed a fat scorpion into the crevice.

Guillermo mouthed, *Now.*

Diago shook his head. *Not yet.* The sigil needed time to reach its destination. He'd spent his fury on these stones, and between his hunger and exhaustion—*and my sanity*—he'd only be able to execute this spell once. He drew his knife and motioned for Guillermo to keep talking.

Guillermo's lip curled, but he complied. Again, he moved from his cover and glared down at Sitz. "Give me my brother's terms."

Diago risked another look over the ledge.

The German licked his lips and sidled closer. With him came his men.

Sitz craned his neck to look up at Guillermo. "Come back with us and renounce forever your right to rule Los Nefilim.

Pronounce your brother as the true king. Then he will call back his assassins. He swears never again to make another attempt on either your life or that of your daughter. Refuse, and you'll condemn that child to the constant shadow of death." Stepping forward again, Sitz led his men onto the ledge. "Your abdication for your daughter's future, Herr Ramírez. Those are the terms."

This is as good as it gets. Diago slashed his palm with his knife and allowed his blood to fall into the crack, doubling the sigil's power. He sang the glyph to life with a furious shout.

Sitz turned toward Diago, and his mouth dropped open. Recovering quickly, he drew his pistol, but he was too late.

The ward flamed, striking the limestone's fractures with short hard bursts. A cascading avalanche of ruptures spread through the sediment.

Diago's chest vibrated with the earth's groan. Beneath that noise, he heard another sound. *Nefilim. It's nefilim, and they're singing, their voices bound together, rising in pitch . . .*

A loud crack thundered beneath him. The edge of the ridge shook with the force of his spell. Too weak to rise, he pushed himself backward.

Too slow, I'm too slow.

I'm going down with them . . .

[2]

The ridge buckled and shuddered. Then the rope cinched tight and dug into Diago's hips. His coat rode up and the cold ground ripped into his stomach as Guillermo hauled him backward to safety.

Gunshots echoed around them. Diago guessed the panicked soldiers were firing indiscriminately.

Well away from the crumbling edge, Guillermo dragged Diago to his knees. Diago waved his friend away as he loosened the knot with shaking fingers. The big nefil released him and took cover behind the boulder. Within seconds, Diago freed himself and joined Guillermo, maneuvering into position to attain a clear view of Gunter's squad.

A tall nefil with a bullish face lifted his hand. With a flash of yellow light, he sang his spell to life. Veins of amber crisscrossed beneath the soldiers' feet.

Diago sheathed his knife and reached for his Astra. The holster's flap stymied his frozen fingers. Fumbling for the clasp, he watched in horror as the nefil's angel-born magic solidified the ground beneath the Nationalists. Limestone crumbled to the left and right of the soldiers, but the ledge itself held.

Guillermo jerked his gloves from his hands and snatched a beam of the day's last light. Twisting the pale gold shaft into a ball, he shouted his song. The air crackled with the electricity of his aura. A stream of orange fire blazed from the stone set within his signet and encircled the glyph. Sparks showered the air.

Guillermo lobbed the sigil down onto the soldiers.

The ward smashed the Nationalist's glyph. Diago's viridian flames shot up through the earth. The beams of light spread through the limestone until the rock disintegrated beneath the squad's feet.

Sitz's foot slid backward and found nothing but air. Throwing his torso forward, he grabbed for the sheer wall and missed. His screams followed him down into the valley.

The second nefil fired his pistol in Guillermo's direction. Three wild shots punctured the air. Diago heard the snap of a bullet. Another tore a chunk off the boulder. The last shot disappeared into the ether with the shooter.

The third soldier made a wild leap. His fingertips caught a thin shelf of stone. Grimacing, he tried to hold on to the mountainside. Sweat coated his face. His lips trembled with his exertion. "Please."

The wind caught his whisper and carried it upward.

Guillermo lifted his Mauser and fired once. Blood spurted from the top of the man's head.

A fourth soldier threw himself back the way they'd come. He landed on a solid shelf of limestone. Getting his feet under him, he started to run.

Guillermo chambered another round. He aimed and fired. The soldier lurched sideways, teetered on the edge, and then plunged down the side with his comrades.

Diago tried to rise, his gun half drawn. Darkness edged his vision. The strange song he'd heard when he cast his spell touched the back of his mind again. The chorus grew, their voices focused and deliberate, each note a study in precision— there and gone as quick as one of his husband's stolen kisses.

What the hell . . . ?

The arrangement wasn't his, nor did it originate with the spell he'd just performed. He tried to discern the cadence so he might learn the source, but the chords danced just beyond his grasp before disappearing altogether.

Did I imagine it? Blinking sweat from his eyes, Diago fought against the numbness flooding his limbs. *Or did I finally poison myself to the point of no return?*

Guillermo pushed Diago's pistol back into the holster and secured the gun. Then he helped him stand. "Are you okay?"

Vaguely aware that his palm still bled, Diago withdrew a handkerchief with a shaking hand. He felt dirty, like he'd been swimming in a sewer, contaminating himself with foul deeds and thoughts until he'd never be clean again.

Avoiding Guillermo's question, he said, "I sensed something."

"What?"

"I don't know. When I sang, something touched my mind."

"Daimon? Angel-born?"

"Yes . . . no. Maybe both." He pressed the handkerchief against the gash on his palm and snapped, "I don't know."

Guillermo's grip tightened. "Look at me."

"I'm fine." The words were out of his mouth before he could consider the ramifications of lying to Guillermo. *I'm fine. I've got to be fine.*

"Then look at me."

Inhaling the cold air in short hard sips, Diago didn't have the strength for a prolonged argument. He met his friend's gaze. Flecks of gold blazed with angelic fire and swirled in Guillermo's light brown irises.

Diago instinctively flinched from that conflagration of power. Guillermo brought his hands to both sides of Diago's face, holding him still. Their auras converged.

The sudden influx of power erupted in a vision:

He floats in the heart of a nebula. Disembodied and weightless, he sees through eyes that are not eyes, not like those he wears in the mortal realm. Here in this vast void, his aura is the only manifestation of his being. He is a cloud of sound and light without a heart that beats or a brain that thinks.

The stars spread around him, infinite and terrifying. A river of white fire flows between the nebula's heliotrope clouds. He cannot define the river's source or its end.

Ophanim, the lords of fire, float just beyond the river's shore. Shaped like blazing wheels, they revolve in place, and he perceives a thousand eyes behind the Ophanim's flames.

Over their heads are mirrored shards that spin and flicker, black like ice shattered by midnight. Complex glyphs shimmer within the shards, held in place by the Ophanim's song.

Not mirrors, but gateways, portals. As he watches with his eyes that are not eyes, angels flash through the portals and dive into the river's flames. Messengers and Principalities, each group distinguishable by the number of wings and eyes intrinsic to their class. They are composed of colors the mortal eye cannot comprehend or even name.

They drink from the flames and emerge renewed. Rising

once more, they return through the portals, back to whatever realms await them.

In his body that is not a body, Diago drifts close to the river. When an angel dives, a molten drop splashes his aura. The fire laces his song and burns . . . it burns with the fire of the sun . . . and as it touches him, he feels the weight of time bearing down on him, pushing him back to the flesh that anchors him like a chain to the mortal realm . . .

Diago broke free of Guillermo's grip. Staggering to one side, he vomited. With so little in his stomach, nothing came up but bile and a single scorpion—small and misshapen, encircled by a thread of silver that seemed pale in comparison to the afterimage of angels fluttering against his mind. A golden ember dropped from the arachnid's tail, then the scorpion withered and died.

Diago gasped. "What the hell did you just do?"

"Nothing to do with hell at all. I lent you some of my power. You gave me everything and you were so gray, I was afraid . . ." Guillermo let the sentence trail into silence as if he feared to even complete the thought. "Are you okay? What happened?"

Diago wiped his mouth. "I had a vision. Angels, feasting on a river of fire."

"I'm sorry. I overwhelmed you. I didn't mean to." Guillermo's misery was palpable.

Christ, he's like a boy who doesn't know his own strength. "It's okay." Diago sniffled and lifted his hand. A drop of blood fell to the ground and sizzled against the stone. Golden light surrounded the wound on Diago's palm, pulling his flesh together until it was as if he'd never cut himself. He shifted his gaze to Guillermo. "What did I just witness?"

"The angels drink from the river of fire to heal themselves. You probably envisioned angelic forces, replenishing their power after a battle."

"And Ophanim singing open the portals between realms." He paused, unsure how to describe them, or why they'd terrified him so deeply.

"They do more than that. The Ophanim also guard the river and make sure the territory remains neutral so that any can drink. They realize the fleeting nature of the angelic conflicts. The river must never fall to one side or the other."

"A drop . . . of that fire touched me. Healed me." He held up his hand. "Is that why Jordi wants the signet so badly? So he can drink and replenish himself?"

"Yes. If he can win the Thrones' trust, then they'll assign him a consort, and he'll be able to go to the river in his flesh, just as I have done."

Diago tried to comprehend visiting that molten river in his mortal form, and for the first time in his life, his imagination failed him. "In your mortal body?"

Guillermo nodded. "But only by Juanita's side. Without her protection, my flesh would be burnt to cinders. With her, I can drink and renew both my power and that of the Thrones' tear in my signet. That is the Thrones' true blessing."

"Jesus."

"Yeah."

"Jesus Christ," Diago repeated. "Can you imagine someone as cruel as Jordi with that much power?"

"It's why I haven't given up the signet. Sitz claimed that giving Jordi the ring would remove the shadow of death from both Ysa and me. But that is a lie. Jordi intends to bring war over the entire mortal realm in order to subjugate the mortals to his will. And what is war but death?" Guillermo sighed and went to their packs. "Do you remember how, in our firstborn lives, our responsibilities were similar to those of the Ophanim, guarding these portals and the magic so that the mortal realm remained neutral for all creatures?"

Diago shouldered his Mauser. "Now we're more like the angels . . . constantly fighting among ourselves."

Guillermo tossed Diago his pack, and then he paused, looking back toward Spain. "Sometimes I wonder if I'm doing this wrong."

"I don't understand. What could you possibly do differently?"

"We need to find a way toward some kind of peace—for the sake of the mortals. Then we can go back to our original purpose as guardians, not soldiers."

"That's a fine ideal, but you can't make peace with someone like Jordi." *When did our roles reverse?* "Listen, I advocated for a truce early in this conflict, but you and your council overrode me. You were right. I was wrong. There is no accord with someone like him."

Guillermo twisted the signet on his finger. "My brother and I have spent five incarnations fighting over this ring. What if I could convince Jordi that his way is wrong? What if I could change his way of thinking? About the mortal world and the nefilim's role in it?"

Diago gaped at him. "We've got to get you off this mountain. The high altitudes are depriving your brain of oxygen."

Guillermo chuckled and grabbed his own pack. Walking toward the cave, he waited for Diago to join him before he spoke again. "You're the one who always says our incarnations change us."

"In Jordi's case, that's true. Unfortunately, he doesn't seem to change for the better. You could never trust him." Diago cut off Guillermo's protest with a shake of his head. "He owned the signet in his last incarnation, and he abused the Thrones' trust by forming a pact with a renegade angel. No matter how much Jordi possesses, he is never satisfied."

"He's my brother, Diago."

"He's your half-brother."

"Still, there must be some good in him."

"I lived with him in our last incarnation." Diago moved in front of Guillermo and forced the other nefil to stop. This wasn't a conversation he wanted to have in front of Carme and Feran.

Guillermo lifted his finger. "You were working as a spy."

"And I'm a damned good one. I saw him in . . . his most intimate moments. He thought I loved him, Guillermo, and he shared with me his aspirations. And his abuse." He held Guillermo's gaze with his own. *How can I make him understand?* "Your brother isn't a good person. I don't know if he can be."

Guillermo inhaled deeply and looked away, as if working to bring his temper under control. "So you've already rendered judgment."

"I'm giving you the benefit of my experience."

"And you're saying he can't be saved."

"I'm saying he won't let himself be saved. He has no desire to become someone different, because he likes who he is. Worse, he's winning this war. He has no impetus to change."

Guillermo nodded. "I don't disagree with you. I know

that any proposal I give to him must come from a position of strength on my part."

"I think you need to accept him for who and what he is—a sadist and a killer."

Guillermo's mouth tightened and his eyes narrowed. Without a word, he stepped around Diago and set out again.

Swell. Diago hurried to catch up to him. *I shouldn't kick him when he's down, but this is madness.* "You know, everyone wants my honest opinion until I give it to them."

"I never asked for your opinion. I was simply thinking out loud." He lengthened his stride, forcing Diago to hurry.

As if their misery weren't complete, the rain turned into snow. *The weather, Christ, even the weather is turning on us. And we can't afford to turn on each other.* "I'm sorry. I shouldn't have been so blunt. Sometimes it's hard for me to remember that you're brothers, and when you start talking about forgiving him, it scares me."

Guillermo shook his head and slowed his pace. "Maybe that's part of the problem," he admitted with a sigh. "I'm scared, too. I realize what my brother is capable of doing, but I'm looking for a way out."

The strain between them diminished, and Diago was glad. "We've got some time. Jordi is going to secure Spain under Franco, and then try to negotiate with Queen Rousseau. She's no fool. He'll have a hard time convincing her to turn us over to him. He's tied himself too tightly to Queen Jaeger." And the German nefilim were chafing for another chance to bring France to heel.

"I think you're right. Jaeger is biding her time until she's ready to goad Hitler into an attack on France."

Knowing all this, how can he possibly believe that he

can change Jordi? Not wanting to provoke Guillermo again, Diago held the thought close and peeked at his friend as they trudged side by side. Weariness and resignation surrounded Guillermo. *He's tired and mourning the good nefilim he lost during this war.* He just needed to grieve and rest. Then he'd regain his equilibrium and forget this insanity of trying to change Jordi.

Hoping to be out of the wind soon, Diago checked the distance between them and the shelter. Just ahead, beneath the veil of snow, the cave's mouth grinned at them. The dry stinging flakes came down harder, carried by the howling wind.

As opposed to the storm, the quiet emanating from the cave seemed ominous. A flash of pale blue wiggled along the lip of stone.

A sigil. Diago saw it just as Guillermo pointed it out.

Like every angel's glyph, each nefil's technique worked like a signature, and this ward carried familiar vibrations. From the color and harsh angle of the lines, Diago recognized Carme's song.

The snow quickly extinguished the already dying light. The ward's intent was unclear. Still, wounded nefilim rarely used their energy for a sigil unless provoked . . . or threatened.

Diago chambered a round in his Mauser. "Do you think other members of Sitz's squad managed to circle behind us?"

"Not likely." Guillermo formed a protective ward. Angelic fire crackled around them, lashing snow and darkness alike. It wouldn't stop a bullet but worked like a flare to distract the enemy's attention. He gestured for Diago to go left.

Diago put two meters between them. At Guillermo's signal, they rushed the cavern's entrance.

[3]

As they charged forward, Guillermo tossed his glyph into the cave. Diago followed the ward. He went in at a crouch and fell to one knee. Beside him, Guillermo drew his pistol and ducked beneath the overhang. They made a quick sweep of the area, searching for obstacles and potential threats.

The cavern was wide and surprisingly tall in places. Shaped like a clamshell, it narrowed toward the rear. A few spent casings dotted the smooth floor. Boulders and flowstone formations spread close to the walls, giving a sniper plenty of room to hide.

Diago searched for human shapes, or the glint of light against metal, which might reveal the muzzle of a gun. No shots rang out, nor did he detect the telltale scuffle of movement that might precede an ambush. *That doesn't mean one isn't coming.*

Guillermo's sigil burned low and then went out. Shadows devoured the faint streams of gray twilight that managed to slip inside. The cave felt strangely empty.

Now that he was out of the wind, Diago's sense of smell

returned. The electric odor of dying sigils reminded him of fried wiring. Wisps of smoke rose from the scarred flowstone.

The remains of a few fading glyphs sputtered against the walls and slithered among clusters of speleothems. Diago recognized the colors of Carme's and Feran's songs on the fading wards. Given the condition of the sigils, the battle had been short and intense. Whatever the fight, no third party seemed to have been involved.

A thick brown streak of blood led from the center of the chamber to a squarish boulder the size of lorry. *Crawled or dragged?* Diago wondered as he examined the trail. The amount of blood on the floor indicated an injury much graver than Carme sustained on the hill. The profusion of wards sizzling around the heavy stone clearly belonged to her.

Rising, Diago edged forward, vaguely aware of Guillermo covering his advance. As he neared the rock, he found two spent cartridges and a boot with the foot turned at an odd angle.

The shoe's cracked sole and the worn sides told him it was Carme. He whispered her name and hoped the foot would move. She didn't.

Diago swallowed hard. *Damn it, Carme. What happened?* He nudged the boot with his rifle's muzzle. "Come on, Carme. You're too goddamned mean to die."

At the sound of his voice, an indigo glyph slithered over the top of the boulder. Diago froze. The ward was mere centimeters from his eyes. It rose like a snake, weaving its head back and forth. Serrated red sparks throbbed along the slender body. He recognized it immediately. It was a particularly nasty spell, and one of Carme's specialties. She'd named it after the fungus it represented: Devil's Fingers.

"Carme." Guillermo whispered her name like a prayer. "We're here now. Kill the ward."

Diago risked a glance downward. The boot remained still. *She's dead.* Which meant the ward would fulfill its design.

But it's weak. She must have been near death when she formed it. Diago kept his hand low and formed a protective ward of his own. Using a low growl at the back of his throat, he charged it with the power of his voice.

Shades of green, threaded with silver, ignited around the six entwined circles he'd created. Embers of gold embraced the glyph's edges.

Diago scowled. *That never happened before.* Nor did he have time to analyze it. Carme's ward swelled. *And when it matures, it will explode.*

The shimmer of golden light around his glyph didn't seem to damage it. Quite the reverse. Like the silver from the angel's tear in his ring, the golden rays seemed to enhance the power of his ward. As Carme's sigil expanded, so did his.

Without warning, the indigo snake burst. Millions of serrated fragments sailed through the air. Diago's glyph shot upward and outward. The circles spread to shield both him and Guillermo, absorbing Carme's spell. The spores fell to the cavern floor, where they withered and died.

Diago exhaled. "That was close."

"She must be unconscious." The denial in Guillermo's voice wrenched Diago's pity into his throat.

He wants her to be alive so badly. Lying to him helped neither of them. "She's dead."

"You don't know that. You can't see her."

"I know it like I know—" Diago snapped his teeth together

before he could finish the sentence. *Like your brother thrives on hate.*

The accusation touched the roof of his mouth. The daimon-born nature he'd awakened on the ridge wanted him to say it aloud, not only because it was the truth, but in order to gouge Guillermo's heart so Diago could feed on his pain.

The craving was like a drug, one that required a higher dosage with each encounter. Nor was it an addiction that Diago wanted.

He closed his eyes and took a deep breath, remembering his husband's advice to follow his actions to their logical conclusion. *If I lash out at Guillermo, his pain will become my guilt, setting up an endless cycle of retribution between us. We will stab each other, first with words, and then with our actions, until one or both of us are dead.*

In another incarnation, he might have expressed the sentiment without caring. No more. Miquel had taught him he needn't be enslaved to his daimonic passions. He could lead Guillermo to the truth without antagonizing their friendship.

Guillermo's aura threw off dangerous sparks. "You know it like you know what?"

"Nothing. Where's Feran?"

"Where indeed?" Guillermo snarled.

Full dark descended outside the cave. Even with his superior night vision, Diago found it hard to see. Shouldering his Mauser, he traded the rifle for his pistol and a torch.

Guillermo likewise drew his torch, shining it into the chamber's crevices. Together they secured the perimeter with a full investigation and found no further threats. Nor did they locate either Feran or his body.

Diago returned to the site of Carme's last stand. He

stepped around the boulder to find her corpse. She'd died as she lived—with her gun in her hand. A half-formed ward sputtered beside her hip. Fresh lacerations covered her face, probably from the pieces of stone that were obviously chipped by either wards or bullets. She'd been stabbed in the gut. That explained the trail of blood. A bullet had been placed between her eyes. If the powder burns were any indication, it was the coup de grâce.

Diago knelt beside her body. "She's dead."

Guillermo seemed to shrink two sizes beneath his disappointment. "Are you sure there's nothing we can do?"

His friend's plaintive tone made Diago glad he'd exercised restraint earlier. "Yes. I'm sure. Her soul is gone. I don't even think your river of fire could bring her back now." The fact that Guillermo didn't try told Diago that he knew it, too.

"Goddamn it," Guillermo muttered as he turned away and pretended to scan the cave, but not before Diago saw a tear slip from his eye. "I never saw it coming. Feran is . . ."

"The kind of person your brother draws to him." Diago kept his tone mild and carefully checked his motives. The need to hurt Guillermo had vanished, but lying to him could cause more pain in the long run. He arranged Carme's jacket and stroked her cold cheek. Choosing his words with care, he pressed his case against Jordi. "Feran is hungry for shortcuts to fame, and that is Jordi's way, too."

"You don't even know for certain that he's working for Jordi."

"Think about it: Feran wanted to stay with you on the ridge, probably to act as a fifth column for Sitz. You're distracted with the squad"—he lifted his hand and pointed his finger at Guillermo's head—"then bang. After that, he and

Sitz storm the cave and take down Carme and me. He was working with them. I'm sure of it."

"This is not a conversation we're going to have right now. Let me in there."

Maybe not now, but it was a discussion Diago intended to continue. *Later.* He backed out of the alcove and moved away a respectful distance.

Guillermo knelt beside Carme and kissed his palm before placing it over her throat. When he spoke, his voice was tight with rage. "I will watch for you, my good servant, Carme Gebara. We will sing of you in France. Listen for our song."

When Guillermo left her side, Diago returned to say his own goodbye. "Sometimes respect has to be enough." Touching her throat and then her heart, he said no prayers, but instead gave her the nefilim's promise: "I will watch for you."

Guillermo turned a slow circle in the center of the room. "This"—he gestured at the carnage of perishing glyphs—"was one hell of a fight. How is it we didn't hear it?"

"I heard gunshots and assumed they were from Sitz's men. Then we were occupied with our own fight. Look around you. This began and ended within moments."

Guillermo conceded the point. "Fair enough. But how did Feran slip out under our noses?"

Diago examined the perimeter with a new interest. "Who said he left the same way he came in?"

"I didn't see any passages when we canvassed."

"That doesn't mean one isn't there. He said he'd used this cave before." Diago climbed a pile of loose stones and shifted several to one side. The wall behind them was solid. He moved a few meters to the right and chose another mound of rocks. These were heavier, some as large as crates.

Guillermo followed him with his torch. "What can I do to help?"

"Just give me light."

Guillermo obeyed him. All Diago found was more wall. He moved to the next pile, working the smaller clusters first. At the fourth section, he found an inch of darkness in the cleft between two rocks. He pressed his fingers against the hole and felt the whisper of warm air kiss his flesh.

"I think I found it."

Guillermo put down his torch and helped. Together, they moved the stones aside. The cleft widened.

Diago shone the light into the shaft. "It's narrow, but I think I can get through it."

He went to Carme's body and took her coat. Using his knife, he cut two long strips and fashioned a pair of knee-pads from the wool while Guillermo continued to move the rocks.

When he'd cleared as much debris from the opening as he could, Guillermo squatted and shone his light inside. "Don't go far."

"I won't." Diago dropped to his hands and knees; he pushed his torch in front of him and then inserted his head and shoulders into the passage. Smooth stone surrounded him.

After a thorough check for sigils, he inched forward. His back scraped the tunnel's ceiling, forcing him to lower his torso and drag himself forward on his elbows. The stone grew slick and damp. Eight meters in, the passage widened. Each breath came easier as the stone receded.

He wiggled through an arch and found himself with

enough room to stand. Moisture coated the reddish-brown stones in a thin film. The low passage continued for thirty paces before twisting around a bend.

Diago ran his beam along the floor. Stones had been recently turned by footsteps. *Feran.*

Moving stealthily, he went to the corner and checked the passage's length. The next section continued until the darkness swallowed the beam of Diago's torch.

Standing perfectly still, he listened. The only sound of movement came from behind, where Guillermo waited. *Feran is gone.*

"Are you okay?" Guillermo's whisper carried his anxiety.

Diago returned to the tunnel. "Yes. I'm fine." He crawled back to the cavern and reported what he had found.

"None of this makes sense." Guillermo exhaled in frustration. "He murders Carme while we're distracted and then flees into the caverns. Why run? He could have ambushed *us* as we entered the cave. What was he after?"

Diago ran his light over the floor again. "Do you see Carme's pack?"

Guillermo swept the beam of his torch near the mouth of the cavern. "No."

"She carried a notebook of contacts with her." Diago returned to her body and searched her clothing. The notebook was gone. Never mind that the pages were protected by sigils and the names written in code. During wars, glyphs were untangled and codes broken. Icy tendrils of fear plunged into his stomach. "Feran missed the opportunity to take you out, so he cut his losses and grabbed the notebook. Believe me now?"

Guillermo nodded. "I'm afraid I do."

"If he takes that to Jordi, we're going to lose our spies in Germany and Italy."

"Shit and bitter shit. We've got to go after him."

"These mountains are riddled with labyrinths. He could be anywhere down there."

A dark glimmer flickered in Guillermo's eyes. "Do we dare follow the cobra into his nest?"

"Do we have a choice?"

While Guillermo secured the packs with a length of rope, Diago cut a piece from his blanket. He used his knife to make a pinprick hole in the wool. Wrapping the cloth around the head of his torch, he secured it with surgical tape.

"Give me your torch." He held out his hand.

"Why?"

"I'm hooding them. We don't want to give Feran too much warning that we're behind him."

"Won't it be completely dark down there?"

"Yes, but there will be twists and turns. A full beam might throw shadows and attract his attention. We'll have to leave the rifles behind, though. They'll be too cumbersome to carry in the tighter passages."

Guillermo didn't question the decision. He went to work removing the rounds and redistributing them between the packs. The ammunition could be repurposed if necessary. He then picked up his rifle.

"What are you doing?" Diago went to work fashioning a set of kneepads for Guillermo.

"Decommissioning them." Using his thumbnail, he traced a line along the bolt. Then he hummed a deep note, charging the sigil until it glowed in reddish hues before it sank into the

metal. "I'm fusing the bolt to the extractor and firing pin."
He set his gun aside and then picked up Diago's, repeating
the procedure.

When Guillermo finished, Diago helped him adjust the
kneepads.

"I'll go first." Taking the end of the rope that tied their
packs together, Diago got to his feet and started for the cleft.
"Once I've dragged the packs through, you come next." He
realized Guillermo wasn't following him. "What now?"

Guillermo glanced toward Carme's body. He absently
reached into his breast pocket for a cigar that wasn't there.
Letting his hand fall, he fumbled for his lighter and gripped
the device with the fervor of a man holding on to a life preserver. "I'm so tired, Diago. I don't know how much longer
I can do this."

The wind howled outside the cave, almost drowning the
sound of Guillermo's grief, but Diago heard it loud and clear.
His daimonic need to aggravate that pain rose in Diago's
chest, but he knuckled it down.

He returned to Guillermo's side and touched his friend's
wrist. "Whenever you're unsure of yourself, lean on me, and
I'll hold you up until you're rested and ready again. I'll guard
your back and help you make good decisions. Just like you
did for me all these centuries."

Guillermo pinched the bridge of his nose and shut his eyes.
*He's trying not to cry. He never wants us to see him
weak. These are the moments he saves for when he's alone
with his wife.* But Juanita was in France with the children,
and Guillermo needed help now. Diago had no idea how she
comforted him, so he did what he knew to do for Miquel
and waited patiently for Guillermo to regain control.

Guillermo opened his eyes and chuffed an embarrassed laugh. "I didn't support you all those years expecting reimbursement."

"I know. That's what makes us friends."

Guillermo smiled, and some of the weariness left his countenance.

But not completely gone, Diago thought as he returned to the cleft. *He needs time away from all this in order to heal.*

We all do.

"We should go."

With a last sad look in the direction of Carme's corpse, Guillermo nodded and pocketed his lighter. "Okay. Let's get this bastard."

Now he sounds more like himself. Diago felt his own confidence return as he ducked back into the tunnel, dragging the packs behind him. The stone pressed against him again, pushing him down, but he kept Feran's face firmly in his mind's eye. Feran, who dared insinuate that Diago couldn't be trusted based on nothing more than his daimonic lineage, was the worst traitor of all.

I will hunt you, Feran Perez. In this incarnation and all others. I will find you. "That is my oath," Diago whispered as he reached the passage. *And I will teach you to fear the dark.*

[4]

Diago watched Guillermo drag himself through the narrow tunnel. Twice the big nefil had to stop, his breath loud in the enclosed space.

The scent of Guillermo's fear, sharp in the cold air, aroused a pleasurable warmth in the pit of Diago's stomach. His tongue flickered between his lips, and he tasted the big nefil's panic, tangy and sweet.

I can't let myself get used to this. "Guillermo?" He shone his light into the tunnel.

The beam caught the top of Guillermo's head, where his cap sat askew. He looked like a boy caught in a bad place.

Pity tugged at Diago's heart, and again he heard Miquel, patiently teaching him: *Be aware of your feelings. Nurture your empathy for others, and the evil within you will die.*

Diago focused on his compassion for Guillermo. "What's wrong?"

"I'm okay." His hoarse whisper was barely audible. He didn't lift his head. "Just a little claustrophobic. It'll pass."

"Claustrophobia doesn't pass."

"I know." Guillermo took several short breaths before he

continued. "I can control it." Then, softer, more to himself, he muttered, "I *must*."

"What can I do to help?"

"I need a breeze. Just to feel the air moving."

"Then come to me. The air is moving here." Diago lowered his torch and held out his hand.

Guillermo lifted his head and crawled forward a few more centimeters before he stopped again. "I think I'm stuck."

Diago aimed the beam over Guillermo's back. "You're not stuck. Your coat is caught. Back up a few centimeters . . . there, that's enough. Now pull your coat tight . . . that's good. Come forward. I'm here. I won't let anything happen to you. Keep coming. Good, very good." He reached through the arch and took Guillermo's wrist. "You're almost done. Can you feel the breeze?"

Guillermo heaved himself through the arch. He scrambled forward and drew his knees against his chest. "Oh fuck, that was tight." Gasping for air, he tilted his head back against the wall.

Diago kept his voice low. "Just be glad you lost some weight. You wouldn't have fit six months ago."

"Always looking on the sunny side, aren't you?" He gave Diago a shaky smile and got to his feet. Freckles stood stark against his pale cheeks and a thin sheen of sweat covered his brow.

"Okay?" Diago touched his shoulder.

Guillermo nodded. "I'm just too old for this."

"We're not old." Diago shoved Guillermo's pack into his arms. "We're venerable." He paused and examined Guillermo's features in the dim light. "Are you sure you can do this?"

Guillermo nodded as he shouldered the rucksack. "Before

the war, Juanita was helping me control the claustrophobia with something she calls exposure therapy. We'd . . . I would force myself to endure the very thing I feared. It must be working." He gestured at the tunnel they'd just come through. "I couldn't have done this five years ago." A few more deep breaths, and his color returned somewhat. "I'm going to be all right."

Diago almost believed him. "Maybe you should go back and wait for me in the cavern. We might hit tighter spots than that down below."

Guillermo shook his head. "No, this is good for me. I'm going to beat this." Before Diago could argue, Guillermo turned to the wall and traced a location glyph on the stone. The ward shimmered for a moment and then faded; it would remain hidden to anyone but them. "That's our anchor. Every ten meters, we'll add a ward to link back to it. That should keep us from getting lost."

"Good idea." Diago noted that his friend's hands steadied as he created the sigil.

Guillermo gestured with his torch. "Then let's move out."

Diago led the way, picking a careful path over the rock-strewn floor. Every click of the stones sliding beneath their feet seemed magnified in the silence.

Nothing to do but hope Feran doesn't hear us coming. Diago shone his light over the walls, searching the niches for active sigils. Although Guillermo didn't protest the slow pace, Diago felt the other nefil's sense of urgency pressing at his back.

The passage looped to the left before descending again. The distance between floor and ceiling narrowed until they were forced to walk bent at the waist. Diago glanced back, but so far Guillermo seemed to be handling the enclosed spaces without any further signs of panic.

They came to a junction between two tunnels. Diago gestured for Guillermo to wait. He followed the left passage. Away from Guillermo, he sniffed the air. All that met his nostrils was the metallic scent of water.

Cave straws hung from the ceiling. They easily snapped beneath his touch. No one had come this way, especially no one moving fast.

Diago returned to Guillermo and signaled for him to remain still. He ventured down the right-hand passage, shining the beam of his light across the floor. A partially clear puddle of water indicated the silt had yet to fully settle. Feran had passed this way not long ago. Another two meters in and Diago found the thin cave straws were snapped close to the low ceiling. A handprint muddied one wall.

Inhaling, Diago caught the scent of Feran's terror clinging to the damp air. This time he made no effort to silence his daimonic longing to taste another's fear.

Licking his lips, he backtracked to Guillermo. "This way."

Guillermo anchored another sigil to the wall. "Are we far behind him?"

"Hard to say." Diago considered the question. "Twenty minutes, maybe thirty."

Guillermo finished the ward and gave Diago a sharp nod. "Let's see if we can narrow that time frame."

They moved as silently as possible in the tight passage.

Because he was relying almost as much on his sense of smell as his eyes, Diago was the first to notice the moist air carried a different odor. The stench of blood and rot crept over the scent of Feran's anxiety.

Shining his light along the walls and floor, he soon found a splash of blood near the base of the wall. Red shards flickered over the stones. Rising from the bloodstain was the slender arm of a fungus. Dotted in black, the red pulpy flesh resembled a sinister finger.

Diago squatted beside the fungus.

Guillermo crab-walked to his side and whispered, "I didn't know stinkhorn grew in caves."

"It doesn't. Carme must have hit Feran with the Devil's Fingers."

"What?"

"The same spell that almost caught us back in the cave. I thought you knew."

Guillermo shook his head. "I just figured if it was coming from Carme, it was lethal."

"She patterned it after a species of stinkhorn she discovered in Australia. Essentially, when the sigil explodes, it jettisons smaller glyphs under the victim's skin, where they become spores." Diago pointed to the red shards darting through the bloodstain. "They surface as painful boils, and as they mature, the fingers"—he pointed to the withering finger on the stones—"begin to push through the victim's flesh. Of course, once the fingers reach the air, they emit the same foul odor as the fungus."

Guillermo paled. "That's horrible."

"Yeah, I know." Diago couldn't keep his admiration from seeping into his voice. "She always had a daimon's love of nature."

"I'm glad you never said that around her." Guillermo frowned. "If it's a fungus, can he spread the spores to other people?"

Diago shook his head. "It's harmless to anyone who wasn't the recipient of the spell. But the spores do continue to spread through the victim's body until they either reach the internal organs or the victim takes his own life."

"How long does he have?"

"Weeks, months." Diago shrugged. "She designed it as a slow kill."

Guillermo shuddered. "I wouldn't wish that on anyone . . . except maybe Feran."

"Oh, his fucking days are numbered now." Diago didn't try to keep the glee from his voice. Only a nefil in his second-born life would be so arrogant as to take on an old nefil like Carme, who was in her fifth incarnation.

He probably thought her injuries weakened her. If so, that was a bad judgment call on Feran's part, and very likely his last in this incarnation. Diago got to his feet. "How are you holding up?"

Guillermo nodded. "I'm okay. Let's move."

Diago did just that. A few meters farther, they came to a rockfall that blocked the entire passage.

Guillermo swore. "What now?"

"Hold my light." Alert for sigils, Diago eased forward and examined the spill. "Looks like the one back at the cave. It was deliberately set."

"He knows we're following him."

"Maybe. And then again, maybe he knew we would and this was simply a precaution to slow us down. If he suspected we were close on his heels, he would have set more traps along the way."

Guillermo didn't seem convinced. "He didn't leave traps for us because his fight with Carme weakened him."

Diago looked over his shoulder. "How can you be so sure?"

"I know my nefilim. Feran still hasn't learned to pace his song in a battle. He gets overexcited and belts out his attacks allegro." Guillermo indicated the quick tempo with lively snaps of his fingers.

"Do you study us all so thoroughly?"

"It's my job. Like I know you've been fighting your daimonic desires ever since you carved the stone back at the ridge."

Diago's fingers slowed, but he didn't turn. "Am I that obvious?"

"Only to me. And I'm sorry. I shouldn't have asked you to do such a thing."

Diago turned and met his friend's gaze. "You did right. It's like your claustrophobia—it never goes away. But Miquel has given me the tools to control it. Besides, it's helping me track our friend." Returning his attention to the rockfall, he brushed the smaller stones aside and caught a whiff of Feran's terror wafting through the rubble.

Maybe it was time to use his daimonic talents again. Just as he'd carved the stone on the ridge, he might have a chance to punch through Feran's obstacle. "Stand back. I'm going to try something."

Guillermo retreated several paces and knelt. "Is there anything I can do?"

"Make a protective ward in case Feran left us a nasty surprise on the other side." Diago traced small sigils over the rocks, linking them together with short, hard notes. When he finished, it looked as if a web of black dots covered the rockfall.

A quick glance over his shoulder showed him that Guillermo nurtured a ball of golden light in one hand. He waited until the big nefil finished his song.

Diago placed his palms on the stones. "Ready?"

"On your signal."

"On three . . . One, two, three!" Diago cried out a sharp note. His tenor slammed hard against the sigils. Striking the rubble with his palms, he pushed against the center of the ward. The black dots wiggled into the crevices between the stones. Threads of silver and gold accentuated his spell, strengthening his song.

Suddenly the rocks fell away from his hands. Instead of a continuation of the passage, he found himself facing a sheer drop into darkness. Unable to stop his forward motion, he reached for a handhold. His hands found only air.

Plunging over the ledge, he lost his balance and skidded first to his knees and then onto his stomach. Dust flew in his face, blurring the steep incline. Rocks tumbled around him.

He twisted hard to the left and onto his side. A fist-sized stone barely missed his nose. As he shifted his position, he glimpsed a large boulder directly in his path.

Caught in the avalanche, he couldn't slow his descent. Then the chamber brightened as a fiery ward flew over his head.

Guillermo's sigil.

The waves of sound landed between him and the boulder. The glyph expanded and formed a cushion between the rock and his body. A shock went through him when he struck the light. It was like landing on a hard mattress. Still, the weight of the ward slowed his downward plunge and pushed him to one side. His hip grazed the boulder, and then he slowed to a stop.

A cascade of smaller stones peppered his body before the landslide subsided. Diago's heart hammered as the ward shimmered and faded. Staggering to his feet, he stumbled a few steps on shaky legs and then turned to look upward through the churning dust.

Guillermo stood on the ledge and lowered his hands. "Are you all right?"

A coughing fit interrupted Diago's answer. He spat and measured his breathing until he regained control. Then he brushed the dust from his clothing and tested his limbs. Years of dancing had taught him to be sensitive to torn tendons and pulled muscles. He seemed to have dodged any serious injuries. "I'll be bruised and battered"—he gestured at the boulder—"but not dead."

"Good." Picking his way carefully down the slope, Guillermo made a much more judicious descent. He reached Diago's side and gave him his torch and pack as if nothing untoward had happened. "Are you sure you're all right?"

"Yeah." Diago sighed as he took the items. "Thanks to you."

"Hey, we're a team. You talk me through the tight spots, and I'll keep you from breaking boulders with your head." Guillermo freed his torch from its hood and dropped the cloth to the ground. "No use sneaking around now. If Feran didn't hear that, he's either deaf or long gone from this place."

Diago didn't argue. He released the hood from his light and shone it upward. The chamber was huge. Adorned in golden hues of browns and reds, the domed cavern rose over twenty meters high. The shape brought to mind the natural stone formations Gaudí mimicked with his architecture. Flowstone draperies swept across the walls. Stalactites and stalagmites joined together to form columns rising majestically throughout the room.

A clear pool of water occupied one side of the chamber, encircled by a narrow shore. When Diago moved the beam of his torch away from the water, the glassy surface turned black. *Like the portals over the angels' river of fire.*

Whether for fear of echoes or from reverence for the natural splendor surrounding them, Guillermo kept his voice low and murmured, "Looks like Feran has disappeared again. He's turned into quite the magician."

"He relies on his environment for his tricks. There has to be another exit." Diago shone his light along the shore.

Across the pool, a flash of orange flickered behind a curtain of flowstone. The familiar crackle of a sigil flickered, hissed, and then went silent.

They switched off their torches. Diago traced the lines of a protective ward in the air. Beside him, Guillermo did the same. They moved in unison, their hands gracefully shaping their shields. As they sang their glyphs to life, their voices joined together, forming a melodious echo in the chamber. Guillermo's shield blazed in fiery shades of red and orange; Diago's burst into viridian hues laced with streaks of silver and gold.

Diago frowned. "My sigils have never burned gold before."

Guillermo glanced at the ward. "It's probably because of the river of fire."

"What the hell did you do to me?"

"You're angel, too. The fire that touched you is manifesting in your song. That's all. It's probably nothing you didn't already have inside yourself."

"Why do you keep saying 'probably'?"

Before Guillermo could answer, the glyph across the room flashed again. He seemed relieved by the distraction. "Come on." He crept toward the sporadic flashes. "It's a dying sigil."

"Are you sure?" Diago drew his pistol and followed.

"Reasonably sure."

"That's not sure."

Guillermo didn't answer. Intent on the aurora borealis of hues shimmering over the flowstone, he stepped beneath a natural arch.

Diago took a slow breath and followed. Behind the flowstone was a much tighter passage. He had just enough room to stand shoulder to shoulder with Guillermo.

Three meters away, a sigil stretched from one wall to the other. The threads of light anchored against the stone like a giant spider's web. Blasts of pure red traveled across the symbols embedded in the glyph before dimming into rose and ivory.

"What—"

Guillermo cut him off. "Listen."

Diago detected the sound of nefilim, singing with broken voices. "That's the chant I heard when I carved the stone."

"Read the symbols."

Diago peered at the sigil. "Infinity, gamma . . ." He frowned at the string of numbers embedded in the ward's innermost circle. "Degrees of longitude and latitude?"

Guillermo retrieved a scrap of paper and jotted them down. "It's a portal to a pocket realm."

Unlike an angelic realm, which created pathways to completely separate dimensions, pockets remained just under the veneer of the mortal realm, like a body beneath a blanket.

They were often used by nefilim as bunkers or covert black sites. *And they're damned hard to maintain.*

"Look at the shape of these lines." Guillermo ran his finger close to the glowing orange threads without touching them. "See the image of a labyrinth beneath infinity? The light orange vibrations overlaid with gold?"

Only one nefil's song carried those hues. "Jordi."

"Oh, my brother, my clever brother is operating a black site in the Pyrenees." A hint of admiration touched the pronouncement. "Right under our fucking noses."

"That explains why Sitz and his squad herded us in this direction." Diago pointed to three broken circles within the design. "But it's not meant to be a permanent gateway."

"Which is why Feran didn't wait to ambush us back at the cave after he killed Carme. He didn't want to be caught on the wrong side."

Diago noted the bitterness in his friend's voice. *Feeding his rage won't get us anywhere.* He gestured to the glyph. "Where do you think it goes?"

"Straight up the devil's asshole."

And from there right into Jordi's lap. Diago gripped his pistol tighter. "That decides us, then."

"What do you mean?"

"You can't go in there. Too risky. I have to go and get the notebook." *Alone. Behind enemy lines.* It wasn't the first time he'd taken such a chance, but in those cases he'd always known exactly what kind of situation awaited him. There were plans and contingency plans.

This time, however . . .

We know nothing about what's on the other side of that glyph.

But that didn't matter—it had to be done. "Wait for me back in the cave. If I don't return in a few hours, then head to France, and take care of my boy."

Guillermo hissed for quiet as he studied the glyph. "Look at this." He pointed to another set of lines throbbing in time with the nefilim's song. Greenish-brown hues clung like tar to the brighter orange. "Have you ever seen anything like that before?"

Diago edged closer. "No. There's too much light for it to be the threads of a daimonic ward." Nor was it angelic—at least, not like any angelic sigil Diago had ever seen.

The ugly lines on the glyph swelled like pus behind a wound.

Guillermo's frown deepened. "I'm not sending you in there alone."

"Don't be foolish—"

Guillermo cut off the protest with a gesture. "We've taken down rogue angels together." He turned his fiery gaze on Diago and emphasized the last. "*Together.* Besides, it's like Miquel always says, 'We've made it through worse than this.'"

"He only says that when he's scared shitless and doesn't want anyone to know it." *I wish he were here with us. I doubt I'd be half as afraid if he was.* But he held that thought close to his heart, like the memory of his husband's touch.

Guillermo shrugged. "Doesn't matter. We've got a better chance of beating this thing together."

The ward pulsed ominously, fading almost dark before it surged to life again.

Guillermo touched Diago's arm. "We're going through. On the next flash. You go left, I'll go right. Stay low until we know what we're dealing with. If you see anything move, open fire." He chambered a round in his pistol. "We'll ask questions when the smoke clears."

Diago gave a terse nod.

The nefilim's chant intensified. The haunted chorus struggled to carry each note.

But at what price? They cannot sing like this for long. No one could. The thought gave him a chill.

A long moan vibrated around them, rising in timbre. The sound came from everywhere . . . from nowhere . . . it undulated, touching their flesh and shaping the stone with waves of sound. The glyph brightened again, signaling the pathway between realms had opened.

"Now," Guillermo hissed.

They stepped into the ward simultaneously. Reverberations of the nefilim's song reached a fever pitch.

The curvature of space and time warped the flowstone around them. Colors merged and bled hot, streaking past them as if the world had turned fluid in a sickening flood of shades, where brown turned to black and red to gray.

The velocity of their forward motion increased. The trajectory flattened Diago's flesh against muscle and bone. After one final surge of the chant, the world solidified around them.

[5]

Diago's boot hit metal. Blinking hard to clear his vision, he immediately turned left and dropped to one knee. His improvised kneepads absorbed the shock from the latticework floor of a catwalk.

The conflagration of light slowly receded. Industrial odors of oil and steel replaced the mineral scents of water and stone. They were on a catwalk high above two rows of train tracks, which were separated by a strip of concrete.

Freight cars sat on one side of the island, empty metro cars on the other. The metro cars' distinctive red and green paint, for first- and second-class passengers, respectively, indicated they were French. Both the freight and metro cars were nestled in a line, which ended in front of a brick wall.

This was obviously a storage area. *But does that mean we're in France?* It was impossible to tell. To their left, the rails continued into the distance and disappeared around a curve.

A guard's roost stood on the walkway. The enclosed structure jutted beyond the catwalk by a meter, supported by metal struts. Grimy windows overlooked the tracks. Spray-painted over the door in blue was 5-z.

Diago zeroed in on the doorknob, but it didn't twitch. No one emerged to inspect the portal. The hut possessed a vacant air.

Or maybe that was wishful thinking. Diago kept the door in his sights, ready to squeeze the trigger at the first sign of trouble.

Near his left arm, the portal sputtered and darkened. The webbed sigil flashed one final time and ejected a bright flash. The light crackled over their heads and latched onto a cable. Sparks showered the walkway as it rushed toward a larger glyph in the shape of an alarm that clung to the side of the guard hut.

Diago rose and traced a sigil for darkness. He coughed a scorpion the size of his palm into his hand. Even this spell maintained that annoying golden light, but he had no time to complain.

He flung his scorpion onto the cable with more force than necessary. The spell practically overshot the wire. Reaching out with one claw, the arachnid managed to latch on to the cable. Chasing the bright sigil, Diago's song doused the warning glyph just before it reached the guard shack.

"Good save," Guillermo murmured.

"Thank you." Diago kept his bead on the door.

"Do you think someone missed all that noise?"

"Maybe. There is still enough room to hide in there. They could be out of sight behind one of the doors."

Guillermo stood. "If anyone was coming, he would have shown himself by now."

"Unless he radioed for backup."

"Move on it, then. Even if it's empty, we're too exposed up here." Guillermo scowled at the scene. "Let's find some stairs."

Shrouded by shadows, Diago led the way forward. At the hut, he examined the door for any protective wards. What he found was a smear of blood by the doorknob. Fading around the bloodstain were the bright crimson fragments of the Devil's Fingers. Feran had passed this way. *And not long ago.*

"We're on the right trail. But it's locked." He stepped aside to give Guillermo room to work. "This is your territory."

Wasting no time, Guillermo knelt and inserted a thin strip of wire into the lock. Within seconds he'd tripped the mechanism. They slipped inside and shut the door. The room was tight and held the scent of Feran's fear.

A stool and a small table that apparently served as a desk occupied the area by the back wall. Another door, opposite the one they'd entered, led to the next section of the catwalk. No more guard shacks were visible from this post, but a field radio occupied the shelf opposite the table.

Switching it on, Guillermo lifted the headset and listened. Frowning, he gestured for Diago to join him, tilting the earpiece between them.

A voice spoke in Castilian ". . . Operation Red Soldier goes into effect in twenty-four hours . . . all units in sectors Blue, Green, and Gold are on standby . . ." A burst of static interrupted the transmission. ". . . melee in Choral Room Two needs cleanup . . . Portal Five-Z is officially disabled. Choral units will shift attention to Operation Fall Gelb. Base camp out."

The transmission ended.

Guillermo switched off the radio. "Fall Gelb. It's German."

"Case Yellow?"

Guillermo nodded. "From what Miquel's intelligence operatives in Germany have discovered, Operation Fall Gelb is Queen Jaeger's plan to invade France."

A shot of fear chilled Diago's veins. "And Jordi is helping her."

Outside the hut, the lights dimmed on the catwalks but didn't go out. Guillermo scowled at the darkened area. "Do you see what they're doing? The choral units are like generators, pulling their energy from one area in order to strengthen another." Guillermo tapped the glass with one blunt finger and pointed at the metro cars. "Somewhere in this base is a portal that enters France, and if there is one, there might be more."

Diago looked down at the tracks. "But metro cars? Don't you think armed soldiers on metro cars would draw attention?"

Guillermo shook his head. "They'll go in as civilians and set up residences within the cities. Jaeger and Jordi are moving a fifth column into place to assist the mortal invasion along the border."

"If the Germans are involved, do you think there are portals from Germany into France?"

Guillermo nodded. "It's very possible. Which means our plan hasn't changed: we need to get Carme's notebook, or we lose a crucial spy network. Then we've got to locate the maps of these portals. We must learn where each one is located so we can shut them down. We'll start here." He pointed to the table behind Diago. "See if there is a map of some kind in there, or notes—anything to tell us where we are."

Diago opened the drawer and rummaged through the papers. "Blank requisitions. Some are in Castilian, some in French."

Guillermo joined him. "Requisitions for what?"

"Transporting pharmaceuticals."

"What?"

"Could that be Operation Red Soldier?" He gave the forms to Guillermo.

"Maybe, but I doubt it. Red Soldier sounds more like a tactical exercise."

Diago continued his search. Taped to the back of the drawer, he found an envelope. Curious, he withdrew it.

The flap was soiled and well worn. Inside were photographs of various naked and semi-naked women in pornographic poses. Diago cleared his throat. "Well, that's, um . . . not what I was expecting."

"What's there?" Guillermo looked over his shoulder.

"Blondes, brunettes . . ."

"Wow. That's . . . quite a collection."

"Explains why the floor is so sticky." Diago tossed the envelope back in the drawer and wiped his hand on his pants.

"Don't be so sanctimonious. You were once a young nefil lusting after mortals."

"I think that was you."

Guillermo folded one of the requisitions and stuffed it into his pocket. He glanced out the window. "We've got company."

A nefil in a Nationalist uniform trudged along the catwalk, looking at his feet. Maybe he'd escorted Feran to whatever destination lay beyond the tunnel's twists and turns before returning to his post. He certainly didn't move like he suspected interlopers.

Guillermo positioned himself behind the door. "You're the bait."

With a soft curse, Diago returned to the stool and drew his pistol.

The nefil unlocked the door and stepped inside. He looked up and saw Diago. "Hey!" His fingers scrabbled against his holster's flap. "You're not supposed to be—"

Diago lifted his pistol just as Guillermo shoved the door shut. With one beefy arm around the young nefil's throat, Guillermo used his other hand to silence the youth's squawk of protest.

"Hands up," Guillermo whispered in his ear.

The nefil obeyed him.

The raw elixir of terror flooding the small office rocked Diago's head and threatened to undo his sense of control. Wiping his mouth, he closed his eyes and fought against his natural instinct to provoke the youth into deeper paroxysms of terror.

Within moments he regained command of himself and assessed the soldier. The boy looked young, but nefilim didn't age like mortals. The true key to a nefil's age lay in his eyes.

Stepping forward, Diago disarmed him. As he did, he examined the nefil's gaze for any sign of sophistication, or the deep knowledge that might indicate a nefil of experience or power.

The innocence he saw reflected in those hazel eyes told him more than a thousand confessions. The guard was in his firstborn life, and if his physical body was any indication, he was only a couple of years older than Diago's son, Rafael.

And I'd want my son treated with dignity.

Still, all three of them knew the rules of war. If they intended to kill the youth, Diago didn't want to prolong his suffering.

He looked over the boy's head to Guillermo. "Kill him or question him?"

The guard's eyes went wide. "Wait!"

Guillermo tightened his grip. "What can he possibly know? Nefilim don't get shit details like this because they're smart."

The nefil's mouth worked silently, his eyes begging Diago for his life.

Having empathy for the boy made his job harder, but Diago didn't flinch from what needed to be done. He holstered his gun and drew his knife. "Were you the one who led Feran into the compound?"

"How do you know about—"

Guillermo rapped the side of the youth's head. "Where is he?"

The nefil shook his head. "I don't—"

Diago raised the knife. "I saw his blood on the door. Don't make me add yours to it."

The nefil made a small sound somewhere between a mewl and a groan. "Lieutenant Espina."

"Who? Espina?" Guillermo's forearm tensed, choking the youth silent. "What is Lieutenant Espina's first name?"

"B-B-B-Benito."

Guillermo's eyes clouded with rage. "Did you hear that, Diago? Our old friend Benito Espina has been promoted to lieutenant."

"Easy," Diago murmured, though he wasn't quite sure

whether he addressed Guillermo or the guard. Once a member of Los Nefilim, Benito Espina abandoned Guillermo to work for Jordi. "Stay focused."

If Feran reached Espina with the notebook, their job just got harder. Espina knew Carme's sigils were deadly. He wouldn't rush to break her wards. Nor would he wait too long.

A note of hope touched the boy's voice. "Do you know Lieutenant Espina?"

Guillermo growled. "Benito Espina used to be a member of Los Nefilim. Then he turned traitor and fled to Portugal in 1932. We've been hunting him for some time. And now I've found him."

The nefil paled. "Oh."

Moving slowly, as if stalking a rabbit, Diago caught the youth's gaze with his own. "What is your name?"

"Private Enrique Martinez."

"How long before your relief arrives?"

"Any minute."

That was a lie. If they were shutting down the portal, they'd have no reason to post a guard.

"How many are coming?"

"Twelve."

More bullshit. Diago assessed Martinez's fear. He wouldn't be this terrified if he knew help was on the way. "You're lying to me, aren't you?"

"You're going to kill me." His voice trembled slightly before he regained his defiance. "Why should I tell you anything?"

Because I can force you to tell me, little fool. Diago maintained eye contact with Martinez. Just as his spell on the ridge required his daimonic talents, so did this one. The angel-born could sing a mortal or even a very young nefil into a compliant state, but the cost to both the nefil and the mortal was great. For the daimon-born, it was a simple matter of clouding their victim's vision. Having been the target of such a spell, Diago rarely used it.

But war changed everything, and morals that once possessed clear lines faded into shades of gray. They needed Martinez's information, however scant it might be, and time was against them.

Keeping his left hand low, Diago pinched a dark shadow from the air and rubbed it between thumb and forefinger. A scorpion with halos of silver and gold emerged between his fingers. He lifted his arm in such a way as to cause the band of his watch to catch the light. He hummed his glyph to life and tossed it at Martinez's left eye.

The young nefil blinked. The scorpion ran across Martinez's iris, dragging a shadow in its wake. Two heartbeats passed before Martinez's shivering eased.

But not completely. Without enough time to perform a stronger spell, Diago relied on his voice to keep the youth calm and talking. "How long before your relief arrives?"

"No one is coming."

"How long did it take you to escort Feran to Espina?"

A shrug. "Fifteen minutes. Maybe twenty."

That was a long walk and made for a huge pocket realm. *How the hell can they maintain something this big?* Diago shuffled the question to the back of the queue. Martinez certainly wouldn't know the answer. "How do we find Espina?"

"He's on the second level, but you don't want to find him. He's either with the generalissimo or questioning prisoners."

"Operation Red Soldier, what is that?"

The youth's confusion was real. "I don't know. This was a temporary assignment. My orders are to lock down the station and then return to my unit topside."

Taking a step backward, Diago opened the table's drawer and withdrew a blank requisition, which he placed face-down on the surface. He located a grubby pencil and set it beside the paper. Keeping his knife in one hand, he gestured to the stool with the other. "Come on, Martinez. Sit and draw me a map."

Martinez shook his head. "I can't. I just got here yesterday."

"Do the best you can." Diago tugged the frightened youth free of Guillermo's arm and directed him to the stool. "Here, right here."

Martinez sat. Diago rested one hand on his shoulder, all the while keeping his blade close to the youth's throat.

He spoke gently. "How many levels are in the compound?"

"Four underground, three above."

"Let's focus on the underground."

Martinez whispered, "You're going to kill me, aren't you?"

"Draw me a map." Diago glanced at Guillermo, who monitored the walkway. *But he's hanging on to our every word.*

"I can't draw." A soft sob. "You're going to kill me."

"Draw four lines."

Martinez scratched four shaky lines.

"Is this the surface?" Diago pointed to the top line.

"No. The fourth level is underground. The surface begins here." Martinez drew three more lines and encased them in a rough dome. Then he touched the dome's first floor.

"Where are we?"

Martinez touched the very bottom line, indicating they were in the deepest part of the basements.

"What's above us?"

"The second level is the prison and interrogation rooms. The third is the infirmary and where some of the choruses are kept."

"What do you mean, 'the choruses'?"

"They're the ones who maintain the pocket realm and the portals. They never stop singing." Martinez licked his lips and shivered. "Ever."

Diago glanced at Guillermo, who merely frowned at the information. "How do they never stop singing?"

"The Germans are in charge of them. When one dies, they bring another to replace him."

Diago stifled a shudder of his own. "Are they all on the third level?" Because if they were, shutting down this pocket realm might be easier than they initially thought.

"No. There are groups on each level, except the prison level."

Of course there were. Nothing was going to be easy. "Where was Espina when you last left him?"

"Second level. That's where he took Feran."

Find Feran and Espina, find the notebook. "You did well, Martinez. Now sit still. I'm going to sing you to sleep and then all this will be over."

He sheathed his knife and moved his hand from Martinez's shoulder to his cheek, brushing a tear from the corner of the youth's eye. *Let his last memory from this life be the kindness of a quick death.*

"Will it hurt?" Martinez whispered.

"No." Diago grabbed Martinez's chin and twisted his head upward and at an angle, hard enough to snap his neck.

The dark sound of Martinez's death oozed through his lips as if his song were reluctant to release its mortal coil. Then a black light flashed—*like the mirrored glyphs over the Ophanim's heads*—and Martinez's soul blinked out of existence.

Diago stared at the spot. That wasn't normal. He wondered if it was because they were in a pocket realm. Perhaps his soul only seemed to disappear because they were so close to the mortal realm. It was plausible.

Guillermo's soft rumble interrupted Diago's thoughts. "I would have done that for you."

"I know. But you would have scared him worse. Help me now. He's about my size."

Guillermo joined him. Together, they eased Martinez to the floor and relieved him of his uniform. Diago stripped to his undershirt.

While Diago dressed in Martinez's shirt and jacket, Guillermo searched the youth's pockets. Martinez carried nothing but two small bottles of pills. The bright red, white, and blue container looked cheerful enough. Diago glimpsed the word *Pervitin* in white.

Guillermo frowned. "Do you know what this does?"

He untied his improvised kneepads and shoved the rags under the desk. "It's a synthetic version of methamphetamine."

A blank stare.

"Methylamphetamine."

Still blank.

"It's a powerful stimulant—an amphetamine that makes America's Benzedrine look like candy."

Guillermo opened one of the tubes and spilled the white pills into his palm. "Why would he need so much?"

"I don't know." Diago quickly buttoned Martinez's jacket.

Capping the bottle, Guillermo slipped it and the other one into his pocket. "Quick: salute."

Diago gave him a closed-fist Republican salute. *Fuck.*

Guillermo raised his finger. "You'll only get to make that mistake once. Again."

Diago gave the fascist salute.

Guillermo nodded. "Don't forget it." He tossed Diago the tasseled infantry cap and pointed to his head.

Diago traded hats. "What do you think?"

Guillermo assessed his appearance with a critical eye. "You should do tassels more often. That look works for you."

Diago shot him a baleful side-eye.

"I've seen that face. I don't think it means you're happy."

He shot him the look again, and Guillermo grinned.

Gritting his teeth, Diago said, "Will I pass for Martinez?"

"As long as no one gets too close. Keep to the shadows if you can. You heard him speak. Do you think you can imitate the register of his voice?"

"When one dies, they bring another to replace him." Diago achieved a reasonable delivery of Martinez's Aragonese.

"I'm impressed."

Diago switched his pistol to the new holster, because his weapons were in excellent working order. He wasn't sure if Private Martinez was as diligent with his gear. They split the rest of the ammunition between them.

Touching his own cap, Diago said, "Ditch your hat. And the kneepads. We need to find you a fascist uniform. Preferably one with a higher rank."

"I'm sure there are more of Jordi's nefilim to kill."

"What about Martinez?" Diago avoided looking at the youth. *I shouldn't feel guilty.* But he did.

"Leave him. They probably won't notice he's gone until roll call. And stop looking so morose. The boy knew the score the moment he donned that uniform."

Diago shook his head. "He was just a kid. I doubt he thought he would ever die."

"He was a kid on the wrong side." Guillermo tossed his kneepads next to Diago's and then finished loading the ammo into his pockets. When he was done, he paused, glaring at the door. "He's also not the first youngster we've had to kill, and unless I can find some way to persuade my brother into a truce, he won't be the last. Let's move."

Diago followed him to the door. He doubted he'd ever achieve Guillermo's and Miquel's angelic detachment for killing during a war. They were soldiers, bred to fight, with the angels' martial bearing ingrained in their very songs.

But not me, not anymore.

His incarnations had changed him. And in this one, Miquel taught him empathy in order to save him from self-destruction. Maybe he'd taught him too well.

Diago glanced at Martinez's face before he shut the door. All he saw in the youth's death mask was his son, yearning to follow in Miquel's footsteps. The thought of Rafael entering a war this brutal scared Diago more deeply than Jordi's combined forces.

Yet it was also all the more reason to give his son a good

example to follow. If the others saw mercy as weakness, then so be it.

Adjusting his cap, he stepped forward and led the way along the catwalk. His nerves jumped with every clanking step on the walkway.

Metal wheels and valves jutted along the walls. Accompanying pipes shot upward into shadows. Whether the fittings carried liquid or gas, Diago couldn't readily tell, but the equipment gave them a few recesses for potential cover.

Luck was with them and they made it to a flight of stairs without further incident. On the ground level, alcoves were spaced every few meters along the narrow walkway that ran beside the tracks.

Diago stayed in plain sight while Guillermo flitted from one alcove to the next, hiding in the shadows until Diago gave him the all clear to move again. They'd walked close to ten minutes when the sound of activity slowed their approach.

Diago motioned for Guillermo to wait in one of the recesses. Several meters away the tracks disappeared around a curve.

At the bend the rails branched to the right, away from the walkway, continuing to another platform farther down the line. A freight train waited by the platform. The faint shapes of people moved purposely around the cars. They were too far away for Diago to make out their uniforms or faces, but he had no trouble noting that some of the figures held rifles. From the way they positioned themselves, it was obvious they guarded either the workers or the cargo.

Diago's sidewalk continued to the left, where a metal door stood propped open. He detected movement on the other side. Slowing his pace, he crept forward and listened.

Someone shouted a command. The squeal of metal wheels on concrete set his teeth on edge. Something heavy fell. Curses filled the air, followed by the sound of someone being struck—one, two, three, four blows.

Why don't they cry out? He walked through the door.

It was a warehouse. Pallets of crates stood at attention in eight neat lines.

Near another door across the room, three boxes lay on the floor next to a handcart. A soldier beat a man in a striped uniform while three other guards watched. At the sixth or seventh blow, the huddled form collapsed, either dead or unconscious. Ten other prisoners, guarded by six more soldiers, stood at attention, obviously forced to watch.

The soldier with the truncheon straightened and glared at the other prisoners. He stabbed his baton at two different men. "You and you, get him the fuck out of here. López, go with them."

A Nationalist, a permanent leer stamped across his mouth, nodded and followed the prisoners out the door.

"The rest of you, get back to work!"

The prisoners didn't wait to be told a second time. They righted the crates on the pallet and wheeled them out of sight.

Now that the excitement was over, the rest of the soldiers stood at ease. They held their weapons loosely.

Diago shifted his attention to a nearby pallet. Through the wooden slats, he was able to make out RESEARCH INSTITUTE OF DEFENSE PHYSIOLOGY stamped on the cardboard box.

What the hell is defense physiology?

"Martinez! Is that you?"

It was the same guard who'd beaten the prisoner.

Diago whirled, making sure the shadows obscured his

rage. Although he refused to give his base nature the satisfaction of enjoying a kill, he'd be damned if he'd mourn the death of a sadist such as this.

The nefil wiped his truncheon on a rag as he strode toward Diago. He wore the stripes of a sergeant major. "Are you fucking lost again?"

"No, sir!" Diago snapped a quick salute.

The sergeant major didn't bother to return it. "Have you sealed that hut already?"

"There's a problem, sir." Diago mimicked Martinez's accent and added a note of urgency to his voice. Turning his back, he half jogged toward the door.

"Fucking idiot boy." The sergeant major hesitated, but only for a second, before he followed. "Do we need to sound the alarm?"

"No, but you should see this." *Oh, how I want you to see this.* Diago picked up his pace and went through the open door. He quickly ducked around the corner, passing Guillermo's hiding spot.

"Hold on!" The soldier followed, merely a few paces behind. "Private!"

Guillermo lunged out of the darkness and grabbed the nefil. He slammed him against the wall, spitting in his face. "This is for Carme," he hissed to the stunned man before he broke his neck.

The dark sound of the nefil's soul disappeared in a flash and a blink just as Martinez's had.

Guillermo dragged the body into the recess. "You couldn't find a taller one?"

"I didn't *want* to find this one." Diago returned to the door and kept watch while Guillermo changed clothes.

Guillermo grumbled, "The sleeves are too short."

"Roll them up." Diago glanced over his shoulder.

Guillermo created a sigil, charging it with a quiet note. The glyph formed wavy lines and descended over the corpse, deepening the shadows and hiding it from view. "We've got about an hour before that fades."

"Then we'd better vacate the area." Diago motioned for Guillermo to join him.

They returned to the warehouse. The other soldiers remained about thirty meters away, blocking the only other exit from the room. They seemed more relaxed with their commanding officer gone. Laughing at some jest, they shared a cigarette and gave the prisoners half their attention.

Guillermo moved toward one of the pallets. "What's in the crates?" he whispered.

"Items from the Research Institute of Defense Physiology. What do you know about that?"

Guillermo's scowl deepened. "According to our intelligence, the institute is under the direction of a mortal, Professor Dr. Otto Ranke."

"I'm familiar with the name. He's working with a pharmaceutical company in Germany . . . Temmler, I think it is. The Germans are doing drug experimentations on mortal soldiers to enhance their stamina with . . ." His voice trailed off. The Pervitin in Martinez's pockets suddenly made sense. "Amphetamines. They're using Pervitin."

Guillermo scowled and touched his pocket, but he didn't withdraw the tubes of pills. Instead, he unsheathed the heavy knife he carried. "Keep talking." He slipped behind a stack of crates.

Diago watched the soldiers and prisoners as he murmured,

"The goal is to create a super-soldier, except instead of breeding a better fighter, they're taking a shortcut with the drugs."

"Shortcuts," Guillermo muttered. "You were right. That's just like my brother." A loud pop indicated he'd succeeded in prying the lid off one of the crates.

Diago flinched at the noise, but neither prisoners nor guards seemed to notice. The large room was filled with the echoes of movement and hushed conversations among the guards.

Glancing over his shoulder, Diago saw the inside of the crate Guillermo had opened was filled with cardboard boxes.

"They're like fucking matryoshka," Guillermo muttered in exasperation, referring to the Russian nesting dolls. Slicing through the tape on the cardboard box, he lifted a smaller unit in a red, white, and blue box. "Goddamn it."

Pervitin. Diago stared at the hundreds of crates. "Jesus Christ. Do you realize how many pills are here?"

"Enough to supply an army?"

Klaxons suddenly screamed overhead. Emergency lighting sent red waves washing over the area.

Diago's heart hammered in his chest. He drew his pistol, determined to put a bullet in his brain before he allowed Jordi to orchestrate his death.

Guillermo dropped behind the crate and drew his own gun.

Diago held his breath and listened. No footsteps moved in their direction.

A door on the other side of the room slammed open.

"Move! Move! Move!" shouted an authoritative voice.

Diago risked a peek around the stack of crates that hid them.

An officer pointed at four burly nefilim. "You, you, you,

and you, come with me. We've got an escapee." He paused and surveyed the group. "Ortega, where is your commanding officer?"

Ortega gestured at the door behind Diago. "I saw him leave with Martinez a few moments ago, Lieutenant."

The lieutenant spat. "Shit. The idiot." Whether the comment was directed at the sergeant or Martinez, Diago didn't know or care. "Then you're in charge, Ortega. Secure the prisoners and report to level three!" The officer ran off with his handpicked squad in tow.

Ortega wasted no time. The officer had barely cleared the door before he began barking at the soldiers. "You heard him! Move!"

Diago waited until the last door slammed. The lights shut off. Sirens continued to blare. Although they were alone, he kept his voice low. "Do you think this is Operation Red Soldier?"

Guillermo shook his head. "Whatever Red Soldier is, it goes into effect in twenty-four hours. This is something different and, judging by the guards' reactions, unanticipated." His eyes narrowed as he glared at the rows of crates. "Why would you need that many nefilim to capture one escapee?"

Diago stifled a chill. "Because they're testing the Pervitin on nefilim, trying to enhance their powers. And it's working."

"Exactly. We need Carme's notebook and to find a way to sabotage this operation."

"The choruses. If we can shut one of them down . . ."

"Good thinking." Guillermo adjusted his sleeves and headed for the door. "Let's get a feel for the layout. We'll have to make this up as we go along."

My least favorite kind of plan. Nonetheless, Diago nodded.

The hallway outside the storage facility was deserted. A long ramp followed a natural slope upward. Diago kept close to the wall, watching for doorways or alcoves that might give them cover. They'd gone roughly seventy meters before they reached a junction.

Footsteps approached from an adjacent corridor. Guillermo veered right, walking with his head up and eyes forward, as if he had every right to be here. Diago kept pace with him.

Office doors lined the hall. A concrete floor replaced the natural stone.

They rounded a corner. A group of three soldiers, all privates, jogged toward them from the opposite direction. There was no place to hide.

Diago fell back a step behind Guillermo as dictated by their rank. The trio gave Guillermo a perfunctory salute as they passed, which he returned without slowing his stride.

The corridor widened until it branched into five different directions. Here, they found more soldiers. Two units hurried past them, obviously an armed response to the klaxons. Others carried on as if nothing unusual were happening.

Diago edged ahead of Guillermo and chose a deserted corridor that appeared to go upward. Guillermo followed.

At the first empty office, he slid inside, with Guillermo on his heels. A lab coat hung on a rack by the door. Medical books with German titles lined the shelves and rested beside a stack of files on the metal desk.

Closing the door, he quickly removed the makeshift map Martinez had drawn and filled in the corridors they'd just traversed.

"What are you doing?" Guillermo whispered.

"This place is a labyrinth. We need to keep track of where we go."

Guillermo went to the files. "All German names."

"Martinez said the Germans controlled the choruses."

They exchanged a glance.

"You're the medic." Guillermo returned to the door. "See what you can find out. I'll keep watch."

Diago pocketed his map and went to the desk. He opened the first file: JANNIK KRAUSE. Age eighteen. Second-born life. Singer. DECEASED.

A black-and-white photograph was stapled to the top right-hand corner of the page. The picture showed a healthy youth with a pugilist's face and fair hair, light eyes.

Flipping to the next file, Diago merely glanced at the name. Another singer, also deceased, age sixteen, firstborn life. This boy thinner, with a piercing gaze.

"Fourteen," he muttered the next boy's age. *The same as my Rafael.* "Firstborn life." He'd actually smiled for his photograph.

Diago went to the next one, and the next: fifteen, seventeen, twenty-one . . . third-born, firstborn, firstborn . . . all dead. He switched his attention to another set of files. These showed an even grimmer picture. Twelve boys, all exhibiting signs of psychoses. "Jesus . . . they report heart attacks, hallucinations, sleep disturbances, five of them have gone insane."

Guillermo's eyes narrowed dangerously. "What's the link?"

"Aside from their ages? Nothing. They're all from different choral groups." He thought back to all the crates in the warehouse. "Unless it's the Pervitin."

"Possibly." Guillermo reached in his pocket and flicked his lighter's lid. "That transmission we picked up in the guard shack . . . wasn't there something about a melee in a choral room?"

"Choral Room Two," Diago muttered as he continued to read.

"Why would there be a melee in a choral group?"

Diago lifted his head. It was a good question; one that the files failed to answer.

Outside, the klaxons continued to blare.

Dawn

la arentitis

(sanditis)

[6]

Shivering in the cold damp air, Miquel squatted in the center of the room and hugged his shins. Bricks studded the cell's floor, jutting upward in the concrete to create a labyrinth of obstacles designed to impede free movement. Walking required great care lest he twist an ankle or knee.

Angelic glyphs writhed on the walls and provided the only light. The razored sigils were rendered in sharp, high notes, each designed to slash his tongue and mouth should he sing a glyph of his own. Already his lips were scabbed from his first test of the wards' power.

In his last clear memory, he saw himself walking through the French internment camp on the beach of Argelès-sur-Mer. He'd passed the hovel belonging to a mortal who occupied the long monotonous hours by packing and repacking his two suitcases while muttering his wife's and daughters' names like a prayer.

Héctor was his name. Héctor-something from Málaga, he was an accountant for a union and had fled up the coast, staying just ahead of the rebels with each move. The gendarmes had taken his wife and daughters to a different camp and he claimed that only through assiduous packing would the French allow him to join them.

Miquel recalled pausing beside the tent. Héctor looked up and smiled. His lips moved, and he said in French: *El bête angélique.* And then Miquel's world had gone black.

The angelic beast? What could that possibly mean? And what possessed Héctor to suddenly speak French? Miquel couldn't answer any of those questions. He touched the lump on the back of his head, working his fingers through the dried blood caking his hair. Nor did he know how many days had passed since Argelès. *More than one, less than twenty?*

Nothing but jumbled images filled in the blanks, a collage of pain and discomfort. He'd awakened on the floorboard of—*a van, a lorry? Did it matter?*—bound and naked, a black hood over his head.

Fading in and out of consciousness, he'd sensed others on the hard floor with him. Someone had injected him with . . . *what?* A narcotic of some kind. It flushed his body with heat and dried the spit in his mouth, cramping his stomach and leaving him disoriented.

He touched the needle marks on his arm. Twelve. Twelve shots of the drug.

Frustrated by his inability to summon the details of his capture, he clenched his fists. The impression of his wedding band remained on his finger, but the ring had disappeared. He felt that loss more keenly than the rest. *All those years I chided Diago about wearing his, and now I've lost mine.*

Stolen, not lost.

That was the least of his worries.

Had they returned to Spain? It was possible. Except a

return to Spain meant interrogations. Thus far, there'd been no questions.

Because this is simply the first stage. Clenching his jaw, he closed his eyes. He understood the process, having performed it enough times on behalf of Los Nefilim. Isolate the subject. Warp their sense of time and place. Sleep deprivation and disorientation were the goals. Questions would come later.

If they find out who I am . . .

A shudder ran through him on hobbled feet.

Don't buy trouble. Cramps seized his calf and refused to let go. He stood and limped through the room, careful to place his feet between the bricks. Eight steps from the door to the back wall. Four from side to side. He paced through twice, but on the third circuit, his exhaustion caused him to stumble. The arch of his foot landed on a brick at the wrong angle. His toes scraped the floor. He hissed with pain and returned to squat in the center of the room.

Think. Go back to the beach. Re-create it. Closing his eyes, he imagined the lean-tos the prisoners had constructed from sheet metal and blankets. The French internment camp stretched over a landscape of barbed wire and sand, endless sand. Miquel had searched the other men's eyes, looking for his nefilim, or any rogues who might have seen them. All he found was hope souring into despair.

Héctor. Go back to Héctor and the beach.

Héctor chanting the names of his loved ones: *Magdalena, Ariana, Clara, Magdalena, Ariana, Clara, Magdalena . . .* He looked up from his suitcases and focused on Miquel. Then he said, *El bête angélique.*

There. Miquel stopped the reel of film running in his

mind's eye. *Héctor used the masculine article "el."* The correct article for angel was the feminine "la," so Héctor referred to a male angel. Had the mortal mistaken a nefil for an angel?

Maybe. Miquel reached deeper. He reconstructed the moment. Soft gray light had suffused the waves. The Pyrenees' icy breath rushed down onto the beach, lifting the sand, pushing it into every crevice of his body, burning his eyes, infecting his pores, crunching between his teeth in the bread he ate.

Ocean waves licked the shore but couldn't ease his thirst. Only by digging did he find a puddle of dirty water, which tasted of excrement and sand.

He licked parched lips. *I am a desert, dry and barren and filled with sand.*

Something trickled between his toes. He opened his eyes. The sigils on the walls throbbed like a headache, pulsing in bruised colors, wine-dark like the sea.

Grains of sand bounced merrily between the bricks, as if the earth quaked, but the floor didn't move. *There is no quake. I'm going insane.* The refugees even had a name for the psychotic break induced by the camps: *la arentitis— sanditis.*

Miquel bit his torn lip. Pain shot through him. He tasted blood. The scene remained.

The grains doubled, then tripled, until they coated the floor, rising to cover the soles of his feet. His flesh crumbled and disappeared into the sand.

"This isn't happening." His murmur caused the sigils on the walls to churn harder.

Miquel rose as the sand reached his ankles, then his knees. *An illusion. It has to be an illusion.* But when he reached down to touch his leg, his fingers found no flesh, only sand.

Instinctively, he traced a ward of protection in the air. The first note to charge the glyph barely passed his lips before he caught himself. A sigil peeled from the wall, its bright saw-toothed edges churning as it flew at his face. He ducked. The glyph smashed against the opposite wall, leaving silver sparks in its wake. It skidded to the corner, where it spun and careened back toward him. The blades ripped a gouge from his ear to his chin.

His blood clotted the sand that was now up to his chest. The grains tickled his chin and then his lips, rose until they filled his mouth, he twisted his head and tried to spit, but his lips were gone, and then his tongue, and he couldn't scream . . .

The cell door slammed open.

The sand disappeared.

Miquel blinked at the floor, empty now save for the zig-zag pattern of bricks. His legs were whole. Blood wetted his chin. He touched his cheek where the sigil had torn him. *What the hell?*

He absently rubbed the needle marks on his arm as he looked toward the open door. Two burly nefilim in Nationalist colors flanked a smaller nefil, who wore a lab coat over his Italian uniform. He was roughly Diago's size, with black hair and the same dark-lashed eyes. But where Diago's irises were green, this nefil had gray eyes with pale hints of blue.

Miquel's heart kicked in his chest. Nico Bianchi. Jordi Abelló's lover. And if Nico was here, Jordi couldn't be far behind.

Goose bumps erupted over Miquel's flesh. *I'm dead. It's*

just a matter of when. He thought of Diago and Rafael—their faces as they'd said their goodbyes. *We knew this day might come.* Still, he felt cheated. *We didn't have enough time together in this incarnation.*

He swiped his palm over his torn cheek. Pain extinguished the self-pity. *Focus. Focus or I'm lost for certain.* He had to devise a way to commit suicide before they pried Los Nefilim's secrets from him. A way and the will to do it.

His first thought was to rush the group, but he didn't give the plan room to grow. They wouldn't murder a valuable source so wantonly. Although both guards were armed, neither of them held their weapons, which meant they'd subdue him with sigils, or their fists, and then monitor him much more closely.

Diago had taught him to watch for the right moment. And this was not it.

As he looked beyond the trio blocking his escape, the spark of live sigils wafted over the door of the cell opposite his. Another captive resided within. *Another member of Los Nefilim? If so, who? And how much have they already revealed?*

"Your papers identify you as Miquel Fierro," said Nico. "Is this your name?"

The Italian's gaze crawled over Miquel's body—not with the cold disdain of an interrogator appraising a source of information, but the way one man would size up another for his bed.

When Miquel didn't answer, Nico smiled and asked, "Is my Castilian this bad?" He held up the papers. "Your name?"

"Miquel Fierro." He found his voice, hating himself for

giving the wards a furtive glance as he answered. The sigils didn't change color again.

"Miquel Fierro, then." Nico jotted a note on his clipboard, shaking his head as if disappointed in the answer. "I am Dr. Nico Bianchi. You have heard of me?"

Miquel nodded.

"Good. We know you as Miquel de Torrellas."

Across the hall, something heavy hit the door, rattling it in its frame. Everyone, even the guards, jumped. The sigils glowed white like irons held in the fire. Someone groaned—a low, lonely sound.

No one went to the prisoner's aid.

Nico's mouth twitched. He picked at the clipboard with one ragged fingernail. "Bring him," he snapped before he turned and walked away.

The bigger nefil waited until Nico's footsteps receded down the hall. He tossed a black canvas hood into the cell. "Put it on."

Miquel reached down and grabbed it. Grains of sand fell from the folds. Mouth dry, he lifted it over his head, hoping the guards didn't see his hands shake.

[7]

Miquel sat on the wooden chair, his wrists cuffed behind him. A gag cut into the fresh wound on his face. The strap across his chest held him against the chair. Not that he intended to move. With the hood on, he had no idea if active sigils, perhaps designed to punish motion, were on the walls. All he could do was remain still while sweat stung the gash left by the sigil from his cell.

One of the guards remained with him. Miquel heard the whisper of fabric as the man shifted position. Somewhere nearby, a low growl rolled like white noise in the background.

A generator? He immediately discounted the idea. The noise was too uneven. It felt more like the restless grinding of stones after an avalanche.

A door opened.

Miquel started, hating himself for jumping. But that's what they wanted. Uncertainty, fear. Unfortunately, he knew this game all too well. Except instead of being the interrogator, it was his turn to play the source. Nor was it the first time. He knew how much punishment his body could take.

But this was different. Always, in the past, he'd depended on Los Nefilim to watch his back. Interrogations were a matter of holding out until a rescue was orchestrated. There would be no liberation here. No one knew where he was.

Someone stepped into the room. "Leave us."

Nico again. Interesting.

"Are you sure you don't want me to—"

"Out."

The guard left.

As soon as the latch clicked into place, Nico loosened the hood and pulled it off.

Blinking in the sudden brightness, Miquel took in the room. He faced a metal desk and a rolling chair. Cracks and patches of missing plaster ran along the walls, exposing the bricks beneath. Blotches of mold darkened the crumbling stones. No windows. The only light came from the naked bulb overhead.

And no sigils on the walls. At least none that were evident to a nefil's eye.

Nico set his black doctor's bag on the desk. He tossed the hood down beside it. Then he removed the gag, gently working the cloth away from the wound on Miquel's face.

After a quick examination, he retrieved a bottle of alcohol and some gauze from his bag. "We don't have much time before your interrogator arrives." He dampened the gauze with alcohol and pressed it against Miquel's cheek.

The alcohol scalded the open wound. Miquel tried to jerk his face from Nico's reach.

Nico caught his hair and held him still. He didn't relax his hold until Miquel ceased to struggle. Gently massaging the back of Miquel's neck, he leaned close and whispered,

"We have three minutes. I have to get out of this place. I need your help. I'm leaving Jordi. Get me to Calais. I want to go to the United States. I need tickets, money, papers. You have a network in place."

The sentences came hard and sharp, like needles in his ears. *Does he think I'll lead him to members of Los Nefilim for false papers and a boat to America?* "I can't . . ."

"Sam has gone to Barcelona—"

"Who?"

"The Grigori. He has gone with the generalissimo to meet with Franco."

Now he knew Nico was lying. "Grigori?" he scoffed. "The Watchers were banished from the angelic realms. The legends say they corrupted the mortals, and for their sins they were placed in everlasting chains under darkness."

"And what is more everlasting than the darkness beneath the mountains?" Nico replied.

Beneath the mountains. They were in the Pyrenees, probably on the Spanish side and close to Barcelona if Jordi and the alleged Grigori were traveling back and forth.

Nico interrupted Miquel's rampant thoughts. "Jordi found the Grigori's prison and freed one."

The certainty in his voice sent chills cascading across Miquel's flesh. If this was true, then the implications were staggering. Suddenly suicide was out of the question. *I've got to get out of here and warn the Inner Guard.*

Miquel stalled, hoping Nico would inadvertently slip him more information. "What business would a Grigori have in Barcelona?"

"The generalissimo and Sam are helping Franco coordinate the new government."

Twice now, he'd referred to Franco *and* the generalissimo as two separate entities. The fact that Nico considered Jordi the generalissimo told Miquel volumes about how the other nefil saw the world.

The mortals were nothing to them. Franco was simply a prop that Jordi would destroy when his usefulness ran out, and apparently Nico saw nothing wrong with that. *Because they're the same, and Jordi is probably behind Nico's ruse.*

Nico checked the gash. "Will you help me?"

If he made an oath to Nico, he was bound by it. "If I say no?"

Nico glanced at the door as he returned the alcohol to the bag. A thin sheen of sweat covered his brow. "Do you really need to think about this, Miquel?"

Miquel shook his head. "This is—"

Nico gestured for him to lower his voice.

"—too easy. You're playing me. What's the catch?"

"No catch. Help me and I will get you out of here. You, in turn, will get me across the Atlantic and to freedom."

Miquel licked his lips.

"We have one minute."

And what have I got to lose? Miquel's heart ached at the thought of his husband and son so far away. With their home destroyed, they were forced into a retreat no one wanted. Hadn't they lost enough?

The temptation to say yes was intense. But Miquel wasn't fooled. Instead of sending an interrogator to beat the information out of him, they'd sent Nico to play on his empathy for others, thinking Miquel would take him to safety. *Leading them and the Grigori straight to the heart of Los Nefilim.* He shook his head. "I can't."

Nico inhaled sharply. The answer wasn't what he expected. "You don't understand. Jordi has changed."

Miquel lowered his voice. "Jordi hasn't changed. He just stopped hiding his true nature behind caresses and compliments, because now he's gotten everything he wants out of you. That is how Jordi works. You knew what he was when you went to his bed."

Nico straightened. Miquel expected rage.

Instead, Nico's lips were white with fear. "I'm begging you."

Voices drifted down the hall. With a nervous glance to the door, Nico pulled a short rubber tube and a syringe filled with cloudy liquid from the bag. "You leave me no choice. Remember that." He tightened the tube around Miquel's biceps and made quick work of the injection, jerking the tube free as he depressed the plunger.

Miquel jumped when the needle pierced his skin, but he didn't struggle. The last thing he needed was a torn vein. From the heat suffusing his body, he assumed it was the same substance they'd injected him with during the trip here. The warmth turned to fire as the drug entered his bloodstream. He felt flushed and hot. A cramp twisted his stomach. He gritted his teeth and sweated through it.

The door opened and a familiar voice said, "Are you done?"

The metallic taste of fear filled Miquel's mouth as a name jumped into his mind. *Benito Espina.*

Nico removed the syringe and quickly taped a piece of gauze over the wound. "Just finishing." He restored the items to his bag and didn't glance at Miquel as he left.

Benito waited until the door shut before he moved again. A large nefil with a congenial manner, he lumbered to the rolling chair and tossed a file to the desk. The springs squealed beneath his weight and then fell silent.

Benito grinned. "Miquel, how are you doing, my friend?"

"I'm not friends with traitors."

"You just fuck them, right? By the way, how is Diago? Better yet, *where* is Diago? Because the last time he was seen, it was with Guillermo, and we need them both." Benito lit a cigarette, squinting at Miquel through the haze.

Miquel stared back, projecting a calm he didn't feel. This was another interrogation trick: mention a loved one and watch the source carefully for a twitch, or a tear, or a blink. Anything to indicate the jab hit a nerve. Miquel knew that if he showed the slightest interest in Diago's welfare, Benito would use Miquel's fear as a cudgel. *Don't blink.*

Benito exhaled a cloud of smoke and sighed. "I didn't expect it would be that easy." He tapped ashes onto the floor. "I've got to admit, for several years I thought I'd be the one sitting in that chair, pissing myself, while you smoked and asked questions."

Miquel felt his cheeks warm with his humiliation. He hadn't exactly pissed himself yet, but if Benito mentioned it, Miquel was sure it would eventually happen. *Don't blink.* "Who knows? You might still find our roles reversed in the near future."

Benito guffawed. "Oh, I'm glad you still have your sense of humor." Still chortling, he sniffed and opened the folder. "You're going to need it."

"What happened to make you leave Los Nefilim, Benito?"

The other nefil looked up. His eyes went hard like hate. "You don't ask questions, Miquel. Today, you just answer. Entiende?"

Miquel nodded. He understood.

Benito dropped the cigarette to the floor and crushed it beneath his heel. Removing a notebook from the file, he nudged it across the desk. "Recognize this?"

Miquel glanced at the composition book. "You're going back to school?"

Another grin, but this one was tight. Benito held up the book so Miquel could see the sigils glowing across the cover. "Answer the question, Miquel. Do you know what's in this book?"

His heart went cold as he recognized Carme's glyphs. She was supposed to be with Diago. Had they been separated somehow? He had to assume yes. They wouldn't be wasting time with him if they had Guillermo. All he knew for certain was that Carme was dead. She never let that notebook out of her sight, much less her possession.

Goddamn it, not our Carme. He clenched his fists behind his back. *Don't. Blink.*

Sick with fear, he shrugged and stared at the desk's leg, waiting for Nico's injection to compel his answer. But it didn't. *Why give me that drug prior to an interrogation? Was it a placebo?* Judging by the way it had burned through his body, it couldn't have been.

Yet I've got complete control of my faculties. As a matter of fact, his brain leapt from subject to subject so fast, he could barely keep up with his own thoughts.

"Answer me, Miquel." Benito broke through the raging chaos in Miquel's head.

He considered giving Benito a false answer, but it wouldn't be believed. *Not this soon in the game.*

The silence ticked between them. Benito gave him a full minute to answer. "Don't make it hard, Miquel."

"What do you want, Benito?"

"We need you to break these sigils so we can read the book."

"Decipher them yourself." That would be fun to watch, because Carme was the master of landmine wards. She'd probably planted enough death in that book to take out an entire regiment.

Benito slammed the notebook onto the desk. "Do you want to see your family again, Miquel?"

He's not as good at this as he thinks he is. "Fuck you, Benito. You and I both know I'm never leaving here alive."

"Okay." Benito went to the door. "Cabello! Losa! Get in here."

The guards who'd accompanied Nico earlier stepped into the room as Benito resumed his seat. They took positions just behind Miquel's chair.

Someone else moved into the room with them. "Don't you want me, as well, Benito?"

Miquel twisted in the chair. He knew that voice. "Feran?" Had they captured him, too? No, that didn't make sense. He wouldn't be wandering the compound if he was a prisoner.

Cabello, or Losa—Miquel wasn't sure who was who—put his hand on Miquel's shoulder.

Beneath the sharp odor of Feran's cologne was the distinct smell of rot.

Stopping behind Benito's chair, Feran ran his palms over his new Nationalist uniform. It was a slow, deliberate move meant to impress Miquel.

In other circumstances Feran's preening would have merely aggravated Miquel. In here, to know someone like Feran had power over him was terrifying. *Just don't show it. Don't blink.*

He was too late. Feran had obviously seen his fear, because he grinned a hungry grin fed with his bile. Bright red sparks flashed through the whites of his eyes. A thin sheen of blood coated his upper teeth.

Holding Miquel's gaze, he reached into his mouth and plucked a needle from his gums. He held it up to the light and examined it curiously, as if he'd found a piece of spinach stuck between his teeth but couldn't quite make out how it got there.

Miquel watched him curiously. *That's a new one.*

Noting Miquel's stare, Feran's grin grew more feral. He pretended to pick his teeth with the needle, and then tossed it to the floor. "I'm a hero. I killed Carme Gebara."

A boil erupted on the side of Feran's neck. Thin crimson fingers of mold wiggled beneath his skin.

Now, that one Miquel knew. *The Devil's Fingers.* "It looks like she killed you back."

Feran blustered, but he failed to cover his fear. "Quit stalling. Decipher the book, and I'll talk Benito into letting Diago live."

They didn't have Diago. If they did, Benito would have gleefully dragged him into the interrogation room and cut his balls off just so Miquel could watch him bleed. "Carme hit you with the Devil's Fingers, didn't she?"

Feran stiffened.

Even sitting bound, I made him blink. "Do you know how the sigils mutate? I do."

Feran's eyes went wide. "Then you know the counter ward."

If one existed, Carme had taken it into her next incarnation, but Miquel would be damned if he'd say that. He shrugged. "I'm in no condition to counsel you."

Hope flickered in Feran's gaze.

But is it enough to entice him into helping me? Miquel wouldn't know until later.

Feran opened his mouth.

Benito silenced him with a glare. "Get out, Feran. The stink of you is giving me a headache."

"But I—"

"Out. He's bluffing you. If there is a cure for Carme's spell, you'll have to find it yourself." When Feran didn't move, Benito pointed to the door. "Go see Nico. Maybe he can help you. Go on." He said the last almost gently, as a commander would console a dying soldier.

Benito's sad inflection seemed lost on Feran. As he passed Miquel, he leaned down to whisper, "I'm a hero."

Miquel couldn't summon enough saliva to spit on Feran, otherwise he would have hurled more than words at the smirking nefil. "You're a traitor. And I will watch for you."

Feran lifted his fist, but Benito caught his arm. "No. He's mine. Now go." He maneuvered Feran toward the door. "Go see Nico."

Miquel heard the latch snick shut. Then Benito returned to the desk and lifted the hood, smoothing the canvas with a gesture that was simultaneously gentle and threatening. "See? Nobody smart fucks with Carme. That's why we sent Feran. We knew he was ambitious enough, and dumb enough, to provoke her. But we're not stupid. What we need you to do is spare us Feran's fate. Tell us how to break the sigils in the notebook, Miquel."

"I can't do that."

"We'll see." Benito settled the hood over Miquel's head and cinched the drawstring tight around his throat.

Miquel's pulse raced. He closed his eyes, waiting for the blows he knew would come next. The torture relied on not knowing where or when the strikes would land. It was brutal and surprisingly effective.

Benito's chair gave another shrill cry as he lowered his bulk onto the seat. The smell of sulfur followed the scratch of a match, and then the pungent odor of cigarette smoke drove the last of Feran's stink from the air.

Benito gave a contented sigh. "Carme was a vicious bitch, but she trusted you. Sing me the counter sigil to unlock it."

Miquel barely heard him. The canvas was hot. He found it hard to breathe. Sweat prickled his scalp.

One of the guards shifted his weight. Miquel tensed, anticipating the first blow. Nothing happened. *Yet. Nothing yet, but it's coming.*

Benito's question interrupted Miquel's low-grade panic. "What key is the sigil in? B? C? Come on, Miquel, give me a clue."

Miquel licked his lips and tasted grit. He heard the whisper of sand slithering across the hood's fabric. *No, this isn't happening.*

His heart accelerated until it became a piston, hammering his chest with quick hard blows. *Too fast, it's beating too fast, and I can't make it slow.*

The terrible flush from the drug filled his veins with fire.

Silt irritated his nose and clung to his cheeks. The insidious hiss of sand began to fill the hood.

"No." *Shit. I blinked.* Miquel bit his tongue to keep himself from giving them another twitch to indicate his discomfort.

"'No.'" Benito mocked him. "No isn't an answer, my friend. Tell me how to break Carme's codes. Then I'll take it off. You'll be able to breathe. You like breathing, don't you, Miquel?"

Miquel whipped his head to the right. Wet sand stung his cheeks and matted his hair. The drawstring didn't loosen. If anything, it tightened. He twisted in the chair. Hands landed on his shoulders, startling him. The guards held him firmly in place.

"What's the counter sigil, Miquel?"

The sand reached his chin. Miquel bucked against his bonds. "Take it off!" He flung his head to the left. Sand stung his eyes and clogged his nose. A sob scraped through his throat.

"You're disappointing me, Miquel. I thought you'd last longer." A hint of amusement touched Benito's voice. "Say you'll decipher it for me, and I'll take off the hood, give you a chance to win my trust. What do you say?"

Miquel parted his lips. His mouth filled with sand and choked off his scream.

Day

los exilios

(exiles)

[8]

Beneath his winter quilts, Rafael drifted between wakefulness and a light doze. He stretched until his toes poked over the mattress's edge. At the first nip of cold air on his flesh, he immediately curled up again, drawing his coltish legs deep beneath the covers.

Sleep reclaimed him, dragging him down with dark wings. This time, he dreamed of Miquel.

His father sat on a chair, and for some reason he kept his hands behind his back. Shadows covered his face, obscuring his features . . .

Miquel whispers, "You've been through worse than this, my little bear. You can do it."

Rafael shakes his head. He knows he cannot. This thing Miquel wants him to do is too hard. It shreds his heart and breaks his voice. He cannot.

But Miquel doesn't relent. He never yields. Papá will change his mind, but never Miquel. "You *must* do this, Rafael. Remember your lessons. All the things your papá and I taught you. Your voice is the key to all your power. Move the breath of darkness from your diaphragm up through your throat and into your song. Remember the steps . . . you must dance close to the border before you can cross over, but once you go, you must never look back."

Over Miquel's head, a dark mirror as black as his eyes spins in time to his words. He looks up, and then he smiles a sad smile. "I'm so sorry, my osito, but this is how it must be. Watch for me."

The mirror cracks. A darkness deeper than any known in the mortal realm leaks over Miquel's face, erasing first his forehead, then his eyes, and then his mouth.

Rafael rushes forward. If he's fast enough, he'll save Miquel. He grabs his father, but instead of saving him, they're both dragged down below, where nefilim sing, their eyes hollow, their fingers bleeding as they dig, dig, dig down into the dark . . .

Rafael sat up, his breath coming in ragged gasps. "Miquel," he murmured to the empty room. "Oh shit, Miquel, where are you?"

Outside his bedroom, Juanita spoke to Ysabel. The closed door muted her words. The click of heels on the floor meant they were already dressed for the day.

How late have I slept? The urgency of the nightmare pushed him out of bed. Sunlight speckled the floor as he crossed the narrow room and went to the wardrobe. Digging through his clothes, he found a clean shirt. He snatched a pair of pants from the back of a chair and pulled them on before reloading his pockets with his money and identity papers. His only homage to his homeland was his lucky scarf, a bright yellow neckerchief that he wore tied at a jaunty angle at his throat.

Pausing at the desk that held their radio, he rooted through the wires between the transmitter and microphone to work Suero's notepad free. He checked the pages. The last notation indicated Suero had taken a report at 00:18.

The transmissions were coming further and further apart. As the war dragged to an end and the nefilim fled, the bursts of static and disembodied voices fell silent.

Soon we'll all be ghosts.

Suero's slanted handwriting revealed no mention of Don Guillermo, Papá, or Miquel. Rafael tapped the paper with one restless finger. The deep red angel's tear nestled in the setting of his ring winked in the light. Just beneath the stone's surface, veins of gold swirled in agitated streaks. The tear was all his angelic mother left him before she died, and Don Guillermo had made Rafael a ring that matched the one his papá wore.

Papá will know how to find Miquel. Except his papá traveled incognito with Don Guillermo. *They should have let me stay with them in Spain.* He tossed Suero's pad to the desk and glared at the microphone. It stood at attention, tempting him to break the rules and check in with the nefilim in southern France.

Except radio silence was the rule unless a crisis demanded communication, and this was no emergency.

Besides, what do I tell them? I had a nightmare and now I am afraid? They'd admonish him for being a child. Nonetheless, his fingers itched to press the mic's button. *Surely someone has heard something by now.*

Maybe this was the time to break the rules. No one would know if he dialed in for a moment. He could always say he knocked the mic over and when he picked it up, he touched the button, accidentally opening the line.

Rafael reached for the microphone.

A knock on his door caused him to jerk his hand back. His blood pounded in his ears. Closing his eyes, he inhaled deeply and counted to ten, waiting for his heart rate to slow. Then he went to the door.

Juanita stood in the short corridor outside his room. Her black hair was smoothed into a bun and she was dressed in her usual flowing pants and blouse. She examined his face for a long moment, as if she could read the guilt in his eyes.

The idea of breaking the rules always felt brave until he found himself face-to-face with the angel. Her mortal form did nothing to extinguish either the threads of gold burning through her irises or the subtle lines of her aura, which smoldered around her in shades of midnight blue.

"Are you all right?" she finally asked. "You're flushed."

"I'm fine," he blurted a little too quickly. "I just thought I'd . . . overslept, so I hurried." Rafael twisted the ring on his finger. "Did I? Oversleep?"

She looked beyond him to the radio.

She suspected something. It took every ounce of his willpower not to look over his shoulder.

"No," she said at last. Meeting his gaze again, she smiled, but the effort at normalcy seemed strained. "You're not late, but you want to come now before Carlos gets here. We're hoping he'll have news of Miquel."

"Do you think he will? I mean, the last three members we've spoken to all said they hadn't seen him." *And I just had a dream, a terrible dream* . . . "What makes you think Carlos is different?"

"He is one of Miquel's capitáns. They would have come across the border together. Now comb your hair and come out when you're ready."

Before he could ask for more information, she turned and walked away. Rafael exhaled slowly through parted lips. That was close.

As his godmother, Juanita had as much of a hand in his upbringing as his parents. Where Papá could be lenient and Miquel often delegated correction to Papá, Juanita remained a stern disciplinarian. Rafael never doubted her love for him, but he likewise understood affection wouldn't deter either her reproach or the severity of her punishment.

And her sigils burn like fire. He didn't tempt himself with the radio a second time. Instead, he ran his fingers through his curls and stepped into the hall, closing the door behind him.

While the apartment was expansive when compared to the residences of other nefilim displaced by the war, it was only because Ysabel commanded Los Nefilim in Don Guillermo's absence, and they required more room. Even so, both Ysa and Doña Juanita were conscious of appearances. They didn't want to be accused of living in opulence while others struggled, so they kept their living arrangements austere.

A pair of tall windows opened onto a balcony that overlooked the street below. Sigils of silence churned along the window frames and over the doors, flashing like silverfish when they caught the light.

An upright piano stood against one wall. Miquel's guitar

leaned against it, and Papá's violin case rested on the top board. Beside the violin was a satchel containing the notes from Papá's collaborations with Don Guillermo.

My mission accomplished. It was the only job his fathers had given him: to get the score for the Key into France and keep it out of the enemy's hands. Terrified that he'd lose the valuable papers on their way out of Spain, he'd memorized them and practiced re-creating the pages until he could faithfully reproduce each note without referencing the originals.

Except no one had given him a job beyond protecting the scores. *And now I'm just useless.*

End tables held boxes of files and a couple of the grimoires they'd brought. The rest of Los Nefilim's extensive papers were entrusted to the library at the University of Toulouse.

Beyond a pair of open doors, the cluttered living room gave way to the dining room, where the table contained a few files. Suero sat there, making notes.

Blond in the way of the Spanish, he was a lesser nefil, but Ysabel kept him close as her father did. His incredible memory coupled with his ability to navigate bureaucratic entanglements made him a vital part of her household.

"Any news?" Rafael asked as he approached.

Suero didn't bother to ask what kind of news Rafael wanted. He merely shook his head sadly. "Nothing yet." He looked up from his notes. "They've been through worse than this, you know. They'll be fine."

Ysabel emerged from the bedroom she shared with her mother. She carried an open file and skimmed the page as she walked.

Rafael noticed Carlos Vela's name on the tab. She was probably reacquainting herself with his profile.

Today, she'd tamed her auburn curls into a fashionable style, and like her mother, she wore long pants and a blouse. Being in command suited her, adding a new dimension of confidence to her beauty. She looked sharp enough to cut out a man's eyes.

A twinge of jealousy tugged at Rafael's heart as he watched her. It must be good to have work to distract her from her father's absence. When it appeared as if she intended to walk past him without acknowledging his presence, he said, "Good morning, Ysa."

Looking up from her file, she paused beside him and smiled. Only then did he notice the deep circles beneath her eyes. "Good morning, my dark rose. Did you sleep well?" The lines etched into her face said she hadn't.

Not wanting to give her more to worry about, he lied and said, "Yes. Yes, I did."

Three hard raps sounded at their door.

"That must be Carlos," she said as she turned back toward the living room.

Suero rose and strode to catch up with her. "I'll get it."

"I don't see why . . ."

Suero whispered, "These men will try to take your power if they can. They think they're smarter than women. Let him see you in charge, not acting as a domestic. Go. Sit at the table."

Rafael mentally kicked himself. *I should have realized that and offered to answer the door.* He needed to learn to be like his papá so that Ysa would see him as someone intent on preserving her prestige as Don Guillermo's ambassador.

Moving quickly, he went to the head of the table and held the seat for her. It was the right move.

"Thank you," she murmured as she allowed him to push the chair closer to the table. "Sit beside me."

"Just a moment." He ducked into the kitchen. "Do you need any help, Doña?"

Juanita looked up from the tea platter. Her gaze swept over him. "I thought I told you to comb your hair."

"It looks like this all the time."

She sighed and shook her head, but affection touched her smile. "Grab that tray of pastries and bring them to the table."

He did as she asked and then resumed his place beside Ysa.

At the door, Suero admitted Carlos, a scruffy nefil, who held his battered hat between his hands. He wore a rumpled suit with a striped shirt, the collar buttoned tight against a patch of stubble on his neck. His eyes were hard and gunmetal blue, his hair blurred into nondescript shades of gray intermingled with black. He shuffled into the living room, feigning a weariness that couldn't disguise the cunning appraisal he gave their furnishings.

When he noticed Juanita, he presented her with a deep bow. "Doña."

She nodded to him as she took her seat at Ysa's right. "Welcome to France, Capitán Vela."

Ysa rose and met him at the dining room doors. She took his hand in both of hers with a grip that Rafael had seen Don Guillermo execute a thousand times. It was simultaneously warm and friendly, yet Ysa handled the gesture with a certain detachment that Don Guillermo never managed to convey.

"Capitán."

He bowed his head to her. "Doña Ysabel, I am so glad to see you are safe."

Ysa guided him to the table. "Please sit. Tea?"

"Thank you."

Suero poured as Ysa resumed her place at the head of the table. Once more Rafael held the chair for her, not because she needed anyone to assist her, but as a sign of respect for her position. Once he'd seen to her comfort, he took his place at her left hand. Suero sat between Carlos and Rafael with a blank pad of paper. He lifted his pencil, his cue that he was ready to begin taking notes.

Carlos eyed the food and then glanced nervously first to Juanita and then to Ysabel. "Don Guillermo will be proud to see the young woman you've become, Doña Ysabel."

The compliment dripped with condescending overtones.

Ysa's lip twitched with her irritation, but she handled her reply with diplomacy. "My heart never left Spain. If I had my way, I would have stayed for the fight."

"It's good you left, Doña. It's not a fit place for anyone now, especially a lady such as yourself."

She gestured for him to help himself to the pastries. "Please, eat."

Carlos took one of the pastries and wolfed it down in two bites. After a moment of hesitation, he ate another before he sipped the scalding tea.

While he picked the crumbs from the plate, Ysa opened a file and scanned the page. "You were liberated by members of Les Néphilim from the French internment camp at Argelès-sur-Mer last week, yes?"

Carlos cleared his throat. "Yes, Doña."

"What is it like in the camps?"

"It's not good. The French mortals practically starved us to death with just two sardines a day. They ration the bread;

two kilos between twenty of us." He looked pointedly at the spread of food before him.

Rafael tried to see the table through Carlos's eyes. *He's probably thinking that nefilim starve in the camps while Don Guillermo's court feasts like the bourgeoisie.* Nothing could be further from the truth. Breakfasts like this were brought out for visiting nefilim and weren't the standard fare for Ysa or any of the high-ranking members of Los Nefilim. But Carlos didn't know that.

When no one bothered to defend the lifestyle, Carlos continued, "The French put the Senegalese over us. Algerians, too. Sometimes they dumped the bread on the sand and watched us fight over it. Dirty bastards, all of them." He shot Rafael a scornful glare.

We're everything he hates, but me especially. Carlos saw nothing but Rafael's dark skin, which was merely a shade lighter than Miquel's smoky brown coloring. *Because people like Miquel and I aren't supposed to have power over people like him.* The prejudices were nothing new. Fortunately, Miquel had taught Rafael to stand up for himself.

"I'm not Algerian, Carlos." Papá came from the Berber tribes, and Mamá took the mortal form of a gitana so Papá would find her attractive. Rafael didn't remember much about her, but once he'd enticed Papá to sketch her face, and the likeness between her and Miquel was that of siblings. "You know that."

"I never said you were Algerian."

"Your face did."

"You're a ridiculous boy."

"And you're an ass."

"Rafael." Juanita's stare worked like a slap.

He lowered his head and let his hair shadow his brow so Carlos wouldn't see his blush. Papá would have silenced Carlos with a glare, and Miquel would have thrust one sharp word into the conversation like a blade. *Why can't I be like them?*

Beneath the table, Ysa's hand snaked onto Rafael's knee. She gave him a gentle squeeze before withdrawing.

At least Ysa was on his side. Her touch heartened him and took the sting from her mother's reproach. He feigned indifference to Juanita's admonishment, placing his cup back in its saucer, proud that his hands didn't tremble with his humiliation.

Carlos glowered at him. "Is that how your papá has raised you?"

Rafael met Carlos's stare but made no apology for his insult. "No. Miquel taught me to swear."

Carlos's lips puckered.

Before the older nefil could retort, Juanita cleared her throat and gestured to Ysa.

With a nod to her mother, Ysa smoothly put the conversation back on course. "Tell us how you've been, Carlos."

"My stomach still isn't right. The water was terrible and we . . ." Carlos reddened and wiped his palms across his thighs. "This isn't talk for ladies. Forgive me."

Juanita's eyes narrowed at the comment, but she held her silence and allowed Ysa to carry the retort.

"You forget, Carlos, Mamá is a doctor, and I've assisted her in the clinic. We've treated the shits as well as gunshot wounds. So there's little you can say to shock us *ladies*." Her light orange eyes sparkled fiercely and failed to match her conciliatory tone. "We know you've had a demeaning experience."

A smile of approval tugged at Juanita's mouth. Ysa's expression didn't change.

Because she is afraid. Rafael saw it in her posture and the tightness of her mouth. She was scared and didn't want it to show.

She pinned Carlos with a glare. "Did you cross the border with Miquel's unit?"

Carlos glanced nervously at Juanita. "Yes. But we were separated at one of the checkpoints. I arrived at Argelès first and watched for him."

Rafael's tension lessened. If they made it to the border, then Miquel was probably somewhere in France right now. Once Miquel was home, they'd find Papá and Don Guillermo. Miquel could handle anything. Rafael exhaled slowly and gave his ring one satisfied turn.

"And did you locate him?" Ysa watched Carlos as intently as Rafael.

He shook his head. "The only thing I found in the camps was la arentitis."

Rafael looked down so no one would see his disappointment. The carmine angel's tear glittered sadly in its setting. *I've lost my mother and now my fathers.* He placed his palm over the stone and clenched his jaw.

Ysa leaned forward. "La arentitis? Sanditis? I don't understand. What does that mean?"

Carlos flicked his wrist dismissively. "It's what the mortals call the madness induced by the conditions. They're already traumatized by the war, and then the French force them to live on that cold beach with no shelter. The conditions have driven some of the mortals insane. One man, he packed both his suitcases and put on his best suit, and then he just waded into the sea. Said he was going to walk to Mexico." Carlos laughed at the image. "Crazy, huh?"

How can he possibly think that's funny? Rafael bit his bottom lip to keep from speaking out of turn again.

A quick glance at Juanita told him that he wasn't the only one upset by Carlos's lack of empathy. Shades of indigo bled into the whites of Juanita's eyes—the first clear indication of her anger. She quickly regained control of herself and blinked once. When her eyelids parted again, she looked like a mortal woman with striking blue eyes.

The fire of Ysa's aura snapped once in a bright halo of rage. Suero continued to write, but his cheeks flared red with displeasure as well.

Carlos must have read their reactions as clearly as Rafael. He coughed uneasily. "Anyway, they call it la arentitis— because of the sand. Sanditis."

Before he could stop himself, Rafael blurted, "That won't happen to Miquel." He was their rock. When the rest of the world crumbled, he stood firm. "Miquel doesn't break."

Carlos turned his pitiless gaze on Rafael. "Everybody breaks, boy. Give them enough pain and take away their hope, and anyone will falter."

A chill ran through Rafael's chest.

Ysa snapped her pencil against the table. "And you found no trace of Miquel?"

Carlos shook his head, but his regret seemed insincere— the callous glint in his eyes spoke more of vengeance than sorrow. "Nothing. Perhaps he was sent to another camp."

From the corner of his eye, Rafael saw Ysabel trade a cloaked look with her mother. *They don't trust him.*

Ysa made a note on her paper. "Thank you for your report,

Carlos. Are you comfortable? Do you need anything? Money? Clothes? Food?"

A muscle along Carlos's cheek jumped when Ysa addressed him by his first name and with such familiarity. Suero was right: in Carlos's eyes, Ysa was a child.

Rather than chide her, he kept his tone civil. "No, Doña. You've been most generous already. I found a job working in the metro."

"Are you sure you wouldn't like something less taxing? We own a cabaret on the Pigalle, Folies Divine. We would welcome you there."

"Thank you, Doña, but I'm fine. I like the physical labor. Soon I'll be ready for the fight again." He rose. "I hope you will forgive me, but if there is nothing else, then I should go. My shift starts soon."

"Of course. Thank you for coming."

"Wait a moment." Juanita went into their bedroom and returned with her black doctor's bag. She portioned out several white tablets and placed them in a glass vial for Carlos. "For your stomach. Take one before each meal." Then she wrapped two pastries in a cloth and gave them to him, as well. "For later."

"Thank you, Doña."

When he reached for the items, she wrapped her hands around his and emphasized, "Nothing has changed, Carlos. Come to us if you need anything." The color of her irises seeped into the whites again, but this time the transmogrification seemed intentional. She turned her eyes into threatening orbs of lapis lazuli that pulsed with her authority. "And be prepared should we need you."

The double entendre didn't go unnoticed by anyone in

the room. They were here to help him, or destroy him, the choice was his.

Carlos bowed his head and gave her a slight nod, but not before Rafael noticed the color rising to his cheeks. He wouldn't meet Juanita's gaze.

Is he ashamed, or afraid?

His hands trembled slightly when she released him. "Of course, Doña." He mumbled the promise before bowing deeply. Then he turned toward the door.

"I'll see you out," Suero said after a quick nod to Ysabel.

When the door shut behind them, Ysa glared at Carlos's empty seat. "He's lying about something."

Rafael wanted to be strong, like Miquel, like Papá. But if the hollow feeling in the pit of his stomach was any indication, he wasn't doing it very well. "They were separated at a checkpoint. Miquel should have been right behind him."

"Patience," Juanita advised. She pushed a plate toward Rafael and then turned to Ysa. "What about the other camps?"

"According to our contacts within Les Néphilim, they have found and freed all our nefilim."

Feeling guilty for having something to eat while Miquel probably went hungry, Rafael merely picked at the croissant. "Maybe he is on his way here? He could have gotten out on his own. He could be walking to us. Do you think that is possible?"

Juanita returned to her seat. "Anything is possible, Rafael. Don't lose hope."

"No one simply vanishes." Ysa stared at her report as if it might magically produce answers. "But counting Miquel, we have nineteen nefilim whose whereabouts are currently unknown. Our milicianos are coming across the border and then disappearing in the camps." She made a short notation on the page. "Which are run by the French."

Juanita raised one eyebrow incredulously. "You suspect members of Les Néphilim are involved with whoever is taking our milicianos?"

"You said it yourself, anything is possible. Rousseau wants me to think she's my friend, but she's not. Papá is right. The kings and queens of the nefilim are rivals even when they're allies."

Rafael didn't try to keep the resentment from his voice. "Carlos didn't vanish."

"No. He didn't, did he? Carlos isn't telling us everything." Ysa made a note. "I want Suero to put someone on him. I want to know who he works with, who he sees."

Undercover. That was it. Rafael lifted his head. "Let me go to the camps. I can pose as a soldier, or even a guard. Carlos said Algerians were helping. And the French don't know an Algerian from a Berber." Warming to the idea, he talked faster. "The disguise would give me access to the rolls. I can see if our nefilim are being sent elsewhere."

Juanita's voice was firm. "No. No one will believe you're a soldier at your age."

Unfazed, he pressed his point. "What about as a servant? I don't care what kind of cover you give me. I had a nightmare this morning. Miquel is in trouble. I'm sure of it." He quickly described the nightmare's sequence to them, hating the way his anxiety caused his voice to break when he spoke of Miquel's distress. "Don't you see? Miquel is telling me to leave the safety of my home and to come to him. We've got to find him, and the camps are the place to start."

Juanita shook her head. "I cannot see Miquel sending you into the internment camp at Argelès."

She was right. It was too far away and their resources were limited. *Papá would compromise. Meet her halfway.* "Okay. Fine. Then let me follow Carlos. That I can do here. Under your supervision." He turned to Ysa. "Make that my assignment."

Before Ysa could answer, Juanita said, "No, Rafael. You're fourteen—"

"And in my firstborn life. I know, I know, but Miquel and Papá have taught me well. I can do this."

Juanita showed no sign of relenting. "You're not your papá. You're not Miquel. You don't have their experience—"

"Why do you keep interrupting? You let Ysa handle Carlos. Let this be her decision."

Juanita's palms struck the table hard enough to rattle the china. Veins of blue seeped into the whites of her eyes and she didn't blink them away as she did with Carlos. "Because I am your godmother, and I will have to answer to your fathers if something happens to you."

Painfully aware that he echoed Ysa's constant refrain to her father, he didn't back down. "How will I ever get experience if I don't try?" He turned to Ysa. "Give me a chance."

Ysabel opened her mouth, but she glanced at Juanita.

From the corner of his eye, he saw Juanita give an almost imperceptible shake of her head.

He fought to keep his voice from rising with his frustration. "Ysa. All I want is what you wanted. To prove myself."

Looking down, she shook her head. "No. I cannot lose you, too."

"Two years ago, I took a bullet for you!" He jabbed his

finger in Ysa's direction. "When I was twelve. Twelve! We were in the streets when we were cornered and I pushed you out of the way. And later, later, when the bombs were falling all around us in those last days, I carried missives between the nefilim, and no one caught me. No one! I was too fast for them. Don't you remember?"

Ysa wouldn't meet his gaze. "I remember . . ."

He whirled on Juanita. "And didn't I outwit my grandfather, a god among the daimons? I tricked Alvaro into showing me the truth of his nature, and Papá let me. Papá was there. He believes in me. Why don't you?"

Juanita's gaze softened, and for just a moment, Rafael thought he might have won her over, but then she shook her head. "This isn't Barcelona, Rafael. The same rules no longer apply. The answer is no."

And that was it. They didn't treat him like a member of Los Nefilim, but more like a possession—a rare treasure that mustn't be lost. "That's not fair."

Ysa stood, finally meeting his gaze. "Please, my dark rose, it's not about being fair. I understand your pain, truly I do. But we're in a very precarious position here. Give me a day to think of something. Just one day."

How can she do this to me? After all the years I stood up for her when she challenged her father? All she had to do was support his case. Instead, she capitulated to her mother without a fight.

The apartment suddenly felt too close, too hot. Rising, Rafael went to the door and put on his coat.

Alarm washed over Ysa's features. "Where are you going?"

"Out." *Out, where I can walk and think and please stop*

hating you. The thought stunned him practically as much as Ysa's refusal to stand behind him, but he knew it was true.

"Rafael—"

"Don't, Ysa." *Please stop talking before I say something I'll regret.*

"All I'm asking is that you trust me!"

He paused on the threshold and met her gaze. "Like you trust me?"

Turning away from her hurt, he shut the door and went down the stairs. As he passed Suero, he lowered his head.

"Hey, where are you going?" Suero asked.

Rafael tried to push by him without speaking. The narrow stairwell gave them little room to maneuver.

Suero grabbed his arm. "Rafael?"

"Out. I'm going for a walk." *Because that's what Miquel would do. He'd walk to Barcelona and back before he'd hurt Papá with harsh words.* Rafael twisted free.

A wave of uncertainty crossed Suero's brow. "Be careful."

Rafael put his back against the door and rolled his eyes. "I'm always careful." He escaped outside before Suero had a chance to retort.

The damp air did little to extinguish his anger as he strode toward rue du Calvaire at a hard clip. Bowing his head, he pretended the brisk wind caused the water in his eyes. He pushed his way past other pedestrians, not slowing his pace until he reached rue Drevet.

Turning right, he followed the block until he arrived at the next intersection, where he took the stairs down to rue la Vieuville. As he passed beneath a window, he caught the muted refrain of Robert Johnson's "Hellhound on my Trail" uncoiling beneath a phonograph needle. The song followed him down the steps.

Normally, he'd pause and listen. He loved the Mississippi Delta blues because the music shared the same deep expressive style as flamenco's cante jondo—deep song.

And it's Miquel who sings cante jondo the best. The thought of his father resurrected his dream, and he realized he'd accomplished nothing by running away. Slowing his pace, he allowed himself to be carried along with the flow of pedestrians until he found himself on rue des Abbesses. There, the entrance to the metro beckoned him.

A plan formulated in the back of his mind as he crossed the street. The metro was a common destination for a lot of people, and his time was his own. *I don't need Doña Juanita's permission to follow Carlos.*

What could it hurt to go down and just look around? No one need ever know how he spent his day, unless he came across some worthwhile information. *Then Juanita will have to admit she is wrong about me.*

Smiling to himself, Rafael went down into the station and purchased a second-class ticket. Miquel always said the best plan was a simple one. *Ride the trains and watch for workers.* He just needed to spot Carlos's crew and get a fix on his location. Then he'd decide what to do next.

A few people loitered on the platform and more descended the stairs behind him. It wasn't long before the station was full. He took a spot near the tiled wall and watched the people, wondering what it was like to be a mortal, living in ignorance of the supernatural threats surrounding them.

His reverie was broken by the jostling of bodies near the

stairs. Eight young men descended in a cluster, shoving their way through the crowd.

The youngest was a thick-bodied boy with greasy black hair and a pimply face. He looked to be close to Rafael's age. The others were older, ranging from sixteen to twenty. The fact that their suits were frayed hand-me-downs did nothing to take the swagger from their walk. They wore their fedoras tilted at jaunty angles on their slick hair.

Rafael recognized them. They were members of Le Milieu, France's underworld.

Goodfellas. The spit dried in his mouth as he lowered his head, hoping they hadn't marked his presence. This group belonged to a gang in the Pigalle, which was run by Pierre Loutrel, who was known more commonly in Le Milieu as Pierrot le fou, or Crazy Pete.

They called the tall boy with steely eyes Blondie. If he owned any other name, Rafael didn't know it. Blondie was a fixture in the Pigalle. He'd visited Los Nefilim's cabaret twice, looking for Loutrel's protection money. Ysa refused to deal with underlings and channeled her payments through more reliable sources. When she told him so, Blondie called her a liar.

At that point, a few members of Los Nefilim had taken Blondie and his comrades into the alley and had given them a beating over the insult. The yellowish ring of a bruise still encircled Blondie's eye. Word on the street was that Blondie swore revenge for the humiliation of that beating.

And he'll definitely remember I was there. Because Rafael had placed himself between Blondie and Ysa, pushing back at the goodfella's threats with bravado of his own.

Keeping his head down, he observed their progress. They

were headed straight toward him. *They likely saw me before I realized they were here. Swell.* His first foray into spycraft, and he hit a snag before he even found his prey.

Blondie tossed his cigarette aside and pointed at Rafael. "You little fucker. I remember you. You live with that Spanish bitch."

A fight was out of the question. He couldn't take on eight of them alone.

Nor could he use his song against them. Ysa made it clear that members of Los Nefilim were to remain as inconspicuous as possible, not just to keep the mortals from sensing their presence, but to stay well beneath Queen Rousseau's notice, as well.

Taking care of an extortion racket with the mortal means of a beating was one thing. Singing down a gang of goodfellas with sigils in a crowded train station was something altogether different.

And I need to prove that I can handle myself. Rafael exhaled softly. His papá said that being smaller than everyone else left only two choices: be the most vicious or the most cunning.

Then it's time for cunning. Rafael moved into the crowd, keeping other mortals between him and Blondie's crew. The people parted around him as if they sensed he was the target of a dangerous predator. A woman gave him a guarded look, drawing her young child against her hip. A man carrying a briefcase sidled away as Rafael drew near. If Blondie attacked him, these strangers wouldn't get involved.

Because they're afraid. Knowing that didn't make him feel better. For the first time since he'd left the apartment, he found himself hoping Suero would show up on some pretext.

Blondie cut through the crowd like a panther through gazelles, with his very presence splitting the herd. He nipped close and bumped Rafael with his shoulder. "What's the matter, little man? Someone steal your fire?"

A spark of rage momentarily extinguished Rafael's fear. "Piss off."

"'Piss off.'" Blondie sneered. "I'm going to piss on your face, you little shit." He snatched Rafael's wrist and twisted his hand backward.

A shock traveled up Rafael's forearm. He swallowed a yelp.

Eyeing the gold ring with its carmine angel's tear, Blondie licked his lips. "That looks expensive. I'll forget the beating if you give up the ring."

Rafael clenched his fingers into a fist. He'd die before he'd give up his mother's tear. "Fuck you."

Blondie slapped him.

Rafael spit in the gangster's face and brought his knee up, aiming for Blondie's groin. Blondie anticipated the move and shifted to the left. Rafael's knee met the air, but the new position allowed him to jerk free of the taller boy's grip.

He ducked between two of Blondie's bigger goons and dived deeper into the crowd. A quick check told him he was too far from the stairs, he'd never clear the station without getting caught.

Next time, keep a position close to the stairs.

If there is a next time.

Rafael kept moving. The train wasn't an option. Once isolated in a car with the gangsters, he'd have no way out.

"The tracks, then," he whispered. Years of Barcelona street-fighting had taught him to use the tunnels. In the darkened passages, he'd have ample opportunity to lose them.

Time was short. The next train was due any minute. To outrun it, he needed enough of a head start to reach one of the alcoves designed for the maintenance crews. The recessed areas allowed workers a safe place to wait for the trains to pass.

But the first alcove is far down the tracks. Even with his supernatural speed, Rafael anticipated a close shave.

The train's distant horn echoed down the tunnel. Blondie gestured to his thugs. They spread out in the crowd, ready to herd him into a car.

Rafael dashed past a woman, reached the edge of the platform, and jumped.

9

Rafael missed the hot rail by centimeters. Someone screamed.

A man hurried to the edge of the platform and offered his hand. "Come on, son! Get out of there before you get killed!"

Rafael barely noticed the commotion. The vibrations of the oncoming train rattled the gravel beneath his shoes. He had less time than he thought. Taking off, he'd barely gone three meters when someone shouted a second time. Glancing over his shoulder to see why, Rafael stumbled.

Blondie had leapt from the platform. He staggered before he got his legs under him. "It's all right!" He gestured to the crowd. He held one hand close to his thigh. "I'll save him! Come back, *son*." He sauntered forward a few steps before breaking into a run. "Come back, you son of a bitch!"

A pinprick of light sparkled in the distance and grew stronger by the second.

The train. Rafael took off again. The report of a gunshot followed on the heels of the bullet that struck a pipe. Steam hissed in the cold air.

Rafael veered left, leaping over the tracks to stay close to the wall. Another wild shot took out a light.

The train didn't stop at the platform as it usually did. Rafael didn't look back to see why. The tunnel brightened beneath the lead car's headlamp, illuminating the recess a few meters away.

The smell of hot metal choked the air. Rafael chased his shadow. Summoning a burst of supernatural speed, he hurtled forward.

Blondie screamed. It was an inarticulate sound of animal rage and fear, drowned by the sudden blast of the train's horn.

Rafael dived into the alcove. He came in too hard. His shoulder struck the bricks and his arm went numb.

The rumble became a roar. The ground shook as the train thundered past with cars swaying. The mortals' features loomed ghostly behind the windows.

As soon as it passed, Rafael remained still and listened. All he heard was his own ragged breathing, loud in the sudden silence.

Blondie might have survived. It was possible but not likely. *Take no chances.*

Using the last of the train's resonance, Rafael traced a man-shaped sigil on the ground. He sang it to life with the power of his voice and sent the decoy onto the tracks, where it moved to the center of the tunnel at a crouch.

Several moments passed before the image faded. No gunfire erupted in the passage.

Rafael crept to the edge of the recess and risked a peek. Blondie was gone. A man's shoe with the foot still inside lay beside the rail.

After the atrocities he'd witnessed during the war, Rafael thought himself inured to the horrors of death. Yet something about the jagged bone gleaming whitely over the polished shoe sickened him.

Because it's the same as Blondie's grin; all splintered ivory and hate. Even in death, the gangster seemed triumphant.

Rafael leaned forward and vomited. Bracing his palm against the wall, he waited until his dizziness passed. *I've gotta go—get out of here.* Yet no matter how he tried, he couldn't force his feet to move back the way he'd come. The dark sound of Blondie's death might be there, waiting for him.

Wiping his eyes, he turned left and wandered deeper into the metro. Blondie's friends had seen them both disappear into the tunnel. *They'll say I murdered him.*

And hadn't he? He'd known the mortal wouldn't survive a race with the train. *But I never expected him to jump.*

That wouldn't mean anything to nefilim like Carlos. They'd accuse him of using his song to lure Blondie to his death. The ultimate sin for a nefil.

The severity of the situation dug its teeth into Rafael's heart. "Shit!" He kicked the black rocks in frustration. "Fuck, fuck"—he slammed his fist against the wall—"*fuck!*"

He risked losing all the goodwill his papá had worked so hard to gather. The ones like Carlos, who were jealous of Papá's influence with Don Guillermo, would seize Blondie's death to prove the daimons couldn't be trusted.

I've endangered them all—Papá, Miquel, Ysa, Don Guillermo . . . And that's what hurt. He'd just proved Juanita right. "Shit. They'll never let me out of their sight again," he muttered. Unless he proved Carlos couldn't be trusted.

Of course. Carlos. Carlos might be his damnation, but the other nefil could very well be his salvation. Surely he was down here by now. *But where?*

Rafael stopped and considered his surroundings. The Pigalle station was in the distance ahead, but Blondie's goodfellas knew the metro as well as Rafael. Several of them probably awaited him there.

But there were other ways through the tunnels.

He edged along the wall until he came to a passage. Gravel covered several steps that ascended to a worker's tunnel, which continued for a hundred meters before connecting to the line leading to Anvers. He waited for the next train to pass before he took to the tracks again.

Walking in the darkness, he shut out his fear and concentrated on finding Carlos. Sounds that escaped mortal ears reached him in that lonely tunnel: the scratch of a rat's paws as it scuttled across the gravel; the low buzz of electric lights; voices from the people who waited on the Anvers platform.

Keeping to the tracks and the smaller passages, he followed the rails from one line to the next, taking care to remain hidden from the mortals' sight. With good timing and great caution, he passed Anvers unseen, then Gare du Nord, where he picked up the number five line to Gare de l'Est. Three times he came upon work crews, but their voices were mortal and none of the men resembled Carlos.

Between the Lancry and République stations, he found a passage that he hoped would take him around the busy platforms at République. Fifteen stairs descended to a tunnel. The clatter of tools and voices reached him. Descending warily, he checked both directions. No workers were in sight.

But they're here. He stopped again to listen. This time he caught the distinct sound of men talking. *To the left.*

Edging into the tunnel, he crept along for eight meters before he saw their shadows. One of the men's voices resonated deeper and more musical than the others. *With the timbre of a nefil.* Rafael held his breath. *Carlos.* He was sure of it.

A recessed area of the wall gave Rafael a hiding place. He settled in to wait.

Carlos said, "Okay, I'm going to the station and will bring the cars forward."

Another man, this one mortal, grunted. "Bring it around the loop and meet us at République."

"Give me an hour." Carlos lumbered into view, carrying a small rucksack of tools.

Rafael huddled against the wall and watched Carlos pass. He held his breath until the other nefil walked by the stairs leading toward the main tracks.

Exhaling softly, Rafael leaned out just enough to see. Carlos proceeded for a few meters before he stopped and looked toward his coworkers. Rafael ducked back into the recess, his pulse thundering in his ears. He counted to ten. When he looked again, Carlos was gone.

What the hell? Where did he go? Rafael left his hiding spot and crept down the tracks, expecting Carlos to grab him at any moment.

But Carlos had disappeared. Rafael slowed, glancing back toward his hiding spot until he felt he was close to where Carlos had stood. Examining the wall, he found a much narrower niche in the bricks. The low door led to a corridor that opened into another tunnel.

Peeking around the corner, he glimpsed Carlos's back as the nefil rounded a bend. Without his daimonic sight, Rafael wouldn't have seen Carlos at all. *The only time when being daimon works in my favor.*

Rafael glanced over his shoulder. When he explored the metro alone, he placed sigils on the intersections to mark his way, but to do so now would alert Carlos to his presence. Instead, he removed his bright yellow scarf and tucked it close to the corner with the tail pointing toward the way out.

Stepping lightly to avoid making a sound, Rafael stayed clear of the broken slats between the rails. Caged lights populated the walls every few meters, but the luminance was minimal at best, leaving the concrete to glow eerily in sepia tones. Thick cables snaked along the walls and ceiling.

Sneaking around the bend, Rafael glimpsed Carlos's shadow as he approached an intersection and went right. Rafael followed. When he reached the corner, he left his metro ticket beneath a piece of gravel.

Carlos walked toward a spark that flared in the distance. Snapping his fingers, he hummed a tune and took his voice through the scales. When he found the right pitch, he filled the tunnel with his song.

The spark flared again in red and gold, brighter this time, stretching across the tunnel like a spider's web. It *was* a glyph. The lines grew stronger, but they still weren't clear enough for Rafael to gauge the ward's purpose from this distance.

Moving gingerly around the rotting boards, he tiptoed forward. As he neared, he detected the faraway sound of voices. It was a choral arrangement all tuned to the same frequency and sung by nefilim, but something about the chant sounded off . . . *like they're straining for notes far beyond their reach.*

Another blast of light flooded the tunnel. When it ended, Rafael found himself less than a meter away from Carlos. *But I didn't move . . . did I?*

Preoccupied with his spell, Carlos didn't notice Rafael. He traced a sigil, like a mirror image of the one blocking the tunnel. When he finished, he raised his arms and joined his voice with those of the unseen nefilim.

The chorus reached a new crescendo. The glyph's sparks bathed them in fiery light.

Rafael's flesh goose-pimpled. This was neither natural nor right. He backed up a single step. His foot skidded in the grit and he fell, sitting hard on the gravel. Before he could rise, the ward flared, the heat of it flowing around him like a river of fire. His ears felt full, stuffed up like when he had a cold. He forced himself to yawn, but the pressure didn't ease.

Rafael froze and listened as his father taught him. *Analyze the enemy's song to understand their intent. Then you can construct a defense. Don't react. Act.*

The passage amplified the arrangement: tenor, tenor, bass, bass . . . all male. The motif was a signature of Die Nephilim.

The tenors ceased to sing, leaving only the vibrations of the bass in the measure. Once more he heard Miquel say: *Move the breath of darkness . . . through your throat . . . your throat . . . throat . . .*

The boards shook beneath him. Dust drifted downward from the ceiling. The tracks blurred. The tenors rejoined the movement. Reverberations echoed in the darkness.

Red-gold beams flooded the passage along with the sound of the nefilim's voices, breaking as they sang.

The passage tilted sideways. Rafael cried out. He covered his head. His flesh pulled tight around his skull. Biting back a second scream, he leaned forward.

As abruptly as it began, the nefilim's song stopped, and the sigil's fire rushed back into the glyph, leaving him to shiver in the sudden cold. Lowering his trembling hands, he dared to look.

Rafael couldn't believe his eyes.

10

The rough boards of the metro were gone. The tracks around Rafael looked new. Several meters away, two sets of rails formed a Y-intersection; the traversing line merged with the tracks that Carlos and Rafael occupied, and then continued forward to a pinprick of light in the distance.

Carlos whirled. "What the hell? You little fuck!"

Rafael scrambled to his feet and traced a protective ward between them. "Stay back, Carlos!" *Where the hell are we?* Or maybe a better question was: *How do I get back to Paris?*

The sigil was gone. No, that wasn't right. He glanced over his shoulder and saw it behind him, still stretched across the tracks, but now the lines of the ward were dead and gray.

Shit, shit, shit. Rafael struggled for calm.

From behind Carlos, someone moved out of the adjacent tunnel. He was a tall man, possessing Don Guillermo's imposing height and bearing. "Who is there?"

The deep resonant voice belonged to a nefil, and the question was spoken in Castilian, not Catalan or French.

From the accent, Rafael determined the man was either from Madrid or had spent a great deal of time there.

Carlos's back stiffened. He flexed his fingers at his side and gave Rafael a poisonous glare. It took Rafael a second to realize that Carlos was afraid.

If Carlos is scared and he is supposed to be here, what does that mean for me? Rafael took another step backward.

Meanwhile, Carlos answered, "It's me, sir. Carlos Vela."

A second figure lurched from the depths of the adjoining tunnel. This man's body was bent and crooked. He spoke but the words were virtually unintelligible, as if his mouth couldn't form the syllables. His voice rang with unpleasant vibrations.

Like the echo from an abyss. It was a strange thought, but once it lodged in Rafael's mind, he couldn't shake it loose.

"K 'asa?" he asked.

Qué pasa? Is that what he's asking? What's happening? Rafael edged closer to the sigil behind him.

The strange humpbacked man lurched forward, pushing his way between the tall nefil and Carlos. He pointed one four-fingered hand at Rafael. The creature's thumbs were as long as his index fingers, a distinctive physical trait that belonged to the angels in their natural form.

Then where are his wings? Struggling past his fear, Rafael recalled Father Bernardo's lessons on the fallen angels. For once, he didn't resent the long hours spent transcribing angelic names while the other children played. Only one breed of angel possessed no wings. *Grigori.*

Rafael's throat tightened. He gasped in short hard breaths. *No, it can't be. They're supposed to be imprisoned deep beneath the earth.*

Puckered scars rose over the portrait mask that covered

the lower portion of the angel's face. The tin mask created a mortal visage with prominent cheekbones and finely shaped lips pursed in a scowl. "K'ien . . . ?"

Quien? Is he asking who I am?

The tall nefil stepped forward. "Who indeed?" he asked Carlos. "Who is this and how did he follow you?"

Carlos turned to the nefil. "I'm sorry, Generalissimo. I had no idea he was there."

Generalissimo . . .

That's what they called Jordi Abelló. Rafael switched his attention back to the nefil. His red-gold hair was lighter than Don Guillermo's auburn locks, but the brothers shared the same mouth and tawny eyes.

But how is he in Paris? Rafael stumbled but still managed to keep his ward between them. *Unless we're not in Paris anymore.* He finally found his voice. "Where am I?"

Jordi held out his hand in a gesture of peace. "Easy, son. What's your name?"

"He's Rafael Diaz, Diago's brat," Carlos snapped as he made a grab for Rafael's arm.

Dancing out of reach, Rafael answered them with a shout that charged his sigil, lighting the tunnel in shades of amber and green. Lines of gold from the carmine angel's tear in his ring reinforced the glyph's power. Curved edges spun around the ward's perimeter, and the gold sharpened the blades with angelic fire.

The Grigori took quick brittle steps, as if he walked barefoot on shards of glass. He and Jordi lifted their hands together to shape a sigil that glittered black like ice. The Grigori howled a withered note and spat it at the glyph. With a flick of their wrists, they flung it at Rafael's sigil.

The shard of black cut through Rafael's ward as if it weren't there. Instinctively, he lifted his hands to shield his face. Black lines encircled his wrists like cuffs made of broken glass, fishhooking into his flesh, rooting deeper under his skin with every movement.

Rafael cried out and stumbled sideways, trying to throw off the bonds. Before he regained his balance, someone kicked him behind his leg. He went down. One knee struck a railroad tie, the other bit into the gravel. He tried to form another ward, but the cuffs gouged deeper into his wrists, reaching for the tendons.

Panic blinded him. Someone jerked him to his feet and pinned his arms to his sides. *Carlos, it's Carlos.*

Rafael threw his weight forward, hoping to tip Carlos off balance. The bigger nefil barely moved.

A pair of polished boots entered Rafael's range of vision. *Jordi.*

The nefil grabbed a handful of hair and jerked Rafael's head back. "Is this true? You're the son of Diago Alvarez?" Snapping his fingers, Jordi fired a ward for light.

Jordi's face blurred in the sudden brightness. Rafael blinked the tears from his eyes. He glimpsed the large gold signet Jordi wore. A dented and misshapen angel's tear crouched in the setting. Lacking the clarity of a true angel's tear, milky veins of umber spurted across the scarred surface of the pale green stone.

Rafael turned his face, as much to avoid recognition as the nearness of that cancerous tear, but Jordi held him tight.

"It's true." Jordi breathed the words reverently as if he'd stumbled on the most precious of songs.

A flush of heat surged through Rafael's body. Darkness

edged his vision. *Don't faint, don't faint . . .* He bit the inside
of his cheek until he tasted blood. Pain drove back the shadows. The vertigo passed. *Look in his eyes. Don't be afraid.*
He forced himself to do the first, but couldn't find the will
for the second.

Jordi's smile broadened. "What an exceptional gift you've
brought us, Carlos. Come see, Sam."

As Sam—the Grigori—approached, Rafael noticed the
tin mask's scowl had changed. Now the lips were spread in
a line with one corner quirked upward in an expression of
curiosity. The angel's scarred eyes burned milk-white with
chartreuse veins. He stroked Rafael's cheek with one gray
finger. Spiders walked as lightly as his touch. "Do you know
what we are, boy?"

Though the angel's pronunciation was no better—*his
mouth, there's something wrong with his mouth*—Rafael
quickly learned to parse the broken syllables so he could understand. "Grigori."

"Hmm, yes." The glass chains on Rafael's wrists hummed
in time with Sam's vocalizations and grew slick with blood.
"Very good. So you know our power."

"You rebelled against the Thrones and were cast into the
abyss. You're criminals."

The Grigori's eyes whorled in purulent hues. "A historian,
hmm?" Sam dug his fingernails into Rafael's cheek, dragging
his claw downward and leaving a trench of fire in its wake.

The scream slipped through Rafael's lips before he could
stop it.

The angel chuffed a harsh laugh, which was absorbed by
the tin mask. "Criminals." He spoke the word with a growl.
"We lost a war, like you did. That was our only crime." He

leaned close, his fetid breath seeping around the mask to bathe Rafael's face. "And if that makes us criminals, what are you?"

We haven't lost. We're in retreat. But Rafael didn't answer the Grigori. Anything he said would be the angel's excuse for more cruelty. His papá always said the smart nefil knows when to shut up.

Then again, a smart nefil wouldn't be here in the first place, he thought bitterly.

Sam's eyes crinkled and matched the mask's tin smile. He tapped the ring on Rafael's finger. "Give it to us."

"No." Rafael clenched his fist.

Jordi's eyes widened in surprise at the refusal, and something else flickered in his gaze . . . a hint of admiration.

"What is this?" Sam's slap rocked Rafael's head.

Stars burst across his vision. His scalp burned and he realized Jordi had released his hair. He tasted blood again and would have fallen, but Carlos held him upright.

Sam turned to Jordi. "Is it demented?"

Why does he want the ring? Everyone knew an angel's tear was useless to anyone but the recipient.

"Leave it on him," Jordi said. "We'll soon control him and his song. Let the angel's magic augment his voice. We'll use it to our advantage."

Satisfied with the answer, Sam snaked his hand into Rafael's pocket. "Let's see what else it has."

Rafael twisted his hips, but the Grigori wasn't to be denied. Barely able to move, Rafael closed his eyes and submitted to the angel's groping. Coins rattled onto the gravel, bouncing along the railway ties, followed by a few francs.

Jordi glanced toward the faraway light. "What do you

say, Sam? Shall we postpone our trip to Barcelona for a few hours?"

The Grigori nodded. "This will prove entertaining."

A cold knot of fear twisted in Rafael's stomach.

Jordi signaled to Carlos with an absent wave of his hand. "Let him go."

Carlos released Rafael and snatched the fallen money from the tracks.

Fucking scavenger. Rafael resisted the urge to kick the older nefil in the head.

Jordi nudged the center of his back. "See that light?"

Rafael nodded.

"Start walking. Carlos, keep an eye on him."

Carlos pocketed the money and then gave Rafael a shove, practically knocking him off his feet. "You heard the generalissimo. Get moving."

Stumbling forward, Rafael righted himself. The glyphs covering the cuffs bit less deeply into his wrists as long as he didn't struggle. "What's going to happen now?"

Carlos smacked the back of Rafael's head. "You're going to shut up."

Trembling less, he licked his swollen lip and used the time to consider his situation. This was no different from escaping Blondie. *Stay calm. Pay attention. Look for the right moment to get away.* But no matter how he tried, he couldn't get his heartbeat under control.

Before he'd formulated even a flimsy plan, they drew closer to the light. A train engine squatted on the tracks, seething steam into the air. On the platform, soldiers in Nationalist uniforms directed the prisoners, who unloaded crates from the freight cars.

Carlos pushed Rafael toward a set of concrete stairs that ascended to the platform. The rough steps were high. Rafael stumbled on the first one. Carlos grabbed his arm before he could fall and half supported, half dragged him the rest of the way.

As they reached the last step, the soldiers turned toward them. Rafael saw nothing friendly in their faces. He looked away from their smirks, feeling the blood rush into his cheeks with his own humiliation.

Carlos maneuvered him toward a door. Inside, a sergeant sat at a rusting metal desk and spoke into a field radio. At the sight of Rafael and Carlos, he abruptly ended his conversation and slammed the handset into the case. "Where the fuck have you been, Vela? You were supposed to be here yesterday."

"I had an appointment this morning that I couldn't put off."

Jordi entered the room. "It's all right, Sergeant. Carlos brought us a guest."

The sergeant shot to his feet and saluted Jordi. "Generalissimo!" He turned to the angel and bowed. "Your Eminence. We thought you'd already left for Barcelona."

Sam's portrait mask leered at the sergeant. "Surprise."

The sergeant's expression said there was nothing pleasant about this particular surprise. He gestured to Rafael. "Shall I process him?"

Rafael wasn't sure what that meant, but he didn't like the sound of it.

Jordi shook his head. "Carlos will see to it. Take him to the interrogation room. Give him a thorough search and then wait for us."

Rafael's fear returned in a rush. *Interrogations?* What could he possibly tell them that Carlos already hadn't?

Carlos's grip became a vise on Rafael's biceps. "Why me?" the older nefil asked.

Jordi lit a cigarette. "Because I trust you won't fuck up."

Klaxons suddenly went off, startling everyone to a standstill.

Jordi's head snapped up. "This wasn't supposed to happen until tomorrow."

"Good thing our little friend delayed our departure." Sam's mask displayed a death-head grin, the alarms obviously music to his ears. "Soon we'll know how effective our work has been."

Carlos hesitated. "Should I put him in a cell and help with the search, Generalissimo?" Every note of the question said he hoped the answer was no.

"Only if you want to die." Jordi made a dismissive gesture with his hand. "You have your orders. Carry on."

Glad to be away from both Jordi and the fallen angel, Rafael didn't resist when Carlos hauled him back onto the platform. They left the train behind, moving in tandem with a group of prisoners, who were herded forward by more armed guards.

Rafael sneaked glances at their faces but saw no one he recognized. Judging from their features, none were Spanish. *Are they Internationalists?* He listened for a word, or even a murmur to give him an accent, any clue as to the men's nationalities. Yet none of them made a sound.

Just beyond the platform, the corridor narrowed and branched. The prisoners were directed to the left. Carlos took the hall to the right.

They passed several wooden doors that would look more at home in a monastery, than a military compound. Rafael heard locks click into place as they passed.

They're locking down. Even if he could get away from Carlos, there was no place to hide. He hurried to keep up with the older nefil, doing everything he could to memorize the route.

Talk to him, form a connection . . .

Rafael licked his lips and whispered, "You're afraid of them."

Carlos's fingers tightened, but he made no reply.

The only light came from overhead, where naked bulbs were strung by a wire along the ceiling. The main corridor continued with two adjacent halls splitting to either side. Carlos veered to the left.

"We never made you afraid, Carlos. Did we? Didn't Doña Juanita—"

Carlos shoved Rafael against the wall and slammed his palm across Rafael's mouth. "One more word and I'll gag you. Do you understand?"

Feeling the blood pulsing hard in his veins, Rafael met the other nefil's gaze and nodded. *But this isn't over. I'll try again. You're scared of them and unsure, and I'll find a way to exploit that.* He had to. Carlos was his only connection to Paris right now.

Carlos jerked him back into motion.

They continued down the hall. Other than patches of plaster that crumbled and revealed the patterns of bricks beneath, or the long handrail bolted to the wall, there wasn't much to distinguish the flanking hall from the main corridor they'd just left. No offices lined the arched walkway—just meters and meters of emptiness. A smell of rot permeated the damp air. The boards under their feet absorbed the sound of their footsteps with the spongy give of rotten wood.

They arrived at a narrow stairwell. Carlos gestured for Rafael to go first.

Rafael climbed on shaking legs, counting the steps to take his mind off his fear. Forty-eight steps later, they reached the landing.

To the left was an alcove, where a nefil sat on a hard chair in front of a rickety table. Beyond the nook, a second stairwell descended to a steel door. A long hall extended from the alcove into darkness. The corridor didn't look well used.

That might be my way out. He sidled to the right.

Carlos caught his arm again. "You're going the wrong way."

The nefil looked up from his game of solitaire and assessed Rafael with icy disdain. "We don't have a children's section, Carlos."

Carlos ignored the jibe. "The prisoner's name is Rafael Diaz."

The nefil sniffed and withdrew a worn notebook from the desk's drawer. He scribbled Rafael's name on a dirty page. Rafael couldn't help but notice the number of names with lines drawn through them.

Dead? Is that why their names are crossed out? Are they dead?

"Does he have a number?" The nefil picked his nose.

"Not yet. He's here for interrogation."

So soon? We're here so soon? He still didn't have a plan. *What if they ask me questions? What do I say?*

"Hmm." The guard shut the notebook and stood. Leaving

his rifle propped against the wall, he withdrew a set of keys from his pocket and went to the next set of stairs.

Carlos prodded Rafael forward.

Moving on numb legs, he descended to the steel door. The nefil unlocked it and stood aside so they could pass. "Hey, Cabello, you have company."

Without waiting for an acknowledgment from Cabello, he slammed the door shut behind them. The key clacked in the lock.

Rafael flinched and then hated himself for letting his fear show.

Cabello occupied a table just as small and shaky as the one above. He put down his novel and addressed Carlos as he stood. "Who do we have?"

"Rafael Diaz."

While Carlos and Cabello talked, Rafael looked down the corridor. A handrail ran along the left wall. Four doors with bolts on the outside were on the right. At the end of the hall was another door—also steel and also shut.

Cabello gave Rafael's good cheek a light slap. "Hey. Wake up. Room two." He pointed down the hall.

Rafael didn't move. *I can't do this. I always thought I could, but now I'm here and I can't do this.*

Carlos poked him. "You heard Cabello. Room two."

Rafael couldn't get his breath. His throat felt swollen.

"Jesus, Carlos, you've scared the shit out of the kid. You can't do that if you want to get anything out of them." Cabello guided Rafael into motion. "Come on. Do as you're told, and you'll be fine."

Somehow, Rafael doubted that.

[11]

Miquel awakened back in his cell. One eye remained swollen shut, the lids of the other barely parted. Blurred images swam into focus.

That fucking hood. He glared at it. Cabello—he now knew who was who—had dropped it on his way out. There it remained, crumpled on the floor, innocuous enough until someone slipped it over Miquel's head. Then, in that hot darkness, the sand crept between his lips and into his throat.

Agony gnawed his muscles. One of the bricks dug into his broken rib cage, another tormented his hip. He vaguely remembered dislocating his shoulder while struggling to free himself from the cuffs, and if he didn't pop the joint back into place, it wouldn't heal correctly.

Struggling into an upright position, he leaned against the wall. With a trembling hand, he grabbed the wrist of his injured arm and pulled it forward and straight. The joint popped back into place. A sob stabbed his chest with rusty nails. Something was broken deep inside him. He tasted blood in the back of his raw throat.

The hood rustled. He froze, barely daring to breathe. Grains of sand leaked from the canvas.

"La arentitis." *I'm going insane.* Or maybe he wasn't *going.* Maybe he'd already arrived.

The canvas bunched together and slithered forward several centimeters. It fluttered as if touched by a breeze, or a sigh.

Miquel's eye widened. *That's not happening. The hood isn't moving.*

In the corridor, a door slammed. Miquel's flesh crawled at the sound. Had Feran taken the bait? Or was it Benito, coming for the next round of questioning?

No. It was too soon. Or was it? Wasn't that how it worked? Come back at odd times, remain unpredictable, throw the source off balance?

Terror reached up from the pit of his stomach to engulf his heart. If they took him now, he would break for certain.

A key clicked in the door's lock.

"No, please . . ." He clamped his mouth shut, but the litany continued in his head: *Please, please, no more, not yet, no more . . . let it be Feran . . . I can bluff him . . .*

The door opened. He shut his eye. Someone whispered his name. *Nico.*

Miquel opened his eye. "I can't . . ."

"Shh," Nico whispered as he dropped a rucksack to the floor. Kneeling, he gave Miquel a quick examination. "Anything broken?"

Miquel indicated his shoulder. "I popped it back into place."

"Is this the first time you've ever done that?"

Miquel shook his head.

"Then I'm going to trust you did it right." Nico withdrew a red, white, and blue vial and tapped four pills into his palm. Before Miquel could resist, Nico pushed the tablets between his lips.

The Italian leaned close. A sweet, musky scent followed the swing of his hair. "You don't have to swallow. They'll dissolve under your tongue. Just relax, relax. It's Pervitin. We give it to the mortals to keep them awake. It helps nefilim heal faster and sharpens our songs. Let it heal you. I need you. Please. Please." That one word whispered over and over like a prayer.

The Pervitin, as bitter as the pain, melted on Miquel's tongue. Tracking the second hand of Nico's watch, he distracted himself by counting the minutes ticking past. At five, his empty stomach cramped.

A seizure racked him. Nico slipped something hard between Miquel's teeth. *Wood . . . it's a piece of wood.*

He chewed the small block as another tremor rattled his body. The heat surging through his muscles turned into a conflagration, accelerating his healing, and bringing horrendous pain in its wake.

Nico held his head and stroked his hair. He whispered a litany of, "Please, please, please . . ."

And Miquel joined the prayer with one of his own: *Kill me, please, let this kill me . . .*

He didn't die.

Blackness edged his vision and held him in its grip. Another seizure rattled through him before the darkness receded in slow stages. The agony subsided. A strange euphoria washed through him, relieving him of his suicidal thoughts.

He lifted his hand. The bruises had yellowed, not quite

healed but no longer the throbbing black malignancies covering him moments ago. The lacerations scabbed, and that broken thing within him cried out when he moved but no longer sucked his breath away.

Nico guided a canteen to Miquel's lips and gave him water.

Miquel had never tasted a drink so sweet. He tried to take the flask from Nico, but the Italian withdrew it. "Too much and you'll be sick."

Setting the canteen aside, Nico pulled clothing from the pack and dropped it on Miquel's thighs. It was a Nationalist uniform that matched those of the guards. With an urgent nod, Nico gestured for Miquel to get dressed.

This time, Miquel didn't argue. All that mattered was getting away from these poisoned sigils and that damned hood. He dressed and quickly laced the boots. *Now comes the real test.*

Nico offered his hand, but Miquel ignored him and stood unaided. The broken thing within him wailed. He slowed his movements. The pain dimmed. As long as he remained careful, he should be fine.

At the door, Nico signaled all was clear. Miquel adjusted the tasseled cap and stepped into the corridor. He closed the door, sliding the lock into place. The cell opposite his was silent. Had the occupant died?

The small window beckoned his curiosity. Before Nico could stop him, he unlatched the peephole's cover and peered inside.

A nefil with a vacant stare squatted on the floor. Sigils wrapped his torso, erupting like veins along his arms and chest. He clawed at the wards. His blood seeped into the ligatures and lines, charging them with power.

Another glyph—thick and brown, the color of rust and bruised apples—snaked into his mouth and forced his jaws wide. A low moan emanated from deep within the man. He whipped his head from side to side, obviously panicked. Without warning he rose and charged the door, slamming his body against the metal.

Miquel jumped back. "Jesus Christ, what's happening to him?"

Nico slammed the peephole cover shut. "What's going to happen to you if you don't move."

"Can we save him?"

"Are you mad? You can't save anyone here. Listen to me: The Grigori thinks the Messengers were wrong to consign themselves to breeding programs. He believes the superior soldier must be created with drugs, or surgeries. We failed with this nefil. He's gone insane." He gestured at the row of cells. "Like the others."

Miquel counted eight cells, including his own. "We should kill them."

"If you do, the Grigori will know. And then he will send guards who will find you gone." Without another word, Nico walked toward the exit.

Miquel looked at the rows of doors and shuddered. He backed away and followed the Italian. *I'm a coward.*

They reached another metal door. Nico inserted a key into the lock.

Miquel put his hand on Nico's arm. "I didn't say I would help you."

"But you will, because I know the way out of here."

Fair enough. Miquel licked his lips but made no promise. "Where is here?"

"You're in a pocket realm guarded by sigils, and because it's maintained by nefilim, it's unstable. Now stop talking and let's go."

Nico opened the door to reveal a narrow hall that gradually ascended away from the cells. The floor itself was uneven and covered with rough boards. A metal handrail ran along both sides of the rock walls, probably to help guards stabilize themselves as they transported unruly prisoners.

Halos formed around the naked light bulbs that hung suspended from the center of the ceiling. The filaments hissed, like whispers.

Or sand moving over stone. Miquel blinked the sweat from his eyes. *It's the drug. It did more than heal me.* The Pervitin heightened his senses, making him hyperaware of every sensation.

Nico snapped the last bolt into place.

Miquel's skin crawled at the clank of metal on metal. His fingers twitched and he wished for a gun. *Why hadn't Nico brought one?*

Licking his lips, he kept his voice low. "How long does the Pervitin's effects last?"

Nico appraised him carefully. "Given your size and the extent of your injuries, I'd say you have maybe an hour." He set off at a sedate pace.

Miquel fell into step beside him. "So soon?"

"Are you disappointed?"

Yes. "Relieved. I don't like using drugs."

"The effects are short-lived. Our test subjects rapidly

build a tolerance, so the dosages must constantly be increased."

"Is that what I am? A test subject?"

Nico didn't answer. He signaled for silence as they neared two closed doors. The lack of exterior bolts meant offices, not cells. Fortunately, they remained shut. If anyone noticed two shadows passing beneath their thresholds, they made no outcry.

The incline grew steeper. Although Miquel had been hooded whenever they took him from the cell, the route felt familiar to his feet. He also recalled steps, and soon enough, they reached the stairwell.

The uneven stairs led upward to a sharp bend. *Then twenty steps, I counted twenty steps.* At the next landing was an alcove. The recess was empty except for a rickety table and chair.

Where is the guard? He didn't have time to consider the problem. Nico was moving too fast.

They crossed the landing, went down another flight of stairs, and through a long corridor without any doors. The hall merged into a main passage.

Nico turned right. Miquel paused at the intersection. On the other side of the wide hall, he noted another corridor similar to the one they had just left. Did that go to the interrogation rooms? If he walked across and counted the steps, he could be sure.

He looked to his left. The passage continued into the distance, although it seemed to grow wider rather than narrower.

Nico tapped his shoulder. "Don't get lost," he hissed.

Miquel nodded and followed him. They continued along the main corridor and came to more stairs. At the next level,

Miquel noted several nefilim in white lab coats. They stood outside a door and smoked. One lifted his hand to Nico.

With a nod, Nico passed them. The plaster seemed newer here and well maintained. They encountered adjuncts, who carried clipboards or files and moved with the studied purpose of men on important errands. A few marked Nico's face and nodded to him, while others made eye contact with Miquel before shifting their gaze quickly away.

Rooms with open doors branched out on either side of the corridor. One contained a map room. A full-scale map of the Barcelona metro occupied the wall facing the door.

Miquel memorized the details of each room. The information would be valuable for Los Nefilim.

The corridor ended by another set of stairs. They climbed again, one flight and then two. At the next landing, Nico paused and checked his watch.

They were alone. Miquel seized the opportunity. "You said this is a pocket realm. How do we get out of it?"

"Sam has managed to create two main portals: the first begins at the abandoned fort at the top of this mountain. That portal remains open at all times. That's where we're going."

"How do we reach it?"

"Via an elevator that goes to the surface."

"And the other gate? Where does that go?"

"Into Barcelona. It's how Jordi is able to move quickly back to Franco's side if he's needed. They're also working on an adjacent gate that will open in Paris."

Miquel went cold. He feigned ignorance. "What could possibly be in Paris?"

"The German Inner Guard is preparing to move their

armies into France. They call it Operation Fall Gelb. They've used their mortal puppet, Hitler, to manipulate enough German support for another war. With the mortals and her nefilim, Jaeger intends to attack France from Germany."

Miquel knew about the plan, but he held his silence to see if Nico revealed anything new.

"While Jaeger attacks from the east, Jordi will launch a surprise maneuver through the Parisian portal. They'll sandwich Rousseau's forces and annihilate her."

All this is worth it for that piece of information alone. Jordi's involvement through a portal realm was the nugget they didn't have. Miquel's mind raced.

If Jordi and Jaeger were successful, the German nefilim would be in the perfect position to take England. Then, with the Spanish, French, and English divisions of the Inner Guard under Jaeger and Jordi's control, Guillermo would lose the last of his allies. He'd be forced to either abdicate or flee into exile somewhere in the Americas. Their chances of reclaiming Spain grew more remote by the hour.

Miquel had to get to France and warn Rousseau. They might not stop the mortal invasion, but they could certainly mitigate the damage on the Inner Guard's front. "What are we waiting for?"

Nico looked up. "The shift change. The elevator runs continually during that time, so we shouldn't be noticed."

Miquel nodded. "Are there more gates than the ones you've mentioned?"

"Yes. But they're not stable. Sam is using nefilim to avoid alerting the angels and the Thrones to our presence. Nefilim's vocal cords aren't designed to reach the required notes to sustain the Key, so the Grigori is using multiple choral groups and drugs to make up the deficiency. The more gates, the greater the strain on the chorus to maintain the few that work. Trust me, this is the surest way out."

The last thing Miquel wanted to do was trust Nico. But so far, he'd guided him true, and, really, he had no other options that he could see. So when Nico signaled it was time to go, Miquel nodded. Nico opened the door and they emerged on a platform. Rows of armed soldiers stood in squads of eight.

Miquel felt their eyes on him as he passed. *Stop being paranoid.* Yet he couldn't shake the feeling that the men were waiting for something other than the elevator. *Does it matter?*

Just ahead, the corridor ended in a T-juncture. Nico went left. A cargo elevator stood at the end of the hall. It was all Miquel could do to restrain himself from running to the cage.

I'm going to make it out of here and see my family again. A great surge of hope filled his chest. The Pervitin sent a spiral of euphoria through his brain. *Just a few short steps and then we're free.*

A box hung from a long cord. Nico went to it and pushed the green button. Gears growled. The cables behind the cage began to move.

Slowly, too slowly.

Klaxons suddenly went off. Red lights flashed along the ceiling.

Miquel's hope soured in his stomach. "Does that mean an escape?"

A short jerky nod was his only answer.

Miquel glanced over his shoulder.

Ten soldiers stood at the juncture, blocking the way back. Three pointed their pistols at him. The other seven stood together in formation. One man stepped forward and began the first line of a sigil. Behind him, the other soldiers mirrored his movements.

They're preparing to sing against me. "You set me up, Nico."

"No." Eyes wild, the Italian backed away. "This wasn't supposed to happen."

Miquel almost believed him. *Because I'm a fool.*

Then the elevator churned to a halt and a voice shouted, "Miquel de Torrellas!"

Chills goose-pimpled his flesh as he shifted his attention to the elevator's car. A Grigori in a Nationalist uniform wrenched the gate open and stepped into the corridor. He wore a grinning portrait mask over the lower part of his face.

Milky eyes assessed Miquel from head to foot. "We remember you from your firstborn life when you were Benaiah, son of Jehoiada, chief of Solomon's army."

Miquel swallowed hard. He glanced around. Nico reached the line of nefilim and stopped.

Sweat slicked Miquel's body, yet he wasn't scared. He had nothing to lose. His only choices were escape or die. Anything less jeopardized Los Nefilim.

Miquel backed away from the Grigori and stopped himself at two meters. Every step backward was a step away from freedom. *Unless Nico was lying about that, too.* He didn't allow the doubt to nag him.

With the soldiers behind him, the elevator was his only route off this level. The other squads they'd passed had to be waiting around the corner. That's how he'd plan an ambush. Leave ten men exposed. If one fell, others were ready to step into his place.

They finished their sigil and watched the angel.

Miquel turned to the Grigori and asked, "Who are you?"

"We are Samyaza."

One of Satanael's generals. At least Jordi was consistent in associating with the most dangerous of the fallen angels. Miquel straightened. The Pervitin hummed through his limbs.

Samyaza stepped closer. "It was you who slayed Solomon's brother Adonijah at the altar. Oh yes, we remember you. And the time for your reckoning has arrived."

Adonijah. Known in this incarnation as Jordi Abelló. "I remember him." Miquel snatched a silvery thread of the soldiers' fear from the air. He combined it with the grays of Samyaza's arrogance to trace a glyph with barbed teeth and sharp notes. "Bring him out. Let him weep on the altar while he begs for his life." Miquel hummed and charged the glyph with the resonance of his voice. "Let me murder him again."

He flung his sigil at the Grigori with little hope of striking his target. Only a king or queen of the Inner Guard possessed the necessary speed and thrust to injure an angel. He hoped for a distraction. If Samyaza danced even a few steps to the left, Miquel had a clear shot at the elevator.

Miquel's glyph momentarily disappeared from sight and then returned to view. It grazed Samyaza's brow. The Grigori howled but didn't relinquish his position in front of the lift.

Stunned by his success, Miquel hesitated, but only for the fraction of a heartbeat. Reflexes honed by centuries of battles kicked in and he quickly fashioned another ward, this one more complex and made with bright pearlescent ropes designed to bind the angel.

Never before in all his incarnations had he performed with such speed and precision. *The Pervitin. It has to be the drug, and it's working like a sip of fire.* He finished the last line and sang the ward to life, forcing it toward Samyaza.

The Grigori gestured to the soldiers. They charged their sigil and channeled it to him. The angel used it to sever the ropes of Miquel's glyph.

Once free, and working with angelic speed, Samyaza created another ward. Then he forced the soldiers to sing.

Miquel looked from the terrified men to the angel. *His voice is damaged and he's somehow singing through them. But how?* The drug snapped through his brain, shifting his attention away from the question and back to survival as he noted the intent behind Samyaza's new ward. It was the mirror image of Miquel's, but rather than light, the strands roiled in shades of black and gray.

As the sigil rushed toward Miquel, it spread, reaching out with thick tendrils, like the arms of an octopus, ready to chain his arms to his sides and fill his mouth. *Like the prisoner in the cell below.*

Horrified by the image, Miquel grabbed a beam from one of the overhead bulbs to form a shield of blistering white between him and the Grigori. He lifted his arms and crossed his wrists behind the buffer.

Samyaza's sigil struck the defensive ward. The concussion jolted the breath from Miquel's body. He didn't fall, but the pressure intensified. The soles of his boots skidded on the slick floor as he was pushed backward.

Darkness washed over him, momentarily blinding him.

The wails of dying angels buzzed through his head. Midnight hues crashed against him and he raised his eyes in time to witness Armageddon raining down in ashes, settling like snow—*black snow filled with flesh and bones and oh, how they died and burned and burned and burned because mortals forget but angels never do*—in a miasma of death like nothing the mortals had ever known; cities smoldered beneath the bombs, falling like tears from the sky; dark mirrors reflected two realms: one a terrible kingdom filled with death, the other brighter, but still borne on sorrow . . .

A sliver of black ice penetrated Miquel's shield, the point coming mere centimeters from his forearm. The vision came to an abrupt halt.

Miquel resumed his song. His shield flashed bright beneath the power of his melody. The black ice snapped in half. He drew the measures tight to wrap the song around his body.

"Fight us, you bastard." Samyaza stalked Miquel, lobbing more spikes of black ice that bounced off the shield to scar the floor. "Fight us!"

From deep within himself, Miquel felt a primal urge to do just that. A foreign rage surged through his chest and reached for his throat, demanding to be released in a refrain of violence.

He choked it down. The Pervitin sharpened his fury into a living thing, but he had to control it.

"Show us what the Messengers wrought with their careful breeding." Samyaza's mocking eyes danced over the mask's lurid grin. "Or did they fail with you?"

The enraged song burned against Miquel's vocal cords. He clenched his jaw until he thought his teeth would crack.

If he dropped his defenses, he'd present Samyaza with an opening. Striking the angel with a ward of his own was out of the question. In another incarnation, Miquel might have fought to the death, but Diago had taught him to retreat in strength.

I've got to move, though. If I don't, I'm dead. Pushing the toe of his boot against the floor, he summoned his strength and managed to gain eight centimeters. Precious, precious little, but more than he'd ever thought he'd manage under such an assault.

Samyaza thrust another spear of darkness into Miquel's shield. The force of the blow shuddered through his body. The pearlescent hues of Miquel's song gave way beneath the ugly edges of Samyaza's ward. The shadowy ice pricked the light and wiggled closer to Miquel's heart.

"Fight us as if you were in your firstborn life. Miquel is weak. Fight us as Benaiah."

Miquel suddenly heard Diago as if his husband stood beside him: *Benaiah is dead, leave him in his grave. Come home to us. Come home.*

But where is home? The terrible fury within him screamed. *Buried beneath their bombs! Crumbled by their tanks!* For the first time since he'd admitted to himself that they'd lost the war, he had a chance to exact revenge. With one well-placed blow, he'd wipe the smirk from Samyaza's mask. *Move quick, move decisively. Pummel him back into the abyss where he belongs. Do it, do it, do it!*

Miquel clamped the manic song behind his lips and closed his eyes. He envisioned Diago and Rafael, whispered their names aloud. Though he knew the thought was selfish, he thought it anyway: *If I die, who'll protect them?*

Samyaza strolled close to the fire of Miquel's shield. The angel's taunt nibbled at his resolve. "The Messengers bred you for war, but you've let Diago cut off your balls and make you weak. You're not a soldier anymore. You've lost your purpose, Miquel." Samyaza scoffed. "And to think we used to fear you."

The Grigori flicked a single shard into Miquel's shield. The black ice cut through the light and sliced into Miquel's chest, reawakening the terrible pain behind his ribs. The agony set off a chain reaction within him, torching his rage into a conflagration of power.

Miquel realized he'd never make it to the elevator. This exercise was merely a game to the angel.

Then give him the anguish he deserves.

Straightening his body, he at last opened his mouth and sang. The notes reshaped the light of his shield into a lance. Ignoring the torment burning within his breast, he twirled the spear, shattering Samyaza's black knives.

The Grigori's eyes widened, first in shock and then in pleasure. He screeched and drew down the night.

Particles of darkness flew around Miquel, cutting into his skin like grains of sand propelled by a gale. Narrowing his eyes, he focused on the angel's form, flitting from side to side. Already he felt the rage leaving his body. When it did, he wouldn't have enough power to challenge the angel.

How much longer before the Pervitin wears off? Nico said an hour, but how long ago was that?

Doesn't matter. I've only got one chance to strike Samyaza. Lifting the lance, he charged straight toward the Grigori. At the last moment, he let his lance fly with the speed of light.

The tip of the spear caught Samyaza's shoulder. The Grigori howled—not in anguish but in triumph. He jerked the lance free.

Miquel whirled and ran for the elevator's metal gate. From the tail of his eye, he glimpsed Samyaza as the angel caught another of the soldiers' glyphs, one without sharp edges. A ward meant to stun. Samyaza raised his arms and released the sigil.

Miquel dodged left. Too late.

The glyph barreled down on him, catching him between his shoulders. He was driven against the wall. The ward slammed the breath from his body.

Darkness flew into his eyes, dimming his vision, until all that was left were the howls of demented angels ringing in his ears.

[12]

Diago considered Guillermo's question about the melee in Choral Room Two. Why *would* singers turn on one another?

He went to the filing cabinet and opened the top drawer, hoping to find the doctor's notes, or even a summation of his findings. Instead, he found more files.

The first one belonged to a woman, and her country of origin was listed as Spain. Alejandra Escobedo.

Diago's heart pounded as he opened the file. Two small photographs—one full-face, the other in profile—were stapled beside a blue triangle. If he'd entertained any uncertainties about the name, the woman's face dispelled any doubts. She was one of Miquel's milicianos.

At the triangle's base was the prisoner's number. Drawn within the triangle was Guillermo's seal.

From his place by the door, Guillermo spoke. "What is it?"

"One of ours. Alejandra Escobedo." Diago licked dry lips. "Consigned to the pit."

"Keep watch." Guillermo left the door and took Diago's place at the filing cabinet. " 'Consigned to the pit.' " He repeated the phrase as he read. "What the hell can that mean?"

"Dead?"

Guillermo winced. "Maybe, or maybe it's code for the prison."

Diago wasn't convinced. "A pit signifies someplace in the ground. Are there others?" *Any old ones, like us, in their fifth-born life?* But he didn't ask that question. He didn't want to know the answer, because then his imagination would put Miquel in this hellhole.

"Too many." Guillermo opened the files one by one and tore the sheets free.

Diago counted at least twelve pieces of paper that represented members of Los Nefilim. Guillermo folded the sheets in half and stuffed them under his shirt.

Near his heart.

"Maybe they keep the prisoners nearby." Guillermo rounded the desk and swept past Diago.

When he opened the door, the klaxons' howls filled their ears. The crisis apparently continued unabated.

Guillermo didn't check the corridor. He turned right.

Diago glanced left. So far, they still had this area to themselves. How long their luck would hold, he had no idea. He followed Guillermo. Time ticked away from them with every step.

Around a sharp corner, the corridor ended abruptly at a door. A handwritten sign indicated the room housed CHORAL ROOM 2.

Guillermo drew his pistol. "The infamous Choral Room Two." His whisper was barely audible beneath the unrelenting sirens.

Diago paused beside the door and tried to listen. The scorched stench of dying glyphs stung his nose. Beneath that, he detected a more ominous scent: blood.

Unable to discern whether the room was occupied or not, he opened the door and entered as if he had every right to be there. The room was empty.

A string of bare bulbs along the ceiling bathed the chamber in cold white light. Three of the six bulbs were broken.

It was a recording studio. Sigils crackled along the walls, the lines erratic and disjointed, like they were made by madmen. The fractured songs and broken magic washed over Diago's flesh and raised the small hairs at the base of his neck.

None of the glyphs were defensive wards. *It's like they all attacked one another simultaneously.*

Tossed beneath the soundboard were two rolling chairs. The wheels were coated with pieces of hair and scalp.

Near the ceiling, mounts in opposite corners indicated that speakers had once occupied those spots. Diago edged deeper into the room. Empty tubes of Pervitin crunched under his boots.

A cracked two-way mirror revealed the studio. The walls were washed in blood spatters. Someone had carried the speakers into the room and smashed them on the floor. Diago suspected that if he went inside, he'd find bits of brain and blood on the speaker cones, too.

A single microphone hung from the ceiling. The cord had been twisted to form a noose and was wrapped around a young man's neck. His toes were mere centimeters from the floor. The body rotated slowly.

Diago recognized him. *Fourteen, the same age as my son, in his firstborn life. He'd smiled for his picture.*

Now his face was blue and he smiled no more.

Diago turned away.

"Jesus." Guillermo squeezed in beside Diago and shut the door. "What the fucking hell happened in here?"

Retrieving a tube of Pervitin from the floor, Diago held it up. "I think we can confirm our link."

Something crashed far overhead. The light bulbs flickered and the corpse in the studio jittered at the end of the cord.

Diago and Guillermo instinctively ducked. When no further shocks hit the walls, they straightened and looked up at the ceiling.

"What the hell was that?" Diago murmured.

"It sounded like an explosion."

"Who would attack them? We've got no more planes, and the French aren't in a position to strafe them."

Guillermo shook his head. "That wasn't an attack. Not with just one explosion. Could have even been an accident."

"Or it hasn't bled to this level yet."

"Whatever it was, it means our time's up. We need to find the notebook, our people, and then get them the hell out of here. Let's go."

They quickly retraced their steps. A light shone under the door of the doctor's office. Diago tried to remember if they'd shut it off when they left. He was certain they had.

Guillermo's gaze cut toward the threshold, and though he frowned, he didn't break his stride.

The door suddenly opened. A tall blond nefil with pale eyes and a ruddy complexion stepped into the hall. He wore a white lab coat over his uniform and when he spoke, he used German. "You! Why didn't you take down the body?"

Guillermo glanced over his shoulder. "Um . . . the alarms. We're to report to level two."

"Three," Diago corrected him.

"What?" The doctor turned on Diago.

"Three, we're supposed to go to level three."

"Right." Guillermo reached the confused doctor in two quick steps and shoved him back inside the office. "But first we have a few questions."

The shocked nefil knocked Guillermo's hand off his shoulder. "You do what you're told, soldier. Now go to Choral Room Two and get that body down. The rest of the crew will be here any minute for cleanup."

Diago's heart skipped. *A crew.* Taking out the doctor was one thing. A crew was another matter entirely.

He followed Guillermo into the office and shut the door. "We can't take long."

The German reached under his lab coat, fingers scrambling for the holster at his hip. He opened his mouth to shout for help.

Guillermo's fist shot out and caught the German on the side of his face. The man went down.

Diago disarmed him and stood back.

The doctor didn't move.

"I think you hit him too hard," Diago whispered.

Guillermo reached down and jerked the nefil upright. The German's eyes rolled backward until only the whites showed beneath his parted lids. An ugly bruise spread across the side of his head.

"What's wrong with him?" Guillermo asked.

Christ, he really doesn't know his own strength. "I'm guessing a concussion."

Outside, someone shouted so he'd be heard over the alarms. "I'll ask Dr. Bormann."

"That's too bad." Guillermo snapped the German's neck. "Dr. Bormann isn't available."

The dark sound of the doctor's soul flickered and was gone.

Diago frowned. "Something very unnatural is happening here." He quickly explained the bizarre way the dark sounds were disappearing. "I've never seen anything like this."

Guillermo dragged the body behind the desk and muttered, "We'll get answers."

Someone knocked on the door.

Diago tucked the doctor's pistol under some files and tapped his sleeve to indicate his rank. A doctor might not distinguish between a private and a sergeant major, but a soldier would.

Guillermo motioned that he understood. He went to the door and opened it, stepping into the hall. Diago locked the door and pulled it shut. Together, they faced six young Germans.

Guillermo took the lead. "Dr. Bormann isn't feeling well." He tapped his temple. "Headache from all these damned alarms."

One of the youths smirked. Guillermo glared the sneer off the boy's face and began giving orders. "You"—he pointed to the two biggest youths—"take down the body. The rest of you get to work on neutralizing those sigils. Did anyone bring bleach?"

One enterprising youth snapped his heels together and

lifted a bucket filled with rags and cleaning supplies. "Yes, sir!"

"Good. Take it to the walls and clean up that blood. We've got orders to have that choral room functioning again as soon as possible. Which one of you is the electrician?"

They looked at one another in confusion and then back to Guillermo. The shortest one said, "None of us are, sir."

"Well, goddamn. Didn't I ask for an electrician, Martinez?"

Diago played his role. "You did, sir."

Guillermo's cheeks reddened. "Mother of Jesus. I have to do everything myself." He whirled and took three steps before he roared over his shoulder, "Move it, soldiers!"

Diago tilted his head toward the choral room. The soldiers took the hint and scrambled down the hall, eager to flee Guillermo's wrath.

Guillermo slowed his stride and gave Diago a chance to catch up. "Do you think I overplayed it?"

"No, you were perfect."

"Really?"

"A perfect asshole."

"Coming from the master, that's quite the compliment."

They fell silent as they rounded the corner and entered the next corridor. The short hallway reached a dead end.

It's like a warren. Gesturing to Guillermo, Diago signaled that they should keep moving. The big nefil didn't argue.

The next ramp they found led upward. Without hesitating, Guillermo took it. The sound of approaching footsteps sent them into another deserted section.

Three doors lined one side of the hall.

"Shit," Guillermo muttered.

Diago noted the metal plates on each door. One of them bore the name of Lieutenant Benito Espina.

He nudged Guillermo and pointed. "We may not need to go to the next level."

Guillermo followed his gaze. "Oh goddamn. This is too good to be true." He went to the office and examined the latch, checking it for sigils. Finding none, he picked the lock and opened the door.

[13]

Rafael sat on the hard chair, desperately trying to curb the tremors shuddering through his body. Ribbons of dried blood caked his wrists and splashed his forearms. His fingers tingled with the numbness of damaged nerves. But that could have been caused by Carlos, who'd slammed Rafael's arms onto the metal desk and held him while Cabello's hard hands violated every secret place of Rafael's body.

Fuck them. Fuck both of them. He clenched his jaw and glared at Carlos, who sat behind the desk. *I didn't scream.* It was a point of pride that he'd made it through the search without crying out. *Stop thinking about it.*

Unable to remove the jacket and shirt because of the cuffs, Cabello had simply cut them off. They'd left Rafael his undershirt and pants, but Cabello disappeared with the rest of his clothes, including his shoes.

Still, the room wasn't cold. *I shouldn't be shaking.* Concentrating on his breathing, he inhaled deeply and exhaled slowly until he managed to regain control over his body. *Get calm. That's the first step.*

Carlos lit another cigarette and dropped his match to the floor. The room was blue with smoke. It was worse than a cabaret on a Saturday night.

Rafael's cheek itched horribly as his flesh tried to heal around the Grigori's deep scratch. He recalled his papá's illness when an 'aulaq bit off his finger. The vampire's toxic bite had nearly killed Papá.

And Juanita said only an old nefil such as Papá could survive so much poison. But angels' claws didn't carry the same venom as a vampire's bite. Thus far, the swelling on his cheek turned his words lopsided, and he had to be careful not to slur; otherwise, he seemed okay. Even the tremors were beginning to subside.

Carlos watched him through slitted eyes. "They say a nefil's transition from their firstborn life into their second incarnation is the most dangerous. Did you know that?"

He's trying to spook me, keep me on edge.

And it was working.

Fear curdled in his stomach and left a pain as sharp as hunger. *Stop it.* He had to quit letting Carlos scare him. *Papá deals with the here and now.*

Rafael suddenly understood why. If he dealt with the problem before him, he didn't give his fear the power to debilitate him. *What is it Miquel always says? Don't blink. Don't let them see you scared or they'll keep using your fear against you.*

Keeping his voice low, Rafael met Carlos's gaze. "I'm not dead."

"Yet." Carlos puffed and grinned through the smoke. "If Samyaza has his way, you won't get any further than the second death."

The death from which no nefil can reincarnate. Rafael touched the angel's tear in his ring. Although the nefilim usually reincarnated, their souls could die. The lonely sounds heard in abandoned places were said to belong to nefilim too weak to be reborn. Others were murdered, their songs unraveled by angels. Even his angelic mother, a high-ranking Messenger, had been given the second death by her kin. *And what is a Grigori but an angel?*

"Who is Samyaza?"

"The Grigori. We only call him Sam when he goes among the mortals."

Rafael's heart thumped faster in his chest. *This is bad. Really bad.* He caught his runaway thoughts before they could scatter his wits. *Think, damn it.* The angels created the Inner Guard to protect mortals from the fallen as well as the daimons. *Miquel would remind Carlos of his duty.*

Rafael summoned the righteous tone he'd often heard his father use when confronted with another nefil's misdeeds. "If you think the Thrones will look kindly on this transgression, you are sadly mistaken. They'll punish Jordi and all who follow him."

Carlos actually paled.

I've made him afraid. Rafael didn't believe Carlos would change his allegiances, but he took courage from the fact that he'd made the older nefil blink. *This is why Papá says knowledge is power.*

Carlos's fingers trembled slightly before he plucked the cigarette from his lips with forefinger and thumb. "*You're* the criminal now. That's what happens in wars, whether they're just or unjust. Winner declares the laws. You'll be questioned and tried. If you're lucky, the generalissimo will have you shot. A quick death is the kindest mercy one nefil can give to another. Otherwise, he'll turn you over to the Grigori, and you'll go to the pit. And if you think those hurt"—Carlos pointed at the sigils binding Rafael's wrists—"you wait until Samyaza chains your song."

Against his will, Rafael looked down at his bound hands. The shards of black ice widened and throbbed with more power each time his blood touched them. They left him feeling filthy.

To imagine the Grigori with that kind of control over his song sickened him. But he couldn't stop them. He was helpless here. No one in France knew where he'd gone, much less how to find him. Panic infiltrated his newfound confidence.

A slow smile spread over Carlos's mouth.

Shit. I blinked and he knows it. He had no threats to use against Carlos. Rafael touched his ring. *Except maybe the future.*

Rafael met the other nefil's smile with a glare. "Those tables turn, too, faster than the Thrones will notice. And the nefilim's memories are long; it is our blessing. It will be your curse."

Carlos's smile froze and then hardened. Rafael counted the blink as a victory, but he didn't let it inflate his ego. Prevailing in a skirmish wasn't the same as winning the battle, or even the war. *I've got to find some way to gain his trust.*

He thought back to Carlos's flush of shame as he accepted the medication from Juanita. "Help me understand why you hate us."

Carlos shrugged. "It's not about hate. It's about watching out for me and where my interests lie. I'm casting my lot with the winning side. You might want to consider thinking the same way."

"We watch out for each other in Los Nefilim—*that* is our way."

"That's Miquel's way, and it's dying."

"No . . ."

Carlos slapped the desk with his palm. "Do you see him here? Or Ysa, or Juanita? Where are they? They'll abandon one nefil for the common good. That's not watching each other's backs." He relaxed in his seat and spread his hands. "They're not coming for you. You're alone."

A loud crash startled them. The light bulb flickered and swung from its cord as if someone had dropped something heavy on the floor overhead. A hairline crack zigzagged from one corner of the ceiling to another.

"What the hell is going on up there?" Carlos extinguished his cigarette and rose.

The door opened.

"Generalissimo!" Carlos snapped a hasty salute.

A bolt of fear shot through Rafael's chest. He kept his gaze locked on the wall behind Carlos. His papá warned him the day would come when his only weapons would be his cunning and his tongue. Carlos had merely been the warm-up act. The real test of his skills was finally here.

"Get out, Carlos." Jordi sounded perfectly at ease. That meant whatever was going on upstairs must be under his control.

Carlos saluted again and then gave Rafael a nod as he passed. Rafael heard the lock click into place. Clasping his hands in his lap, he waited. His papá rarely spoke of his association with Don Guillermo's brother, which left Rafael at a disadvantage. *I've got nothing on him.*

Jordi didn't move for several moments. The silence

stretched long between them. Finally, he asked, "How is your father?"

The question was soft, melodious, and Rafael immediately thought of Don Guillermo's voice. *But he's not Don Guillermo.*

He looked down at his white knuckles. Consciously, he forced his hands as far apart as the cuffs allowed. His tongue felt loose, ready to wag in an effort to delay any pain. Unsure how to respond, he remained silent and waited.

An edge seeped into Jordi's tone. "I expect an answer."

Why doesn't he move where I can see him? "I don't know."

"You don't know how your father is?"

"I don't know *where* he is. I haven't seen or heard from him since April last year." *Not entirely the truth, not entirely a lie.*

"The war has caused many causalities." Jordi's perfectly manicured fingers slid onto Rafael's shoulder.

Rafael started at the sudden touch.

The signet with the Grigori's malignant tear winked into view. "I hope he isn't one." Jordi tightened his grip. "It is my wish"—he leaned close to whisper in Rafael's ear—"that he lives to see his son again."

The scent of the nefil's strong aftershave filled Rafael's nose and mouth. He remained still.

Jordi's fingers released their hold as he circled to perch on the edge of the desk, forcing Rafael to look up at him.

He's trying to intimidate me. It was working. Rafael tilted his head and met Jordi's gaze.

The older nefil's eyes were light brown and flecked with gold. Centuries of knowledge burned in those bright irises. It was like looking into the countenance of a hungry dragon.

Where Don Guillermo was freckled and worn by the wind, Jordi's unblemished skin was the color of cream. While his nose was less prominent than Guillermo's, his cheekbones were more pronounced, giving his features a rapacious cast. His aura sparked around him in a savage nimbus of orange and red, quelled at times by deep golden hues.

In contrast to Don Guillermo's coarser features, Jordi possessed both the refinement and grace that his brother lacked. Don Guillermo looked like a soldier, Jordi a king.

"Has your father frightened you with stories about me?"

"No. He rarely speaks of you at all."

"Interesting." Jordi didn't seem offended by his lack of popularity. "Maybe he feels guilty."

"About what?"

"His lies." Jordi lit a cigarette. "Do you lie like him?"

Only when it suits me. "No."

Jordi's palm struck Rafael's face. It happened so fast he never saw the blow coming. His head rocked and his cheek stung more from humiliation than from pain.

Jordi continued smoking as if nothing had happened. "You address me as Señor General. Do you understand?"

Rafael licked the blood from his lips. "Yes, Señor General."

Jordi nodded. "How old are you now, Rafael?"

"Fourteen, Señor General."

Jordi pursed his lips thoughtfully and in doing so he resembled Don Guillermo in one of his reflective moments. "Fourteen, that's a hard age. You're still a boy, but you're trying to be a man."

He's trying to establish a bond with me. Rafael wasn't sure how to play the moment, so he did as his father often counseled him to do: when in doubt, wait for a clear direction to emerge and then move accordingly.

"Do you love your parents?"

He's talking to me like I'm four, not fourteen. Rather than risk another slap, he kept up the game. "Of course, I do . . . Señor General."

"Even when they're wrong?"

"They're not wrong."

Jordi lifted his hand.

Rafael hated himself for flinching. "Señor General," he blurted, and relaxed along with Jordi.

Jordi gave him a parental smile that didn't touch the rage burning deep within his irises. "Perhaps, *misguided* is a better word. My own father was beguiled into passing my birthright to Solomon in our firstborn lives. Did you know that?"

Rafael considered his answer. If he said yes, then he validated Jordi's position. But according to Don Guillermo, their father wasn't fooled into naming Solomon as his successor. King David had known Adonijah would abuse his power over the nefilim, so he'd skipped over his firstborn son and bequeathed the signet to his last son, Solomon, who in this incarnation became Guillermo.

"It's not a rhetorical question, Rafael." Jordi glowered at him.

And what will the wrong answer provoke? Another slap? Or something worse? It was time to be careful. Measure every word. "I've heard the stories." He waited two beats and then added, "Señor General."

To his relief, Jordi seemed satisfied with the answer. "Diago was called Asaph in his firstborn life. You knew this?"

Rafael nodded.

"And Miquel was called Benaiah in those days."

Another nod. "And Don Guillermo was called Solomon and you were his brother, Adonijah." The carmine angel's tear in Rafael's ring caught the light and flashed like a warning. "Señor General."

Jordi seemed pleased. "Very good. You *are* the little historian, aren't you?"

The patronizing tone rankled Rafael. Rebellion seized his tongue and he forgot himself. "You died hugging the altar, begging for your life, Señor General."

Jordi's right eye twitched and a muscle jumped along his jawline.

Shit. Went too far. Rafael held his breath, waiting for another slap. None came.

Nonetheless, Jordi's tone carried a hint of restrained violence, and Rafael heeded it. "But Adonijah is dead, as your father likes to say." He took a slow, deliberate drag from his cigarette and observed Rafael through the haze.

He's reevaluating me. The game is about to change. Careful not to twitch, Rafael held the old nefil's stare.

"Do you know why the other nefilim don't trust your father?"

"Because he is half daimon—"

"Because he betrayed Solomon and Benaiah. He stole the signet from Solomon, and he gave it to the king of daimons, Ashmedai." Jordi crushed the cigarette against the corner of the desk. Sparks melded with his aura as they descended to the floor. "When Asaph's deeds were discovered, Solomon had him imprisoned, and Benaiah turned his back on Asaph. Benaiah left him to die. Alone. So much for their true love."

He's trying to bait me into an argument. Rafael held his tongue.

Indifferent to Rafael's silence, Jordi went on. "What you must understand, my little historian, is the past foretells the future. Miquel will love your father unless Diago betrays Los Nefilim. If he does, then Miquel will turn his back on Diago again."

"No," Rafael whispered. Yet the word sounded weak as it slipped through his lips. Although his fathers never hid the story of their beginning, they rarely spoke of the past.

On the nights they did, Papá often withdrew quietly to one side, lost in memories he never shared. Only Doña Juanita seemed to notice the reflective quiet emanating from his corner of the room. On those nights, she watched Papá with a calculating gaze that gave Rafael chills.

Jordi folded his arms across his chest. "What are you thinking?"

"They don't ignore the past. They remember it so they can learn from one another. As they passed into new incarnations, they tried to become better people."

"You're a dense boy."

Rafael flinched from the contempt in the older nefil's voice.

Jordi's words were tight and landed like blows. "Let me spell it out for you. Your father cannot change the course of his destiny. None of us can. Our firstborn lives dictate our alliances, the very nature of our existence. We are locked into our roles by the decisions we make. That we *made.*"

Rage flashed through Rafael's chest, momentarily obliterating his fear. He met Jordi's glare with one of his own. "Have you ever again died clinging to an altar and begging for your life?"

The air around Jordi's body crackled with energy. Red-gold sparks snapped between them and sent goose pimples over Rafael's skin.

Jordi lunged. His hand encircled Rafael's throat and he jerked him forward, half lifting him from his chair. "I have died honorably in every subsequent incarnation."

Hoarse with his own terror, Rafael still managed to gasp, "Then you changed your destiny. Señor General."

Jordi's eyes narrowed. His gaze grew sly. Once more Rafael detected that strange mix of surprise and admiration Jordi exhibited when Rafael refused to give Samyaza his ring.

Without a word, he shoved Rafael back into the chair, which rocked beneath his weight.

Rafael slammed his foot to the floor and barely prevented the chair from overturning. *I've shocked him twice now.*

"You've got your father's wily tongue." Jordi's voice dropped an octave. "Have a care I don't slice it out of your head."

Chilled, Rafael made no reply.

The door slammed open. Samyaza entered the room, his milky eyes leering at them over the mask's painted mouth. "Operation Red Soldier is a success." He pointed to smoking wounds on his brow and shoulder. "Two strikes while on extreme dosages of Pervitin. We need to use older nefilim and give them more of the drug." He jerked Rafael out of the chair. "How is our baby nefil?"

Rafael twisted his face away from the Grigori's hate.

Samyaza didn't wait for an answer. He stretched his arm, and Rafael found himself airborne. His back struck the wall, driving the air from his lungs.

Awakened by the sudden movement, the glass cuffs

gnawed at his wrists. Rafael slid to the floor, tears of pain blurring the room. He forced himself to be still. The sigils slowed and then ceased to bite into him. With a ragged gasp, his body remembered how to breathe.

Jordi faced the angel. "What the hell are you doing?"

"Making room for our esteemed guest." He gestured to the door, where Cabello and the other guard, a nefil named Losa, dragged a bound man between them. They dropped him into the chair, buckling a thick lash across his chest.

Rafael stared at his father in disbelief. "Miquel?" *What have they done to him? He's too thin, too frail.*

The sleeves of his shirt were ripped. Lacerations covered his forearms. A jagged gash that mirrored Rafael's ran down the side of Miquel's bruised face. He lifted his head. His eyes were unfocused. A string of bloody drool escaped the corner of his mouth.

"Don't let his appearance fool you," Samyaza murmured as he slithered close to Miquel. "He was magnificent. The control . . ." The Grigori growled low in the back of his throat. "Once provoked into the fight, he became a true berserker." He lifted his hand to touch Miquel's brow.

"Don't touch him!" Rafael struggled to his knees, the vicious cuffs gobbling his flesh as he did. *Oh fuck. The ultimate blink.* But he couldn't stop. All his rage poured through his lips. "You get your goddamn hands off him."

"Or what?" Samyaza tilted his head and fixed his milky gaze on Jordi. "It still nips and yaps. Haven't you brought it to heel?"

"Leave him alone," Jordi murmured. "He's mine."

Ignoring the exchange, Rafael rolled to his feet. Cabello touched the grip of his pistol. Rafael froze.

Jordi examined Miquel, lightly slapping his cheeks to bring him around. "Wake up, Miquel. You have a visitor. Someone you'll want to see." He gestured for Cabello to bring Rafael. "Bring him."

That was all the permission Rafael needed. Without waiting for Cabello, he approached Miquel. Cabello trailed on his heels like a sinister shadow.

"Miquel," Rafael whispered, reaching for his father.

Jordi grabbed his arm. "Not too close. He's out of it. He might not recognize you," he whispered in Rafael's ear before he turned to the angel. "Give him a pill. See if that brings him around."

Samyaza withdrew a vial from his pocket and tapped two white tablets into his palm. Using his claw, he pushed the pills between Miquel's lips.

Moments passed and Miquel's eyes finally focused. "Rafael?" He grimaced and twisted in the chair. The strap creaked but didn't budge.

Now Rafael understood his dream. Miquel wasn't holding his hands behind his back. Metal cuffs restrained him. He wanted to address his father with authority. Instead, he sounded like the child he was. "I'm here."

Blinking at Rafael, Miquel winced and then shook his head. "No . . . you can't be . . . I'm hallucinating again . . ."

Jordi's grip relaxed. Rafael twisted free. He dropped to his knees in front of Miquel. "This isn't a dream. It is me."

"Oh no." Miquel bent forward until his forehead touched Rafael's brow. "No, my little bear, please don't be here."

Never in his life had Rafael heard Miquel sound so broken. *I'm sorry, I'm so sorry.* But he couldn't say that, not with Jordi and Samyaza hanging on to their every word.

Then speak in Caló.

Of course. All three of them used the language of the Iberian Romani when they wanted no one else to understand them. Papá had learned from Miquel and Rafael from his fathers.

Using their secret language, Rafael murmured, "Tell me what to do and I'll do it. Tell me how to fight them."

Jordi rammed a sharp finger between Rafael's shoulders. "Speak Castilian or this little family reunion is over."

Miquel answered in Castilian. "Leave them to me. You can't fight and win. Trust me. Will you trust me and do as I say?"

Rafael met his father's gaze and nodded, following Miquel's lead. "I trust you forever."

Miquel kissed Rafael's hair. "Everything will be okay."

Will it? Rafael made no effort to rise.

Jordi folded his arms across his chest. "Well, this is touching, but I'm short of time, Miquel. It's been brought to my attention that you refused to decipher the notebook Feran brought to us."

Miquel turned his head and spat a wad of bloodied phlegm at the floor. Then he met Jordi's gaze evenly. "Let your own people break Carme's glyphs. It'll be educational for them."

A surge of pride filled Rafael's chest. *He's not scared. He's not scared of anything.*

"I see you need convincing . . ." Jordi pushed away from the desk. "Gentlemen, let's take a little walk, shall we?"

Rafael knew what that phrase meant. In Barcelona, he'd listened by the door while Miquel talked to recent escapees from a Nationalist jail. They spoke of a priest, Father de Fustiñana, who walked the streets in shoes caked with

Republican blood. They said when that bird of ill omen invited a prisoner for a walk, the stroll always culminated in death. Any hope he had that they might survive died with Jordi's simple utterance.

It wasn't fair. He needed time to tell Ysa he loved her. And Papá . . . what would happen to Papá without them? He said his love for them held back the darkness in his life. What would happen if they died? Or, worse, what if Papá never knew what became of them? How would he find them in their next incarnation?

I'm so sorry, Papá. He swallowed his tears and forced himself to stand.

Miquel's expression didn't change. "You watch for my soul. I'll lead you into your next incarnation."

I don't want either of us to die. Rafael watched numbly as Cabello loosened the strap that held Miquel to the chair.

Miquel let them pull him to his feet, and then he kicked the chair away from his legs. He paled, momentarily favoring his left side before forcing his torso straight.

He's hurt but he doesn't want them to know.

Looking down at Rafael, Miquel muttered so softly in Caló that neither Jordi nor Samyaza seemed to hear. "Don't blink."

Don't blink. If Miquel can hide his pain, so can I. Drawing a small measure of courage from his father's presence, Rafael allowed Jordi to lead him into the hallway. He could be brave, but that was just on the outside. Inside, he was still in turmoil.

Because, like the arrival to the interrogation room, everything was happening too fast.

[14]

Rafael glared at Samyaza's back. Instead of going to the exit that led to the surface, the angel went in the opposite direction, toward the mysterious door at the end of the hall. As the Grigori sauntered down the corridor, he snapped his fingers and hummed "A Gypsy Told Me."

He's mocking us. Rafael opened his mouth to retort. From the corner of his eye he glimpsed Miquel, who gave an almost imperceptible shake of his head. Shutting his mouth, Rafael squelched his retort. Without any idea of what Jordi had up his sleeve, he decided to follow his father's lead. It could be that Miquel had a plan.

Samyaza turned the latch and opened the door. A breaker box spewed electrical cords down one side of a spiraling staircase.

From somewhere below, nefilim sang a haunting song, their voices rising and falling in unison. The chant began as a requiem in G, the ponderous tempo carried by the bass singers. *A long chord follows a short chord, then the major lifts.*

Caught up in the song, Rafael slipped on the first step. Jordi gripped his arm and held him steady.

Why is he keeping me safe if they're just going to shoot us? He glanced at the tall nefil. The lines around Jordi's mouth softened. He appeared almost sorry for what was about to happen. *But is he really?*

A terrible stench rose from the darkness.

Rafael gagged and then swallowed his bile. He recognized the odor from his days of hiding in the metro as the Nationalists bombed Barcelona. The stink of terror and moldering flesh had filled the tunnels.

This is where they dump their dead. Rafael's throat constricted at the thought. A quick glance over his shoulder assured him that Miquel's demeanor hadn't changed. His father fixed his gaze on Rafael and gave him a stern nod.

Don't blink. Right. The icy floor sent chills up through Rafael's soles and into his body. He clenched his jaw to keep his teeth from chattering and concentrated on the nefilim's song, which grew in volume, raising the hair on his arms. His throat ached listening to them.

Jordi's palm slid down over Rafael's forearm, tracing the line of his muscle. The touch felt more like a caress.

Unnerved by the sensation, Rafael pretended not to notice. *It's just another way to rattle me. Maybe he's hoping I'll beg him for our lives.*

At the foot of the stairs, Samyaza went through a doorway carved in stone. Rafael's mouth went dry as he followed.

The domed chamber yawned open like a mouth, the roof extending high overhead, where the natural stone was pocked, like a sinus cavity. The walls carried the nefilim's vocalizations up high and into the mountain, channeling the song through the tighter passages.

On the floor, portable electric lights were arranged to illuminate an immense pit filled with sepia-colored boulders, some that must have weighed well over a ton. Two guards occupied a camp table to one side. They rose so quickly, their flimsy chairs upended and clattered to the floor. They saluted Jordi.

He acknowledged them and then said, "At ease."

Neither of them returned to their seats.

Rafael hardly noted them, though. Instead, he focused on the prisoners in the pit. Clothed in rags, the nefilim were barely more than walking skeletons. Ashen skin stretched taut across their skulls, making their heads seem birdlike in the gloom. Their vacant eyes stared straight ahead, their thoughts obviously no longer their own. They surrounded a large boulder.

The Grigori's manacles of black, like the ones encircling Rafael's wrists, bound their arms to onyx rods that disappeared beneath the stones. In unison, the group traced a sigil with their broken, bloodied hands. As Rafael watched, he realized the nefilim weren't moving of their own free will. Something beneath the rocks used the rods to manipulate their hands while forcing them to sing.

Midair over the cavity was a single mirror, which whirled lazily. The colors of the prisoners' song rose up and disappeared into the glass, only to return as darkness, deeper than any darkness in the mortal realm. Ichor from the mirror dripped over the boulder and sizzled across the nefilim's upturned faces.

Rafael cringed from the smell of scorched flesh. A low moan burned at the back of his throat as he remembered his nightmare and the spinning mirror over Miquel's head. *No. Not my Miquel.*

The sable light from the mirror's sigil leached into the boulder's cracks. The quiet roar of a muffled blast sent puffs of dust into the air. The fissures widened. The nefilim's hands moved, and the process began again.

Samyaza reached behind his head and loosened the strings holding his mask in place. When he turned, Rafael recoiled from the angel's ruined face.

His wide mouth practically split his misshapen head in half. A thin whipcord tongue snaked between his serrated teeth. The profusion of scars traveling from his chin to the corner of his eyes seamed his face like an old leather sack.

"Isn't it magnificent?" Samyaza gestured to the pit. "Jordi's nefilim stumbled on our prison while they were blasting a tunnel through the mountain. He freed me, but our brethren are buried much deeper. We feared using more dynamite would bring the whole cavern down, so we devised a subtler way to break the stones."

He strolled along the edge of the platform, admiring his handiwork. "We give them manacles, like those we gave our little historian." He bestowed on Rafael a hideous grin. "And then we bring them here, let them see what awaits them."

Suddenly Rafael realized this performance wasn't for his benefit. *They want Miquel to see. They want him to lose hope.*

Jordi's voice purred close to Rafael's ear. "And they talk, Miquel. They spill all your secrets, thinking they'll escape the pit. That's how our troops won the battle at the Ebro. We knew you were coming long before Colonel Campos warned us of Republican movements across the river. It's how I convinced Franco to turn his eyes from Valencia and halt his operations on the Levante front."

Rafael couldn't see Jordi's smile, but he heard it in his voice. "We broke your nefilim and they gave us your codes. Your operation was doomed from the beginning by your own people."

Miquel gazed into the pit, his lips moving silently. His face was almost as ashen as those of his milicianos in the pit. He swayed on his feet. Rafael realized that he whispered their names.

Reveling in Miquel's horror, the Grigori held out his arms as if to embrace the milicianos. "Once they confess all that they know, we give them a sedative before we drop them into the pit. Unconscious, they can't resist when our brethren take control of their minds. But our kin are weak from their long internment. They can manipulate the nefilim's song, but not their bodies. So I designed the sigils on the manacles to lengthen into supple rods that descend into the Grigori's prison."

"You turn them into puppets." Horrified, Rafael looked down at the sigils on his wrists. And now he understood what Jordi meant when he said they owned his song. *They'll force me to sing, and my mother's tear will augment my magic.*

"Miquel . . ." The murmur was the same as a blink. Rafael didn't care. He couldn't stop his panic. "Miquel!" He twisted in Jordi's arms. *Save me, make them stop . . .* Terror lent him strength, but the older nefil held him tight.

Miquel tore his attention away from the pit, but instead of

rising up and breaking his chains, he seemed to grow smaller in the shadows. The realization of what they intended to do drained the color from his face.

Samyaza crooned, "And when they die, their souls are taken into the mirror and channeled to our brethren down below. In the abyss, the Grigori twist the resonances of the nefilim's auras—what the daimons call the dark sounds—into glyphs that they use to hammer their prison's walls. By working the stone from above and below, we'll release them faster."

Destroyed by the angels, the nefilim condemned to the pit died a second death and never reincarnated. Rafael suddenly craved the quick death a bullet would give him.

Jordi laughed. "Oh, don't look so shocked, Miquel. We only use the criminals who fought against us." The generalissimo leaned forward and hissed in Rafael's ear. "Remember what I told you about the allegiances in your firstborn life, Rafael? Those nefilim"—he gestured at the pit—"have consistently aligned themselves against me. They're incorrigible. They cannot be redeemed, so their deaths mean nothing to me."

"Miquel." He whispered his father's name before he bit his lip. *I've blinked three times now and it's like I'm driving spikes into his heart, because he's as helpless as I am. But . . . but I cannot stop.* He held his breath, craving a miracle.

None came. All Miquel had was words, and even they sounded weak beneath the nefilim's constant chants. "You've learned nothing, have you, Samyaza? You and your kin were like parasites, coupling with mortals and taking their minds. You turned them into slaves." His voice broke on the last word. "For those sins, the Thrones damned you. They tore off your wings so you could never again ascend to the heavenly realms. They banned you from drinking the healing flames from the river of fire. And to silence your song, they covered your mouths with stones. Do you think they'll turn a blind eye to your games with the nefilim?"

"It doesn't matter what the Thrones do." Samyaza reached Rafael in two strides. "It'll be too late for this one." His claws snatched a handful of Rafael's hair. He pulled his head backward until Rafael thought his neck would snap.

The Grigori lifted a vicious-looking syringe filled with cloudy liquid, holding it high enough for Rafael to see. "Where do we give it to him, Miquel? In his throat?"

The needle dipped out of sight. Something cold touched Rafael's neck. His pulse filled his head.

"Stop." Miquel took a step forward before his guards grabbed his arms.

"No?" The needle moved again until Rafael felt the tip resting on the soft flesh beneath his eye. "Or his eye . . . such dark-lashed eyes."

Rafael choked back a sob. His terror froze his brain and stole his will.

"Stop!" Miquel's calm assurance was gone. He bucked against his captors' grip, but his guards held him back. "Jordi Abelló, if you're a party to this, then you can forget ever seeing the king's signet on your finger again."

Jordi shook his head. "No, Miquel, this is on you. Give me a promise to break the sigils in that notebook. Do it and I swear I'll keep Rafael from the pit. I'll see to it that he reaches maturity."

Rafael closed his eyes. *Miquel will say no. He has to*

say no, and then Samyaza will drive that drug into my body . . . unless . . . He opened his eyes again. *Unless I jam the needle into my brain first.* Suicide was his only option. He wondered if he would die before the drug took effect. *Before the Grigori can take over my body.*

He couldn't get his breathing under control. *On three. Do it on three, don't think, just do it.* He had to ram his face down hard. When he tensed, he glimpsed Miquel again. *I'm sorry, I'm so sorry, Papá . . .*

"Okay." Miquel sagged in his captors' hands. "Okay. I'll do it, but I need your word, Jordi."

As if sensing Rafael's suicidal thoughts, Samyaza jerked the needle away, but he didn't relinquish his grip on Rafael's hair.

In spite of himself, Rafael retched a sound that rang somewhere between relief and sorrow. *Too late. I'm too late again.* Miquel never gave up, he never relented . . . until now. *I caused him to fail.*

He was strong until me.

Jordi's grip tightened, as if he expected Miquel to renege on his offer. "I swear to you Rafael Diaz will live at my side. And if you successfully decipher that notebook, I'll see to it that he reaches maturity."

Miquel looked down in defeat. "You have a deal."

"Let the boy go," Jordi said to Samyaza, who obeyed him. "Now I need an oath from you, Rafael."

He shook his head. *What will Papá think of me? That I betrayed his husband to save my life. Worse, what will the other nefilim think of Papá? They'll say he raised me to be a traitor.*

"Do it, osito," Miquel said.

Rafael forced himself to meet his father's gaze. "I can't."

Miquel didn't relent. "You can. You must."

And here was Rafael's nightmare come true. *It was a prophecy. But can I change it?*

Miquel held his gaze. Speaking in Caló, he said, "Come on, now. We've been through worse than this. Keep your head."

"Castilian, Miquel." But Jordi's command held no teeth.

"Find the elevator to the surface. That's your way out."

"*Castilian,* Miquel." Jordi nodded at the guards.

Cabello drove his fist into Miquel's stomach.

Miquel wheezed around the words, but he continued in Caló. "You've got to warn Los Nefilim about what's going on here. Now humor him and leave the rest for me. Find the elevator to the surface. That's your way out."

He's got a plan. Rafael gaped at him, astounded by his father's ability to think under pressure. *But if I go, will I be able to bring Los Nefilim back in time to save him?*

"Last time, Miquel. Speak Castilian." Another gesture from Jordi sent Cabello's fist into Miquel's jaw.

Miquel spat a mouthful of blood to the cavern floor. When he spoke again, it was in Castilian. "Trust me, Rafael. You said you trusted me. Prove it. Do as I say."

"I will." Anything to make them stop hitting him. They had a miracle; a small, frail thread of hope. *Nurture it and make it strong.* "I promise."

Jordi released Rafael and forced him to turn. He held out his hand. The Grigori's tear throbbed and pulsed in the signet's setting. "Submit yourself to me, Rafael, and I will honor my word. I will even free Miquel once he translates the notebook."

Rafael licked his lips. He didn't believe that. *All his promises are barbed with lies.* Revulsion twisted in his gut.

Jordi held out his hand. "Swear you will submit yourself to me."

"Do it," Miquel whispered in Castilian.

"I swear . . ." Rafael hesitated, unsure of how to proceed. *What do I say?*

Jordi encouraged him with a smile. "Repeat after me: I, Rafael Diaz, do hereby pledge my body and magic to you, Generalissimo Jordi Abelló, a true king of the angel-born nefilim's Inner Guard. I swear to uphold your laws and remain faithful to you and the angel-born nefilim in this life, and in all my lives to come."

No. That wasn't what he intended to say. *Remember your lessons.* Papá taught him that oaths were sacred and that he should be careful never to say what he didn't mean.

He met Jordi's gaze and said, "I, Rafael Diaz, swear to submit myself to you, Jordi Abelló, in exchange for the life of my father, Miquel de Torrellas. If you forswear your part of this bargain, I will hunt you in this life, and in all my lives to come."

The nimbus of Jordi's aura pulsed around his body as he considered Rafael's oath. A slow smile spread across his lips. "I will accept that oath, Rafael Diaz. Come." He held out his hand. "Kneel and kiss the ring."

Wincing with his revulsion, Rafael went to one knee. He barely brushed his lips across the stone. As he did, he saw heavy flakes of black snow . . .

. . . not snow, but ashes . . .

. . . drifting over a street, coating the pedestrians with soot . . .

. . . the dead are falling from the sky . . .

. . . where chimneys glowed red against the dark, and the trains kept rolling, rolling, rolling all night long *. . .*

Rafael gasped and jerked back so fast he sat hard. His teeth clicked together painfully and he tasted blood. *What the hell did I just see? A vision of what's to come?* He didn't dare ask. He was afraid of what the answer might be.

Jordi, for his part, merely smiled. Something gray slithered across the iris of his left eye, dimming the fire of his gaze, and then it was gone.

A trick of the light? Rafael had no idea.

Suddenly Samyaza's body was between him and Jordi. The Grigori touched the cuffs. The sigils chaining Rafael's wrists fell away, leaving angry raw circles of chewed flesh.

But I'm free to move unhindered. He got to his feet and walked to Jordi's side. The taller nefil clamped his hand on the back of Rafael's neck before he turned to Cabello. "Take Miquel to the interrogation room. Give him whatever he needs. I expect those sigils to be broken within twenty-four hours." He shifted his attention to Miquel. "Keep your end of the bargain, and maybe one day you'll see him again."

Rafael met Miquel's gaze. "I will watch for you."

"And I for you." His father smiled grimly. "Now go. Don't look back."

Jordi shoved him toward the stairs. Rafael blinked hard to keep the tears from spilling over his cheeks. He loathed the relief flowing through him. *I'm a coward. I don't deserve to call myself his son.*

The walk back to the interrogation rooms took less time than going down. At the top of the stairs, Jordi shut the door. "Face the wall."

Is he going to shoot me, after all? It wouldn't surprise him. They extracted information from the nefilim and then gave them to the Grigori in the pit. It wasn't that Rafael didn't expect to be betrayed; he just didn't anticipate it happening so soon.

After the horror he'd seen below, the thought of a quick death actually relieved him. Still, he hesitated. *Why make it easy for him?*

The back of Jordi's hand caught the corner of Rafael's mouth. The signet tore into his lip. His head rocked back and struck the wall. Shadows clouded his vision.

Jordi's voice reached through the darkness. "You swore to submit yourself to me. Now face the wall."

Swallowing the blood in his mouth, Rafael obeyed him.

"What did Miquel say to you?"

"He said I was to tell Papá that he died honorably and to give him his love. That is all. He was saying goodbye." Rafael's voice caught on the last word. The first part might have been a lie, but the second part was true. *He was saying goodbye.*

Jordi remained silent for close to a minute. The seconds ticked by painfully slow. "Two steps behind me at all times. Do you understand?"

Rafael nodded.

Another punch, this time to his kidney. Rafael cried out and twisted. Jordi grabbed his shoulders and jerked him upright. "Your father coddled you to uselessness."

Rafael gritted his teeth against the pain. If by coddling Jordi meant that his fathers never raised their hands to him, then yes, they coddled him. But neither parent hid him from the ugliness of the world.

Jordi's breath drifted over the back of Rafael's neck. "But that's okay. I'm going to teach you. The first lesson: You don't nod or shake your head to me. You speak, and when you do, you speak to me with respect."

Rafael glared at the wall. "Yes, Señor General."

"Very good. How many steps behind?"

"Two, Señor General."

"Fuck up again, and I'll send Miquel straight to the pit." Jordi whirled and started down the corridor.

Rafael knuckled his anger under control and hurried to catch up. Falling exactly two paces behind Jordi, he considered his options. Miquel wanted him to flee and tell Los Nefilim about Jordi's black site. Except Rafael had no intention of leaving his father behind.

With his oath to Jordi, he should have some freedom of movement. *I don't need a lot.* Just enough to find that elevator and plan a way to break out Miquel.

He didn't have a gun, or even a good idea of the compound's layout. *But I've got twenty-four hours.* It would have to be enough.

[15]

Miquel turned his head to watch Rafael climb the stairs. *It's all right, osito. You won't have to submit yourself for long.* If his plan worked, Rafael would be free of his oath by dawn, and their souls well on their way to a new incarnation. Diago would have to understand. *Forgive me, my bright star, but this is the only way.*

When the door at the top of the stairs shut, Miquel turned his attention to the pit. He saw his milicianos—the men and women who'd fought by his side. *They followed me. Even when I led them surely into death, they kept their faith and followed me.*

And now I've murdered them with their allegiance.

He named their names, said them aloud, and suddenly he understood why Héctor . . . Héctor-something from Málaga, relentlessly packing and repacking his suitcase, suffering from la arentitis, but somehow never giving up the hope he'd be reunited with his family . . . said the names of his wife and daughters over and over in that hovel on Argelès-sur-Mer. Names held power. Say their names and he made them more than shadows. "Vicente, Alejandra, Juan, Luciana, Remedios, Indalecio, Gaspar . . ."

Yet no matter how loudly he called them, he couldn't bring them back from the dead. All he could do was bury them in his heart. *But I will not forget you. I will not let Los Nefilim forget you.*

It tore him apart that he couldn't say he'd watch for them.

Samyaza followed his gaze and grinned. "You can't save them. They're already dead. They just don't know it yet. Like you."

And you. Miquel smiled at the Grigori.

The angel clicked his claws together in slow ticks, apparently unnerved by Miquel's smile.

How about that? I made him blink.

Finding his balance again, the Grigori stepped forward. "You must understand, the Messengers have beguiled you with their propaganda. They've enticed Los Nefilim into a military rebellion against the Thrones. You're about to find out what it means to be on the losing side of those lies."

Miquel shook his head. "You're twisting the truth. This isn't the first time the angels have warred. We'll put this rebellion down, too."

Samyaza's gaze traveled from Miquel's face to his bound arms and back again. "Forgive me if I doubt your boast."

Warmth flushed Miquel's cheeks, but he didn't retort. *Let him have his little jab. It'll damn well be his last.*

Retrieving his portrait mask, Samyaza brushed the dust off the tin and tied it back into place. "Or you can change sides. Like your son. You'll be able to watch over him. Keep him safe from Jordi."

Miquel pretended he believed Jordi would keep his oath. "Jordi said he'll reach maturity."

"Do you believe that?" Samyaza laughed. "Fool. Jordi will make that boy pay for his father's sins, and to Jordi, Diago's crimes are legion."

And now for the biggest bluff of all. Miquel shrugged, as if Rafael's fate were no matter for him. "I have twenty-four hours to decipher that notebook, Samyaza, and you're taking my time."

Samyaza turned back to the pit. "Give him whatever he needs."

Miquel turned toward the stairs. The pain in his chest flared, an ugly reminder of his own mortality, but he didn't resist either the discomfort or Cabello's hand.

Let them believe they're in control. From this point forward, subterfuge was his only weapon—that and his rage. The fury was all that kept him on his feet, because the Pervitin was wearing off. Exhaustion crept into his muscles and then his bones.

I need those pills, but will they give them to me? He wouldn't know until he asked.

When they returned to the interrogation cells, Cabello guided him to a different room. In this one, a straw pallet was on the floor beside a D-ring, which was embedded in the cement. The short chain led to a cuff. Carme's notebook rested on the pallet.

They knew I'd say yes in order to protect Rafael. But did they guess the rest? Could they?

Only one way to find out.

Cabello pressured Miquel to the floor. "On your knees."

He obeyed the guard. Cabello latched the cuff attached

to the short chain to Miquel's right wrist before he removed the other restraints.

Bound this way, he could still form sigils, but he wouldn't have the range of motion necessary for an attack. "I need paper and a pencil."

Cabello turned to Losa. "You heard him. The generalissimo said to give him whatever he needed."

"Are you okay alone?"

Cabello waved him off.

When Losa left, Miquel said, "I haven't slept for a long time. Do you have any Pervitin?"

Cabello hedged. "I don't know if we should give you that."

"Samyaza gave me two to bring me around earlier. The generalissimo said to give me whatever I need. If you want me to stay awake, I need the Pervitin."

Cabello sighed and tapped eight pills onto his palm. "That's all you're getting. It's not the same as the shots, so if you're thinking of taking them all at once and re-creating your upstairs performance, you'll be sadly disappointed . . . and dead."

Miquel put the pills on the floor, just under the lip of the pallet.

Losa returned. "Mora wants you upstairs. Go ahead, I've got it here."

Cabello nodded and left the cell.

Losa tossed the pencil and paper to the mattress. "Anything else?"

"Pervitin. I haven't slept in days, and I'll need all my faculties to get past Carme's sigils."

Losa didn't question him. He found his bottle and tossed it at Miquel. "You've got twelve in there."

Miquel caught the container. He waited until Losa left the cell and snapped the bolt into place. When the guard's shadow moved away from the threshold, he slipped the bottle into his pocket.

Cabello's eight with Losa's twelve gave him twenty, but he didn't put them together. Instead, he took four of the pills he'd hidden beneath the pallet and left the other four within easy reach.

Within minutes, the stabbing pain in his chest momentarily took his breath. His heart rate kicked higher. Four might have been too many. *Too late now.* He turned his attention to the items before him.

Sigils writhed across the cover of Carme's notebook, and he had no doubt more were embedded within. He also knew Carme. She had two or three favorites. One was the ward killing Feran. The other worked like an explosive. The unfortunate party who tripped that particular glyph set off a chain reaction that caused the notebook to explode with the intensity of a bomb.

And that's just what I need. Because once he found that ward, he could design a second one to amplify it, and with the Pervitin, he intended to bury Samyaza, his fucking Grigori, and Jordi's whole operation.

If the Grigori in the pit managed to catch his and Rafael's souls before they fled the mortal realm, then they would die the second death here. But that was a chance he had to take. The Grigori couldn't be allowed to escape. "Forgive me, my Diago. Please forgive me."

Miquel took a deep breath and opened the notebook.

16
February
1939

Night

les bêtes angéliques

(angelic beasts)

[16]

FOLIES DIVINE
26, RUE PIERRE-FONTAINE
PARIS, FRANCE

It was after midnight. Ysabel stood by the bar and watched the club's entrance. "Where is he?"

Juanita nursed a glass of wine and shook her head. "I don't know. He's just like his father. Diago will disappear for a good sulk whenever he doesn't get his way."

"But Rafael never misses a night at work. Even if all he does is spend the evening throwing dark looks at me, he comes to the club and stays to closing." She signaled Bernardo for a drink.

As big and ugly as a bear, Bernardo reached for a bottle of wine, but Ysa shook her head. She pointed to the whiskey and indicated that she wanted two fingers.

He frowned and glanced at Juanita, who nodded for him to give Ysa what she wanted. "If she's old enough to lead, she's old enough to drink. She has her father's tastes."

"Would she like a cigar, too?" Bernardo quipped but otherwise didn't contradict the angel.

Ysa almost said yes, but she feared she'd give the old nefil a heart attack. She couldn't blame him for being overprotective. In Santuari, Bernardo had served Los Nefilim as the village priest, but when the majority of clergy followed the Nationalists, he found himself hunted.

Knowing Bernardo's talents as a compassionate priest easily transferred to bartending, Guillermo suggested that Ysa employ Bernardo in the cabaret when they arrived in Paris. As usual, her father was right.

Because Papá knows his nefilim's strengths and how to assign them to jobs they're good at. Unfortunately, that was a learned skill, one she had yet to acquire.

Bernardo placed the drink in front of her. "Do you think something has happened to our Rafaelito?"

"I don't know. I hope not." She forced herself to meet his gaze and projected as much confidence as she could. "Suero is looking for him, and if anyone can find him, he will."

Bernardo nodded and patted her arm. "I'm sure you're right. He'll be fine."

When Bernardo moved to serve a mortal customer, Ysa touched the cool glass and lowered her voice. "I should have given him a job, any assignment."

Juanita lifted her finger in a warning gesture. "Don't you dare blame yourself. Rafael is responsible for his own actions. I know you think of him as a sibling, but he's not a child anymore. Neither are you.

"You must distance yourself from him, and treat him like the other members of Los Nefilim. All good leaders love their followers, but you cannot become too emotionally attached to them."

"You mean the same way that Papá isn't emotionally attached to Uncle Diago?"

Juanita exhaled sharply and shook her head. "Your papá . . . made many mistakes in his firstborn life, and his guilt follows him from one incarnation to another, because he will not let go. I'm trying to prevent you from suffering the same fate. Listen . . ."—Juanita twisted on the stool until she and Ysa were face-to-face—"Rafael, like his father, is part daimon, and the daimons are more . . . temperamental than the angel-born. They don't have our singleness of purpose. The angels know how to work together, and so do our nefilim. The daimons are more independent of one another—they're moody and base. It's why we were able to defeat them."

Ysa gaped at her mother. While she'd always known that Juanita held on to many of the angels' prejudices, this was the first time her mother had actually vocalized her biases so bluntly in front of Ysa. *It's like our relationship has moved to a new level.* "And you think Uncle Diago is base?"

"Diago is the exception, not the rule. He fights his daimonic predispositions, keeps them under control, as he should."

Ysa killed her drink with one shot. *Jesus.* She had no idea how to respond to her mother. Did she feel the same way about Rafael? Ysa didn't ask. She knew the answer, although she didn't agree. It seemed very unfair to demand that Diago and Rafael deny their heritage simply because their songs were more resonant of the daimons' shadow worlds.

Yet she knew her mother would never back down from her stance. Perhaps if she spent more time trying to understand the daimons, she might not find them so different from the angels. Ysa didn't make the suggestion, though. Not tonight. Not with Rafael acting from the very impulsivity that Juanita derided.

And not without Papá to back my argument.

On the club's stage, the jazz band finished their last number with a flourish and saved Ysa from having to respond.

A few groups of mortal patrons still occupied the tables, their boozy laughter loud in the sudden quiet.

"We'll talk about this more later." Juanita finished her wine and gestured to Bernardo. "It's time to close for the night."

As Juanita joined Bernardo, Carme's daughter, Violeta, left the stage and came to the bar.

A young nefil well into her first incarnation, she wore her sleek black hair clipped short and slicked against her head. With her pants and bolero jacket, she was sometimes mistaken on the street for a man, an occurrence that never ceased to delight her.

She poured herself a drink. "Rafael still hasn't shown?"

Ysa shook her head.

Violeta downed her drink and glared at the club's door. "Don't worry," she whispered. "We'll find him. We're the Three Musketeers. Remember? We took the oath." She raised her glass.

Ysabel swallowed past the lump in her throat. "We were children."

"Some of us still are," Violeta said with a grin. "But we love him, anyway." She bumped shoulders with Ysa. "All for one. We'll find him."

Ysa offered her friend a wan smile.

Bernardo gently urged the mortals still perched on the

stools to finish their drinks and settle their tabs. Once he finished at the bar, he proceeded to the tables, and one by one the last of their patrons weaved and bobbed into the night.

Eva Corvo emerged from the kitchen with an empty tray, followed by her twin, Maria, who carried a bucket. Like Bernardo, Eva and Maria had been with the family's household since the early twenties. Eva had served as Rafael's governess, and Maria watched over Ysabel when she was younger. In some ways, she still did.

Maria busied herself wiping down the scarred tables. "No one has seen Rafael?"

"Not yet." Juanita tied an apron over her evening dress. "Suero is looking for him. He'll call as soon as he knows something. While we're waiting, the rest of us have work to do. Ysa, it's time to count the till."

"Of course." *Mamá is right. Keeping busy will keep our minds off his absence.* She went to the register and opened it. Taking the cash drawer to an empty table, she sat facing the entrance.

Violeta poured two more drinks and brought them to Ysa's table. She sat next to Ysa and lit a cigarette, while Ysa busied herself with the sodden francs.

Eva shot Violeta a nasty glare. An old-school nefil, she didn't believe in becoming too familiar with either Don Guillermo or his family. "You think yourself high and mighty, Violeta Gebara? What would your mamá say about your behavior?"

She's so old-fashioned. Ysa's love for Eva was all that prevented her from saying so in front of the others. "It's all right, Eva. We don't stand on the old formalities here. The world is changing."

Eva sniffed. "And not for the better."

Unperturbed by Eva's reproach, Violeta smoked and re-laxed. "My mamá was with Don Guillermo in his firstborn life. We *are* one of the old families."

Which made it easier for Ysa to overlook Violeta's friend-liness. "Let's not argue tonight." She entreated Eva with her eyes.

The older nefil shook her head, joining her twin to wipe down the tables.

Ysa glanced at Violeta. "You were good tonight."

"I'm good every night." Violeta winked. Opening her sil-ver cigarette case, she offered one to Ysa. "Smoke? They're American."

"Maybe later." Ysa tallied the numbers in her account book. It amounted to short work tonight. They'd taken in barely enough to cover the liquor. *And we need the money.* Spain's war had cost them in both nefilim and finances. While she couldn't do anything about the loss of life, she could certainly find ways to increase Los Nefilim's coffers, and she intended to recoup as much money as she could before her father arrived.

The club's doors opened. Ysa felt, rather than saw, Violeta stiffen beside her.

Bernardo, whose back was to the door, called over his shoulder, "We're closed."

"I know," said Sabine Rousseau, the queen of Les Néphilim. A heavy-bodied woman, she sported a thin scar from her right brow to her chin—a souvenir from the Great War. Like Ysa, she was dressed in the evening clothes she wore when hosting guests at her club, the Bal Tabarin.

Rousseau's dress sparkled with sequins and intricate

embroidery; the white stole around her neck was definitely mink. Ysa smoothed her palms over her own, less extravagant silk dress, which looked like a gunnysack next to Rousseau's rich gown.

Violeta crushed her cigarette in the ashtray and practically jumped away from the table. She might be comfortable sitting with Ysa among the other members of Los Nefilim, but she possessed her mother's sense of protocol and knew that overfamiliarity might make Ysa seem weak in Rousseau's eyes.

That's what makes her my friend, my Musketeer. Ysa rose more sedately and approached Rousseau.

Beyond Les Néphilim's queen, the door opened to a rainy winter's night and the shiny black car parked at the curb. *Merely a block away, and she had her driver bring her.* Ysa nursed a mild stab of jealousy. Los Nefilim had commanded such wealth in Spain.

Biting down on her resentment, she took the other woman's hand as she'd seen her father do so many times. "Madame Rousseau, you honor us. Please, come and sit. Bernardo, would you bring madame something to drink?"

Rousseau caught Bernardo's attention with a graceful motion. "Coffee, if you have it, monsieur."

Bernardo bowed his head to her. "I'm afraid that all we have is chicory, madame."

Rousseau smiled. "Chicory will do."

Bernardo hurried into the kitchen.

As they walked to the table, Rousseau's angelic consort, Cyrille, entered the club. Like Violeta, Cyrille's short red hair was slicked against her skull. She, too, wore a man's suit.

Utilizing all three sets of her vocal cords, Juanita greeted Cyrille in the language of angels. Cyrille's answer was equally respectful and just as melodic. Their songs conjured images of fiery oceans and springtime moons.

Everyone paused to listen. Even passersby on the street slowed their step to revel in the heavenly tones.

The angels spoke at some length before they embraced. Then, arm in arm, Juanita led Cyrille to the table.

As if awakening from a trance, the room burst into movement again. Violeta held Rousseau's chair for her and then hurried to do the same for Ysa.

Rousseau took a long moment to admire the club's décor. "You've done well with this place, Mademoiselle Ramírez. Your father will be pleased."

"Thank you, madame. We're hoping he will join us soon."

Rousseau lit a cigarette. "Wars are messy. It may well be another month before he can get to France."

Ysa smiled and nodded, because that was what Rousseau expected her to do. *But why does she say so with such certainty? Does she know something I don't?* Although Juanita didn't believe Rousseau was involved with Los Nefilim's missing members, Ysa still wasn't entirely convinced of Les Néphilim's innocence. *But I'll never get one as old and wily as Rousseau to slip.*

Bernardo returned from the kitchen with a tray. He placed four cups on the table and poured for the group. "I'm afraid all we have is saccharin and milk."

Rousseau waved the apology aside. "When the mortals are done with their useless wars, we'll indulge with sugar and cream again."

Bernardo bowed and left them.

Rousseau withdrew a flask from her bodice and splashed a shot of liquor into the cup. "That'll sweeten it."

Ysa waited until Rousseau took a sip and then asked, "What may I do for you this evening, madame?"

"See?" She wagged one finger at Cyrille. "I told you. Guillermo, he spends time chatting, feeling out the other person, but Ysabel—she is straight to business. I like that."

Ysa wasn't sure if Rousseau had just complimented or insulted her. "Forgive me, madame. I didn't mean to be rude. It's been a very long day."

"It has been for me, as well, which is why I appreciate your tendency to dispose with banalities." Rousseau placed her cup on the table. "To the point, then: I need your help with a somewhat delicate matter."

Oh, Rafael. Please don't let this be about you. "Of course, you know I am ever at your service."

"Pierre Loutrel came to see me this evening."

Fucking Crazy Pete. Ysabel raised her eyebrows. "Are we remiss in a payment?" She knew damn well they weren't, and she had the books and receipts to prove it. *Or does this have to do with Blondie's beating?*

Rousseau shook her head. "It seems that one of Loutrel's men, some punk that goes by the moniker of Blondie, was killed on the metro this morning. Rafael was involved."

Ysabel didn't have to feign her astonishment. *Oh, my dark rose, what did you do?* "Excuse me? You think Rafael killed Blondie?"

"We're not precisely sure what happened. My people are still questioning witnesses, but it seems there was an altercation between Blondie and Rafael on the platform. Rafael jumped to the tracks and Blondie followed him."

Juanita frowned. "Then how does Loutrel connect Rafael to Blondie's death?"

"It seems Blondie was hit by the train."

"I'm quite sorry to hear that," Ysa responded. She wasn't, but her platitude sounded reasonably sincere even to her own ears. *I'm getting better at this.* "Did Rafael push him in front of the train?"

Cyrille shrugged and inserted a cigarette into a long black holder. "All we know for certain is that they're still scraping bits of Blondie off the number twelve line." She lifted the cigarette holder to her lips.

Violeta stepped forward to light the cigarette for her, trading a frown with Ysa as she did.

The angel barely noticed their expressions. "Thank you, lovely." Cyrille took two puffs and then said, "Frankly, no one cares about Blondie. Loutrel is more worried over the loss of face in the matter."

Mortals. *Male* mortals and their wounded masculinity would be the death of her someday. "I don't understand. How does Loutrel lose face?"

"One of your people was involved," Cyrille said through a cloud of blue smoke. "And because it seems like a small-time Algerian has wiped out a Frenchman in Loutrel's gang, Loutrel is in fits. Mortals." She sneered the word with the same contempt Ysabel heard royalty use when discussing the nouveau riche.

"Indeed." Rousseau sipped her chicory. "My concern, and that of some of my ranking officers, is that Rafael might have given in to his daimonic nature and sang Blondie onto the tracks, thereby facilitating the mortal's death."

Ysa's blood turned to ice. "Rafael would never do such

a thing." She gestured to Violeta, because she definitely needed that cigarette now. Her friend didn't disappoint her. She stepped forward and snapped the case open. Ysa retrieved a slim cigarette, proud that her hands didn't tremble as she allowed Violeta to light it for her. "Rafael is far too conscious of the ramifications of such an act, especially given his heritage. Have your people check with witnesses, but I'll stake my reputation on the fact that Rafael did not sing Blondie onto those tracks."

Rousseau accepted Ysabel's defense with a nod. "I hope you're right; however, his lineage complicates matters. I have a detective on the mortals' police force. He is looking into the incident for us." She placed her cup on the saucer with a slow, deliberate movement. "Understand me, Ysabel, I have a great deal of respect for your father."

But not for me. Though Rousseau didn't say it, the point was clear. Nor did Ysa expect Rousseau to give her deference based on bloodlines. *Like Rafael, my youth works against me.*

Rousseau added another dollop of liquor to her chicory. "I also have people within my own ranks who are looking for any excuse to push the Spanish nefilim out of France. Unfortunately, we are now experiencing the same political . . . upheaval . . . your father suffered in Spain. These officers of ours feel you are interlopers, who are intent on taking France and merging Les Néphilim with Los Nefilim. I'm telling you this not to frighten you, but to make you aware of the vulnerability we both face."

"I understand." Frightened nonetheless, Ysa reconsidered the untouched shot on the table. She casually poured the liquor into her own cup. Taking a sip from the liquid courage, she hazarded into territory she'd hoped to leave for her father. "My own nefilim are fractured and frustrated, as well. We've had reports today that some of the incoming refugees have disappeared after reaching the French border."

Rousseau raised an eyebrow. "And you think members of Les Néphilim have something to do with it?"

"We don't know who is involved. It could be mortals, and since you've asked us to follow French law, I have been hesitant to intercede."

"I see." She clearly wasn't pleased, nor did she immediately discount Ysa's concerns. "I will look into that on your behalf."

Heartened by the response, Ysa allowed herself to trust the older woman. "Thank you, madame. Meanwhile, I can assure you Rafael often used the metro in Barcelona to flee from pursuit, especially when outnumbered. He's small and quick and has an innate feel for the tunnels." *And suddenly, now that he's gone, I'm beginning to see his strengths.* "He probably didn't expect Blondie to follow. It sounds to me like the mortal was too slow."

Rousseau nodded. "I believe you. My detective's investigation is merely a formality to clear Rafael's name among my own nefilim. Loutrel, on the other hand, presents another problem for us. He suffers from the misperception that Rafael successfully conducted a hit on Blondie. No matter how indirect you and I understand that hit to be, it makes Loutrel appear weak."

"That sounds like a mortal problem to me."

"Yes, but we want to keep the mortals happy."

Because if they grew unhappy and discovered the nefilim's supernatural nature, they might turn on us as they did throughout the Middle Ages and during the Inquisition. Only now we'd be studied like insects under a microscope. Ysabel didn't need those basic facts explained to her, and she was gratified that Rousseau didn't instruct her like she was a child.

Ysabel took a sip of her drink, allowing the heat of the liquor to flow through her chest before she asked, "What can I do to make this right, madame?"

"Loutrel wants a bigger cut from your take."

Fucker. "How much?"

"Twenty-five percent."

Fuck, fuck, fucker. "For how long?"

"A year."

"Blondie couldn't possibly be worth that much. Six months."

"I didn't come to barter with you, Ysabel. If you truly want to make this right, twenty-five percent for a year."

Ysabel glanced at her mother.

Mouth tight with her own anger, Juanita nodded.

Shit and bitter shit. Ysa sighed and lifted the cloth from the cash drawer. Counting out Loutrel's extra take, she covered the till again so Rousseau wouldn't see the bare drawer. "My apologies for your trouble, madame."

Cyrille scanned the room. "And where is Rafael?"

"We don't know. Suero has been looking for him all evening. It's not like him to disappear." Her voice caught and she covered the lapse with a sip of her tepid, bitter chicory. Not even the liquor took the edge from her apprehension. Her hand trembled as she eased the cup back to its saucer. "He never misses work. Never."

Juanita covered her hand with a reassuring touch. "I'm sure it's nothing. He's fourteen and struggling to find his place in the world."

"Our firstborn lives are the hardest." Rousseau pushed the stack of cash back toward Ysa. "Keep your money. I'll cover the amount this week. Next week, you pay."

"I can't ask you to do that."

"You didn't. I offered."

"I don't know what to say."

"Thank you, would be a good start."

"Thank you."

The club door opened. Bernardo looked up from his place at the bar, but he didn't admonish the newcomer. It was Suero. He was filthy, covered from head to foot with the black soot from the metro.

Ysa stood, pushing her chair backward so fast, it tilted over. "Did you find him?"

Suero bowed his head to Rousseau and Cyrille. "Madame Rousseau, Madame Cyrille. Forgive me for interrupting." He placed a soiled yellow scarf on the table.

Ysabel would have known it anywhere. It was Rafael's.

Suero wasted no words. "You need to come, Doña Ysabel." His gaze swept over the others. "All of you must see this."

Ysa picked up the scarf and held it to her lips. It still smelled of Rafael. *Where are you, my dark rose?*

Violeta came forward and stood by Ysa's side. Even Eva and Maria, who in their respect for the nefilim's royalty would never encroach on a private conversation between two queens, drew close to the table. Eva looked as if she wanted to snatch the scarf from Ysa's hand.

Oh, she loves Rafael as if he were her own child. Ysa

didn't banish either of them back to the shadows. Instead, she held out her hand to motion them closer.

"Where did you find it?" Eva asked.

"In the metro. You'll all want to change clothes. We're going into the tunnels. There is a strange sigil there, and I believe it leads to a portal realm."

Rousseau rose from her seat and towered over Suero. "What?"

"Coordinates for longitude and latitude were embedded in the glyph."

"That is definitely a portal realm." Cyrille put out her cigarette and joined Rousseau. "Where is it?"

"Close to the station at République."

Had Ysa been in Spain, she'd have no doubt what to do, but Paris wasn't her territory. She looked to Rousseau. "Madame?"

Rousseau flexed one gloved hand. Ysa had the distinct impression that the impracticality of the gown was all that kept her from immediately charging into the metro. "I keep a change of clothes at the Tabarin. We'll meet you back here in an hour."

"Should I alert my nefilim?"

Rousseau paused, obviously considering the situation. "We don't want to arouse the mortals' suspicions if we can avoid it. Put your nefilim on stand-by. Do you have twenty you can call in on short notice?"

Ysa glanced at Bernardo. He nodded.

"I do."

"Go ahead and post five nefilim aboveground and five in the station at République. Have the rest of your people meet us here. We'll begin at the ward Suero found."

Ysa nodded to Bernardo. He bowed his head and lifted the phone from behind the bar. His soft bass rumbled like the percussion of war drums as he issued orders into the receiver.

Rousseau acknowledged Suero as she passed. "Good work, Suero." She lifted her hand to Ysabel. "In an hour, mademoiselle. Tell your people to come armed."

After Rousseau and Cyrille left, Juanita turned on Suero. "And Carlos?"

"Carlos seems to have disappeared, as well."

That was definitely not what Ysa wanted to hear. "Do you think Rafael followed Carlos?"

Juanita's eyes flashed in the dim light. "After we told him not to? I certainly hope not."

Ysabel twisted the scarf between her fingers. *Damn it, Rafael, what have you done?* He should have known better than to follow an old nefil into those tunnels. *And I should have known better than to think he wouldn't.* "He wanted to prove himself. This is my fault."

"The hell it is." Juanita whirled and walked toward the back room. Her heels cracked against the floor. "Rafael Diaz has brought this on himself."

Violeta came to Ysa's side. "We'll find him. All for one."

"And one for all." Ysa tied Rafael's scarf around her wrist. *Hold on, my rose. I don't know where you are, or what is happening, but we're coming.*

[17]

THE BLACK SITE
UNDISCLOSED LOCATION IN THE PYRENEES

At the main level, Jordi set a grueling pace. Climbing the hills of Paris to the clubs in Montmartre had strengthened Rafael's legs, but now he suffered from the lack of both food and sleep. He struggled to keep up with the generalissimo.

As they entered a new corridor, soldiers stopped and snapped their heels to salute Jordi. Their stares burrowed into Rafael from all sides.

A youth, who didn't appear to be much older than Rafael, gave Jordi a smart salute before making eye contact with Rafael. The soldier waited for Jordi to pass, and then he swept his foot at Rafael's ankle.

Rafael danced sideways and whirled. He kept his balance, but barely.

Jordi halted at the soldiers' laughter. He turned his head and snapped his fingers. Rafael moved forward cautiously.

"Did you do something to amuse them?"

Rafael's heart hammered in his chest. "I almost tripped, Señor General."

"Because?"

The older men grew silent.

The young soldier paled.

Rafael shifted his gaze to the floor. Getting the other youth in trouble wouldn't help his cause. *And right now I need friends.* "Because I am clumsy."

Jordi struck him without warning. The slap landed on the same cheek Samyaza had clawed.

Rafael's head whipped back. Blood flushed his face, reawakening whatever poison lay beneath his flesh.

"That's good. Because I haven't given anyone permission to touch you." Jordi glared at the young soldier who'd attempted to trip Rafael. Ten seconds ticked by before he started walking again.

Numb from his pain and humiliation, Rafael followed. He didn't look back.

Miquel said to find the elevator to the surface. He held on to that thought as his life preserver. He had to get away from Jordi long enough to secure the elevator's location, but the twisting labyrinth of corridors now all seemed the same. Stairways led up and then down as if the entire structure had been molded against the mountain's contours. Before he could formulate both a plan for breaking out Miquel and getting them to the elevator, he first had to learn the layout. A task that grew more daunting with every step.

Keeping his head lowered, he watched each area for distinguishing characteristics. No signs indicated the floor they were on, but colored squares marked some sections as blue and others as green or gold.

They turned down another corridor, which was more deserted than the others. A white square with a red cross indicated the universal sign for medical care.

The infirmary. The sectors are color-coded. Of course. It made sense given the mixture of German, Italian, and Spanish soldiers. The older nefilim might be fluent in all the languages, but not the younger ones.

The realization was a small victory, but an important one nonetheless. He felt a little more in control.

Turning his attention back to his surroundings, he noted several doors lining the hall. A short, round nefil wearing a white lab coat slipped out of one room and consulted a paper on his clipboard. The sign by his shoulder designated the chamber as CHORAL ROOM 5.

Rafael wondered how many choral groups it took to maintain the portal realm. *Are they willing participants, or are they forced to sing?* He thought again of the nefilim in the pit and shuddered.

The short nefil looked up and saluted Jordi, snapping his heels together. "Generalissimo!"

Jordi returned the salute without pausing.

"This is very fortunate." The nefil hurried after them. "May I have a word, please, Generalissimo?"

Jordi halted so suddenly, Rafael skidded and barely kept from crashing into the taller nefil. From the glare Jordi threw at him, Rafael suspected making Jordi look like a fool would earn him a few more kidney punches.

Or worse. He edged behind Jordi, careful to stay out of sight and at the requisite two steps.

"Forgive me, Generalissimo, but I'm sure Lieutenant Espina notified you that one of the singers expired this morning."

"You mean died?"

The round nefil waved away the distinction as if it were a bad odor floating between them. "An unfortunate occurrence, but between the loss of that nefil and the melee in Choral Room Two, we are in desperate need of replacement singers."

"I understand that, Dr. . . . ?"

"Jimenez. Doctor Jimenez."

"Well, Dr. Jimenez, I'm sure Lieutenant Espina can find you a replacement."

"I'm sorry, Generalissimo. I had hoped this was our new singer." He gestured to Rafael. "I mean, he's young, so he'll last a bit longer than some of our older nefilim."

"He'll be useless to you. His voice still breaks. Find someone else." Jordi turned and continued down the hall.

Jimenez produced a cigarette and lit it. As the hall filled with the smell of nicotine, Rafael felt the nefil's eyes on his back.

That's twice now I've practically been inducted into the horrors of this place. He had a bad feeling his razor's edge of luck was about to run out. Rafael twisted his ring and touched the angel's tear in the setting. *Mamá, give me strength.*

But it wasn't his mamá's voice that he heard in his heart. It was Miquel's. *Don't blink. Find the elevator, warn Los Nefilim, but whatever you do, don't blink.*

Jordi wanted to keep him off balance, because that kept him compliant. *And I keep blinking. Damn it.*

At a nondescript door, Jordi didn't bother to knock. He turned the knob and entered, surprising the occupants.

It was an examining room. A nefil with thick black hair and soft gray eyes whirled at the intrusion. He opened his mouth, most likely to admonish whoever was so bold as to barge into his lab. When he saw Jordi, his demeanor changed.

Clearly unnerved by the interruption, he dropped a scalpel into a metal tray with one shaking hand. "Jor— Generalissimo. What a surprise."

Lavender sigils washed the walls and covered the odor of rotting meat that wafted from the nefil sitting on the table. Red fingers spotted in black peeked from the boil on his neck. Judging from the placement of the towel on the man's shoulder, the doctor was preparing to remove the lesion.

The nefil shot to his feet and saluted Jordi. "Generalissimo!"

Jordi returned the salute. "What have we here, Nico?"

"An interesting case." Nico pointed to the patch of protrusions that resembled curving fingers. "If you'll remember, Feran brought us Carme's notebook."

Traitor. Rafael glared at Feran.

Feran didn't seem to notice. His eyes smiled with pride and he saw no one but Jordi. Before speaking, he fished in his mouth and withdrew a thin needle about two centimeters long. Blood coated his teeth. "Generalissimo, I am proud to suffer in your name." Red spittle dotted his chest.

Before Feran could move, Jordi drew his pistol and shot him between his eyes.

Rafael backed against the wall in shock.

The dark sound of Feran's death blinked out of existence as soon as it appeared.

The Grigori ate him, Rafael thought wildly as he put his hand over his mouth and choked on his cry.

Nico glanced at him.

Rafael lowered his hand and tried to compose himself. *Don't blink. Don't die.*

Jordi holstered his pistol. "You couldn't save him, Nico."

Nico stared at the body slumped on the examining table. "He was trying to . . ."

"It doesn't matter what he was *trying* to do. He failed. I can't abide failure." Jordi's gaze locked on the doctor. "You came close this afternoon."

Nico paled. "What?"

"With Miquel. Samyaza was ecstatic with the results of your experiments with the Pervitin. And to think we nearly missed viewing it."

"I don't know what you mean." Nico retrieved Feran's towel from the floor and used it to cover the dead nefil's face.

"Operation Red Soldier." Jordi watched him as dispassionately as if Nico were mopping up spilled wine. "You released our Red a day early."

Typical rebel, assuming we're all Communists. Rafael resisted the urge to spit.

Jordi continued. "It was merely a stroke of luck that Samyaza and I hadn't left for Barcelona when we did."

Understanding dawned on Nico's features. His countenance darkened. "You can blame Benito and his thugs for that. They beat Miquel so badly, he was dying. I had no choice but to begin when I did. Once I applied the dosage, I couldn't stop. I knew that even if we cleared the compound, you'd find us." He met Jordi's gaze evenly. "I wasn't worried."

A spark flashed across Jordi's aura at the last sentence. *He's piqued?* Interested by the subtle change, Rafael tried to figure out precisely what instigated Jordi's umbrage. Then it came to him: Jordi had no way around Nico's calm assurance. If he objected, then he admitted to the possibility that he lacked control over either Nico or the experiment, a concession Jordi Abelló would never verbalize in front of someone like Rafael.

But later, in private, this discussion will continue. Rafael had witnessed such moments between his fathers. Except the undercurrents between Jordi and Nico lacked the layer of the love and respect shared by Miquel and Papá. Nonetheless, Nico didn't seem too afraid of the likelihood of answering to Jordi, which meant he either told the truth or his alibi was irreproachable.

Jordi didn't pursue the matter. Instead, he snapped his fingers and pointed to a spot on the floor. "Diaz. Here."

He probably calls dogs with more respect. Regardless, Rafael stepped forward. He was fast learning that Jordi Abelló considered himself the only person of value in the room.

Nico turned his gaze to Rafael. "Diaz. You're Diago Alvarez's son?"

Nico's assessment felt less intense than Jordi's; Rafael was beginning to understand that each nefil measured him differently. Jordi, so far, had been right about one thing: Rafael stood on that perilous brink between childhood and maturity.

Cabello had treated him as he would any other male. Carlos saw him more as a boy and spoke to him as such. Nico would also consider how close Rafael stood to adulthood.

Can I win his empathy, or does he see me as a man and deserving of Jordi's scorn? Rafael lowered his gaze and observed Nico through his lashes. He detected a hint of pity in Nico's soft gray eyes. That small trace of compassion was all he needed. *There's a possibility I can win his protection.*

Jordi traced a small sigil and snapped, "The doctor asked you a question. Don't be rude."

The ward popped against Rafael's arm, leaving a slash of singed hair in its wake. Rafael swallowed his squeak and re-sisted the urge to rub the wound. "Yes, Señor Doctor, Diago Alvarez is my father."

Nico's face reddened as he acknowledged the answer with a nod. He didn't ask any more questions.

Jordi gestured to Nico. "This is Dr. Nico Bianchi. He'll tend to your hands and clean you up. Then he'll bring you to our quarters for our evening meal." Turning back to Nico, Jordi said, "Just have them burn his clothes."

Nico raised his eyebrows but didn't seem to mind the as-signment. "What kind of uniform should I find for him?"

"He won't need one."

"You want me to parade him naked through the com-pound?"

"Do you have a problem with that, Nico?"

Rafael swallowed hard. *Say yes, please say yes, and fight him on this.*

"No. Of course not. It's just . . . I thought . . ." Nico glanced at Rafael, clearly uncomfortable and unsure how to proceed. "I'll take care of him."

Meaning, he'll take care of his own best interests. Rafael looked away from the nefil. Walking through the corridors had been hard enough barefoot and ragged. The humiliation of marching naked before the sneering soldiers made him physically ill. *I'm going to be sick.*

"Good." Jordi turned to the door. "I have a meeting with Samyaza. Dinner in two hours."

Nico shook his head. "Three, at least." This time he

didn't back down at Jordi's glare. "Look at his face and his wrists. He'll need stitches. This is Samyaza's work, isn't it?" To Rafael, he said, "Take off your shirt."

Rafael touched the collar of his shirt but made no attempt to remove it.

Jordi grabbed Rafael and slammed him against the wall. Like the punch to his kidneys, the move happened so fast, Rafael didn't have time to deflect.

He's old and he's fast and he's angry. And now he fully understood Doña Juanita's reluctance to send him up against such an ancient nefil. *Too late. I always understand everything too late.*

Jordi wrapped his hand around Rafael's throat. "You'll submit yourself to Dr. Bianchi with the same obedience you give to me. Understand?"

Rafael squelched the whine from his voice. "Yes, Señor General."

Releasing him, Jordi stepped back. "Well?"

Rafael removed his shirt with shaking hands.

Jordi snatched it from him and flung it over Feran's corpse. "Good." The word floated through the infirmary as gentle as a kiss. "All right, Nico, you have three hours. Don't drug him. I want him to feel everything." He went to the door and left them.

"I'm going to be sick," Rafael whispered, hating himself for the weakness.

"Quickly." Nico grabbed his arm and led him to a metal basin.

A hot wave of nausea washed over him, and for a moment he thought he'd faint. *The ultimate blink, but I can't do this anymore. I'm scared. I'm sorry I ever left Paris.*

Papá and Doña Juanita are right, I'm not ready, I'm not ready, I'm not . . .

He dry-heaved, but there was nothing in his stomach. Staring at the shadowy face in the bottom of the basin—eyes wide with terror and mouth agape—he didn't recognize himself. Behind him, he heard the lock click into place. He whirled.

Nico came forward and cupped his face. They were close in height and the other nefil smelled nice. *He uses the same cologne as Papá.* The nostalgia associated with that scent tickled the back of Rafael's mind with pleasant associations, driving away some of his fear.

"Look at me," Nico commanded him gently. "Take a deep breath . . . in through your nose and out through your mouth . . . do it . . . do it with me. Inhale. And exhale. Just breathe. That's it. Calm. Everything is going to be all right. What do your friends call you?"

"Rafael."

"Good. Keep breathing, Rafael. That's it. Your color is getting better. Excellent. Are you still feeling sick?"

He was, but he shook his head nonetheless.

"How old are you?"

"Fourteen."

"Do you know what Jordi intends to do to you?"

Rafael couldn't bring himself to say the words. "Yes."

"Have you ever had sex before?"

Rafael felt a hot flush wash over his cheeks. "Yes."

"Man or woman?"

"Both."

"Rascal." A faint smile touched Nico's mouth and Rafael felt some of the tension leave the room.

Was I wrong about him? Will he help me? He wiped his eyes.

"Let me see your face." The Italian gently turned Rafael so that his back was to Feran's corpse.

He's doing everything he can to calm me. Glad to have Feran's body behind him, Rafael didn't resist.

Nico went to the counter and retrieved the alcohol and some cotton. He murmured a soft song until he finished cleaning the wound. Rafael let the other nefil's voice soothe his tattered nerves.

After he finished his examination, Nico said, "It's going to hurt, but you're healing fast. I doubt you'll even have a scar." He poured some water in the basin and washed Rafael's wrists.

"Do I need stitches?"

Nico examined the wounds. "No."

"Then why did you say I would?"

"To buy us time." He handed Rafael a bar of rough soap. "Clean yourself up. Be quick."

Rafael washed the blood from his arms and chest. As he worked, Nico touched his back where Jordi had punched him.

"Does that hurt?"

"No." Another lie, but his voice was firm.

"It looks like he bruised your kidney. Don't be frightened if there is a small amount of blood in your urine, but let me know if it goes on more than a few days." He gave Rafael a towel. When he finished drying himself, Nico tended his wrists.

The pain had become so constant, Rafael ceased to think about it. Nico applied a thick salve over the mangled flesh and bandaged his wrists. "Listen to me very carefully." He went to a shelf and retrieved a rucksack. "You're too young for this. He keeps . . ." He seemed to catch himself before he could say more.

"He keeps what?"

Nico didn't answer. He opened the pack and rummaged through it.

Talk to him. Form some kind of connection. Nico stood between him and Jordi. Tenuous as that barrier was, it was all Rafael had. "Please. I don't know what's going to happen. I'm scared."

Nico closed his eyes. When he opened them again, he seemed to come to a decision. "Listen. This isn't about you. It's about how much Jordi hates your father. He believes that every injury, every humiliation he inflicts on you is a strike against Diago's heart. And he's probably correct."

Either Nico Bianchi is the world's greatest actor, or he truly empathizes with me. Don't wait too late again. "Miquel said there is an elevator to the surface."

Nico inhaled sharply. "You've seen Miquel?"

"He has twenty-four hours to decipher Carme's notebook."

"But he's alive."

"He was when I left him."

Nico's eyes brightened with something akin to hope. "Okay. We need to get you into a uniform so you don't attract attention."

"Jordi said no clothes."

"Do you want to help me get Miquel out of here?"

Rafael's heart galloped in his chest. *He's going to help us.* "Oh God, yes."

"Then you have to do exactly as I tell you."

Rafael hid his fear behind bravado. "Tell me what to do."

"Help me get Feran out of his pants and boots. His jacket and shirt are here." Nico pointed to a shelf under the examining table. "Don't worry about the smell. I can make that go away."

Rafael just stared at Nico and then gestured at the dead nefil. "You're not kidding, are you?"

Nico shook his head as he unbuckled the corpse's belt. "Get his boots."

He wasn't kidding. *And I don't have a better idea.* Rafael took a deep breath and went to work. They soon had Feran stripped to his underclothes. Nico formed a pale blue sigil like the ones on the walls and sent it over the uniform. The sigil neutralized the rotten flesh odor wafting off Feran's clothing.

Nico stuffed the uniform and boots into the rucksack. "You're going to have to leave here dressed as you are. If I put you in Feran's uniform now, someone will notice." He wrapped Feran's pistol in a towel and placed it on top. If anyone opened the rucksack, all they'd see was the towel. Then he slid the two extra magazines into his pockets.

When Nico finished, Rafael asked, "What now?"

"I'm going to get you out of the infirmary and to an office that I keep nearby. Once we're there, you're going to put on Feran's uniform before we go after Miquel." At another cabinet, Nico unlocked the door. He removed four syringes and the same number of vials. With a practiced hand, he filled the syringes and capped them, placing them in one of the rucksack's outside pockets. They were deep enough to be hidden, but within easy reach.

"What are you doing?" Rafael asked.

"Making a weapon that is as effective as a gun." Pushing the empty vials to the back of the cabinet, he closed the door and locked it again.

"This is it," Nico said as he grabbed the rucksack. "I know it's embarrassing, but trust me. We can't arouse suspicion. Stay behind me, the same as you did with Jordi. Keep your head down like you're beaten. Take my lead in all things, but if I start to fight, attack with everything you have. I mean it. Sling your deadliest wards and make sure your shot is true. Do you understand?"

Rafael nodded, not daring to believe they would make it out of the complex.

They left the examining room. Nico locked the door and sang a ward over the latch, fusing it shut. Then they walked back toward the main corridor.

Dr. Jimenez chatted with two heavily armed nefilim in front of an open door.

Nico didn't slow his pace, or even seem disturbed by the sight of the guards. He nodded to the doctor. "Jimenez."

"Nico, your escort is here." His greedy gaze went to Rafael.

Nico's back stiffened as he came to a halt just beyond the open door.

He wasn't expecting this. Rafael inched forward until he could see inside the room. Two other doctors sat before a soundboard. A crate of Pervitin was tucked against one wall.

On the other side of a two-way mirror was a group of twenty nefilim wearing German uniforms. They stood in a semicircle and sang into the microphones that hung from the ceiling. Unlike the nefilim in the pit, this chorus willingly carried each note.

Or do they?

Their gazes skittered from corner to corner. Sweat sheened their faces and soaked the high collars of their uniforms.

How long had they been standing there, locked in place?

"Magnificent, aren't they?" Jimenez whispered to Rafael. "You would look handsome in such a group." He used the back of his hand to stroke Rafael's bare shoulder. "Sing for me. Let me hear your voice."

Rafael gaped at the doctor.

"Don't you dare sing a note," Nico snapped at Rafael. He glared at Jimenez. "The generalissimo has taken an interest in this boy. Get another singer from the new recruits." Without missing a beat, he turned to the guards. "What's the meaning of this?"

Jimenez answered for them. "The generalissimo would hate for something to happen to his most valued doctor and friend. So he asked Rana and Valdez to remain with you while you treated your patient."

Nico turned on him with a snarl. "I want you to take your simpering ass back to your job."

One of the doctors at the soundboard turned his head and snickered.

Jimenez cowered at the malice rolling through Nico's voice. "My job is to keep the choruses singing."

"Then do it." Nico waited until Jimenez slinked back into the control booth and shut the door.

Rana cradled his rifle. "We weren't expecting you so soon. The generalissimo said you needed three hours."

"The generalissimo also stipulated that the boy isn't to be drugged. Do you think I want him shrieking so close to one of the choruses? He'll be a distraction to them. I'm taking him to the office near the prison. No one will notice his screams there."

"Then you don't mind if we follow along?" Rana asked.

"Of course not." Nico stepped around the nefil. "I'll need someone to hold him down."

Satisfied with the explanation, Rana and Valdez fell into step behind Rafael.

Rafael kept to his role and remained submissive, hoping Nico actually had a plan.

Diago followed Guillermo into Benito's office and shut the door. Feeling along the wall, he found the switch and pressed the button. The bulbs overhead flickered to life.

A desk and rolling chair occupied the center of the room. Two filing cabinets stood at attention along the left wall. Behind the desk was a huge map.

Guillermo went to the desk and began opening drawers, rifling through the contents. "No notebook, but there are more requisitions," he murmured. "These are completed and some are stamped with Jaeger's seal."

"That's damning." Diago circled the desk and went to the map.

"Not really." Nonetheless, he withdrew one of the forms and carefully folded it before tucking it into his pocket. "At this point, she can claim she doesn't know Jordi's plans, only that she is assisting an ally." He moved to the next drawer. "But I've got names and routes. That's important."

"Only if we get out of here alive." At Diago's angle, the image on the map initially appeared to be that of a skull.

But as he neared, he realized it was the interior of a cavern. Green pins occupied numerous points within a crater.

The map was flanked on the right by an enlarged photograph of the same cavern, and on the left by a typed sheet of paper containing a legend.

"Guillermo," Diago whispered. "Would you call that a pit?"

Guillermo lifted his head and turned, scowling at the images on the back wall. Reaching into the desk, he retrieved a handheld magnifying glass and approached the photograph. "What the hell are they doing?"

Diago went to the legend and read aloud. "'Each green pin represents the location of one of Satanael's generals.'" His stomach cramped with fear. "Satanael. Chief of the Grigori."

Turning to the map, he counted the green pins. Seventy-two. Seventy-two generals, a legion of angels beneath each general. "Oh Jesus Christ."

"Come here." Guillermo pressed his finger on the photo.

Diago reluctantly joined him.

The big nefil passed him the magnifying glass. "Look at this." He pointed to a specific stone.

Diago moved closer to the photo and lifted the glass. Lying between two large boulders was a person. *No, not a person.* A four-fingered hand gripped the stone. The individual's exposed back showed extensive scarring.

Guillermo scratched his chin. "Think back. The portal sigil we passed through to get here. Didn't it have greenish hues?"

They'd clung like tar to the brighter lines of Jordi's song. "Yes, they did." Diago lowered the glass. "Can you handle a Grigori?"

Guillermo tilted his fist so that his signet caught the light. "I can definitely fight one alone, maybe two. But that . . ." He gestured at the map with its numerous pins and shook his head.

Diago returned to the legend. "According to this, they have Samyaza. They don't mention any others. But they are working to free Satanael next."

"Because Satanael will make short work of liberating the others." Guillermo retrieved his lighter and flicked the lid. "When my brother plays with fire, he uses a flamethrower."

Diago tossed the magnifying glass to the desk. "Do you still think you can save Jordi?"

"I never thought you and I would be friends again, yet here we are, having adventures." In spite of his jocular tone, Guillermo's eyes glittered dangerously.

"That's not a fair comparison."

"Maybe not," Guillermo conceded. "But I believe there is a way to reach Jordi. I've just got to find it."

Diago couldn't keep the sarcasm from his voice. "Maybe Samyaza can mediate the discussion."

"Now you're just being an asshole." Guillermo tapped the map. "Do you know what my brother is about to unleash on the mortal realm?"

Diago didn't answer. He didn't need to.

The soft click of Guillermo's lighter popped twice. "Once we've secured Carme's notebook, we have to find that cavern."

"And then what?"

"Bury the Grigori again. Look here." He traced his finger over the higher regions of the caverns. "See the holes? One well-placed sigil will bring all that down on the pit." He pocketed his lighter and started for the door. "Let's see if we can find some stairs."

With a final uneasy glance at the map, Diago followed Guillermo back to the corridor. The klaxons finally ceased to scream. The quiet was somehow worse.

They set off again, finding their way back to the main corridor. A group of soldiers returned from the upper levels. Diago spied Espina among them.

Christ, what shitty luck. Thus far, they'd bluffed their way past other soldiers by simply walking as if they knew where they were going. They'd never fool Espina.

Diago nudged Guillermo toward a smaller passage to the left of the main corridor. The area wasn't as well maintained as the other halls they'd found. Patches of plaster crumbled onto the spongy wooden floor. A long handrail was bolted to the wall and ran the length of the passage.

No offices lined the walkway—just meters and meters of emptiness that left Diago feeling more exposed than he liked. For the first time since they'd started their reconnaissance, he looked over his shoulder more than once as they traversed the hall. The smell of rot permeated the damp air.

They finally reached a stairwell going upward. At the next landing, they found an alcove to their left and a long corridor that extended into darkness to their right. Directly across from the landing was a second stairwell that descended to a steel door.

Inside the recessed area was an ugly guard, who straddled a camp chair. Greasy cards showed a game of solitaire well in progress on the folding table.

"Hey!" The nefil looked up from his game.

Diago's heart kicked in his chest. He rested his palm on

his holster in what he hoped the other soldier would perceive as a casual gesture.

The nefil played a card before he set the pack aside. "What was all the noise about?"

Diago relaxed somewhat. *It's a lonely post and he's looking for news.* "Don't know. We were busy securing a portal."

"The one that bastard Feran came through?"

The guard suddenly had Guillermo's undivided attention. "The very one."

The guard ventured to the edge of the alcove and leaned against the peeling plaster. "Have you seen him?"

"Feran?" Diago asked.

"Yeah. He got hit bad."

Guillermo feigned surprise. "By what?"

"Sigil. Shit. It's incredible. He's got these red fingers growing out of his neck." The guard shuddered. "What kind of sick bitch would create something like that?"

Oh, Carme, you were a piece of work.

Undeterred by their silence, the guard continued, "And he keeps spitting out needles."

Diago exchanged a glance with Guillermo. "You mean like metal needles?"

"Yes! They just . . . ooze out of his gums."

Diago was genuinely astonished. The needles were a new twist. He wondered how she'd managed that.

"Shit," Guillermo murmured. "That's got to be painful."

Don't sound so pleased about it. Diago shot him a warning glare.

The guard nodded. "Looks like it hurts like hell, and the stink! Mother Mary, I'd shoot myself just to get away from the stench."

Wondering if the guard knew of Feran's whereabouts, Diago eased forward. "I've got to see this. Do you know where he is?"

"Infirmary. Dr. Bianchi is trying to remove the latest boil. Hey." He motioned them closer and whispered, "We've got a pool betting on how long Feran will last. You want in?"

Daimons stick together better than this lot. Diago clicked his tongue. "I'd love to, but I'm broke."

"Yeah, me, too." Guillermo patted the nefil's shoulder. "And we have to go. I'm just sorry I can't see that."

"Maybe you can. There's a shortcut to the infirmary." He pointed down the corridor. "That way. Straight ahead and around that bend you'll see a door. On the other side is a corridor. Dr. Bianchi uses it all the time to get to the prisoners in case of an emergency, so he leaves the door unlocked. If you slip through real quiet, you might get a peek at Feran as he's leaving Bianchi's office."

Diago glanced at Guillermo, but he didn't say anything. It was the first good luck they'd had since they'd fled into the mountains, because even if Feran didn't have Carme's notebook, he'd know where to find it.

Guillermo glanced down the hall and then shook his head. "Oh, but we shouldn't. We'll get in trouble."

The guard shook his head and pretended to cover his eyes. "I never saw you." He dropped his hand and winked. "Go on."

Diago nudged Guillermo. "Let's do it."

"I don't know . . ."

"Come on. We'll never get another chance."

Feigning reluctance, Guillermo finally nodded. "Okay. I guess we could. This shortcut, is anyone there?"

The guard shook his head. "Bianchi keeps an office in the corridor for supplies, but he's rarely there. Otherwise, there's nothing between here and the infirmary. Go on. Hurry. My relief will be here soon, and I want to hear what you think."

Guillermo put his finger to his lips and the guard grinned at him. Diago started walking down the hall.

They'd barely turned their backs before the jovial smiles faded from their faces. They found the door and went through.

The corridor was dimly lit. They slowed and eased around a curve. A passage masked in shadows continued for another sixty paces before taking a sharp right.

The sound of footsteps reached them as they neared the corner. Three, maybe four men. Diago lifted his hand and sidled forward. Guillermo flattened himself against the wall.

At the corner, Diago leaned around the edge. A single bulb hung over the storage room's door. The rest of the corridor remained heavy with shadows, much like the one in which they stood.

A nefil wearing a white lab coat and carrying a rucksack walked toward the storeroom. As he reached the pool of light, Diago instantly recognized Jordi's lover, Nico.

A youth trailed behind Nico. The boy was barefoot and shirtless. His bruises and torn pants testified to a hard fight. A pair of guards flanked him.

With that wild hair and the slouch, he could be my Rafael. Then the boy stepped into the light. Diago sucked air between his teeth and ducked back around the corner.

It is Rafael.

The ramifications of seeing his son this far from Paris

whipped through his brain. *Are we too late? Has Jordi already attacked France?* That would explain Rafael's appearance. He'd fought them hard, that much was apparent. *But where are they taking him? And what about Ysa and Juanita?*

Guillermo frowned at him and raised his eyebrows.

The empty hall carried Nico's command to them. "Face the wall."

A flash of rage hit Diago's chest. That was probably given to Rafael.

Guillermo started to move. Diago signaled that enemy soldiers were around the corner.

If they moved too soon, they endangered Rafael. The boy was unarmed, and Diago wasn't sure if they'd somehow weakened his ability to form a sigil. He seriously doubted they'd allow him to move uninhibited through the halls.

Diago drew his pistol and risked another glance around the corner.

Nico fumbled with the rucksack and then unlocked the door. "Get inside."

Rafael obeyed him. One of the soldiers started to follow, but Nico got in front of him. "I need you two to wait out here for a moment."

Diago frowned. *What's he up to?*

The taller soldier appeared concerned about Nico's motives, as well. "The generalissimo said not to let either of you out of our sight. And you said you needed us to hold the boy."

Diago didn't like the sound of that.

The second guard stood just behind the first. He stared into the room, presumably watching Rafael.

Nico struck like a snake, pushing something against the

first guard's thigh. When he pulled his hand away, Diago thought he glimpsed a syringe.

The soldier swayed on his feet. "What did you just do?"

"Nothing." Nico's hand disappeared into the rucksack. "You look tired. Have you been taking your Pervitin?"

The shorter nefil looked to his companion. "Rana?"

Rana choked. A line of foam emerged from between his lips and dribbled down his chin.

"Quick!" Nico dropped the rucksack and gestured to the other soldier. "He's having a seizure. Get him on the floor."

The soldier did as he was told. As soon as his back was to Nico, the doctor withdrew a full syringe. He slipped the needle into the back of the second soldier's neck and rammed the plunger home.

"You son of a bitch!" The guard fumbled for his pistol, but his reflexes couldn't outrace whatever poison ran through his veins. Soon he was twitching beside his comrade.

Nico capped the empty syringe and tossed it into the storage room. "Quick! Help me get them out of the hall!"

Rafael emerged from the room and grabbed the taller nefil's ankles. "Is he dead?"

"He's dying." Nico took the guard's arms.

Guillermo started. "Is that . . . ?"

Diago nodded and stepped around the corner. He lifted his pistol. "Get away from my son."

The pair froze and stared at Diago as if he'd popped up through the floor.

And in some ways, I guess I did. As Diago advanced on them, Rafael dropped the soldier's feet.

"Papá?" Blood seeped through the bandages on his wrists. Three claw marks decorated his cheek.

What the hell did he fight? And then he remembered the photograph and that strange four-fingered hand. *Grigori.*

Guillermo caught up to Diago. His freckles were stark on his pale skin.

He's worried he's going to find his Ysabel here, and frankly I am, too. Rafael's presence led to more questions than answers. *Where is Juanita?* She'd never let either of the children out of her sight for long.

Nico didn't release the nefil's arms or dive for a gun. Keeping very still, he monitored their approach the way a rabbit watched wolves.

Calculating his next move. Diago glanced at the dying soldiers and easily recognized the signs of strychnine poisoning. Nico had hit them hard and with a full vial if their convulsions were any clue.

Rafael gave a hoarse cry and took a staggering step toward Diago. "It is you!"

He caught his son before Rafael could fall. Holding him tight with one arm, he kept his pistol trained on Nico.

And I thought I'd never hold him again. Diago pressed his lips against Rafael's cheek. Choking on a combination of relief and fear, he murmured around the lump in his throat, "Hush. I've got you."

Guillermo pulled Rafael away from Diago. "Is Ysa here, too?"

Rafael wiped his eyes and shook his head. "No. She is in Paris. She's safe."

Nico hissed for quiet. "This hall isn't used often, but it is used. Help me get them out of sight, or we're all going to the pit."

Surprising Diago, Rafael left his side and grabbed the

smaller soldier's ankles again, pulling as if his life depended on it.

Guillermo lifted the shoulders of the biggest nefil and indicated that Diago should take his legs. "Why would they send us to the pit?"

"Inside," Nico whispered as he and Rafael hauled the guard into the storage room.

Diago wasted no time helping Guillermo drag the bigger soldier through the door.

A desk and a rolling chair commanded the center of the room. Boxes clearly marked as medical supplies lined the back wall next to two filing cabinets. Squat bookshelves filled with fat binders occupied the space next to another door.

Nico tossed his rucksack to the desk and went to the door. He fumbled with a set of keys and finally found the right one. Jamming it into the lock, he opened the door to reveal more boxes of medical supplies, some of them marked the same as the ones in storage below: *Pervitin*.

"Get them in here." He shoved boxes aside to make room for the dying nefilim.

And dying they are. Their convulsions were ceasing. The strong odor of urine suddenly filled the room as one of the soldiers lost control of his bladder.

Nico pried open a box containing towels. He went to the corridor and swiped the floor. Then he returned and locked the door.

In the office, he wiped up the trail of urine, and tossed the towel into a corner. Humming softly, he fashioned a sigil that produced gentle violet tones. The glyph enveloped the stinking towel, burning it to ash, but instead of charred cotton, the room smelled of lavender.

"Nice trick." Guillermo complimented Nico before he hefted the guards' rifles and brought them to the desk. "What have we got?"

Diago surveyed the ammunition. "All total: two rifles, four pistols, and I've got four extra magazines for the pistols."

Guillermo nodded. "With mine, we have seven for the pistols." He placed four stripper clips, each holding five rounds, beside the Mausers. "And four for the rifles." He shot the bolt of each rifle in turn. "Both have a full load."

Rafael opened the rucksack and produced a handgun. "Five pistols."

Nico placed two more magazines on the desk. "That's all I've got."

It would have to be enough. Diago turned to his son. "If everyone else is safe in Paris, how did you get here?"

"It's complicated."

"He came through the French portal," Nico said. "It opens in Paris."

Of course, and somehow his enterprising son managed to get sucked through it—which, when he thought about it, also felt like an "of course." He didn't ask how. *But if we survive this and I find out that he disobeyed Juanita* . . . He shut down the thought and noted the bruise over his son's kidney. "What happened to your back?"

Rafael withdrew a uniform from the sack along with a pair of boots. "Jordi wants respect."

Guillermo scoffed. "Then he should try earning it."

Rafael pulled on the shirt and buttoned it. "I'll let you tell him that after we save Miquel, because that's where we're going . . . to get Miquel, and then we're getting out of here. Right, Nico?"

Guillermo froze. "What?"

Diago's knees felt weak. He leaned against the desk. *Jesus. Jesus Christ. How close did I come to losing both of them?* He shut off the thought. They were all still in danger, and the chances of losing one or both were still too high. "Miquel is here?"

"Yes, and we have to hurry." Nico adjusted Rafael's collar.

Diago resisted the urge to tell the other nefil to get his hands off the boy.

Nico seemed to notice Diago's glare. He cleared his throat and stepped away from Rafael. "Jordi is expecting me to bring Rafael to his chambers"—he checked his watch—"in two and a half hours. When we don't show up, he's going to come looking for us with a squad and Samyaza on his heels. He already suspects me."

Watching Nico carefully, Guillermo asked, "What exactly does Jordi suspect you of doing?"

Nico took one of the pistols and checked the chamber. "That I tried to help Miquel."

"And did you help him?" Diago straightened, not liking the spike of jealousy piercing his heart. "Or were you just concerned with helping yourself?"

Nico held his ground. "Both."

Guillermo cleared his throat and shot Diago a warning. "Gentlemen, let's focus on the situation."

Rafael reached for the pants. "Don Guillermo is right, Papá. We have to get to Miquel quick. I'm afraid he's given up."

Could that be? Had they broken him? He searched Rafael's countenance, hoping for some reassurance that they weren't too late.

He found himself staring into the eyes of a man. They'd

been apart for only ten months—a bare blink of time to the nefilim, yet Rafael had grown three inches and the mischievous child Diago had nurtured in Spain was forever gone. The war stole lives in more ways than one.

Another reason to hate Jordi. Yet he couldn't completely blame Guillermo's brother. Rafael was no mortal child. He was nefil. *And Miquel is right, I've got to stand aside and let him grow.*

The uniform was a close fit. Rafael would have no trouble blending in with the other soldiers, except for those wild curls around his face.

Shit. Now for the fight of my life. Diago went to the desk's drawer and rummaged past rulers and pencils to find a pair of scissors. "We've got to do something about that hair." He grabbed another towel from the box. "And for once, don't argue with me about cutting it, because—"

Rafael took the towel and wrapped it around his shoulders as he sat. "Hurry. Miquel offered to translate Carme's notebook for Jordi if I was spared from the pit."

Diago met Guillermo's gaze as the realization of what Miquel intended to do hit them at the same time. Miquel would never give their secrets to Jordi.

"Jesus Christ, he'd only offer to do that if he thought he had a chance to blow the compound," Guillermo said, echoing Diago's thoughts.

Nico suddenly went white. "They wouldn't give him enough freedom to create such a sigil."

"They wouldn't have to." Diago snipped his son's hair in short savage bursts, dropping the curls into the wastebasket beside the desk. "Carme already created the sigil. It's somewhere in that notebook and he intends to find it."

Guillermo nodded. "From there, all he has to do is augment it with his song."

Diago finished with Rafael's hair.

The youth stood and tucked his shirt into the pants. He reached for one of the gun belts. "Now I understand why he wanted me to find a way home so I could tell Los Nefilim about this place. He never intended to leave. Since they're keeping him in the interrogation rooms over the pit, he's probably hoping to rebury Samyaza's kin."

Guillermo stuffed two magazines into his pockets. "Someone needs to explain to me precisely what is going on in that pit."

"We've got to get moving," Diago snapped.

"And we're damn well going to know what we're moving into. The guard said his relief was due soon."

Nico checked his watch. "He's right. It won't be safe for another fifteen minutes."

"Good." Guillermo pointed at Rafael. "Talk fast."

Rafael quickly told them how Jordi and Samyaza had taken them to the Grigori's prison. Diago's blood turned to ice. He looked at the bandages on his son's wrists.

Rafael didn't seem to notice his father's horror. "And there is a mirror over the pit that takes nefilim's souls."

"That's no mirror; it's a sigil." Diago turned to Guillermo. "That explains why the nefilim's dark sounds flicker and vanish. I thought it was because this is a portal realm, and they were reemerging in the mortal world." A chill stampeded down his back. "Their souls disappear because anyone that dies here goes straight to the Grigori."

Numbed by the realization, he thought of Martinez. *Jesus Christ. I sent that child to a second death.*

Guillermo removed the papers they'd stolen from Dr. Bormann's office and looked at his seal drawn within the ugly blue triangles. Slamming the pages onto the desk, he grabbed Nico's collar and forced him to look. "These are my nefilim . . ."

"*Were* your nefilim," Nico whispered through pale lips.

Diago's heart sank another notch. Those milicianos were never coming back.

Guillermo's fingers tightened. The fabric of Nico's white coat ripped.

The Italian flinched but made no effort to escape. "I couldn't stop what was happening, and I can't bring them back. But I can help you make sure no more die."

Diago placed his hand on Guillermo's arm. The big nefil's muscles trembled beneath his hand. "We need him."

"Maybe," Guillermo growled. Slowly, as if it took every ounce of his willpower to let go, he released the Italian.

Nico backed away, rubbing his throat.

Diago ignored him. "Now I understand why Sitz and his nefilim herded us in this direction. Can you imagine a nefil with your power in that pit?"

Guillermo tucked the papers back into his shirt and glared at Nico. "I've had it with traitors, Nico. You've been with Jordi since before he started this war. Before I trust you, I need to know why you're turning on him."

Nico took a shuddering breath. "When Jordi succeeded in freeing Samyaza, the Grigori was so grateful, he gave Jordi a tear and fashioned it into a signet. But something in that stone is changing him. Somehow the tear has given the Grigori a hold on Jordi's mind."

Rafael glared at Nico. "Jordi seems like he's in perfect control to me."

Nico didn't contradict him. "At times, he is. Samyaza doesn't influence his every move. He doesn't want Jordi to suspect that he is being manipulated. It's hard to explain."

"Try." Guillermo's tone left no room for disobedience.

Nico thought for a moment. "There's a parasitoid wasp in Costa Rica, it lays its eggs in the abdomen of an orb spider—"

Diago snapped, "We don't have time for an entomology lesson."

"We do if it's a good one." Guillermo motioned for Nico to continue. "And it better be good."

After another nervous glance at the door, Nico sped up, talking so fast that, in his agitation, his explanation became a mix of Castilian and Italian. "When the wasp larva is ready to pupate, it injects the spider with a chemical so that the spider builds a new kind of web. The lines aren't sticky; instead, they're strong enough to support the larva's cocoon in the heavy rains. Once the web is built, the larva forces the spider to sit in the center of the web. Then the larva eats the spider."

"Jesus," Diago whispered as the implications of the analogy hit him. "He's using Jordi to build the kind of world he wants."

Rafael touched the corner of his eye. "I saw something crawl across Jordi's iris."

Nico nodded. "The Grigori is some kind of parasite." He turned to Guillermo. "That's not your brother anymore."

"You forget," Guillermo rumbled. "This *is* the kind of world my brother wants."

"No," Nico insisted, "*you* forget: Both the spider and the wasp want a web. It's the nature and function of the web that changes. Jordi wants dominion over the mortals and nefilim.

"Samyaza wants a holocaust."

Rafael glanced uneasily at Diago and then Guillermo. "There may be something to this. When I touched the ring, I had a vision of ashes falling from the sky."

"I've experienced the same vision when he makes . . ." Nico stopped talking and looked away from them.

When he makes love to you. Diago finished the unspoken sentence without saying it aloud. "Why have you waited so long to run?"

"You were a rogue, Diago. How far do you think I would get? Jordi will never let me leave." He lowered his voice until he was barely audible. "I know all his secrets."

In that sentence was both a confession and an offer that wasn't lost on either Guillermo or Diago. To help Nico meant they would have access to a mother load of information.

"Go on," Guillermo said.

"When they captured Miquel, I saw a way out. He never said he would help me. I tried to free him anyway, but Samyaza and Jordi didn't leave for Barcelona as planned. They caught us before I could get out with Miquel."

Rafael tilted his head in Nico's direction. "He helped me, Papá. He didn't have to. And he knows how to get to Miquel and he knows the way out of here. There's an elevator that leads to the surface. I say we trust him."

Guillermo put both palms on the desk and leaned forward, pinning Nico with his glare. "If I decide to let you come with us, you have to promise two things."

"Name them."

"You stand by us to the bitter end, no running back to Jordi if we're cornered."

"I accept that condition."

"Two. If we get out of here alive, you will submit yourself to me for judgment for your crimes."

Nico exhaled a shocked laugh. "I have committed no crimes."

"You enabled Jordi with your actions."

Nico's disbelief stretched his voice high. "You're accusing me as his accomplice?"

"From what you just told me, you were fine with Jordi's actions until Samyaza came along. I've lost countless nefilim to this war." He touched his chest. "Some are never coming back. You owe me a debt you can never fully repay."

Nico glanced at Rafael, but the youth pressed his lips together and looked at his boots.

Without missing a beat, the Italian's gaze bounced to Diago and then back to Guillermo. "I could call them all down on you right now."

Guillermo called his bluff. "Do it. Raise the alarm."

But he wouldn't. Diago saw the defeat in Nico's eyes, knew it was there before Guillermo spoke. *He's never been held accountable before in his life.*

Nico's lips trembled, then he blurted, "Pass judgment on me now."

Guillermo shrugged as if the timing were no matter to him. "Fine. If we get out of here, then you'll swear an oath to me that you will stay with Los Nefilim. You will take my sigil and obey my commands to fix this goddamn mess you helped create."

"And after that?"

"I'll think about it."

For a moment, Nico looked as if he might balk. Diago didn't envy him. He recalled weighing the advantages versus the disadvantages of belonging to Los Nefilim long ago when his son was barely six. Rogues possessed unlimited freedom, but that autonomy also left them at the mercy of more powerful nefilim. Without the protection and networks of the Inner Guard, Nico stood no chance of evading Jordi or his agents.

Nico bowed his head. "I accept your sentence."

Guillermo nodded. "We'll make it formal later. Right now we need a plan."

Nico reached into the desk's drawer and withdrew a piece of paper. He quickly sketched the area. "We're here, and we've got to go here."

Back past the guard in the alcove.

Nico checked his watch. "You came from that direction. Did you see a set of stairs going down toward a metal door?"

They nodded.

"Those are the interrogation rooms. That's where Miquel is now. There are four guards: the one in the alcove, another behind that metal door, and two down in the pit."

Rafael traced his finger to the end of the hall. "The entrance to the pit is here."

Guillermo withdrew his lighter and flicked the lid. "Diago, that spell you worked on the ridge . . ."

Diago cut him off before he could complete the thought. "No. That's out of the question. I'd risk bringing the entire structure down on us all."

Guillermo cleared his throat and reconsidered the issue.

"Okay, plan B: We take out the guard in the alcove. Nico, you and Rafael will stay above and keep watch. Diago and I will take the guard at the interrogation level. I'll cover the pit so we won't get surprised from the rear while Diago frees Miquel. Once we're back to the alcove, we're going to . . ." He looked to Nico.

"This is the only level where the elevator doesn't stop. So we go up. I can take us through several adjacent passages where we won't be seen, and I'll get us to the elevator."

Diago frowned. "Which goes right into the belly of the beast." They'd be in the middle of a compound filled with checkpoints and Nationalists. "Why can't we go through the Paris portal?"

Nico shook his head. "The portals are unstable. Jimenez is having a hard time keeping the choruses going. It's comprised of volunteers, but they can only sing so long before they either lose their voices entirely or die."

How casually he expresses it. Diago thought of the dead boy hanging in the choral room and looked away.

Nico didn't notice Diago's revulsion. "Once we're on the tracks we'd be lucky if we could activate the glyph."

Guillermo stared at the sketch. "The clock is ticking, gentlemen, and it's not in our favor. We'll go with our surest bet and take the elevator." He met their gazes one by one. "Any questions?"

Rafael stepped forward. "May I have a moment with my papá?"

"A quick one." Guillermo turned his attention to the guns.

Rafael took Diago's arm and led him to a corner. "I'm sorry," he murmured. "I wanted to help Doña Juanita and

Ysa. I just wanted to prove to them that I could be a valuable part of Los Nefilim, and I messed up. I disobeyed Doña Juanita and followed Carlos. This is my fault."

Diago winced as he realized he'd given his son more than green eyes. *That was my lament for so many years, and my son took it as his own song.* He forced himself to face Rafael's shame. He knew it well, having seen it reflected back at him by far too many mirrors.

"Well," Diago whispered, "you were wrong to disobey Doña Juanita, but all of this is not your fault."

There are so many things I want to say to him. Except there wasn't time. *So say the things that matter.* And those were simply the words he'd always yearned to hear from his own father.

Looking his son in the eye, he said, "I love you. And more than that, I'm proud of you. Never forget either of those things. Not once have I regretted bringing you into my life. You have a place in my heart, and I will always keep you there, close to me."

Rafael's mouth twisted the way it always did when he fought against the urge to cry. "Papá."

"It's okay." Diago kissed his cheeks and tasted the salt of his sweat. "We'll work all this out when we get home. Okay?" He pushed a magazine into Rafael's hand. "You don't have unlimited ammunition. Make every shot count."

Guillermo tapped the desk and pushed three extra magazines to Rafael. "Remember, when you reload that pistol you push in the magazine firmly. Make sure it seats." He patted the youth's shoulder. "I said my goodbyes to my family in Spain. If you make it out and I don't, you watch over my Ysa."

"I will, Don Guillermo."

Nico lifted one of two syringes. "I'll be able to get close enough to the first guard to use this." He offered the second one to Diago. "For the one guarding the interrogation room."

Diago shook his head and lifted an ugly knife. "I've got the only syringe I need."

Guillermo tapped his watch. "Nico?"

The doctor checked the time and nodded. "Shift change should be over."

Guillermo went to the door. "Okay, gentlemen, nice and easy. Nico is in the lead, I'll be behind him, then Rafael. Diago will form our rear guard. Ready?"

Without waiting for an answer, he opened the door.

[19]

Miquel huddled over the notebook and waited for his nausea to pass. His muscles ached. Sweat blurred his vision. He ripped the torn sleeves from his shirt and used them to wipe his face.

With one shaking hand, he formed a protective ward and opened Carme's notebook. Sigils squirmed across the pages in a profusion of colors and shapes, forming chromatic aberrations that caused Miquel to close his eyes until another wave of nausea receded.

When he opened his eyes again, he distinguished individual sigils amid the various shades. The colors vibrated around one another, forming the symbols for clefs, rolled chords, glissandi, portamenti, and ghost notes. Lift one and risk triggering another. The right move revealed the glyphs below; the wrong move led to death.

Carme layered them so the threads of light were entwined. They pulsated like the rhythm of a complex song. A starburst of azure generated lines of teal that led to indigo before darkening to black.

Miquel exhaled through parted lips and began at the top

right-hand corner of the page. He worked right to left, using the pencil to nudge the sigils apart so he could judge the ward's intent. Line by laborious line, he moved down the sheet.

Turning the page, he began the process again. Halfway through the glyphs, he used the tip of his pencil to lift the symbol for a tremolo. The sigil beneath it flew at his face.

He flinched. His protective ward absorbed the blow, sending the glyph back onto the paper, where it bounced forward again. Three times the sigil struck his ward before it finally died, cascading onto the page in a shower of sparks.

When the last of the color expired, Miquel glimpsed another huge sigil. A staccato chord vibrated against his eardrums. The intensity of the sound grew louder, as if thunder clapped within his ears.

Four times the vibrations slammed against him, sending an onslaught of bass tones roaring through his head. He cried out. His protective ward surged and then fluttered beneath the assault. If it collapsed, Carme's song would strike him like blows.

He sang a hard note to reinforce his glyph. The shield held. But barely.

Minutes passed before Carme's song diminished and then faded. Panting, Miquel closed his eyes and rocked his torso until his jitters subsided. His ears rang. A drop of blood seeped from his nose. He wiped it away and turned the page.

Losing himself among the colors, he began again. All the while, an internal clock ticked in the back of his brain. *How much time had passed? An hour? Or two?*

He had no way to know. With Carme's deadly glyphs dancing before his eyes, he navigated through eight more pages. At the ninth, a sigil flared like a flashbulb, temporarily blinding him. Unlike the others, the ward itself was harmless—more like a poke in the eye than an actual blow. He shut his watering eyes and pinched the bridge of his nose.

Thanks, Carme. Sniffling, he waited until the white dots evaporated from behind his closed lids.

Cautiously, he reopened his eyes. Black specks filled the room. He blinked and the dots fell from the air to burrow into the floor. They coalesced into a pool of darkness by one corner. Swirling together, the spots formed the contours of the canvas hood.

This isn't happening. The hiss of sand through the hood sent a chill through him. Glaring at the apparition, he shaped a protective sigil and hissed, "You have no power over me anymore. Begone."

The hood disappeared.

His weak glyph faded.

Miquel released a shaky sigh. A small victory, but a triumph nonetheless. *I'll take whatever I can get.*

Turning his attention back to the notebook, he frowned at the profusion of sigils writhing over the page.

He formed another protective glyph. The shield's pearlescent hues wavered. Small holes appeared in the buffer.

Even with the Pervitin, I'm getting too weak. After so many hours on the brick-lined floor of his former cell, the pallet beneath him felt like a feather mattress. To rest invited sleep, but unconsciousness knew no clock. He couldn't risk closing his eyes . . . not for a moment.

The sound waves of his shield fluttered, snapping him out of his drifting thoughts and back to the job at hand. One of Carme's stronger wards would easily pierce his fragile spell.

Then be careful.

A drop of sweat fell from his brow to the page, blotting the ink beneath the churning colors. A teal clef carried an indigo ghost note across the page. The lines twisted together. He tried to separate them. The tremors returned to rattle his hands.

He needed a caesura—the two diagonal slashes that indicated a brief, silent pause—to insert between Carme's raucous notes. Using his own voice, he hummed until he formed enough blue sound waves to create the caesura. With the pencil, he tried to push the slash marks beneath the teal clef. His hand shook as if palsied. The pencil missed the gap between the clef and the indigo ghost note. On the second try, he caught both lines together and had to let them go. The third attempt brought him success. Peeling back the clef, he found the ghost note's true image. He sucked his breath between his teeth.

Finally. He'd found the sigil for the bomb.

His hand trembled, as much with excitement as with the tremors from the drug. The pencil jittered from his fingers and rolled across the floor. His caesura disappeared, and the teal clef resumed its dominance over the underlying ghost note. The page blurred again.

Clasping his hands together to stop the shakes, he rocked himself back and forth. Anyone looking through the cell's peephole would think he was praying.

His only invocation came from his heart to his love. He thought of Diago. *Help me, my star. Lend me your strength. Help me save our son.*

From somewhere outside his cell, he heard the slam of a heavy door. *A new prisoner? Or are they coming to check on me?*

He had to hurry.

A quick glance told him the pencil was out of reach. *It doesn't matter.* He could use his fingers to insert the caesura between the clef and ghost note, and then, while the rhythm paused, he would have to pluck the ghost note from the page.

Once it was free, he would be able to transfer the glyph to the cell's floor. From there, it was a matter of strengthening its lines without drawing his jailers' notice and then using the Pervitin to intensify his own song.

Of course, to drop or lose the ghost note before securing it to the floor might set off the bomb prematurely.

Miquel gauged the movement of the patterns and licked his lips. *So don't fuck up.*

Forming another caesura with his voice, he created the twin diagonal lines and watched the teal clef. When it shifted to the left, he pushed the caesura between the clef and ghost note. The caesura floated over the clef and disappeared into the sigil.

I missed. Damn it, damn it . . .

"Damn it," he whispered.

The cuff's chain dangled and swayed, destabilizing what little steadiness he had left. Grabbing the chain with his left hand, he slid the cuff past his wrist and onto his forearm.

Lifting his hand, he ignored the clink of the chain and shaped a new caesura with the pearlescent hues of his song. Carefully, he guided the twin slash marks between the clef and the ghost note again.

This time he succeeded. Plucking at the threads of light, as if picking a guitar string, he pulled the ghost note's indigo hues upward and froze.

Beneath the ghost note was the symbol for an arpeggiated

chord. *The broken chord.* And here lay the true glyph for the bomb. *I should have known. A ghost chord doesn't carry the sound needed for a bomb.*

All of which meant he'd misjudged the layers and fallen into Carme's trap. His caesura wouldn't hold much longer.

And when it fails, all three notes will fall together and explode.

The door to his cell burst open.

Miquel looked up and blinked, because he couldn't believe his eyes. The shock practically stopped his heart. "Diago?"

"Hey." Diago's gaze moved from Miquel's face to the notebook in his hands, and from there to the cuff and chain. A mix of sorrow and horror and love filled his eyes. "What are you doing?"

He's not supposed to look at me like that. Humiliation warmed Miquel's chest and cheeks. His hands shook harder. The broken chord hummed dangerously. "Get out. I messed up. Oh God, Diago . . . it's going to blow." He loathed the fear quivering through his words.

"Hold on," Diago whispered and stepped into the cell. "Stay calm and just hold on." Moving quickly, he circled Miquel until he stood behind him. Kneeling, he put his arm across Miquel's chest and examined the notebook.

"The broken chord," Miquel whispered. The fear unraveled him. "I missed it. I should have known."

"Shh," Diago murmured. "Don't let it go." He sang another caesura and with his steady hands he easily inserted it between the notes. The strength of his voice bought them precious minutes to work through the problem.

Another figure filled the doorway. Miquel looked up. "Guillermo?"

The big nefil scowled. "You look like hell."

A sharp laugh erupted from Miquel's throat before he could stop it. "I blinked and they unraveled me."

Guillermo scowled.

Diago's arm tightened on Miquel's chest.

Christ, I sound insane. Get a grip. Give them information they can use. "The Grigori are below us . . ."

Guillermo nodded. "We know. We found Rafael. I'll take care of them. Meanwhile, you two try not to blow up anything while I'm gone." He pointed a finger at Diago. "Stop making that face at me."

Diago waited until Guillermo disappeared, and then he brushed his lips against Miquel's cheek. "I'm here. We'll do this together, okay?"

I'm supposed to be the one saying that. In all the centuries they'd been with one another, it was he who comforted Diago. Not trusting his voice, Miquel licked his parched lips and nodded.

Diago shifted his position to crouch beside him. Their shoulders touched. *It's as though he doesn't want to lose contact with me, because I've scared him.*

And Jesus knows I don't want him to stop touching me.

Diago frowned at the sigils. "What are you trying to accomplish?"

"The broken chord is a bomb. I wanted to peel it from the page and use it to blow the compound. But I mistook the ghost note for the bomb. I picked up the wrong one. If I let it go . . ."

"You activate the bomb. I see it now." Diago examined the intricate lines connecting the sigils. "Okay, hold on to it." Using both hands and soft notes, he padded Carme's spell with more caesuras.

Miquel watched him work. "Do you remember how we first met in this incarnation? How I found you? Beaten half to death in an alley?"

"I remember." He formed a new glyph and sang it to life.

Miquel watched him with admiration. The movements were second nature to Diago. "Do you remember what I promised you? Do you?"

"That you would always take care of me."

Miquel closed his eyes and inhaled the scent of him. "And you were surprised. Do you remember that? You said I was a fool; that only mortals fell in love at first sight, because their lives were like those of butterflies, short and filled with fleeting beauty. You said no one could possibly love you." *But I did, and I do, and this is all backward and wrong, because I should be saving you.*

"I remember." Diago gave him a tolerant half smile. "Let me concentrate."

"How did you know I was here?"

"We didn't. We were chasing Carme's notebook."

"I found it."

"I see that," Diago said, but the words were barely there. *Like a ghost note.* He watched Diago weave the sound of their conversation into his spell and found himself in awe of his husband's talent. *I'm as awkward as a child next to him.*

"Let it go now." Diago nodded at the pearlescent lines of Miquel's song.

Allowing the notes to die, Miquel lowered the shield. He withdrew his fingers from the ghost note.

"Good," Diago whispered. He plucked the threads of Carme's ward from the page line by line. Once the sigil was free, he lifted it from the paper and placed it on the floor as carefully as if he were handling a bottle of nitroglycerine.

The glyph shimmered like a pool of water and then it stabilized.

Diago withdrew a key from his pocket and unlocked the manacle on Miquel's wrist. He eased both the cuff and the chain to the pallet. Then he unshouldered his rifle with the same care. He gave the gun to Miquel. "I need to rig the ward to explode once we're long gone from here. Very, very softly now, I want you to go into the hall."

"I'm not leaving you."

"You're not. You're going down to help Guillermo." Diago gave him a strong nudge. "That's an order, soldier."

"I outrank you."

"Spouses have the ultimate rank. Leave the notebook. I'll bring it with me when I come. Now go. I need room to work."

Still, Miquel hesitated. His heart rattled in his chest at the thought of descending to the pit. *And if I don't go and something happens to Guillermo, I'll never forgive myself. I've always been torn between them,* he realized with a pang. How much longer would he be able to honor them both?

He didn't know. At least today, the choice was clear. Diago was right: Carme's sigil required steady hands and nerves of steel, both of which Diago had in abundance.

Diago must have sensed his indecision. "Trust me, corazón."

Miquel kissed Diago hard and quick. "Swear to me you'll be careful."

A wicked light flashed in Diago's eyes. "I'm always careful."

Rising, Miquel went to the door. Too late he realized he'd forgotten the pills he'd tucked under the pallet. Hesitating at the threshold, he glanced back.

Diago followed his gaze and frowned. "Do you have more of these?"

The truth trembled on his lips. *What will he think of me?* And behind the question came the answer. *That I'm weak. I blinked and gave them power over me.* And he couldn't be the vulnerable one in their relationship. Diago needed him to be strong. "No. Those are all."

Diago's eyes narrowed slightly.

Miquel offered his husband a faint smile. "I'm going to help Guillermo, but I still outrank you."

The comment won him a wry smile from his husband. "If it makes you feel better. Now go. Don't look back." Diago turned to his task.

My words to Rafael. A grim smile touched Miquel's mouth as he moved down the hall. He checked the Mauser's chamber. A bullet, slim and lethal, rested in the groove. He glanced back toward the cell. Diago remained occupied inside.

Before he could think too hard about his actions, Miquel reached in his pocket, opened the bottle, and took two pills. *Ten left.*

The familiar bitterness settled on his tongue. He pocketed the tube as he strode down the corridor. The dying nefilim's refrain seeped through the open door.

Putting his back to the wall, Miquel descended, one slick step after another. The Pervitin soared through his veins. Every sound swept across his flesh, raising the hairs all across his body.

As he reached the last step, he glimpsed Guillermo standing by the archway. The big nefil motioned for Miquel to hold his position.

A sigil shaped like a mortar round vibrated by Guillermo's right hand. With his left, he created a second, smaller glyph, this one with the fire of the Thrones searing its edges.

Hope flared in Miquel's chest as he realized Guillermo's intentions. If he destroyed the angelic sigil over the pit first, then the Grigori couldn't take the milicianos' souls and give them the second death. Once he shattered the Grigori's glyph, he'd use the ward shaped like a mortar to bury the pit.

They'd still lose their milicianos, but *only in this incarnation.*

Miquel held his breath and raised the rifle, his gaze on the archway, watching for the guards. Something tickled his cheek. He touched his face. Grains of sand stuck to his fingers. *No.*

He brushed the grit away and whispered the names of his milicianos, spoke them softly like a talisman against the dark: "Vicente, Alejandra, Juan, Luciana, Remedios, Indalecio, Gaspar . . ."

The sand disappeared.

I'm supposed to save them, but they have saved me. Miquel said their names again, louder now. The vibrations of his voice joined Guillermo's song. The pearlescent strands deepened and grew sharper. Shards of blue and pink and white ice flowed over the smaller glyph.

With a great shout, Guillermo ignited the ward. He flung it at the fallen angels' glyph. The Grigori's mirrored sigil shattered beneath the orange flames of Guillermo's song.

Shouting their names, Guillermo spoke to the milicianos—he sang of his love for them and his gratitude for their sacrifice. Miquel provided the coda, with a promise to watch for them. The power of their voices rang throughout the chamber.

A sunburst of light washed over the pit. Heavy veins of gold burned through the ichor and shot into each nefil, shattering their chains.

Whether the milicianos heard or not, Miquel couldn't tell. Vicente, Alejandra, and Juan had obviously been there the longest. Their papery flesh ignited and they died instantly. Remedios, Indalecio, and Gaspar held hands, falling into a heap across the stones. Whatever words they whispered to one another were lost beneath the roar of Guillermo's fire. Freed from the Grigori's hold, only Luciana raised her voice at the end. Even as her body perished, her song remained, reverberating off the cavern's walls in one long, glorious refrain.

From around the corner, one of the guards cried out. Chairs clattered to the floor.

Guillermo launched the second glyph. The golden light of the ward surged upward into the ceiling's cavities. Ropy veins of lava wormed deep into the crevices, loosening the stones.

A sigil belonging to the guards burst into view.

In their panic, they had created a killing ward.

Jordi will have their balls if he finds they've cheated him of Guillermo. The thought raced through Miquel's brain before he realized his mistake. Instead of focusing on his milicianos with Guillermo, he should have created a protective sigil. It was an apprentice's error, and one that might cost Guillermo his life.

Unless I move fast.

With the Pervitin burning through him, Miquel shoved Guillermo aside, forming a glyph as he did. His shield rose like a wall of light, shattering the guards' ward.

Sweat dripped from his hair. *Barely. I just barely made it in time.*

It wasn't over. The two guards circled the entrance, their weapons held low. Guillermo shot one. Miquel lifted his rifle and took down the other one.

Guillermo grabbed Miquel's arm and spun him back toward the stairs. "Go!"

Miquel didn't argue. Sparks showered them as they charged up the stairs and ducked past the breaker box.

Guillermo slammed the door shut. He sang a hard sigil over the lock and fried the bolts into place.

Miquel slid to a stop in front of the interrogation room. The door was closed. *But where is Diago? Still inside?* He put his hand on the latch.

[20]

Diago stood beside the dead guard and whistled to get his husband's attention. "Next person that opens that interrogation room blows this entire wing."

Miquel remained still. His fingers flexed on the latch, and for a moment Diago feared he'd enter the room in spite of the warning.

He said his husband's name again. "Miquel."

This time Miquel responded. He turned away from the door. "The notebook?"

Diago exhaled softly and patted his pocket. "Got it. Now help me." He gestured to the dead guard.

Together, they moved the nefil into the first interrogation room, placing him alongside the body of the upstairs guard. Miquel yanked the jacket off the larger nefil and quickly changed his torn shirt.

Guillermo joined them. He watched Miquel warily but spoke to Diago. "We've got about a half hour before my sigil blows."

Something happened down there. Diago wanted to ask

what but there wasn't time. "I designed my wards to cushion Carme's bomb from any shocks caused by yours. The only way hers will explode is when that door is opened."

"Then let's get out of here." Miquel passed them. "I'll take the lead."

Before either of them could object, he was climbing the stairs.

Guillermo paused. "What's wrong with him?"

"I don't . . ." *The pills.* "I think I know. I found four Pervitin on the floor of his cell."

"Oh shit." Guillermo gestured for him to go.

Diago saw why. Miquel had already reached the landing. *He's going too fast.* Diago hurried to catch up. Guillermo pounded up the stairs behind him.

Miquel assessed the hall and opposite stairwell, sweeping both with his rifle before turning to the alcove. He froze, his body rigid with fury.

Diago took the stairs two at a time. He was only three steps from the landing when Miquel dropped his rifle and strode into the recess.

"Miquel!" Rafael hissed his father's name, not in relief, but in alarm. "Wait—"

Jesus, what now? Diago gained the landing.

Rafael's voice rose with his panic. "Miquel, don't—"

There was a scuffle, and then the rest of the sentence ended abruptly. *Too abruptly.* Diago quickly scanned the corridor and stairs. So far, no one had stumbled on them. *But that luck won't hold.*

Inside the alcove, Rafael crouched against the wall, gaping at Miquel as if he were a stranger. A new cut marked his forehead.

Miquel backed Nico up against the wall. "You son of a bitch." He raised his fist and brought it down twice on Nico's head.

When Miquel raised his arm for a third blow, Diago caught his biceps and hauled him away from Nico. Miquel twisted. Diago felt him slipping away and then Guillermo appeared. The big nefil wrenched Miquel backward and shoved him against the wall.

Fortunately, Nico seemed to have gone into a defensive position and offered no resistance. If he'd fought back, Diago had no doubt that Miquel might have killed him.

Diago turned on his husband. "What the hell has gotten into you?"

"Stay out of it." Miquel's feral gaze hit Diago like a blow. They'd been together for centuries; they'd argued, even fought, but never in all their time together had Diago seen Miquel's hate aimed at him. *He's like an aggressive dog, ready to bite whoever attracts his attention.*

The aftermath of the melee in the choral room resurfaced in Diago's mind. *They went berserk and they destroyed one another.*

Not realizing the danger, Rafael opened his mouth. *Christ, if he strikes Rafael again, I'll have to fight him.* Diago lifted his hand to silence their son. "Be still," he said to Rafael and then turned back to Miquel. He needed to de-escalate the situation, but he couldn't give in to his husband's demand. Keeping his voice gentle but firm, he said, "I won't stay out of it."

Guillermo spoke softly. "Rafael, go to the stairs and keep watch for us."

The youth shouldered his rifle and scooted past Miquel with the same wary glances he'd give to a vicious bull.

Guillermo tilted his head in Nico's direction. "Diago, can you see to him?"

The other nefil was on his knees, still shielding his head with his arms, and spitting blood onto the floor.

Backing away from Miquel, Diago reached Nico and knelt beside him. When he touched him, the Italian flinched and pushed himself against the wall.

"Ya, ya, ya," Diago sang softly. *He's been abused.* The quick defensive position and the nervousness all indicated this wasn't the first time someone had attacked him. *And he's been conditioned not to strike back.* Whispering, Diago coaxed the other nefil to lower his hands. "Let me see."

Nico spat a molar to the floor. "I'm okay."

He didn't look okay. A bruise enveloped his left eye and another swelled along his jaw. *Christ, Miquel came close to blinding him.* Diago held up two fingers. "How many?"

"Four." Nico wiped his chin with the back of his hand, smearing blood and drool across his mouth.

Shit. Diago traced a healing ward over Nico's temple. *How is he going to shoot if he can't see?*

Guillermo kept his voice low. "He's with us, Miquel."

"The fuck he is." Miquel spat the words. "What did he tell you? That he offered to help me? That he tried to get me out? Well, he fucking lied to you. He made his promises and led me right to Samyaza. Don't trust him. Get away from him, Diago."

Remaining in place, Diago sang the glyph to life. *Never in my life would I have seen this moment coming, where I'm tending my enemy's lover while my own husband is raving against me.*

Nico muttered, "It wasn't supposed to happen that way.

Jordi and Samyaza were going to Barcelona. For some reason they never left."

Rafael poked his head into the room. "He's telling the truth, Miquel. Jordi and Samyaza were on the tracks when I came through the Parisian portal behind Carlos. They mentioned postponing their trip because of me."

Diago snapped his fingers. "Keep watch!"

Rafael disappeared again.

Nico barely acknowledged the interruption. "We were supposed to be gone long before Jordi and Samyaza returned from Barcelona."

"Liar!" Miquel started forward.

Guillermo's palm struck Miquel's chest, stopping him in his tracks. "We're standing on two bombs, and the clock is ticking." His tone left no room for argument. "Nico is with us. That's my order. Obey it."

Miquel's nostrils flared.

Diago worried he'd defy Guillermo. *Then put him on the defensive.* "How much Pervitin did you take, Miquel?"

Nico spat and cleared his throat. "Doesn't matter. He's been injected with it since they found him at Argelès. We've been experimenting with varying dosages to craft the perfect soldier. We succeeded with Miquel."

"Lucky me." Miquel snarled through bared teeth.

Nervous now, Nico looked down. "We've found the drug enhances our powers, but it also makes some nefilim more aggressive."

"Do you see what he is doing?" Miquel stepped around Guillermo and snatched up his rifle.

Everyone tensed. Diago shielded Nico's body with his own.

Miquel deliberately slowed his movements. "He's trying

to turn us against each other." Taking a deep breath, he chambered a round. "Okay? You want him, you be his nursemaid. If he betrays us, I'm putting a bullet through his head."

This isn't Miquel. This is how I used to act all the time. Before Miquel found him, Diago's aggressiveness was his defense and paranoia his code. The behavior his husband currently exhibited was precisely what he feared he'd lapse into once he began using his daimonic song again.

Yet I haven't. Stunned by the revelation, he realized just how much Miquel had helped him change. *And now I've got to remind him of who he was before Nico injected him with the drugs. The same way he taught me: by example.*

Diago helped Nico to his feet and held up his fingers again. "How many?"

"Two."

"Good." *He's healing fast.* Diago took the other nefil's arm and guided him.

Nico jerked free of Diago's grip. He shouldered the rucksack and hissed, "I don't need your goddamn pity."

Diago knew the feeling all too well. "I don't pity you. I just know where you've been, because I've been there, too." Not waiting for an answer, he left the alcove and joined the others.

"Which way are we going?" Guillermo glanced at Nico somewhat uncertainly as he said it.

Nico started haltingly but gained confidence as he spoke. "We can't go through the infirmary, a group this large will be remembered. We also risk someone recognizing either Miquel or Rafael. Our safety lies in hiding among the soldiers."

Miquel's eyes narrowed. "You mean go downstairs and circle around using the main corridor?"

Nico nodded. "And then take the stairs in Gold sector to reach Blue. If we get separated, you know that route. You can find it yourself."

Miquel lifted his gun. "The only thing that will separate you from us is a bullet."

Nico swallowed hard and nodded.

"Okay." Guillermo motioned for Nico to stand beside him. "I'm going first, center aisle. We walk like we own this place. Our uniforms will throw the newer recruits off balance. If one of the old ones marks our presence, shoot and go into an attack pattern." He pointed at Rafael. "Fight with everything you've got. It's you or them. Miquel on the right, Diago on my left. Nico, you're beside me. Fuck up, and you won't have to worry about Miquel putting a bullet in your head. I'll do it. Rafael, you have the rear guard. That means every three steps, you look back and make sure no one is following us. Everyone clear?"

Rafael gripped his rifle. His lips were white, but he gave a sharp nod. Miquel reached for him. Rafael flinched as if he anticipated a blow.

Sorrow touched Diago's chest. He'd hoped never to see his son exhibit that behavior. Still, he held his peace to see what they would do.

"I'm sorry." Miquel lowered his hand. "I'm so sorry I struck you. I . . . I didn't mean . . ."

"It's okay." Rafael touched his father's shoulder. "You're going to be okay." He chambered a round into his rifle and offered Miquel a smile. "We've been through worse than this."

A faint smile touched Miquel's lips. "We have." He wiped the blood from Rafael's forehead and kissed his son's cheek.

"We certainly have. But I'm still sorry, and I'll never raise my hand against you again."

"Family time is over." Guillermo grabbed Nico's arm and started for the stairs. "Let's go!"

Diago waited for them to descend five steps, then he motioned for Miquel to go next. His husband winked at him as he passed, and for the briefest moment Diago saw the man he loved once more.

And I'll get him back. But first they had to get out of Jordi's hell alive.

[21]

At the bottom of the stairs, they fell into formation. As their march gained rhythm, even the old floorboards couldn't muffle the stamp of their boots. Nico shed his lab coat and tossed it to the floor.

Diago snatched a shadow and twisted it between his hands. He listened for his son's footsteps.

One-two-three, turn.

He thought of the humiliations Jordi and Samyaza had inflicted on his family. In doing so, he touched the outer core of his fury and coughed a harsh note into the shadow. The reflex came easier now, as natural as breathing. *And that's not something I want.*

Or was it? Didn't he grow stronger with each song? Wasn't stifling his daimonic nature no different from hiding his relationship with Miquel when circumstances warranted?

One-two-three, turn.

As he shaped the darkness into a sigil, his rage took the form of a scorpion. Gold and silver marbled its back. He ran his thumb over the lines, feeling each ridge of his hate. Wasn't this as much a part of him as his love?

One-two-three, turn.

Maybe. But animosity murdered empathy and gave understanding little room to grow. The darker emotions had their place. Diago glanced over his shoulder and noted his son's grim features. *But they're not to be nurtured.*

One-two-three, turn.

From somewhere behind them, a muffled explosion shook the corridor. Patches of plaster and stone rained down on them.

Guillermo lengthened his stride. "That was the ward I placed in the pit."

Klaxons suddenly screamed in the corridor ahead.

Nico's step faltered, then he regained his pace and kept going. Diago watched him carefully as the group broke into a jog.

One-two-three, turn.

He knew from his own experience that this was a critical moment for Nico. The lure to go back to the abuser was real and dangerous and strong. Jordi, malicious though he was, represented a known factor in Nico's life. Nico understood Jordi's moods and how to mitigate the danger. Stepping into the unknown probably terrified him.

It certainly did me.

Worse, Nico wasn't moving toward a better relationship. Acceptance in Los Nefilim presented a difficult route for him.

One-two-three, turn.

Returning his attention to the scorpion in his palm, Diago adjusted the line of a silver ward, nudging it closer to a thread of gold so that three letters spelled *HCl* and formed the sigil for hydrochloric acid.

One-two-three, turn.

Guillermo wrinkled his nose at the strong odor but said nothing. Nico and Miquel pretended not to notice.

One-two-three, turn.

The passage didn't seem nearly as long on the way out. As they stepped onto the main corridor, a group of five soldiers passed them at a run, heading toward the upper levels. *And why not? That's where the original emergency sent them.*

To the right, the hall was empty. Guillermo turned left and suddenly stopped. They halted in a loose line: Guillermo, Nico, Miquel, Diago, and then Rafael.

Guillermo's gaze remained locked on something far up the corridor. Diago kept his attention on the five soldiers who had just passed them. The group slowed their pace and then moved to the left. As they did, they revealed Jordi, with Samyaza at his side. Four more nefilim followed the Grigori and the generalissimo.

This is bad. Diago took a sliding step forward to block Rafael's body with his own. The act won him a vicious stare from his son.

Nico's lips barely moved. "I'll stall them."

Miquel growled, "Move and I'll blow your brains out."

"Easy," Guillermo murmured.

As the five soldiers fell into formation behind the four already flanking Samyaza, Jordi finally noticed Guillermo. He staggered to a stop and his mouth dropped open.

Had their situation not been so dire, the shock of the moment would have been comical. Unfortunately, Diago had lost his sense of humor somewhere in the Tavascan Pass. All he saw before them now was certain death.

Samyaza halted beside Jordi. "What are you waiting

for?" he screeched at the soldiers. "Take them alive!" His malignant glare landed on Miquel. "Leave Miquel for me."

Samyaza formed a sigil. Jordi's hands moved in tandem with the angel.

Nico is right. Samyaza is using Jordi. Diago riveted his attention on the glyph's lines. With its blunt edges and concussive sound, it was meant to stun.

Miquel reached into his pocket, retrieving a bottle of Pervitin. Popping several of the pills into his mouth, he swallowed and returned the angel's glare. A slow smiled spread over his mouth, chilling Diago to his bones.

The stamp of boots against the floor drew his attention to the advancing soldiers. The time had come to fight.

Diago strode forward. He shouted and whirled, throwing his scorpion to the floor.

The glyph shattered into a million scorpions that scuttled over the soldiers, crawling over their bodies in a relentless cyclone of motion. The Nationalists dropped their weapons and writhed beneath the scorpions' stings. Instead of venom, the arachnids injected acid into the nefilim's flesh. Smoke rose from the soldiers' bodies. Their howls careened off the walls as their flesh melted from their bones.

Samyaza and Jordi shielded themselves with protective sigils. The scorpions flowed around the pair. Neither the angel nor the generalissimo made any effort to aid their men.

Guillermo took the sounds of the soldiers' deaths and wound them into a glyph. He formed a ward made for fire and murder.

Rafael followed Diago's sigil with one of his own. The blinding flash of amber light turned into a golden snake with sparks flying off its scales. It struck the wall and slithered past Samyaza to envelope the soldiers still waiting there. The men jittered in place as if electrocuted.

"Quick! Before their reinforcements arrive!" Rafael pushed Diago toward another hall. "We've got to get to the tracks! I know the way!"

Diago maneuvered behind Miquel and grabbed Nico's arm. "Go," he hissed. "Get to the tracks with Rafael. We'll be right behind you."

Nico hesitated with a fearful glance toward Miquel, but Diago's husband remained fixated on Samyaza.

Jordi's eyes narrowed. "Nico! Get your ass over here now!"

The Italian made his decision. He backed away from the fury in Jordi's eyes and fled with Rafael.

Suddenly Samyaza ran at them with lightning speed. The angel's tin mask was gone. The lower half of his face hung to his chest, as if his jaw had come unhinged and he intended to swallow them all whole. He emitted a ferocious shriek. With his wizened claws outstretched, he lifted his sigil.

Miquel danced forward and whirled. His lips moved as he murmured a litany of names: "Vicente, Alejandra, Juan, Luciana, Remedios, Indalecio, Gaspar . . ."

Then he snatched a beam of light from the bulbs overhead. Molding the electricity between his palms, he fashioned a glyph and sang it to life. A shield rose between their group and Samyaza's ward. Miquel's sigil struck down the angel's concussive glyph and sent it back toward the angel.

Jordi fashioned a shield of his own. He raced in front of Samyaza and skidded to a halt, lifting the ward just in time to block Miquel's glyph. Though the veins in his neck stood out and his face turned as red as his hair, Jordi held the barrier.

Guillermo finished his ward. He sent the sigil forward,

where it burned with the fire of a thousand flamethrowers. The blaze scorched through the hall.

Jordi's glyph held firm, matching Guillermo's ward with angelic fire. The Grigori remained behind Jordi's shield, cowering from the scalding touch of Guillermo's song.

"Quick!" Diago motioned for them to follow Nico and Rafael. To his surprise, neither Guillermo nor Miquel argued.

Guillermo waited until Miquel was past them and fell into step beside Diago. "Did you see that?"

Diago nodded. His husband had just redirected an angel's ward. Only a king or queen of the Inner Guard possessed that kind of power, and even then only through the authority of their signet. "It's the Pervitin."

Yet again, he found himself thinking back to the gruesome choral room; the litany of heart attacks and psychoses that killed the young nefilim. He forced himself to stop thinking. "We'll treat him when we get to France." *We'll fix him. We will. We must.*

Guillermo nodded and broke into a jog. "Take the rear guard."

Diago fell back and turned once. The hall behind remained clear. When he faced forward again, he caught sight of Rafael running down a narrow passage with several wooden doors along the left wall. Nico followed him, with Miquel close on their heels.

As Guillermo drew parallel with the first door, it opened. Without pausing, Guillermo aimed his pistol at the surprised officer and shot him in the face.

Diago leapt over the fallen body and found another nefil blocking his path. He couldn't risk shooting—the bullet could pass through the soldier's body and hit Guillermo.

The assessment flew through Diago's mind in a flash, which was how quickly the other nefil was on him. The soldier had no weapon, but he attacked anyway, his fist narrowly missing Diago's face. Diago jabbed blindly with the rifle's stock. A lucky strike took the other nefil in the diaphragm, causing him to double over. Diago brought the stock up and into the soldier's chin. Three more strikes, and the nefil stopped breathing.

Looking up, Diago noted that no one pursued them, but from ahead, bursts of gunfire suddenly filled the passage. He straightened and tried to ignore the cold fear in his gut. Rafael was in the lead. Had he taken them into an ambush?

Passing the nefil he'd just killed, Diago found Guillermo engaged in close hand-to-hand combat with a third soldier. Their fast, violent blows left no opening for Diago to enter the fray.

Guillermo bent low and threw his weight against the other nefil, pushing him against the wall. He fired point-blank into the man's forearm. The nefil screamed and twisted, giving Guillermo a better target. The next bullet took the man between his eyes.

In the distance, the firefight slowed to sporadic pops. Guillermo moved cautiously. Diago followed with his heart pounding. He prepared himself for the worst.

No one emerged from the last door they passed. Behind them, the corridor remained clear.

The sound of four more shots reached them.

Then Miquel's voice: "You got him, osito!"

Diago's relief almost overwhelmed him. They were both alive.

The hall widened to reveal a platform. The bodies of five

Nationalists littered the concrete. Miquel disarmed a man and then used the pistol to finish off the mortally wounded soldier.

Nico ran out of an office and headed for the edge of the platform. He hesitated on the first step and looked back.

Rafael emerged next with the barrel of his rifle raised. He spun and lifted the stock to his shoulder when he heard Diago and Guillermo.

They skidded to a halt.

Rafael's pupils were dilated with fear. He slowly moved his finger off the trigger. "Papá?" he whispered through pale lips as he lowered the gun.

Christ, he came close to firing on us. "It's okay." Diago eased forward and glanced inside the office. A sergeant sprawled on the floor. Crawling over his dead eyes was a sigil with gunmetal-blue lines; a syringe protruded from his chest.

The song and drugs that killed the man belonged to Nico.

Diago joined Nico and checked the tracks in both directions. He saw no other sign of soldiers. Turning to the Italian, he said, "Good work."

Nico grimaced. "All I've done this day is murder. There is nothing good about that."

"You saved a boy's life. Don't lose sight of that. Because I won't." Diago lowered his voice. "And you're going to help me wean my husband off your drugs. Understand?"

Nico pressed his lips tight and nodded.

On the platform, Miquel shot another groaning soldier.

They all started at the pistol's crack.

The sound jettisoned them back into action. Guillermo grabbed Rafael's arm and rotated him toward the stairs. "Follow Nico!"

Diago tilted his head, and that was the only permission Nico needed to start running again.

Holding his position, Diago waited for Rafael and Guillermo to pass, and then he descended with Miquel covering their retreat.

Thirty meters down the tracks, they came to a junction.

Guillermo paused. "Where does that go?"

Nico slowed but didn't stop. "Barcelona."

Which was crawling with Nationalists by now.

"And the sigil leading into France?"

Rafael pointed down the tracks. "There. You can see the outline from here."

The glyph held the faint glow of red and gold. Complete darkness enveloped everything beyond the ward. Even the tracks disappeared.

Nico merely glanced at the sigil. "We'll never open it."

Undeterred by Nico's pessimism, Rafael led the way forward. "While you were talking to that doctor . . . Jimenez, I saw the choral unit inside the control room, and I heard them. I also remember the song Carlos used to open it from the French side."

Guillermo studied the lines. "Can you teach us?"

Rafael sang a note and gestured for Nico to join him.

Nico hesitated, but only for a second. Then he harmonized with Rafael. A glow of amber light strengthened around the edges of the glyph.

Nico stopped singing and the glyph faded. "We need more voices."

Miquel faced the distant platform and lifted his rifle. "We've got company."

"Guillermo!" Jordi's shout rolled down the tunnel.

They whirled, weapons raised.

Guillermo lifted his hand. "Hold your fire."

Jordi descended to the tracks. Samyaza came next. Several other soldiers hurried behind them, leaping to the tracks and taking up firing positions.

Diago counted twenty. More troops were certainly on their way.

This is going to be a massacre.

"Carlos?" Miquel aimed his rifle at one of the distant nefilim. "Carlos Vela, is that you? I'd know that shambling gait anywhere. You traitorous son of a bitch!"

Guillermo placed his hand on the barrel of Miquel's gun. "He's mine to judge."

Miquel's jaw worked, but he didn't shoot.

Diago whispered to Guillermo, "I've got a bead on Jordi if you can take Samyaza."

"And then his soldiers will open fire and send us into our next incarnation. Wait . . . He wants something. Let's see if we can make it work for us." Guillermo watched his brother.

Jordi walked forward, stretching forth empty hands. "Don't shoot, and my men will hold their fire." He strolled a few paces toward them and then paused in the center of the tracks. "A truce, my brother. You and me. We must speak of the future of the Inner Guard's Los Nefilim division. What do you say?"

Guillermo glared at his brother. "Give us a minute."

"I'll give you two." Jordi retreated ten meters.

Diago kept his bead on Jordi but monitored the other nefilim. They seemed to be in no hurry to start shooting. Given the skittishness of the forward guard, Diago guessed this group had passed their smoking comrades in the corridor above.

Guillermo kept his gaze locked on his brother as he muttered, "Anyone with a bright idea, it's your moment to shine."

Nico hissed, "Destroy Jordi's signet and you destroy Samyaza's power."

Diago murmured, "Samyaza's power, or Samyaza's power over Jordi?" Because those were two very distinct things.

"Both," Nico replied. "The angel is crippled. He cannot sing his spells unless he commands another nefil's song. While he can do it with any nefil that lets Samyaza into his mind, his relationship with Jordi is different. Samyaza is seeded in Jordi's mind through the tear."

Diago thought back to Nico's description of the wasp and the spider. "It's a symbiotic relationship."

"Exactly," Nico whispered. "Take out the tear, and you've shattered the link between them."

Guillermo nodded. "Okay. Rafael, Nico, and Miquel, you work on opening that portal. Diago, can you give them the cover of darkness?"

Diago glanced at the impregnable void behind them. "Leave it to me."

Guillermo lowered his voice. "Get to work while I stall Jordi. I'll buy us as much time as I can."

While Rafael, Miquel, and Nico gathered near the glyph, Diago shouldered his rifle. He snatched a handful of black and turned to assess the soldiers.

The Pervitin left them susceptible to psychoses, which bred hallucinations. And what better weapon to wield against them than the terrors within their own minds?

Shaping the first note of his song, he massaged the shadows between his palms and nurtured his dark emotions. Soon Jordi's men would remember why the daimons were feared.

[22]

Rafael turned to his father and Nico, noting the Italian's nervousness. Recalling his papá's notes on the Key, the angelic song that shifted the realms, he suddenly realized what he needed to do.

The Key is about the angels' exile, their anguish at leaving their home, and their desire to return. To open the realms, they needed to depend on one another. Each angel had to carry their part to perfection, and if one faltered, then another had to lend their strength. *It's about trust. We must trust one another . . . help one another . . .*

"Stand on my right, Nico." That gave the Italian some distance from Miquel. Turning his attention to his father, he whispered, "And stop scaring him. We've got to work together."

Miquel glanced at the soldiers gathering on the platform. "Okay." He met Nico's gaze. "You did good back there. A truce."

The Italian nodded, and to Rafael's relief, he relaxed

somewhat. *As relaxed as we can be standing at death's door.*
Turning his back to Don Guillermo and the soldiers, Rafael
faced the portal sigil.

Singing the first note, he led them through the scales, testing their range. As he did, he recalled his dream.

Miquel gave him the secret: *Your voice is the key to all
your power. Move the breath of darkness from your diaphragm up through your throat and into your song.*

"This is it," Rafael sang as he watched their faces. "On
three . . ." He counted off and they joined their song with his.

Encouraged by the approval in Miquel's eyes, Rafael
gestured for Nico to carry the higher notes while he joined
Miquel in forming the bass. Leading them into the piece bel
canto, Rafael guided them through the song without words,
without emotion, to simply create the sound necessary to
vibrate the glyph's threads.

Nico's gaze moved away from Rafael and to the soldiers
at the platform. His voice cracked with his fear. The light
around the glyph dimmed.

Rafael smoothly shifted his range from his chest to his
head to reach the higher registers. He lifted his hand and at-
tracted Nico's attention. When the other nefil locked gazes
with Rafael, he found his way into their song again. Rafael
smiled and nodded, rolling his voice back down to a deeper
pitch.

The lines of the glyph strengthened and shimmered with
veins of gold and red. The abyss beyond the glyph lightened . . .
black became gray and gray became white.

A shadow moved just past the sigil. Rafael recognized the
shape of Ysa and, beside her, Violeta. *But they're not there.*

That's just my wish. I just wish they'd come and save us. But it's up to us to save ourselves.

Closing his eyes, he focused entirely on their small chorus.

Ysabel watched her mother and Cyrille test the sigil's lines with various tones. They probed it carefully, as one would a bomb.

Rousseau lit a cigarette and offered it to Ysa. "Try and relax. They're going as fast as they dare."

Declining the cigarette, she merely whispered, "I know." If they forced their song on the ward, they risked snapping it and trapping Rafael in that portal realm.

Beside her, Violeta folded her arms across her chest and glared at the sigil as if she could pry it open by sheer willpower alone. When she noticed Ysa looking at her, she winked and mouthed, *All for one.*

Ysa gave her a brave smile and then returned her attention to the angels.

One of Rousseau's guards whistled a warning. Someone was coming. They turned as one to see Suero loping toward them. He carried a map under one arm.

"I found where the coordinates lead." Breathless from his run, he squatted on the ground and spread the paper on the boards. They gathered around and shone their torches on the map. "Here." He jabbed a spot deep in the Pyrenees. "There is an old fort in this pass."

Rousseau looked up. "Charles, what time is it?"

A short, surly nefil who looked quite at home in the tunnels stepped forward smartly. "Four, madame."

"Cyrille?" Rousseau called to her angelic companion. "Any progress?"

The angel shook her head. "The sigil must be operated from both sides simultaneously."

"Shit." Rousseau tossed her cigarette to the boards and crushed it beneath her boot. "The mortals will be arriving for their shifts soon. We're going to have to break off until tonight. Charles, station a guard on that glyph."

"I'll stay, too," Ysa said.

Juanita turned and said sharply, "You're needed above-ground."

"I'm needed here."

Rousseau said gently, "You're no good to your people if you're not rested. Cyrille will stay and watch over the glyph."

Violeta stepped forward. "I'll stay, too." After a sharp glare from Juanita, she added, "With your permission, of course, mademoiselle."

Ysa touched Violeta's arm. "Yes. Yes, I want you here. Report to me immediately if there is any change."

Violeta bowed her head. "I'll be your eyes and watch for him."

Juanita's gaze flickered from one to the other, but she raised no objection to the arrangement.

Ysa shut off her torch. It was no use arguing. Both her mother and Rousseau were right. Yet their reasoning did nothing to negate the feeling that she was somehow abandoning Rafael.

As they gathered their things, Ysa turned back to the sigil one last time. The edges seemed brighter. Frowning, she walked toward the ward.

Juanita's head snapped up. "Stay back, Ysa."

"Look at it," Ysa whispered. "It's brighter."

The clatter of tools diminished as the nefilim turned to look.

Violeta rushed to Ysa's side. "Listen to your mamá and stay back. If it becomes active, it might take you."

"Hush." Ysa gestured for silence. She heard the distinct sound of Rafael's voice. It was distant . . . *Like a radio turned down low. And he's singing.* "Everyone, be quiet."

Juanita shook her head. "Ysa, I know you want to find a way to Rafael, but there's nothing—"

"Wait." Cyrille cocked her head and lifted her hand. "She's right."

Ysa moved closer to the glyph. Red and gold flames shimmered along the edges. A bright flash temporarily blinded them all. When Ysa opened her eyes again, Violeta stood between her and the sigil, a protective ward already formed by her quick hands.

Blinking against the images floating over her retinas, Ysa looked past her friend to see figures on the other side of the ward. They stood in a loose semicircle.

Rafael, Miquel, and an unfamiliar nefil raised their voices together. Beyond them was Diago and her father. Ysa would know their stances anywhere. They faced someone in the distance.

"It's them!" she shouted.

Juanita's eyes went wide. She reached out to touch the glyph.

Cyrille grasped her wrist. "Easy, my sister. You've been too long in your mortal form and you forget yourself." She switched to the angelic language.

A tear slipped over Juanita's lashes as the angels trilled to one another.

She misses Papá. The thought took Ysa by surprise. All these long months and days, and she never considered that her angelic mother might suffer from the mortal affliction of love.

Cyrille smiled and brushed the tear from Juanita's cheek. "Come close, everyone, and do exactly as I say."

Juanita turned, and Ysabel felt a thrill go through her at the sight of hope on her mother's face.

Violeta watched the glyph with shining eyes. It was only then that Ysa realized Carme wasn't on the other side.

Guillermo listened as Rafael led them through the chant twice. Not since Metatron had a nefil exhibited such range. *If we can get him out of here and fully trained, none will ever stand against Los Nefilim again.*

Jordi checked his watch. "Two minutes are up, Guillermo."

Nodding, Guillermo stepped forward three paces. Diago moved so that he remained two steps ahead of Guillermo. Jordi approached until only ten paces separated them.

From the corner of his eye, Guillermo saw Diago blow into his cupped palms. He knelt and poured darkness onto the tracks. Gravel jittered and danced and took a life of its own. Millions of glittering scorpions formed a blue-black wave of sound.

Jordi scowled at Diago. "Call off your daimon."

Guillermo motioned to Diago, who rose and bowed his head.

"As long as your troops don't move, nothing bad will happen to them," Diago said.

"They'll follow orders," Jordi snapped.

"And so will Diago." Guillermo evaluated the situation.

The soldiers might still fill the tunnel with gunfire, hoping to score a random hit, but in doing so, they stood a good chance of striking Jordi, too. *And Samyaza won't let that happen. The wasp needs his spider.*

Guillermo glanced at Jordi's finger, where the Grigori's tear churned in shades of pale green and umber, and then up into his brother's eyes. It seemed as if a film covered his irises, deep and sickly green, which was the same shade as the tear in Jordi's ring.

In the distance, Samyaza seemed content to wait by the platform. *Probably because he can hear every word through Jordi.*

Reaching into his pocket, Guillermo found his lighter. He touched the metal and warmed it with his flesh. Juanita had given it to him on one of their many anniversaries. She'd inscribed it with sigils for wisdom. Whenever he felt the need to make a decision of import, he held on to it; although the glyphs carved in the metal were symbols only. Any wisdom came from him and no one else.

And right now, I'm not sure if what I'm about to do is wise at all. Gripping the lighter in his left hand, he waited for his brother's first move. "You wanted to parley. Talk."

Jordi tilted his head as if listening to a voice only he could hear. "Send Rafael to me." Though he spoke to Guillermo, he watched Diago's reaction.

What mad game is he playing now? "What?"

"He swore himself to me." Jordi lifted his hand, and the Grigori's tear pulsed. "He touched his lips to my ring and took an oath. He's mine."

Guillermo gestured at the portal sigil without turning. "He's busy right now."

To his surprise, Jordi laughed. "Do you think that boy can save you? Let them try. Rafael is talented, but the song that controls the glyph is complex. He'll never work through it in time. You're going nowhere, Guillermo. Hand him over."

"I don't think so."

Jordi's humor was short-lived. A scowl returned to his features, and he growled, "The boy swore that he would submit himself to me in exchange for the life of his father, Miquel de Torrellas."

Cupping the lighter, Guillermo flicked the lid once. Then he used his thumb to begin the first lines of a sigil on the metal's flank. "That sounds like an oath taken under duress."

"It's not yours to judge."

"Of course it's mine to judge. I'm still the king of Los Nefilim."

The comment had its intended effect. Rage surged through Jordi's irises.

Keep him off balance. "And that's something we need to talk about . . . judgment and our firstborn lives." He held his breath and watched uncertainty flit across his brother's countenance.

In the distance, Samyaza edged forward.

Piqued his interest, too.

Jordi shrugged. "You had me murdered, Guillermo."

"I gave you every chance, Jordi, every chance to accept our father's decree—" Guillermo added more lines to the glyph on the lighter's body. He needed his brother to speak so he could wind the vibrations of Jordi's voice into the sigil.

"You stole my birthright and then you wanted me to accept it? And when I protested, you sent your swordsman to do your dirty work. I don't know what you want, Guillermo. My blessing?"

That wasn't exactly how it had happened. Adonijah didn't protest. Rather, he'd tried several machinations to force his way onto Solomon's throne.

It didn't matter. *That's how Jordi remembers it, and the truth is I didn't* have *to order his death.* But he couldn't undo the past, and if he wanted to stop the killing in the present, he had to find some way into his brother's heart. *One of us has to back down.* "I'd do my firstborn life so much differently if I could, but I can't, Jordi. I can't. You're not Adonijah anymore. I am not Solomon. The past is dead."

"No!" Jordi took a single lurching step forward. "The past lives on and on and on, because we cannot escape it. Everything you did, I remember . . ."

"Remember, yes!" Guillermo roared back at him. He inhaled and traced another sigil on the lighter. Lowering his voice, he whispered, "But can you forgive?"

Jordi froze. "What?"

"Forgive me? Can you forgive me?" Guillermo held his breath. *Because I want this. I started over with Miquel, and then Diago. I won them back to my side. If I can win Jordi's trust, then maybe these terrible wars will end.*

He traced another line on his lighter and connected the glyph's symbols. Running the pad of his thumb over the ridges, he hoped he had enough. *It will have to be.* "Please, just think about it."

Jordi tilted his head. "Are you saying you're wrong?"

"I'm saying that I was wrong to have you murdered." Guillermo shifted his position. From the corner of his eye, he saw the portal hadn't opened, but the door seemed to be cracked. Glittering lines flashed. A surge of golden light enveloped the ward. *Almost like the one Diago and I entered.*

Beyond the glyph, the darkness faded. A shape moved.

Are my eyes playing tricks on me? Guillermo frowned.

As Rafael led them through the chant, the sigil paled and Guillermo clearly saw someone moving on the other side. He recognized the shape of his daughter. *Oh, Ysa, my sweet Ysa.*

Aching to feel his family in his arms again, he almost didn't hear Jordi when he asked, "And my birthright?"

Turning back to his brother, Guillermo exhaled slowly. *Careful, now, or you'll never hold them again . . .* "In my firstborn life, when I was Solomon, I was wrong about many things."

Jordi spat in disgust. "Obfuscation! You talk in circles and say nothing! You haven't changed."

"That's not true!"

In the distance, Samyaza must have noticed Rafael's progress on the ward. He formed the first line of a sigil. Simultaneously, Jordi's hand rose and fell, mirroring the angel's movement.

Snipers moved into position. One aimed his rifle at Rafael.

Diago moved between the shooter and his son. Spreading his fingers, he grabbed a handful of shadows and began another spell.

I'm out of time. Guillermo swallowed hard.

Jordi smiled and showed no signs of resisting Samyaza's control. His voice dropped low, barely audible beneath the sound of Rafael's song. "Then give me the ring, Guillermo. If you're sincere, hand over the signet." He traced the next line of the glyph in tandem with the Grigori.

With his hope sinking, Guillermo realized his brother didn't struggle against the angel's influence. "I'm sincere, Jordi. With all my heart, I want to make peace between us." Guillermo passed his left hand over his right and pretended to remove the signet. "I'm so sorry." He tossed the lighter.

Jordi instinctively caught it before he realized that it wasn't the ring.

With a shout, Guillermo clapped his hands and activated the glyph.

The lighter exploded in Jordi's fist.

Jordi's signet, still on his severed finger, landed at Guillermo's feet. Guillermo brought his boot down on the ring, crushing the tear beneath his heel.

Jordi screamed and bent double, cupping one bloodied hand with the other. Before Guillermo could stop himself, he took a step forward, reaching out to his brother.

Jordi's head snapped up. The fury in his eyes slapped Guillermo like a blow.

His brother wept tears of pale green and umber. Vomit spewed through his lips as Samyaza's poisoned magic left his body. He gasped. "What have you done?"

Guillermo looked up. Samyaza lurched forward.

The troops by the platform lifted their weapons. The snipers fired.

Diago gave a terrible scream and flung the shadows into the air. As Guillermo watched, the darkness turned into a wave of scorpions, rising to catch the bullets destined for their small group. The cloud slowed most of the projectiles and dragged them to the tracks.

Diago's head whipped to one side. A thin line of blood appeared on his cheek.

Grazed him. Lucky bastard, Guillermo thought wildly as another bullet snapped by his ear.

More shots seeped through Diago's barrier, puffing the dust around them, ricocheting off the tunnel walls.

Diago spun in a circle. His aura deepened, pulsating in midnight hues. Then he stamped his heel against the ground. A spark of green fire ignited a second wave of the scorpions, bringing them to life. He sent them surging toward the platform with an ominous growl.

Threads of silver and gold snapped like lightning through the cyclone of scorpions. The click of claws filled the tunnel. The arachnids skittered over the soldiers, crawling into their ears.

Some of the men ran screaming. Others cowered and wept. A few formed protective sigils and stood their ground.

"What did you do?" Guillermo shouted over the cacophony of gunfire and screams.

"I sent them their worst fears," Diago replied. He pointed at the advancing Grigori. "But that I cannot stop."

Samyaza, undaunted by the cresting scorpions, continued to run toward Jordi.

No, he's mine. Guillermo returned his attention to his brother, meeting Jordi's glare. "I know you're angry! But think about this: I could have killed you. Instead, I've freed you. I'm sincere. I want your forgiveness. And to prove it, I'll make sure the Grigori doesn't take hold of your mind again."

Without waiting for Jordi to respond, Guillermo traced a blazing glyph, like the one he'd used in the corridor above. Made more vibrant by the Thrones' tear in his signet, sparks flew from his fingertips. He charged the ward with his voice and flung it at the advancing Grigori.

Helpless without Jordi's voice to shield him, Samyaza skidded to a halt when he saw Guillermo's sigil flying at him. Whirling, he fled back toward the platform.

Terrified soldiers clogged the stairs, blocking the angel's path. The flames engulfed both the angel and the nefilim. The Grigori writhed and danced across the tracks. Shrieks filled the passage and almost drowned Rafael's song.

Guillermo reached out for Jordi one last time. "We will talk again, brother! In better times! Watch for me!"

Jordi made no answer.

Red and gold light suddenly flooded the tunnel. Guillermo glimpsed Diago running toward him. Though he was smaller, Diago hit Guillermo low, around his hips. His forward motion carried them toward the flaring sigil.

The last thing Guillermo saw was his brother, rising and running back toward the platform, where his angel burned.

[23]

The colors swept over them, carrying them through the portal. Diago's tackle sent them both to the ground. Guillermo landed on his back. Diago skidded beside him. Carme's notebook fell from his pocket and landed on the tracks.

The world gradually stabilized around them. They were still in a tunnel, except this one was more brightly lit. Excited voices rang through the passage.

French. Diago's stunned mind sifted through the language. *They're speaking French*.

Guillermo stood and helped Diago to his feet. "Okay?"

Diago nodded as he staggered to one side, looking for Miquel and his son. He found them a few meters away.

Rafael struggled to hold Miquel upright. He'd looped Miquel's arm over his shoulder, and Diago could tell by the way Miquel leaned on their son that he was in trouble. Nico reached out, but Miquel knocked the Italian's hand aside. Rafael staggered under his father's weight.

"Let him help!" Diago shoved past two nefilim he didn't recognize.

Miquel looked up at the sound of Diago's voice and smiled, but his face was ashen.

Diago reached them. Draping Miquel's arm over his shoulder, he took his husband's weight. As he did, Miquel whispered in his ear, "I lost my ring, I'm sorry, I'm so sorry, my bright star, I lost my ring and my nefilim and now my heart . . ."

"It's all right." Diago held his husband. "Just hold on, hold on, hold on . . ."

Miquel sagged in their arms. They eased him to the tracks as gently as they could.

Rafael kept his hand behind Miquel's head. "Papá? What's wrong with him?"

"I don't know." Diago lifted his head. "Is Juanita here?" He shouted in Castilian, and then Catalan, before he called once more in French. "Please! Someone find her!" Then he returned his attention to his husband. "Miquel? Miquel, wake up. We're here. We did it. Come on, wake up."

Miquel didn't answer. His skin was icy.

He's too cold. Diago took off his coat and covered his husband.

Nico came to his side. "The Pervitin . . . it weakens the heart. We've got to get him to a hospital."

Rousseau shouted, "Someone get me a stretcher. Charles, we need a train to get everyone out of this tunnel, and then arrange for cars on the surface. Make one of them an ambulance."

Guillermo pushed through the crowd. "What's wrong?"

Cool hands gripped Diago's shoulders and Juanita was suddenly there. "Let me see him."

Diago rose and backed away. Although he was terrified of the answer, he asked, "Can you help him? Like you did me? Can you?"

"Quiet, now," Guillermo murmured as he touched Miquel's brow. "Stand back." He positioned his hands on either side of Miquel's face and bowed his head until their brows touched.

Rafael came to Diago's side. Diago held him close and prayed, but not to any god. He silently urged his friend to save his husband. In their firstborn lives, Solomon had caused their deaths, but now Guillermo stood a chance to save them. *So take him to your river of fire, please, take him and bring him back, because he is my heart.*

A soft glow suffused the trio. Juanita kept her hands on both Guillermo and Miquel. The light grew brighter . . .

Suddenly Miquel sputtered and coughed as if surfacing from a deep dive. The terror constricting in Diago's chest loosened. Beside him, Rafael gave a soft sob.

Guillermo leaned back on his heels, his own face pale, his freckles stark across his nose.

Juanita stroked Miquel's hair and smiled at him. "There. Your family is waiting for you." She kissed his mouth and gave him her breath. Then she rose so they could join him again.

Diago knelt at Miquel's side as Rafael removed his coat and folded it. He lifted his father's head and placed the makeshift pillow beneath him.

Miquel tried to rise. "Did we make it?"

"Yes," Rafael whispered. "Just lie still and relax. We're safe."

Remembering the notebook, Diago looked for it on the tracks. The book was gone.

Ysa saw Violeta reach for something on the tracks. When the young nefil stood, tears spilled over her lashes and struck the tattered notebook in her hands.

Ysa hurried to her side. "What is it, Violeta?"

Scrubbing her cheeks angrily, Violeta sniffed and met Ysa's gaze. "My mamá . . ." She held the notebook like an offering. "My mamá . . ."

Ysa recognized the book. *Carme never let that notebook out of her sight.* Cold with the realization of Carme's death, Ysa embraced her friend. Violeta folded with her grief, taking them to their knees together.

When Ysa heard Miquel gasp for air, she turned in time to see her own mamá and papá rise. *I'm so lucky.* She rocked Violeta but offered her no platitudes.

Guillermo's smile faltered when he noticed the book in Violeta's hands. Still pallid from his own exertion, he came to their side and knelt beside them.

"This isn't how I wanted you to find out," he murmured to her. "Your mamá was one of the bravest nefilim I've ever had the honor of commanding. And because she gave her life for Los Nefilim, my debt to her is great. You will live in my household until you are ready to find your own way. Do you understand me, Violeta?"

Violeta nodded and struggled for control. "We will sing for her?"

"Of course we will sing for her. We will watch for her." He reached out and stroked Ysa's hair. "Can you take her home, Ysa?"

His heart is so great, it might shatter one day. "I will."

"Good. Good. We'll be there soon. Take care of that notebook, Violeta. Your song will be as great as hers." He saluted her. "Capitán."

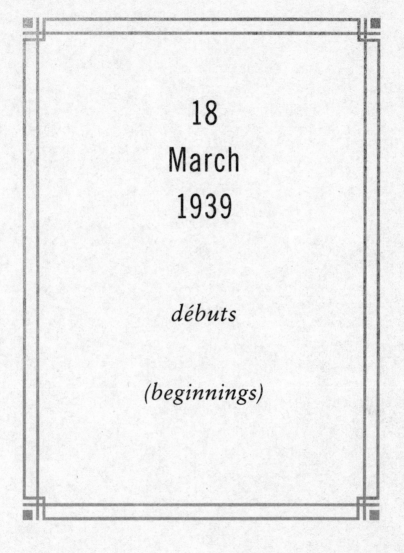

18
March
1939

débuts

(beginnings)

[24]

Only a few people moved through the Pigalle at dawn. The great clubs stood silent and shuttered against the day's gray light.

Miquel refused to stay in bed. Although he was still too pale and thin, he insisted on accompanying Rafael to his hearing. Diago didn't have the heart to deny either of them the comfort of each other's presence, so he hired a cab to take them to the Bal Tabarin.

Rafael rode with Miquel in the back seat, looking out the window apprehensively. He twisted his ring and glanced at his father anytime he moved.

As the cab drifted to the curb, three nefilim emerged from the nightclub. Two flanked the door while the third approached their car. The tall, reedy nefil with angular cheekbones and milky skin was none other than Jean Marchand, Rousseau's second-in-command. His well-fitted black suit did little to hide the pistol strapped to his shoulder holster.

And that is deliberate, Diago thought as he paid the fare. The gun and the reception underlined the severity of the situation.

Diago glanced at his family. He hoped Rafael was paying attention. To his relief, he noted that his son's mouth was tight as he helped Miquel to the sidewalk and gave him his cane.

He needs to know this is no game. Diago exited the car and went to Rafael. He adjusted his son's tie. "You go in, you tell the truth, and if they decide you must be reprimanded, you take your punishment, and just move on."

Rafael nodded. "I love you, Papá."

"We're not saying goodbye." Diago kissed his cheeks nonetheless.

Miquel stood on the curb and nodded to the French nefil. "Jean."

"Miquel, it's good to see you."

"Likewise."

Rafael went to Miquel, who winked at him and indicated that he should go inside. "Don't make them wait on you."

Rafael squeezed Miquel's hand as he passed.

When he reached the door, the two nefilim fell into step on either side of the youth. Jean waited for Diago and Miquel to enter before he followed them inside.

The immense ballroom was dimly lit and possessed a different kind of magic from the kind that graced its halls during the night. The long tongue of the stage held no dancers, but instead a table that was occupied by Rousseau and Guillermo, who were both busy reading files. Cyrille and Juanita stood behind their respective partners. A plump young woman with chestnut hair and lively eyes sat next to

Rousseau with a pad and pen ready to take notes. Suero kept his place near Guillermo.

On the floor in front of the stage, Guillermo's sigil for Los Nefilim glowed against the burnished wood beside Rousseau's glyph for Les Néphilim. The linked edges of the wards symbolized that, while both remained independent, they worked together for the common good of the Inner Guard.

At a nearby table, Nico sat alone with two of Guillermo's nefilim behind him. He wore a borrowed suit that was slightly too big for him. After a nervous glance at Miquel, he lowered his eyes again.

Just beyond him, Ysa sat with a dour French nefil in a rumpled suit. She pretended not to notice Rafael. Her expression told Diago that she was still piqued with Rafael. Guillermo hadn't reprimanded her, but like her father, Ysa hated making mistakes. She saw them as a reflection on her own abilities.

Rafael's guards escorted him to Nico's table. Rafael, for his part, pointedly didn't look Ysa's way. Diago knew his son still hadn't forgiven her for not supporting his request to help find Miquel.

Both of them are full of pride, just like we used to be before the world taught us to treat each other more kindly. He put his palm on Miquel's back, not so much to steady him, but because he simply wanted the comfort of touching him.

Jean cleared his throat and announced them.

Juanita looked up, her gaze going straight to Rafael, who possessed enough grace and humility to bow, first to her and then to Cyrille. He didn't take his seat until Guillermo acknowledged him and told him to sit.

The move seemed to mollify Juanita, though Diago knew

she wasn't pleased with the rash decisions that led his son on his adventure. Then she turned her attention to Miquel. Another wave of displeasure washed over her countenance at his presence today. Though she pursed her lips, she said nothing to embarrass him.

At least now she can see where Rafael learned the art of insubordination.

Guillermo, on the other hand, had no problem shaming his second-in-command for attending the hearing. "Suero, would you please bring a chair for Monsieur de Torrellas, who should have kept to his bed this morning?"

Suero was moving before Guillermo completed the command. He quickly took a chair from one of the tables and offered it to Miquel. Rather than protest, Miquel sat.

Diago put his hand on his husband's shoulder, noting the rapid rise and fall of Miquel's chest. *He's overexerting himself.* All he could do was hope that Miquel's condition might speed the proceedings.

That prospect was dashed when Suero called Nico forward first. He indicated that the Italian was to stand in the center of Guillermo's sigil.

Miquel stiffened. Diago gave his shoulder a warning squeeze. *Easy.*

Guillermo opened a file. "Nico Bianchi, you are here to swear an oath to Los Nefilim and the Inner Guard, that you will honor and obey me as king for the rest of your life in this incarnation."

Nico's mouth dropped open. "You said I only had to serve until the war was over."

Guillermo met his gaze evenly. "No. That's what you heard. No one ever walks away from the Inner Guard. We cannot take the chance that you will sell our secrets to our enemies. Once you take the oath, it's for the rest of your life in this incarnation."

Nico looked physically ill.

A slow smile spread across Miquel's mouth. He was enjoying Nico's discomfort entirely too much.

The Italian's aura popped in shades of gray and blue. Guillermo's sigil burned hotter around him.

Breathing rapidly, Nico made a visible attempt to get himself under control. "And if I refuse?"

"Then you remain a rogue. And I put a price on your head for the murders of my nefilim. You will be hunted for all the days of your life, in this incarnation and all that follow."

The weight of Guillermo's pronouncement caused Nico to stagger. He wandered to the edge of Guillermo's glyph as if he might step over the line and attempt to flee.

They'll cut him down if he does. Diago lifted his hand.

Nico halted, teetering on the edge of that fiery sigil, and locked gazes with Diago.

Careful to keep his expression neutral, Diago lowered his hand and waited. Whatever decision came next had to come from Nico.

The silence stretched through the cavernous room. They all knew Jordi's men hunted the Italian. Add Guillermo's nefilim into the mix, along with any rogue who wanted to cash in on the bounty, and Nico wouldn't survive a week on his own.

They all knew it—no one more acutely than Nico. He turned a slow circle, gauging the expression of each person in the room before he faced Guillermo once more. "Then I have no choice."

Miquel gripped his cane. "You always have choices, Nico."

Diago muttered through clenched teeth, "Don't be an ass-hole."

Miquel took the hint and quieted, but his smile didn't fade.

Nico shot Miquel a dark look worthy of Diago himself. Straightening his tie, the Italian paused for another moment and gathered his thoughts. When he spoke, his voice was even and the colors of his aura calmed. "By all rights, you should put me to death, but you honor your word by giving me a place in Los Nefilim. I accept your proposal and the generosity with which it is given. I offer myself"—his voice broke, but he recovered himself quickly—"to the Inner Guard and will take an oath to serve."

Guillermo rewarded the speech with a curt nod. "Does anyone object to Nico Bianchi taking an oath to Los Nefilim?"

Miquel rapped the tip of his cane against the floor. "I do."

"Noted. Do you wish to speak?"

"I'll say what I have to say during his oath-taking ceremony."

Guillermo exhaled a resigned sigh. "Of course you will. Nico, I will formally take your oath in a fortnight. Meanwhile, Diago will help you prepare."

Diago ignored his husband's sharp stare. Miquel never needed to know that Diago had asked Guillermo to make that assignment. Being Nico's handler meant Diago would oversee Nico's every move, and Diago's close proximity to Miquel gave Nico added incentive to quickly find a cure for Miquel's withdrawal symptoms.

Diago bowed his head. "As you will, Don Guillermo."

Guillermo leaned over and conferred in whispers with Rousseau. When he finished, she said, "That can be arranged."

"Excellent." Shifting his attention back to Nico, Guillermo said, "While you're waiting to formally take an oath to Los Nefilim, you will brief our chief intelligence officers, Sofia Corvo and Lise Fourcade, regarding the Pervitin experiments you conducted for Jordi Abelló and Ilsa Jaeger."

Nico hesitated. "I . . . it's not that I don't want to help. Please don't misunderstand. But I don't have my papers, my notes . . ."

Rousseau appraised him coldly. "You have your memory, monsieur. We need to know everything in order to help the mortals against the Nazi threat, and to protect our own nefilim. Abelló and Jaeger are creating an army of berserkers. We must know what we're dealing with."

Nico rubbed his forehead and glanced at Diago.

Diago gave him the only thing he could: an almost imperceptible nod.

Turning back to Rousseau and Guillermo, Nico bowed his head. "I'll tell you everything I know."

"Good. See? That wasn't so hard." Guillermo's sigil flared once before returning to its soft glow. He gestured to his nefilim. "Escort him back to his apartment." Pointing to the taller nefil, he said, "Alfonse, make arrangements with Mademoiselles Corvo and Fourcade to meet with Monsieur Bianchi. Keep him under close guard for his own safety."

Alfonse snapped a closed-fist salute to Guillermo and gestured for Nico to follow. When the door shut behind them, Suero stepped forward and called Rafael's name.

Rafael rose and took his place within the wards. He stood in the center of Guillermo's sigil.

Rousseau closed the file in front of her and looked at Rafael. "State your name."

Rafael stood with his back straight. "Rafael Diaz de Triana."

"Very good, Monsieur Diaz. Do you understand why you are here?"

He bowed his head to her. "To answer accusations that I sang a mortal to his death."

Guillermo reached into his pocket and withdrew a lighter. Unlike his old one, this one was shiny with the engravings for wisdom sharp and bright.

All ready for new decisions.

Guillermo flicked the lid, one soft click after another. "Tell us what happened on the morning of 15 February 1939."

Rafael recounted the day, pausing only to answer Rousseau's questions. His voice remained strong and his aura pulsed in soothing shades of amber and green. As Rafael spoke, Diago found himself suffering from both sadness and pride. He missed the child who used to touch him so hesitantly and talk himself to sleep each night.

But Miquel and I must have done something right. Because a self-assured young man replaced that shy child, and it was wonderful to see.

When Rafael finished testifying, Rousseau nodded. "Monsieur Ramírez, do you have anything to add or ask?"

"I'm satisfied."

But then again, Guillermo had been from the beginning, going out of his way to reassure Rafael that the entire proceeding was to soothe grumblings from within Les Néphilim.

Rousseau turned to the nefil in the rumpled suit. "Inspector Bisset?"

He stood and bowed. "I, too, am satisfied, madame. Diaz's account is consistent with my findings. The mortal pursued him of his own volition."

Rafael glanced their way and winked.

Oh, he thinks he has gotten away with something. Neither Diago nor Miquel smiled back.

Unsettled by their lack of jubilance over what he clearly saw as his vindication, Rafael turned back to Rousseau.

She made a notation in her file. "Then we move to the matter of restitution for the mortal's death. Monsieur Ramírez?"

Guillermo's demeanor turned grave. "As I'm sure you heard, Los Nefilim is now responsible for reimbursing Monsieur Pierre Loutrel for the loss of his . . . employee, for lack of a better word. I think you should bear some of the burden for those costs, Monsieur Diaz. Therefore, we will be docking twenty-five percent of your pay until such a time as you have compensated Los Nefilim for your error in judgment that day."

Rafael's mouth dropped open. He glanced at Miquel and Diago. Miquel signaled to him that he was to accept the conditions.

To his credit, Rafael gritted his teeth and bowed his head. "Of course, Don Guillermo."

"Very well, then." Rousseau nodded to Jean. "Do we have any other business before us today?"

Jean stepped forward. "No, madame, that is all."

"Excellent! We stand adjourned." With a flick of her wrist, Rousseau extinguished her sigil.

Guillermo did the same.

Rising, she stretched. "I'm famished. Juanita? Guillermo? Will you have breakfast with us?"

"Of course." He pocketed his lighter and stood. "Rafael, we will see you tonight."

Rafael bowed his head again before turning his back on Ysa and walking to stand before his fathers. "Are we ready to go home?"

Miquel remained seated. "You should go thank Inspector Bisset for his thorough investigation."

Rafael glanced toward the inspector, who chatted with Ysa. "I can thank him later. We should get you home."

Miquel made no effort to rise. "Now. And while you're over there, speak to Ysa."

Rafael lowered his voice. "She's the reason for my poverty. She was mad that Loutrel wanted twenty-five percent of the take from the cabaret, so she had her papá take it out of my pocket."

Diago motioned for Rafael to draw close. *He's a man, yes, but there's still a bit of the boy left.* Sternly, he said, "You have received a very light sentence. This hearing could have resulted in expulsion from Paris, or even France, for you. What you did was wrong."

"But everything came out all right."

"That is not the point."

"Your papá is right." Miquel nodded. "And there is a huge difference between twenty-five percent of a cabaret's income and your meager salary. So go thank the inspector and make up with Ysa; however you see fit to do so."

Rafael opened his mouth for a rebuttal, but Miquel cut him off before he could begin. "This conversation is over."

With an exasperated sigh, Rafael turned. Diago, though, had had enough of his petulance.

"Rafael."

Sullenly, Rafael turned around. "Yes, Papá?"

"If you want to be treated like an adult, then you need to act like one. There is no shame in making a mistake. Learn from it. And be responsible enough to admit your error. Then I will believe you have matured."

Rafael glanced at Ysa. "She'll think less of me."

"You might find that she'll respect you more."

Rafael twisted his ring and considered the situation. "Okay. I'll try it your way. But if you're wrong . . ."

"I'm not wrong." He gave his son a gentle nudge. "Now go, make amends and earn back her trust."

Squaring his shoulders, Rafael walked over to the pair and waited for the inspector to finish his conversation with Ysa.

Miquel watched them carefully. "They have to get past this. These little digs begin early and escalate fast. I don't want them to waste their firstborn lives like we did. If I could go back . . ."

"You can't. Even in your heart, you cannot go back and change it." *Neither you, nor Guillermo.* "All we can do is move forward."

"Even so, we can use our bad experience to help them." Miquel nodded at Rafael, who had managed to work his way into the conversation.

When Rafael finished speaking to the inspector, Ysa touched his arm and drew him aside. As they watched, the tension eased between the youngsters. After a few more words, Rafael returned to them.

"Ysa has gone to get Suero. He's going to drive you home."

Diago raised an eyebrow. "Aren't you coming?"

"If it's okay with you, Ysa has invited me to breakfast with her and Violeta, and I'd like to go. For Violeta's sake, you know."

"Of course. For Violeta," Miquel teased. "I suppose I can take care of your papá until you get home."

"Give Violeta our love." Diago slipped his son a few francs. "Go and be good to each other."

Rafael pocketed the money and saluted them.

Miquel returned the salute with a faint smile.

Diago merely lifted his hand. He, for one, was glad to return to civilian life. *For now.*

[25]

PLAZA DE CATALUÑA
HOTEL COLÓN
BARCELONA, SPAIN

Safely ensconced in the haze of morphine, Jordi watched Dr. Jimenez unwrap the bandages on his right hand. A nurse plumped the pillows on his bed while a mortal servant entered the bedroom to draw the heavy drapes.

Spring sunlight flooded the room. Beyond the window's glass, Barcelona's bones rose against the sky, her buildings hollow and starved like the mortals the war left behind. The people remaining in the city were those who couldn't bear the thought of what leaving meant, or those who supported the Nationalist advance.

Regardless, they all belonged to Jordi now. With Franco stamping out the last of the Republicans, the prisons were overflowing and the rivers were red with blood. Soon Jordi's soldiers would locate any nefilim who remained loyal to

Guillermo. They'd be weeded from the mortal chaff and sent into their next incarnation.

Dr. Jimenez murmured appreciatively over the color of Jordi's healing skin. "This is looking much better, Generalissimo."

Guillermo's little trick had severed Jordi's ring finger and the upper segment of his middle finger, but his loss was minimal considering what might have been. For once, he found himself in his brother's debt.

A brother who wants forgiveness.

All Jordi needed to do was figure out a way to exploit Guillermo's guilt. *And that shouldn't be hard.*

Jimenez opened a fresh strip of gauze and proceeded to rewrap the wounds. "How are you sleeping?"

Sleeping. Now, that was another matter altogether. After eschewing drugs for four years, he found himself sleeping so much better with Jimenez's morphine shots. Why had he ever allowed Nico to wean him from the drugs? *Why had I ever allowed him into my life? The traitorous fucking queen.*

Nico had been a mistake—one that Jordi didn't intend to repeat. But all those were thoughts to muse on another day. Certainly none of them were any of Jimenez's business. "I'll need a shot before I sleep tonight."

"Very good, Generalissimo. I'll be here to deliver it personally."

"Thank you, Doctor," he murmured. "That is all."

Once Jimenez packed his black bag and left the room, one of the servants entered. "Lieutenant Espina is here, Generalissimo."

"Send him in."

As the others filed out, Benito entered. He snapped a sharp salute and waited for Jordi to speak.

As soon as all the mortals had left the room, Jordi acknowledged his lieutenant. "So tell me, Espina, what news?"

"Ilsa Jaeger, the queen of Die Nephilim, requests to visit Spain and meet with the nefilim's new caudillo, Generalissimo Jordi Abelló. She says that your experiments were a success and she is ready to implement a new plan for France."

"Magnificent." Jordi smiled. "Please convey to her that I am most pleased to receive her. I trust you'll make the appropriate arrangements."

"Of course, Generalissimo." Benito closed the bedroom doors. "Permission to approach, Señor General."

Jordi nodded and gestured for Benito to draw near.

The nefil placed a plain white envelope on the table beside Jordi's chair. "As you requested, we destroyed any indication that we were ever at the black site. Fortunately, Guillermo's ward removed any evidence of the Grigori without requiring further effort from us."

Another small favor from his brother. Jordi didn't dwell on it.

Espina continued. "I retrieved the personal effects you requested."

"And that is all he had on him?" Jordi indicated the envelope.

"Yes, Generalissimo."

"And of that other matter, the one involving my former personal physician?" Jordi forbade them from mentioning Nico's name. *That one is dead. He simply doesn't know it yet.*

Benito started to say Nico's name before he caught himself.

"The Italian is being hunted. We think he is in France, and our people are drawing close."

"I thought he wanted to go to the Americas."

"It's possible he still does. We're watching the ports. We're also finding evidence that Los Nefilim have moved their operations to France."

Let Guillermo hide behind Rousseau's skirts. Death would soon march on both of them from the east. Even if Franco continued to prove impervious to Jordi's counsel to join Hitler's cause, the mortal still managed to serve his purpose. Franco would honor his arrangement with the Führer, and Spain's natural resources would continue to flow into Germany to build planes and bombs, while Republican soldiers hiding in France would eventually find their way into concentration camps.

It's simply a matter of time. I'll bring a war to Guillermo's doorstep that he will never forget. "Very good. You're dismissed, Lieutenant. Close the door behind you."

Benito saluted again and backed from the room.

Always with the proper respect, Jordi thought as he watched him go.

Settling in the comfort of his bed, he took the envelope and opened it. Wrapped in a piece of velvet was a golden wedding band, carved with sigils. Miquel's most prized possession.

"It's just a ring," Jordi whispered. Turning the band to catch the light, he noted a scratch on the sigil for trust. Humming a tune, he formed a ward of his own and erased a little more of the line. "But rings are potent symbols . . . and some even have power."

He smiled as he settled back into the pillow, knowing his dreams tonight would be of Los Nefilim's end.

EPILOGUE

51, RUE GABRIELLE
PARIS, FRANCE
2 APRIL 1939

The scent of cigarette smoke filtered past the apartment's door. Diago wrinkled his nose as he set down a basket of bread and vegetables. Retrieving his keys, he unlocked the door and picked up the groceries.

His husband sat at the kitchen table. Although it was well after noon, Miquel still wore his pajamas. His skin no longer carried the ashen shades of gray that he'd worn for weeks after their arrival, but he had yet to fully recover. While Juanita remained confident the damage to his heart would heal, it would take some time.

And the more he smokes, the longer it will take. Diago narrowed his eyes at his husband.

Rafael emerged from the kitchen, all innocence and smiles. A cigarette in his hand.

Diago had no doubt that his son had taken the cigarette

from Miquel when they heard the key turn in the lock. *They think they're slick, these two.*

Two files were open on the table next to a pad of paper, a pencil, and a newspaper. Miquel moved a file over the newspaper, but not before Diago saw the headline. Franco had finally declared the Spanish Civil War over.

Jordi must be jubilant. Diago fixed his glare on his son. "I thought we agreed: no newspapers."

Rafael blushed and exhaled twin streams of smoke from his nostrils. "He threatened to go himself and actually had his coat on, so I went."

The statement had the cadence of a prepared lie.

Miquel attempted to deflect Diago's attention from both the paper and the cigarette in Rafael's hand. "Were the markets crowded?"

Rafael put out the cigarette in a tin ashtray. "Do you need help, Papá?" Rather than wait for an answer, he reached for the basket.

Diago turned slightly and looked at the ashtray, counting four cigarette butts. *And I was gone less than an hour.* "Rafael, I thought we *also* agreed you'd smoke outside." He met his husband's gaze. "Especially since Juanita said Miquel needed to refrain from smoking while he healed."

"It's okay." Miquel bit his lower lip and pretended to scan a report. The page trembled in his hand. "He's been helping so much at the club, I didn't want to make him run up and down the stairs."

"Except for newspapers, right?"

Rafael commandeered the basket. "Really, Papá, Miquel wasn't smoking and the newspaper isn't going to hurt him."

No, but it will make him angry. "You're both terrible

liars." Picking up the ashtray and emptying it in the fireplace, Diago returned to the table and sat across from his husband. "What's making you so upset that you're smoking more?"

Miquel thumped the report in front of him. "This one. Jordi is back in Barcelona."

Down on the street, a lorry backfired. Rafael spun and flinched at the sound, his eyes searching for a threat before his brain had time to tell him there was none. Diago knew the reaction well. He'd experienced it often enough during his own postwar days.

Diago held out his hand and without a word, Rafael came to him. "It's all right. It's just noise. You'll get used to it again."

Rafael offered him a tremulous smile and squeezed Diago's fingers.

"Don't get too used to it." Miquel slammed the paper to the table and clenched his fists. "We'll be at war again soon enough. Why didn't Guillermo kill Jordi when he had the chance?"

Reaching across the papers, Diago covered Miquel's fist with his palm. *Good thing I have two hands.* "He has his reasons." But Miquel wouldn't understand those reasons, not now. His husband's wounds were still too fresh. "We have to trust him. Okay? What is it you told me all those years before I joined Los Nefilim? We're stronger together. Right? So we trust." He kept his voice even and didn't stop talking until he felt Miquel's tremors diminish.

Miquel nodded. "Okay. Okay . . ." He drew a shuddering breath and fought to calm himself. Another moment passed and then he said, "You're right." He reached across the table and took a cigarette from the silver case Diago had given him.

Diago struck a match and lit the cigarette for him. As he withdrew, he palmed the case from the table and tucked it into his breast pocket. "There. That's the last one for a few hours."

"You're a miser with them," Miquel grumbled.

"And our son is far too generous." He shot Rafael a withering look.

"I'm sorry, Papá," he mumbled at his shoes without sounding the least bit sorry. His feigned remorse lasted until the clock chimed two. "Is it two already?" He hurried to Miquel and then Diago, kissing both of them on the cheek as he passed. "I've got to get to the club. We're having a rehearsal, and I promised Ysa and Violeta I wouldn't be late."

Miquel fiddled with the pencil. "We're singing for Carme tonight?"

Rafael put on his hat and coat. "Yes, and Violeta is taking her oath so she can step into her mamá's rank."

Fortunately, he didn't mention that Nico was taking his oath to Los Nefilim tonight, as well. Of course, now that Diago thought of it, that also explained why Miquel was so keyed up.

It was never one big thing but a thousand tiny cuts.

Grabbing his guitar case, Rafael opened the door and practically ran into Guillermo.

Rafael stood aside. "Don Guillermo, come in."

"French, Rafael."

"Oui, monsieur. Au revior." He stepped smartly around Guillermo, and then he was gone, clattering down the stairs, out the door, and onto the street.

Where, hopefully, no more lorries would backfire and send him diving for the pavement.

Guillermo shut the door and headed to the table. He carried a bulging accordion file, which likely held another thousand cuts.

Diago met him halfway and took the file. "He needs to rest."

Guillermo relinquished the file without breaking stride. "You've put on weight," he said to Miquel. "Juanita is going to be pleased."

"I'm ready for the field." Miquel smoked and watched the accordion file in Diago's hands.

"No, he's not, and he's worked enough for today." Gathering the other files and the newspaper, Diago deposited everything on a side table. "It's time for him to rest."

"I'm having a cigarette."

"When you're finished."

Guillermo sat beside Miquel. "It'll only be for another month. Your age saved you. A younger nefil would have died four times over with that much Pervitin in their system. So let your body heal."

"For the sake of Los Nefilim, I'll endeavor to carry on." Miquel finished his smoke and stood. In spite of his best efforts to appear alert, his few hours up had taken more of a toll than he would ever admit. He brushed his fingers across the back of Diago's hand as he passed. "Want to come tuck me in?"

"I'll be there in a moment." Diago waited until the bedroom door shut before he joined Guillermo. "Can I get you something?"

Guillermo shook his head. "I can't stay long. Is Nico ready for tonight?"

"I think he is. He seems to have resigned himself to his

oath. In some ways, I don't think he regrets it. He's used to France. He spent some time here in the past, which helps."

The bedroom door opened and Miquel glared at them from the doorway. "He lived with Jordi in Avignon. He's a goddamn Italian and fought with the Black Shirts. He should be shot for what they did in Trijueque back in '37."

Diago reached deep for his patience. They were becoming used to these odd outbursts, but that made them no easier to bear. Taking a slow breath, he modulated a calm tone. "Nico wasn't in Trijueque, and he had nothing to do with the Black Shirts shooting those Internationals."

Miquel wasn't satisfied. Breathing heavily, he jabbed a finger at Diago. "They pulled those men out of a hospital, dragged them to the wall, and massacred them. That's what the fucking Italians do. They wait until you're down and then they shoot you in the back. Mark me."

This isn't my husband talking—it's his fear turned to hate. Diago caught Miquel's gaze and held it. "Miquel, please. Nico may be Italian, he might have served the enemy, but he saved our son's life, and he did that willingly. There is something good within his song. Let's help him nurture it. Like you did with me."

Guillermo cleared his throat. "And he's given us quite a bit of useful intelligence in these last few days. The Germans are preparing to invade France. They're giving Pervitin to the mortals and a select group of nefilim. If we intend to stop their advance, we need to be ready. And united." He shot Miquel a meaningful look. "We must be united."

Though said gently, the admonishment was cold water on Miquel's rage. He lowered his eyes. "I'm sorry." He touched his chest, an unconscious gesture. "I . . . I don't know what

CARVED FROM STONE AND DREAM ■ 343

comes over me. It's like my brain snaps from one topic to another. It happens so fast—"

"It's okay." Guillermo waved his hand as if the outburst were nothing. "It's the Pervitin. It's why we're not giving it to our nefilim."

"Right." Miquel sniffed and allowed his gaze to flicker to Guillermo before landing again on Diago. "And you're right, too. But Nico is yours. I can't work with him . . . not now."

"I know," Diago whispered. "It's too soon."

Mollified, Miquel nodded. "Good. I won't even speak against him tonight. How's that?"

"Thank you."

Stepping back into the bedroom, Miquel closed the door and muttered, "The fucking queen."

Guillermo winced and whispered, "I've never heard him call anyone a queen."

Diago shot the door a concerned look. "Nico and I meet at the café on the corner for breakfast every morning. I can't bring him here . . . for obvious reasons." He lowered his voice. "Even when Miquel is quiet, he makes Nico so nervous I can't get him to open up, so I keep them apart for now."

"Smart move." Guillermo toyed with the ashtray. "How about you?"

"What about me?"

"How are you?"

"Busy taking care of Miquel and Rafael, and now Nico. And that's good." He tapped his temple. "Keeps me out of my own head."

"Really?"

Diago met his gaze. "Really. As a matter of fact"—he rose and went to his violin case, retrieving the satchel that rested next to it—"Rafael and I have been working on the Key. Coming through that portal realm gave us the clue to the next movement." He spread the composition on the table in front of Guillermo. "See? The arrangement begins with the sound of the angels' exile and anguish, but as the song progresses, it builds on the sound of—"

"Trust," Guillermo murmured.

"Yes. On trust. That was Rafael's idea." He gathered the score and returned it to the satchel. "Take it with you. I'm eager to hear your thoughts. Maybe tomorrow we'll work on it some more."

"Sounds good." Guillermo rose and patted his pocket. "Oh, and that thing you asked me for." He removed a small box from his pocket, placing it on the table. "It's finished."

"Thank you." Diago didn't bother opening the package. He knew it would be perfect. Palming the small container, he carried it with him as he followed Guillermo into the hall and closed the door.

Guillermo whispered, "How is he doing? Really?"

"He has more bad nights than good ones." *He won't truly fall asleep unless I'm holding him, because that is the only time he feels safe.* But Diago didn't say that to Guillermo. *That is Miquel's to tell when he feels ready.* "Once he gets back in the field, he'll feel more in control again. Right now he's a terrible patient." Diago shrugged. "But so was I."

Guillermo withdrew a cigar from his pocket. "Juanita wants to come and see him again."

"Tell her to call. I want it to be his idea. He doesn't want to seem weak in front of her. Like I said . . ."

"Control. Okay. I'll see you tonight at the club?"

"You'll see us both. He wants to sing for Carme and the

nefilim he lost to the Grigori. Frankly, so do I. Carme might have hated me, but I miss her nonetheless."

"I don't think she hated you," Guillermo said. "She was . . ." He sighed at his loss for words.

"Carme. She was Carme, and there will never be another like her until she is reborn."

"You're right about that." Guillermo smiled sadly. "Tonight, then."

"Tonight." Diago waited until his friend stepped onto the street before he slipped back inside the apartment.

He went straight to the bedroom, where he knew Miquel would be awake, trying to catch their every word. His husband didn't disappoint him.

Reclining on his side, he pretended to be absorbed in a novel. With his thumb, he rubbed the ring finger of his left hand, where his wedding band had left a permanent mark on his flesh. Even though the ring was gone, his skin remained indented with the memory of the metal that encircled his finger for so long.

Diago kicked off his shoes and eased onto the bed next to his husband. Reaching over Miquel's shoulder, he gently closed the book and whispered the only magic words he knew. "Talk to me."

Miquel shrugged. "There's nothing to talk about."

"You don't call people queens, or rage about war atrocities over which you had no control. Wasn't it you who told me that anger is poison and that it will kill the soul as surely as arsenic will destroy a body?"

Another shrug, but this one was less robust than the first.

"All this resentment, this is not you." Diago stroked his husband's hair. "Talk to me."

Another minute passed before Miquel spoke. Pressing his lips together, he swallowed hard and then asked, "Do you remember when we first met? How I saved you?" He swallowed hard, his eyes glassy in the soft shadows wafting through the room. "Do you remember?"

Diago recalled the taste of blood and grit between his teeth. Then a hand had emerged from the darkness, gently brushing his hair from his brow. "I remember."

"You always said I saved you, but I didn't. It was you who saved me. When I saw you, I knew I wasn't insane. All those memories tumbling through my head abruptly made sense. I remembered our firstborn lives, and how I abandoned you to die alone. And suddenly here you were again, and I knew I had a chance to win you back, and I swore that if I ever did, I would stand by you, nothing would ever part us, not the angels, or the daimons, or even the Inner Guard. Do you understand what I'm saying to you, Diago?"

He's saying he's sorry for something that happened five incarnations ago. Diago drew his husband close, wishing he could stop Miquel's pain with the force of his own body. *And his guilt for that firstborn life is why he always tries to be so strong for me in this one. Now it's my turn to be strong for him.*

"I understand," Diago whispered. "We can use the past to change the present, and then we must let our firstborn lives go." He took the jewelry box from his pocket and placed it against his husband's palm.

Miquel frowned. "What is this?"

"A gift."

Miquel lifted the lid. He said nothing for a full minute. "How did you find it?"

"I didn't. Guillermo made a new one for you." Diago removed the wedding band from the box and placed it on his husband's finger.

Miquel smiled, and for just a moment Diago saw the gentle husband he recalled from before the war. *Such dark eyes, but when he smiles, he fills my heart with the sun.*

Holding up his hand, Miquel admired the gold ring. Like the one he'd lost, the band was inscribed with the sigils they'd chosen to represent their love. "I know you think I'm a fool for putting such stock in these things, but I feel complete again."

"I don't think you're a fool. Our love is greater than any band of gold or silver, but rings are symbols, and symbols have power."

"Like our love," Miquel murmured, his eyes already closing. "Our love has power."

Diago drew him close and stroked his hair. "Like our love."

GLOSSARY

ANGELS Creatures from another dimension that invaded the antediluvian earthly realm. They warred with the daimons for control of the mortals. The angels caused the Great Flood in order to force the daimons to capitulate to their demands. Rather than watch the mortals destroyed, the daimons surrendered. While no daimonic uprising has occurred in centuries, the angels sometimes engage in civil wars. These conflicts often bleed down into the mortal realm.

ANGEL-BORN NEFILIM (OFTEN SHORTENED TO ANGEL-BORN) Nefilim who can claim direct lineage to an angelic ancestor.

DAIMONS The old earth gods who resided in the mortal realm before the invasion of the angelic hordes. Most have retreated to homes deep beneath the earth and have removed themselves from mortal affairs. Others, like Diago's grandfather, Moloch, work toward reasserting themselves and their presence in the mortal world.

DAIMON-BORN NEFILIM (OFTEN SHORTENED TO DAIMON-BORN) Nefilim who claim direct lineage to a daimonic ancestor.

DIE NEPHILIM The German Inner Guard, led by Ilsa Jaeger. Her second-in-command is Erich Heines.

FALLEN The Fallen are angels who have been cast out of the angelic ranks and forced to live in the mortal realm.

GRIGORI Also known as the Watchers. A group of angels that committed vile crimes against the mortals. The Grigori were cast out of the angelic realms. Their wings were torn from their bodies and they were buried deep beneath the stones of the earth, where they live in eternal torment.

IL NEPHILIM The Italian Inner Guard, led by Matteo de Luca. His second-in-command is Chiara Ricci.

INNER GUARD The Inner Guard functions much like a central intelligence agency for the angels. The Inner Guard is comprised of angel-born nefilim that monitor daimonic activity for the angels. Each mortal country has a division of nefilim to serve in this capacity. During times of war, they often fight alongside mortals.

LOS NEFILIM The Spanish Inner Guard, led by Guillermo Ramírez. His second-in-command is Miquel de Torrellas.

LES NÉPHILIM The French Inner Guard, led by Sabine Rousseau. Her second-in-command is Jean Marchand.

MESSENGERS (ALSO KNOWN AS MALAKIM) These angels are the closest in form to the mortals, and because of this, they serve as messengers between the Thrones and the nefilim. They also mate with both the mortals and the nefilim in carefully orchestrated breeding plans designed to produce powerful nefilim.

NEFILIM/NEPHILIM The nefilim are often distinguished as either angel- or daimon-born. All nefilim reincarnate and retain memories of their past lives, with their firstborn and current lives being the most important.

OPHANIM An angelic species, the Ophanim have thousands of eyes and are the lords of fire that float just beyond the river of fire's shore. Shaped like blazing wheels, they spin in place and maintain the complex glyphs that are portals from one dimension to another.

POCKET REALMS Unlike angelic realms, which create pathways to completely separate dimensions, pocket realms remain just under the veneer of the mortal realm, like a body beneath a blanket. Such realms are often used by nefilim as bunkers or covert black sites, but they are extremely difficult to maintain.

PRINCIPALITIES Angels that rule over specific countries in the earthly realm. The kings and queens of the Inner Guard report to their respective Principality through the Messenger angel assigned to their division.

ROGUES Nefilim who do not join the Inner Guard are known as rogues. Rogues move independently among the mortals. While they lack the networks and structure that enable the Inner Guard to move freely during mortal wars, rogues have been known to organize to protect their own interests. They have their own set of arcane codes and rituals, which dictates their behavior among both the mortals and other nefilim.

THRONES Probably the closest thing that stands as a collective godhead to the nefilim. The Thrones are fiery angels that are never seen in the mortal realm.

ACKNOWLEDGMENTS

Special thanks always go first and foremost to my family, especially to my husband, Dick, who does so many things to make sure I have time to write.

To Michael R. Fletcher for reading and rereading my opening sequences until I got the action just right. To Michael Mammay for his military expertise and assistance with military terminology.

For my fabulous first readers: Rhi Hopkins, Glinda Harrison, Courtney Schafer, and Vinnie Russo. To Josep Oriol for his early assistance on Barcelona and for pointing me toward period Catalonian resources. Likewise, to Ollivier Robert for helping me navigate the Paris metro and for sending me links to French resources I wouldn't otherwise have been able to locate on my own.

If I made any mistakes in the facts, they are mine and certainly not theirs.

To the Extraordinary Fellows of Arcane Sorcery: you know who you are. You're a magnificent lot, and I'm proud to say I've been a part of your group.

To Lisa Rodgers, who always has my back and whose mad editing skills help me to be a better writer. And especially to David Pomerico and the team at Harper Voyager, who believed in this series and made it happen.

My deepest gratitude goes to my readers. This book couldn't have happened without you and your support. Thank you for giving this story your time. I hope you enjoyed it.

I will watch for you . . .

SOURCE BOOKS & INSPIRATION

Where Oblivion Lives

Andalusian Poems, translated by Christopher Middleton and Leticia Garza-Falcón.

The Battle for Spain: The Spanish Civil War, 1936–1939, by Antony Beevor.

The Battlefields of the First World War: The Unseen Panoramas of the Western Front, by Peter Barton.

The Dictionary of Homophobia: A Global History of Gay & Lesbian Experience, edited by Louis-Georges Tin and translated by Marek Redburn.

The Evolution of Hitler's Germany: The Ideology, the Personality, the Moment, by Horst von Maltitz.

Hitler: Ascent, 1889–1939, by Volker Ullrich and translated by Jefferson Chase.

The Legends of the Jews (7 vols.), by Louis Ginzberg.

"Los Invisibles": A History of Male Homosexuality in Spain, 1850–1940, by Richard Cleminson and Francisco Vázquez García.

The Occult Roots of Nazism: Secret Aryan Cults and Their Influence on Nazi Ideology, by Nicholas Goodrick-Clarke.

Shadow and Evil in Fairy Tales (rev. ed.), by Marie-Louise von Franz.

The Somme: Heroism and Horror in the First World War, by Martin Gilbert.

The Spanish Labyrinth: An Account of the Social and Political Background of the Spanish Civil War, by Gerald Brenan.

They Thought They Were Free: The Germans, 1933–45, by Milton Mayer.

Carved from Stone and Dream

The Battle for Spain: The Spanish Civil War, 1936–1939, by Antony Beevor.

Blitzed: Drugs in the Third Reich, by Norman Ohler and translated by Shaun Whiteside.

Dark Mirrors: Azazel and Satanael in Early Jewish Demonology, by Andrei A. Orlov.

The Legends of the Jews (7 vols.), by Louis Ginzberg.

¡No Pasarán! Writings from the Spanish Civil War, edited by Pete Ayrton.

The Routes to Exile: France and the Spanish Civil War Refugees, 1939–2009, by Scott Soo.

Sacred Space, Sacred Sound: The Acoustic Mysteries of Holy Places, by Susan Elizabeth Hale.

The Spanish Civil War: Reaction, Revolution and Revenge, by Paul Preston.

The Spanish Holocaust: Inquisition and Extermination in Twentieth-Century Spain, by Paul Preston.